BLACK & WHITE

BLACK & WHITE

Wes Albers

ZOVA Books
Los Angeles

$ZOVA$ BOOKS

This book is a work of fiction. References to real people, events, establishments, organizations, or locales are intended only to provide a sense of authenticity and are used fictitiously. All other characters, and all incidents and dialogue are drawn from the author's imagination and are not to be construed as real.

First ZOVA Books edition 2012.

BLACK & WHITE. Copyright © 2012 by Wes Albers.

All rights reserved.

Printed in the United States of America.

No part of this book may be used or reproduced in any manner whatsoever without written permission except in the case of brief quotations embodied in critical articles and reviews.

For information or permission contact:

ZOVA Books
P.O. Box 21833, Long Beach, California 90801
www.zovabooks.com

ISBN-13: 9780984035076
ISBN: 0984035079

Cover Design © Daniel Pearson

For the street cop.
Each day they willingly leave their homes and loved ones to walk in harm's way never knowing whether they will return or how dramatically their lives will be changed should they make it to the end of their shift.

PROLOGUE

I WISH I COULD remember my last solid shit but I can't. Then again, I wish I could remember a lot of things. I wish I could remember the last time I believed true love really existed or that relationships lasted. That a person could feel excited about something, as anxious for a new experience as they were sure that bad things didn't happen to good people.

I wish I could remember what it was like before the loss of friends in the line and the loss of friends who couldn't forgive a bad day, a mistake, or the breakup of a marriage, those friends who thought their only way out was a bullet that erased the promise of everything they might have been, and tainted all that they were.

I wish I could remember what it was like to not have seen the cold things in this world, the faces of the poor, tortured dead, people who got that way because they were stupid enough to make bad decisions, or simply unlucky enough to be in the wrong place at the wrong time. I wish I could remember a lot of things . . . but I can't.

I didn't start off this way. Does anyone? Certainly no one I know. I started like the rest, a wide-eyed kid focused on the singular thought that I could make a difference in the world, I could help others, and what I did would mean something, that my efforts would be rewarded. Then something changed.

Over the years I've been hit, bit, kicked, and tossed around like a raggedy chew toy in a golden retriever's mouth. I've been poked, stabbed, punched, shot at, clubbed, and pummeled. Getting yelled at is just a matter of daily routine.

When I show up, my contact with you is rarely a happy moment, and even when it is, emotions nearly always run high. You're only glad to see me if I'm doing what you want.

Otherwise, I'm the asshole.

I've felt your discontent, sometimes in the form of a thick ball of slimy spit that rolls down the back of my neck and inside my shirt. And some of the finest of you have emptied the contents of your stomach on my boots just before looking up at me through sweaty, stained, stringy, vomit-soaked hair to demand that I wipe your face and clean you up.

Let's not forget the blood, there's plenty of that. It didn't used to be such a big deal. Nobody worried. It was just blood. There was no need for rubber gloves. Blood, urine, feces, it was all no big deal. I was exposed daily and didn't give the matter much thought. Nasty stuff was part of the job. Not so much any more. Now it's not just the things I can see that I have to worry about, it's the things I won't know are there until some doctor tells me he's sorry. Every time you cough on the back of my neck, I get to wonder whether you're part of the tuberculosis epidemic or whether I'm just gonna get my sixth cold of the season.

When the world explodes and I show up, I get brief moments to correct the convoluted storm of human misery someone else worked very hard to create. If, in the short time I have to regain control of the chaos, I don't do something perfect, you get the next several months—or years—to tell me how I could have done better. If my error is a big deal, you get to tell me how bad a person I am and how my failure to be perfect is one of intent rather than lack of insight.

You expect perfection in me while I deal with your imperfections, things you believe should be overlooked because of any litany of mitigating factors that are a part of your own unfortunate past. It's funny, I've studied the *Bill of Rights* but I cannot, for the life of me, remember the section that outlines the myriad of different things people think they are due. You have a right to make a phone call, but you don't have the right to struggle and resist me until you get it.

And what do I get for all this? A pension when I retire, something you complain about to no end. In your eyes it's totally unfair that I should get to live so well when I retire so early. Never mind that my chances of surviving a career to receive that pension are only slightly slimmer than the likelihood I'll live long enough to enjoy it.

Welcome to my world. There are a lot of things it's not, but it's still my world.

I'm a street cop, the first person who shows up when things go to hell, the first responder who has only frantic moments to take in a great deal of information and formulate a plan on how to stabilize things. If it helps you to believe that I'm lazy, ignorant, generally incompetent and way too overpaid, go ahead. Your future is still in my hands.

So am I bitter? Nah, it could be worse. I have a hot cup of coffee mixed with just the right amount of non-dairy creamer and sugar. Such a brew is a hard concoction to perfect, but when you get it right, so is the world. The smoke from the Marlboro Ultra-Lights I keep trying to get away from rolls smoothly across my tongue, the tobacco a perfect blend to accent the taste of the coffee.

It is moments like this that I really appreciate.

To top off the break, this is my favorite time of day. The hour when the city breathes a collective, exhausted sigh of relief and nighttime holds back, waiting patiently to release the bad things. When motorists cruise home on auto-pilot and the automatic headlights start to pop on. That moment when the day's warmth still hangs in the air, fighting to hold on as the cool evening breeze chills the heat that clings to the asphalt in the streets. Sunset. More specifically, that instant right before dark when the sky grows a deeper blue and the world around is caught in that brief place of twilight where things are nearly luminous.

I've found myself a comfy spot to enjoy the moment. The door of my black-and-white Crown Victoria is the perfect resting spot, as I lean against my car in a parking lot at 52nd and El Cajon Boulevard. This is East San Diego, Mid-City Division.

They used to call it Eastern Division. When I got here, everything south of Interstate 8 was the 310's service area. Comprised of eight different beats, this was flat out the ass of the city. If San Diego could have been given an enema, this would have been where they inserted the nozzle. Everyday we'd drive down I-15, and as we crossed over I-8 and through the canyon toward our beat, my partner would start our day with some quote from Dante's *Inferno*. I'd hear Morrison's "Riders on the Storm," and then the world would explode.

Meanwhile, folks in the real world spent their days watching the dawn of the nineties man, the emergence of a sensitive man in touch with his feminine side who can cry on command.

On a Friday or Saturday night there'd be forty, fifty, maybe more of us, spread over one of the smallest areas of the city. And when we'd clear the station after line-up, there'd be an even greater number of emergency and priority calls waiting for us. No matter how many cops we put out, the calls would never go away. In the course of a night, each unit commonly went to a couple dozen incidents. *We* might have been on the cusp of the nineties, but there was no room for a sensitive man among us.

It was an era of mayhem.

Rock cocaine was at its peak, and methamphetamine was making a rapid climb toward the top of the drug food chain. You couldn't count the number of different gangs—whites, blacks, Hispanics, Asians, and enough subdivisions of each to make your head spin, each of them vying for their share of limited space in which to sell their illicit products. After all, the economy hadn't quite rebounded yet, and when times are bad, people get high. That meant I went to shootings, stabbings, and beatings, sometimes several times in a night. There was so much blood, so much violence that the misery of this place just never seemed to end. When I was young and invincible, this was a wonderland, and every night was an adventure.

But things change.

It's no longer Eastern Division. The Mid-City station opened in '95, built out of the old grocery store at Fairmont and Wightman that was robbed and shoplifted to the point where there was nothing left to sell at the end of the day. If you ask most cops who work there now, they don't remember it was ever anything but a police station.

I do.

I remember rolling around on the ground in what is now the front parking lot of the station with some dreg-thief who was so amped up on god-knows-what he didn't even know I was there. He never felt my nun-chucks even though they were wrapped so tightly around his wrist that they warped and bent. My partner inflicted a similar level of pain, but that misguided creep still fought us until he had no fight left. In the end, when he came down, he didn't remember a bit of his ordeal. He just wondered why he felt so bad.

It was insanity.

So much happens on the streets. They are the conduits through which we live. At least that's how I see it. The streets take me where I need to go. They are the passageway to life, death, and all those moments that fill the in-between. Those same streets have forged my life these past years. But they do wear on you.

We used to tell the tough little gangsters, the dope fiends, the miscreants, "Clean up, no man is tougher than the streets." Who knew that same logic would apply to us? The streets will wear a man down just as surely as they do the tires on my cruiser. Still, sometimes the best you can do is see how much tread you have left and hope you don't hit any potholes.

The sweat still clings to the underside of my vest, and I shiver as the cool wind blows the last of the perspiration off the back of my neck. A good swallow of coffee takes care of that. Hell, a good cup of coffee takes care of a lot of things, and whatever *7-11* is, is not, was, should be, or represents, it can still brew a fine cup of coffee . . . mostly. There is the 3:00 AM sludge, the thick, burned out crust that remains after hours of sitting on the burner. Without fail, it's all that's left when you don't have time to wait while they brew a new pot. That's always when you need to rush off to the next self-generated critical event in some goofball's life. It's the kind of coffee that scalds your mouth and then clings to your taste buds with all the tenacity of a macaroni and cheese dinner that's been burned to the lining of a cast iron pot. Still, usually the coffee is good.

At least some things don't change.

Chapter 1

MY REVERIE WAS INTERRUPTED just as surely as if I'd tripped on any of the multitude of deteriorating sidewalks that make up this neighborhood. My rookie partner felt compelled to disturb me.

"Are you about ready?" he whined. My moment would have been destroyed but for years of experience in tuning people out. "Let's go find something to do."

I groaned. "Give me a moment. Enjoy your Snapple. The bad things will come soon enough."

"C'mon, this is boring."

"Indulge me, sometimes I like boring."

I could feel it waiting. The evening was too quiet, too solemn, but that couldn't be taken as a sign that nothing is happening. The city is like a woman at times, she can speak volumes without even so much as word. Tonight it was as if she was holding some rotten secret she wanted to share just as soon as things got dark enough. That's how it works sometimes, and if you pay attention to her you can sense what she wants you to know. Some call it a sixth sense. I never much paid attention, I just knew that some things can be felt, but not explained.

Not so for my partner. Tonight I'd been made a "Zebra Unit," a two man car, with little Stevie Buckman. Poor kid, he'd likely throw a tantrum if I called him Stevie, but it hardly seemed fit not to. Barely twenty-two, he wasn't even a year out of the Academy and he'd already set his sights on changing the world. It is just his kind of zeal I wish I could remember.

Mostly what I remember are those things that beat such a sense of excitement right outta my hide. He doesn't know those moments are coming, but they are. Hopefully he'll have the guts to stick it out and the good grace to live to an age where he can sit and enjoy a sunset.

I took another swig of coffee, almost to the bottom of the cup. Maybe two sips left, and it was still warm. With any luck I'd get through the whole thing before I got a call or the last gulp got cold. Just another of those small things that brings joy to my life. Not so for Stevie. I could hear him sigh dramatically as if I'd just told him he couldn't watch Power Rangers.

Stevie shifted in the passenger seat. I heard him start typing frantically on the keyboard of the computer inside our car. His was a new generation—cops email and text each other all night long. No one listens to the streets. They keep their heads buried in the monitor or their fancy phones, chatting back and forth as the world moves on around them.

At five-ten and maybe a hundred and sixty pounds, Stevie hadn't had time to fill out his uniform. He kept it clean and pressed, though, no doubt the work of the mother he still lived with. Two years of college, a job, and still at home. That seems the way of Californians. I can only imagine the coronary my father would have had if I'd still been in the nest at his age. Then again, the young people seem to keep getting older. Thirty years of living today gets a person where most used to be at eighteen. Stevie might have the uniform, the shiny leather, the short trimmed wavy brown hair but he still looks like he ought to be in high school. At least he has a full-time job.

Of course, things would be different if we got a call near the University. You can bet there'd be no mention of living at home around all the young college girls. He'd be in heaven, strutting around with his chest puffed out like some rooster in the henhouse.

The next swig of coffee is only warm. One more swallow and I'm back to work. That gives me just a few more seconds to enjoy the moment. My Marlboro has reached the end of its usefulness. I roll the end of the filter until the cherry drops to the ground and then crush the ember with the tip of my steel toe.

The sun is gone, well below where I might catch a glimpse, but still the light fights its last battle of the day. In the sky above I can see the brilliant underbelly of a jetliner. The plane is too high up to make out anything distinct, just the shimmering glow of sunlight reflecting off polished aluminum, the wispy white vapor trail marking a path across the heavens. Too far up to be heading in to Lindbergh Field. Those folks are probably heading to some far off exotic locale.

For a brief moment the thought pulled at me. I ought to be on that plane headed for Hawaii, Tahiti, or the Caribbean. Then reality strikes. It's flying south. Mexico. Damn. Probably headed to some corrupt, drug-running, impoverished shithole where people are traded and life is cheap. So much for exotic. Who goes outta their way to walk in shit?

The radio transmission crackled loudly in my ear, one of the few things that will get a cop's attention, anytime, anywhere. "Cover now," were the only two words I heard, but that was enough.

CHAPTER 2

COVER NOW. WHEN AN OFFICER speaks these words it can mean only one of two things—his world has gone shitty or he is quickly approaching that moment. In either event, the call means he needs help . . . immediately. In the hierarchy of things that are important in my life, there are only two that rate a higher priority. There are the 11-99, which commonly translates to "Send Everyone," and "Officer Down," which needs no translation. A "cover now," on the other hand, still holds promise. If you can get there quickly enough, perhaps then the bad things can be held at bay, turned back toward their inky, dark hiding spot. If not, you're likely to carry a lifetime of troubled thoughts about what you might have done differently.

I never finished that last bit of coffee, never gave it a thought as I pitched the cup at the nearest trash can. I probably missed, but if someone wanted to complain about littering, I'd deal with that later. My hand went straight to keys with as much economy of movement as I could manage. I was in the driver's seat and firing the engine to life as quickly as possible.

Stevie's face bore a mixture of excitement and apprehension. His voice cracked. "He didn't get out his unit number, who was it, where is he?"

He turned to the computer, hoping to glean enough information to determine who the call had come from. Information sure wasn't coming from the radio. There were too many units jabbering at once. That's the way of a call like this. Everyone wants to announce what they're doing, to let everyone know they're on their way. The problem is, the person in trouble can't get on the air to update them.

I'd recognized the voice. At least I hoped I had. Mike Murphy, and as best I could remember, he went out on a stop at 50th and Trojan. If I was right, he was three blocks away.

Stevie nearly tumbled into my lap as I jammed the car into reverse and gunned the accelerator. We screeched backward as I cut the wheel hard to the right. The power steering screamed a protest, and customers gawked wide-eyed at me from the front window of the store.

I tapped the brakes and threw the transmission into drive. The car lurched as I forced gears to work against design. Tires squealed. I flipped the switch for the overheads, and suddenly the street corner came alive with the wail of my siren and the blue and red flashes from my overhead lights.

A couple of seconds, that's how quickly things change. One second you're drinking coffee, the next you're hurling headlong into the unknown. Each time you're never quite sure whether your number is about to get punched.

"No matter what's up, you stay with me," I barked at Stevie.

"Yeah, okay," he muttered, his eyes fixed ahead on the boulevard. We screamed forward and the world narrowed. Two of the things that cause tunnel vision are speed and adrenaline. I was dealing with both, which meant I had to compensate to manage the effects. My eyes scanned back and forth.

Traffic was light. We were nearly on top of the car in front of us before he looked in the mirror and saw our lights. Of course he didn't pull to the right. No one pulls to the right. Instead, he jammed on his brakes, his mind in total vapor-lock about what to do.

"Dumb ass," I shouted as I hit the air horn. That only flustered him more. Precious seconds were wasting. I considered going around him. Bad plan—that is usually the time they figure out what to do and change lanes into you. I wasn't going to do Murphy any good if I got in an accident along the way.

Then the guy moved. I stomped on the accelerator, jamming it to the floor as hard as I could. As we raced past, I saw the driver's deer-in-the-headlights look and wondered how we ever put a man on the moon.

I prepared to cut hard onto 50th to go south. Then I was on the brakes again. This time the delay was for two people crossing the intersection. Apparently they were too amazed by my dazzling lights to bother getting out of the street any more quickly than if they had been on a leisurely stroll on a warm Sunday evening.

"Move," Stevie shouted out the window, the adrenaline constricting his vocal cords.

Once again, I stomped on the accelerator. One more block. Mike should be hearing the sounds of the cavalry, the wail of the approaching siren. Any time I heard it, I found my strength renewed.

The radio crackled. The dispatcher was doing her best to work down the possible list of people who might need help; it wouldn't be long before she figured it out. I thought about transmitting my thoughts. If I was wrong, I'd cost someone else time.

We hit the intersection at Trojan Avenue. I crunched down on the brakes as I glanced out my side window to look for any sign of Murphy.

"Right, right, go right," Stevie shouted.

I looked as I was turning. Murphy was on the ground fighting with someone, and there was a black male watching. I couldn't see his hands. He looked up when he heard our engine. An instant later he was gone, running southbound down the alley. I'd have gone after him, but my priority was the cop on the ground.

I keyed the radio. "831 Zebra, cover now is 5000 Trojan. We are 10-97 with one black male rabbit in a blue shirt running southbound in the alley."

I tossed the radio mic and exploded from the car. Murphy was on top of a second black male. He was doing his best to get the man under control but his opponent was on his hands and knees, pushing up in an attempt to topple the officer on his back. I couldn't see if Murphy was injured. I could see the suspect's hands though—no weapons, at least at this point.

That could change just as quickly as coffee turns into "Cover now."

Rushing forward, I caught Stevie out of the corner of my eye. He was past me in a flash, the benefit of youthful speed and agility. I expected him to be on Murphy a second or two ahead of me, but instead he kept going. Little Stevie Buckman rushed headlong past us and into the dark unknown to catch the man who'd run.

An already complicated situation intensified. I had one officer on the ground with a suspect, and I had no idea if the officer was hurt or if the suspect was armed. My rookie partner was in pursuit of a second possible suspect, and he was alone.

The quickest way to get dead in this job is alone, and the fastest way to get there is to be young and not think about what you are doing.

Murphy's breath was ragged and raspy. He was wearing down. That meant taking over the fight. Every second the struggle lasted was another second Stevie got deeper into the shit.

"Coming up on you, Mike," I shouted. The suspect heard me and heaved mightily. Mike tumbled next to him but stood almost instantly. He wasn't giving up.

The suspect was up even faster than Murphy. He'd looked shorter on the ground. Then again, they all do. We locked eyes. Maybe six foot, he stood about two inches shorter than me, but he was ripped, his muscles cut hard. Probably fresh out of prison. I'd need to end this fast.

I grabbed his left arm and pulled down. He bent and came off balance long enough for me jam my right hand against the back of his elbow. If I could get him in an arm bar, I might be able to leverage him toward the trunk of the car. Precious moments were ticking by. An officer was on his own and hadn't gotten on the radio to let anyone know where he was headed, while I was burning time with this knucklehead.

The suspect countered my move and returned a swing of his fist. I took the blow to my left shoulder. He stepped back to gain distance. I advanced.

"Enough of this stupid shit." I brought my right knee up between his thighs and firmly into his groin. Not a move they'd preach at the academy, but it worked. The blow lifted him up and backwards. Immediately his body froze in preparation of what was about to happen. It was male instinct. Then there was the brief, half-second pause while his brain tried to deny what would follow, and a fleeting moment of reprieve before the nauseating wave rippled up from his testicles into his stomach.

Normally when a guy gets a kick in the nuts he gets the customary honor of being allowed to drop to his knees and gasp for whatever air he might find. Not so in this case. I grabbed his arm and yanked, spinning him toward the car. His groan was only made possible by the air dumping out of his lungs as his diaphragm compressed.

He hit the trunk with a thud, and it took little effort to get him into handcuffs. I couldn't tell if they fit too tightly but didn't have the time to discuss concerns about comfort with him. My hands did a speedy search for hidden weapons, obvious contraband.

Murphy was next to me, opening the passenger door to his car as I moved the suspect toward the back seat.

"Watch your head," I said as I directed the collapsing mass forward, pulling down on his arm to guide him. He crumpled into the back seat and started gasping as I slammed the door shut. My hand was already moving to the microphone on my lapel. "831 Zebra, cover now suspect in custody. My partner is in foot pursuit of second suspect, last seen southbound." As I spoke, I could see Eric Smith had arrived and was out of his car. The engine clicked and popped from the heat that had been generated from the racing motor.

The dispatcher answered me. "10-4, unit with foot pursuit, location?" There was no response.

I was moving as I spoke to Murphy. "You okay, got any holes?"

"Fine," Mike heaved. "Thanks."

Again the dispatcher came over the air. "Unit 831 Zebra in foot pursuit please advise your location?"

Her answer came in short, stuttered words spoken between hoarse, raspy, breaths. "831 Zebra, Buckman, I'm okay but I lost the suspect. If units moving into the area can set up for a search we might be able to locate him."

I sighed and looked at Murphy who was bent over trying to catch his breath. "That guy wanted for anything?"

He raised his head and shook it. "No, we got the person I wanted. The other one was just walking by."

"Nice of him to lend a hand."

Murphy shrugged. "Welcome to the real world," he said before breaking into a coughing fit.

I could hear police cars still racing into the area, sirens wailing urgently. "Units disregard that last. Cover now suspect in custody, outstanding male is not wanted. Have my partner return to the scene unless he needs me to drive to his location to pick him up."

There was dead air until Stevie's agitated voice answered, "Negative. I'll walk."

Two more black and whites raced up. Martinez and Jenkins burst out of the first, Marcus Irving the second.

"Everyone remain calm," Martinez announced when he determined the fight was through. "We are the police, and we're here to help."

He and Rick Jenkins were a matched set that hadn't separated since the academy. Martinez was a medium sized guy with thick, dark hair and a Mexican heritage that left him perpetually tan. Jenkins was a tall, light skinned Midwestern white kid with reddish blond hair. The Navy had been his ticket out of the fields.

Brotherman Marcus Irving had been around nine years, before that the Marines and college. He grew up in the neighborhood and chose to come back for those who remained, those who might still make their way out. Perhaps filled with more bluster and bravado than some cops liked, he was straightforward and loyal. He simply looked at Martinez and rolled his eyes.

My attention returned to Murphy as Jenkins and Martinez started to give him a hard time. We don't hug to relieve stress, we belittle our friends.

"What can I do to help?" I asked.

Jenkins feigned a serious look. "You might want to take his prisoner. SWAT guy like him will never be able to go downtown with those boots looking like they do."

Martinez giggled and made a sad face. "And he got a boo boo on his elbow."

"Kiss my ass," Murphy groaned, then coughed some more. He might spend more time than most in the gym worrying over how good he'd look in his uniform, but vanity aside, he was good to have around when things got stupid. His conditioning likely saved his life.

"Well then . . ." Martinez exclaimed, his expression shifting as if surprised by the response. "I thought you were a ninja. What was knucklefuck's problem anyway?" He asked as he looked through the patrol car window at the man crumpled up in the back seat. "You guys lump him up, or what?"

Jenkins spoke before Murphy could respond. "People can't play nice anymore," he said with as much fake seriousness as he could manage. "It's the new world. Haven't you ever seen a reality show? People are downright hostile. Good thing you had the old man here."

"Excuse me?"

"You are, you're old," he nodded. Martinez mirrored his partner's reaction.

"Well, Padawan, when either of you thinks you're ready for a shot at the Jedi title, you let me know. You might want to get a couple stars in your galaxy first."

Jerkins raised his hands in submission. "I'm just sayin'."

Martinez dipped his head and moved toward his car. "Time to go, things to do, places to be, meth-monsters who need accommodations. If you were a hot chick, I'd be glad you are okay," he said to Murphy as he passed him. "At least you're still around to help with radio calls."

"Speaking of hot chicks, where's Suzie?" Jenkins asked intentionally, matter-of-factly drawing our attention to the obvious, the only member of the squad to not make the cover call. No one answered. I didn't care. Our resident princess was trouble, and I kept a fair amount of space between us despite the fine work the doctor had done with her implants.

With no one to bite on his bait, Jenkins scampered after his partner and then stopped to speak to Mike. "For what it's worth, I'd have beat his black ass too." Startled, he looked at Marcus. This time the look wasn't feigned, "Sorry man, no offense."

"None taken, Corn-fed, just as long as you don't beat his ass *because* it's black."

"Huh? No, that's not what I meant."

"Get the fuck outta here."

Jenkins scrambled back to the car and the two of them sped off.

Marcus leaned in close to Murphy and me. "What is it about that backwater kid that makes him run his mouth about the speed of stupid?"

"Those guys always want to be the comedians," I said. "Unfortunately for Jenkins, being the straight man leaves him looking like a dumb ass when his mouth and head don't communicate."

"No shit," Marcus said. "I mean, I'd a beat his black ass too, but pick your audience."

"Yeah, well, there was no ass beatin' going on," Murphy replied firmly. "I just wanted him to do as he was told." Mike looked at me. "If you have any film in your camera, I could use a couple photos for the report."

"Film? Welcome to the digital age, I always have film."

Stevie returned as I dug in the trunk.

"What the hell was that all about?"

I looked up. "Excuse me?"

"Why the hell did you cancel my search? We might have caught that guy."

I fought as the temptation to lay into the kid threatened to overpower my good judgment. "He wasn't wanted for anything," I said plainly.

"He ran."

"Last I checked, that isn't a crime."

"Well how about this?" he said as he held up the familiar one inch squared zip lock baggie with two tiny white colored rocks inside. "Last I checked, this was a felony."

That did it. At six-two and two hundred pounds, I had a lot of size on the kid. In three long steps I was on him. He tried to back up, but I stayed close until he backed into the door of one of the alley garages. The fire in my eyes wasn't for effect. I was flat out hot as sailor's piss after a weekend leave in the Philippines.

"Lookie here, Stevie," I started. "You might be fast, but that guy was long gone before you even started after him. If he wasn't, he had enough distance that you weren't going to catch him. That is, unless he stopped running and waited for you. At which time you might have got your stupid young ass jumped before you knew what happened—your stupid dumb ass that was alone. And for what? Twenty bucks worth of rock you didn't see him pitch. Even if you could have connected it to him, it would have never made a solid enough felony charge to outweigh the gravity of the other problem you failed to notice."

I took a breath and glared at him. He made eye contact but only briefly between attempts to look around me for an escape route.

"Relax," he said dismissively.

With that, I thought seriously about grabbing him firmly by the shirt collar and raising him off the ground. *That* would have been for effect. Then I remembered the total lack of support a similar move had garnered General Patton in a time when such acts were generally more tolerated. I would have to content myself with yelling. Little in the world really pisses me off, but not looking after your teammates tops my list.

"It's not about the dope, slapnuts. It's about leaving people behind. I told you that on the way over here. We stick together. We do not split up and go our separate ways on the whim of some crack fiend who doesn't want to get caught holding a couple dimes worth of cocaine. You wanna run, make the risk worth something."

His gaze shifted to the ground. "Yes, sir." He coughed.

"Enough, Hatch. He gets it." It was Marcus. I hadn't even noticed him, but like a good partner he'd moved in to look out for me. My point was made. I turned and stepped away without another word.

As I walked back to the car, I passed Smith standing there with a disgusted look on his face. I'd forgotten the pasty skinned, squad apple polisher was even at the call. "The guy's a kid. You always this much of an asshole?"

"Worse," I said, and went back to my car to look for my camera.

Chapter 3

LIFE IS TENUOUS. Considering all our advances, our belief that we have evolved, the world is still a hostile and unforgiving place. Even with our fancy toys, we remain a primitive culture. And for all our attempts to protect the stupid and unaware, for all our annoying court-ordered warning labels placed in brazenly obvious places, life can still change in an instant. Most folks don't realize that but for a handful of times in their lives. But in my world time is metered in fractions of a second.

Stevie and I returned to the mundane part of our job nearly as quickly as we had left. It was now time to take photos and restore order so Murphy could head downtown to process his prisoner. To any bystander, things would seem relatively uneventful. To someone just passing by, the fight might never have existed. They would simply think this was another task that wasted the time of three cops when one might suffice.

As I lifted the camera, my legs wobbled. Nothing visible to anyone else, but I felt the quiver. The adrenaline coursing through my veins caused my body to tremble like a supercharged sports car idling in neutral. There was nothing I could do but take a couple deep breaths and get back to work. I didn't have the luxury of sitting around. Murphy needed to go downtown, and we needed to clear for the next problem. This was Thursday night—my Friday—but the city was coming to life, and my work was far from over.

The moment was worse for Stevie. He might need a few minutes to cool off and bring himself out of supercharge mode. Smith got back in his car and drove off to whatever little cave he hid in. He only ventured out into the mean world when he had to.

I snapped a few shots of Murphy's torn shirt, the bloody scrapes on his arms, and the disarray of his appearance. There was nothing like a few photos to remind a jury that the spit-and-polish officer they saw in court didn't look nearly that nice after rolling around on the ground with the clean-cut defendant now sitting in front of them. Even with the photos, nobody would see the oh-shit look that I'd caught on Murphy's face as he fought; worried that one small error on his part could tear away any remnants of his future. At least for now, we were back in control.

Then the dispatcher spoke. "831 Zebra, are you clearing soon?"

In dispatch terms, that was a loaded question. They don't ask unless they have something crummy on your beat and wanted to give you first chance at taking the call. Oh well, it was my beat. You can't just take the good stuff.

"What do you have?"

"Priority 'check the welfare' coming in down the street. The phone room is still getting info."

I looked across the alley at Murphy. He nodded. "I'm outta here. Thanks, Hatch."

I nodded back. "831-Z, you can show us en route. Can I have the address?"

She gave me a number on the 4200 block of 48th Street.

I made a quick scan to find my partner. He was already in the car, no doubt typing a string of messages to his friends in protest of having to work with me.

I jumped in. "What have we got?"

Stevie seemed startled that I would talk to him considering what just happened.

"Nothing's come through yet," he mumbled. "Think the computer's not catching the signal here."

I fired up the car, and we were off. The dispatcher came back on the air. "831-Z, the caller hung up. All he said was that he just found his wife on the floor, and she's not moving. Medics are en route but standing back."

"10-4." Just wonderful! A check-the-welfare, nothing further, and we would be at the scene long before dispatch could ever get an update. Once again, we were headed into something blind. Experience told me our call was probably less dramatic than it sounded. She'd probably got drunk and passed out on the floor. The husband came home and overreacted. The nagging thought in the back of my brain was that the night could get a whole lot worse.

I was about to ask for another unit when Marcus came on the air.

"834-Yellow, I'm still in the area. I'll take the alley side of that call."

Good man. Normally I preferred working alone. When I didn't, I liked working with the Brotherman. He knew his job.

Of course, if Marcus was reading options, so were others. I pressed down on the gas. The call could be nothing. If so, I wanted it taken care of without turning a drunk into a big deal that wasted a bunch of cops better used someplace else.

I didn't look at Stevie, just kept my eyes on the road. "This time you stick with me. Got it?"

"Yeah."

We were there. I turned onto 48th Street, pulled over, and parked a few houses from the residence. I could see the caller just down the street waving frantically at us. The temptation was to drive right up to him, but in my job distance equals time. If he was some nut hoping to ambush us on arrival, racing up to him wouldn't do us any good.

We got out of the car, and the man—a white male, tan, perhaps Hispanic—moved our direction. I gauged him at maybe five-eleven, two-hundred-thirty pounds. In jeans, tan boots, and dirty white t-shirt, he was clearly a labor oriented person. His powerful arms stretched the fabric of a white cotton t-shirt, and he had a broad chest with just a hint of a gut that had probably been well earned and was still being purchased through regular payments to Budweiser. If we ended up fighting, it would be a rough one.

There was a small nylon case on his belt—probably a knife—perhaps a Leatherman tool. Other than that, I saw no immediate threats.

"Come, come," he said, his voice quivering, then turned and headed back to the house.

My voice came deep, from the diaphragm, slow, loud, and clear: "Stop."

He halted, and then started to turn away again.

"Stop," I said again. "I need you to tell me what's going on, quickly." If she was hurt we couldn't waste time.

He took a hesitant step toward us. "My wife, my—my wife.

I came home and found her in the bedroom. I think she's dead. Please hurry."

Marcus came back on the air. "834-Yellow, 97 in the back."

Then Martinez and Jenkins, "832 Zebra, 10-97 out front with 831-Z." The headlights of their police car came around the corner.

"Is there anybody else in the house, any kids, dogs, anything I need to know about?"

"No, it's just us."

"Which house? Is the front door open?"

"The blue one. Yes, I think I left it open."

"Your wife's name?"

"Esther."

As he answered, Jenkins and Martinez pulled up and got out of their car. "Jess, stick with him. Rick, come with us."

I walked toward the house with Jenkins and Stevie. I looked for signs of trouble. There was nothing. It was a simple, single story 1940s era bungalow, probably a two bedroom. The blue exterior was faded, the white trim cracked and flaking away. The cracked, weedy, concrete driveway was on the right side and led to an unattached single car garage. The door of the garage was closed, and I could see the padlock hanging in place. There was a beat-up, white Chevy truck in the driveway with a tool box in the back. I could see a carpenter's belt and a couple pails of junk in the bed.

The yard was overgrown, tree branches hanging down, some kind of mostly dead ivy covering the chain-linked fence that ran across the front yard. There was a small front porch with a chair and a trash can overflowing with soda and beer cans. Next to that was an old flower pot filled to the brim with cigarette butts. The front door was partially open, but there were no indications of anything more ominous than a couple who liked to drink but hated to work in the yard.

As we walked through the front gate, I pointed to the left and Rick moved to the corner of the house. I got on the radio, "Can 842-Yellow advise if he has eyes on the back?"

"Back is clear," Marcus responded.

"We'll be entering the house," I told the dispatcher.

Stevie and I moved more quickly now. If Esther was hurt, we'd get to her soon enough. The "I think she's dead" part had changed things. Dead is bad, maybe dead is creepy. If she was dead, we had all the time in the world. The difficulty lay in between. She could be passed out, she could be grievously injured. It was the how that I didn't know and needed to worry about.

I called out, "Esther, San Diego Police, you in there?"
No response.
"Esther, it's the police, can you answer me?"
Again, nothing.

I pushed the front door all the way open. The house was in a similar state as the yard. There was a dirty couch, a coffee table littered with filthy plates, ashtrays, magazines, and beer cans. A large television sat on a wooden cabinet that was much too small. There were cables sticking out from behind the TV but attached to nothing.

To the right was a small kitchen with a similarly filthy table and four chairs. On the far side of the kitchen was a door to the back yard. A DVD player and a microwave were stacked on the table.

My gun came out.

I heard Stevie unholster his gun. His came out slow as if he was still unsure why. We moved toward the back hallway.

You'd think these moments would get easier after all these years, but they don't. Walking blindly into a strange place would never become natural—you just learn self-control.

I could hear Stevie behind me. His breath was short and stuttered. He probably wasn't even aware of it. I wanted to tell him to breathe, but now wasn't the time.

The hall was empty. We moved toward the first bedroom, small, maybe nine feet square. It had a twin bed and the rest of the space was cluttered with all manner of junk people keep in the hope such trash will turn into forgotten treasures.

Next was the bathroom. The formerly white shower curtain was now more of a yellowish brown. At the end of the hall was the last bedroom. The door was open, the wood splintered around the frame and a large dent about shoulder height in the middle. Someone had forced it.

The door was at the left end of the room and opened inward, flush up against the wall. On the other side was a dresser with a mirror. Against the opposite wall from the dresser was a queen size bed that nearly filled the room. The mattress was askew. There was a window on the back wall and maybe two and a half feet of floor space on either side of the bed.

I could see Esther's legs sticking out from under the mattress, which had been pulled off the box spring and tossed on top of her. She was alone, jammed between the bed and the wall nearest the door. She wasn't moving. I holstered my gun and immediately moved to the floor next to her. My gut was telling me she was dead, but I had to know.

If she was dead, I needed to disturb as little in the room as possible.

I knelt at her feet and shook her by the calf. Her leg moved easily, warm to the touch with no sign of rigor mortis. I lifted the mattress.

My hopes dwindled. A clear plastic bag covered her head, the kind of plastic that comes over clothes from the dry cleaners. There was no mistaking the white rope wrapped around her neck or her blue face.

There was also no reaching her carotid artery since the rope had been wrapped around her neck several times. I found an arm and checked for a pulse. Nothing—no rise and fall of the chest, no staggered, involuntary rhythm as the body might attempt a gasp for air. I brought my light around to her eyes. They were wide-open, pupils fixed, with the milky glaze of death clearly apparent. Esther was as dead as they come.

I eased back up, careful not to move my feet. I'd already disturbed more than I cared to. "831-Z, we're okay in the house, have the outside units maintain their positions and have 834-Sam respond." I hated to call the sergeant, but there was no getting around it. The circus was about to start.

"834 Sam," the dispatcher called out, "Are you clear to respond to 831-Z's location?"

There was no response.

"834-Sam?" she asked again.

Figures, he was probably buried in the station studying pie charts or something.

Finally, "834-Sam, are you calling?"

"834-Sam, can you respond to 831-Zebra's call." The dispatcher's transmission was a statement, but he didn't pick up on her tone.

"834-Sam, what does he have?"

I got back on the air. "Just have him respond." The last thing I wanted was to make the circus larger. He was clearly disturbed by the interruption, but he'd need to get out of his office and pretend to be in charge for a while. That's what he got paid for. There didn't need to be any unnecessary discussion about why. The less the press picked up from the radio, the longer we had before they arrived. Since this was a homicide, their presence was inevitable, but it was always nice if they didn't get there until after the priorities were taken care of. Until then, they were usually just an additional complication.

I turned to Stevie who stood crammed in the doorway next to me.

"She's dead?" His face was without expression. His breath still came in short, rapid gulps followed by long pauses.

"Yeah."

He stepped backwards.

"Stop."

He froze.

I looked around the room, scanning, taking everything in. The air was oppressively hot. The room stunk of sweat, but a hint of perfume lingered, clinging to the trace smell of death I hadn't noticed before. Maybe I even imagined the scent. The stench was sickening, and I wanted out.

But this was my beat, and she'd died on it. There was a job to do.

"Come on, Hatch, we gotta back outta here. Let Homicide handle this."

"Stand still, quit running your mouth for a second, and you might learn something. We're already in. Once we back out that's the last opportunity we're going to have at this scene. Pay attention while you can."

From this point, the case belonged to Homicide. That didn't mean I was without a role in the investigation. Over the years I'd been to a number of these. I knew the routine but I was also the one who came out to this neighborhood every night. If I hadn't already met the person who did this, we might yet meet. I didn't want to miss anything that might help me identify who that was. I didn't want to miss anything that might help the detectives. I wasn't going to drop the ball.

I knew I couldn't stay long, but I wanted something. As I looked around, I put together a mental picture of what happened. The clearest image was sheer, angry violence. Esther had not gone gently into this good night. She had several straight abrasions on her arm, probably from the rope as she fought to keep it off her neck. Visible skin on either side of the rope showed indications that she'd been fighting as the cord was wrapped around her throat—when pulled tight it pressed deeply into the flesh.

There were shoe marks on the wall, and divots in the drywall where she had kicked in an attempt to get leverage. Next to them were light blue scuff marks. What they were didn't register at first; then it hit me. Those marks were from her jeans. She had been thrown against the wall with such force that her blue jeans left a layer of cotton lint on the wall, much the way a hit-and-run car often leaves a trace of paint. Her shirt was torn, and there was a button on the floor.

Much of what had been on the dresser was now on the floor at the foot of the bed. It was easy to see where the dust had been swept clear by whatever brushed across the wood surface. I imagined it was Esther flailing and struggling for her last breaths.

As I considered the DVD player and microwave in the kitchen, the most likely scenarios came to mind. Poor Esther had come home and surprised a burglar. She got killed for her bad timing. There was, of course, the alternative version waiting outside with Martinez. The husband found her, and that alone put him on the list. The viciousness of the crime helped too. If a burglar killed her, he was a hard-core crook. If the husband murdered her, well . . . no one dies more viciously than those killed by the people who love them.

I turned to Stevie, who had clearly grown anxious, "You ready to go?"

"Yes."

CHAPTER 4

SOMETIMES A HOMICIDE rolls in like a Midwestern thunderstorm. One minute the sky is clear and it's a warm summer day. The next, it's dark and layered with high reaching blue-black clouds. The thunder rolls in from a distance and lightning flashes. The intensity builds as the storm draws closer. Once the clouds have opened, there's no closing them until the torrents of rain have run their course. Sometimes you get hail and tornadoes.

Such can be the nature of an incident like this. Word spreads quickly when someone dies horrifically, and there's little you can do to stop the approaching storm. Each supervisor who arrives adds an exponent of confusion. Very quickly, the one person in charge is replaced by a tribe with too many chiefs and not enough Indians.

Throw in the press, the nosy neighbors, and the parents who bring their kids out hoping to see something and then complaining when their child is traumatized, and the whole damn thing gets worse.

Then you have the cops themselves. Nobody signed up because they wanted to spend hours writing reports. We got into this job because it allowed us to do everything our mothers told us not to. We get to drive fast, play with guns, and talk to strangers—it's expected. That means when the choice is write a ticket, take a report, or go to a homicide, the latter will win every time. There are those strange few who don't think that way, but most are like wide-eyed ten-year olds just aching for adventure.

But a homicide isn't like the movies. What happens in a crime scene must be accounted for. That means you don't get forty people standing in a living room talking and joking while the body lies at their feet. In the real world, once the crime is determined, no one goes into the scene unless they have a compelling need to be there. When they do, that gets documented. For that reason alone, someone has to stand guard so people don't wander where they shouldn't, cops included.

Rick and Marcus got that glory job. They would remain posted to the front and rear of the residence until relieved. We placed the husband in the back seat of our car. He wasn't under arrest, but we couldn't have him going anywhere either. Stevie got in the car to keep him company. Martinez set about blocking off the sidewalk in front of the house with yellow tape. Other than Homicide, no one showing up would need to get any closer than him.

I asked Stevie to get the husband's name, his wife's basic information, and any other general details that might be helpful. Homicide would want that, and they'd treat us like amateurs if we didn't have such basics when they arrived.

I phoned the Watch Commander. He'd be the one to call out Homicide. The faster I got a hold of him, the quicker they'd get here. No matter how fast I worked, how organized and prepared I might be, this was the last call of the night.

After briefing the Watch Commander, I made a list of officers who showed up and what they did. I made notes with information the sergeant would need in order to brief Homicide. This wasn't my job, but doing the work now would save me from having that task delegated down the road.

I was done with the briefing sheet when my sergeant arrived. Theodore Roosevelt. His overly protective parents had apparently thought it would be a cute name for their magnificent little boy. Perhaps thought he was the model of greatness and needed a name befitting his grand future. I'd only worked for him a couple days, but he clearly held the same belief.

As Sergeant Roosevelt stepped from the vehicle, he stretched his back then stood straight as if he might squeeze an extra inch or two out of his average height. At twenty-nine he was the youngest sergeant on the Department, something he made sure everyone knew. The troops call guys like him five year wonders. Not to his face, mind you, but that was the truth. He was a white suburban kid with baby-boomer parents who gauged success by title and income.

Sergeant Roosevelt was the ass-kissing suck-up so typical of nearly any corporate workplace in the country. Of course, in corporate jobs, your lack of experience might not mean the difference between life and death.

He wanted to be Chief. Not only that, he wanted to be the youngest chief in the history of the department. That meant no time to be bothered with something as insignificant as experience. He simply moved from job to job as fast as he could and only stayed long enough to be able to claim a line on a resume. It was never about what he knew, only where he could say he'd been.

I'd taken the time to check him out. Any cop worth his salt always had his sources, and they're never further away than a phone call or a meet for coffee. As soon as I knew I was getting a new boss, I'd done my research.

Sergeant Roosevelt's brow furrowed as he looked around at the yellow tape and the other officers. "What have you got, John? This turn into something more than a welfare check?"

He was brilliant. I saw a grand future for him. "Turned into a homicide, sir." I withheld my distaste. No good could come from belittling a little man. Just ask Napoleon.

"You sure? That's not what the call said." He started moving toward the house as if he was going to need to check for himself, as if he didn't believe me.

"Quite positive."

He stopped and faced me as he processed his next move. I helped him along.

"In the back bedroom, rope around the neck and a bag over her head. The husband said he came home and found her on the ground."

Stevie walked up and stood next to me, "Hatch?"

"Just a second," Roosevelt said with a wag of the finger and his best fatherly tone, "He's briefing me."

My impulse was to pay attention to Stevie and make the sergeant wait, but I continued. "The husband is in our car."

"Hatch, that's . . ."

Again, he was cut short. "You'll get your chance in a minute, Steven. Let's finish the important details."

Stevie shut up but shifted unsteadily on his feet like he had to go to the bathroom.

"We saw a DVD player and a microwave stacked on the kitchen table. On its face, this is looking like she stumbled into the house at the wrong time."

I ran Sergeant Roosevelt through the rest of our observations and told him who was doing what and where everyone was positioned. I finished with, "I wrote up the homicide briefing. I put it on the hood of Martinez's car. The Watch Commander has been contacted, and Team Two is en route."

I turned to Stevie expecting his information would come next. I was wrong.

"You called the Watch Commander?"

"Yes, sir."

"Thanks, but that's my job. That's generally the sergeant's call."

"The briefing itself is all yours, just thought I'd give you a head start."

"Just the same, if I need you to do it, I'll ask."

The spike in my blood pressure was instantaneous. The work was done, and Napoleon still felt compelled to let me know who was in charge. I nodded and drew a long breath. This was about control. I wouldn't make that mistake again.

This time Stevie spoke. Even the new guy picked up on the pecking order. "Sir?"

Roosevelt turned, brought out of his distraction. "Yes, what's so important?"

Stevie's shoulders deflated. "Sir, ah, I was sitting in the car with the husband and, well, I think there might be more to his story than he's telling us."

"You're not questioning this man, are you?"

The expression on his face resembled that of a puppy caught peeing on the carpet. "Ah, no. He just kept asking me if his wife was dead. I didn't know if I should tell him ,but he was nearly crying."

"That's fine," Roosevelt answered abruptly. "I'm sure he figured it was coming. No harm."

"Yes, sir. Thank you." Roosevelt started walking back to his car. "Sir, that's not the problem."

Roosevelt stopped and sighed. It was obvious we were overwhelming him. Considering his background, odds were he hadn't been to many of these. His brain was probably a bit too overloaded to be distracted.

"I mean, I'm glad that was okay, I was a little worried," Stevie rambled. "But, when I told him she was dead, he didn't start crying like I thought. He cussed at her."

"Anger is a natural reaction."

"How about, 'Good, the fucking cunt deserved it'?"

I was as shocked as Roosevelt.

"He rambled on for like five minutes calling her a whore, a slut, and a whole bunch of nasty things. Said he was glad she was dead. I didn't ask him anything, really. I just sat there listening like they told us in the academy. What do you want me to do?"

Sergeant Roosevelt silently processed his next move.

And then the storm arrived, and it was not Midwestern at all. No, much like most California storms, this one rolled in a great deal less impressive than it could have. Two press vans pulled up, but the only people moving quickly were the cameramen who wanted to get as much file footage as possible. The reporters lagged, idling slowly with an indifference that would be reflected in their lack of interest in the story.

Unless something changed and Esther turned out to be the errant daughter of some Senator or the lab found the rifle from the grassy knoll, Esther's death wasn't likely to get more than a brief sound byte from a slow day broadcast and a few lines in the morning paper. Esther was nothing more than space filler. There would be no storm, no downpour of reporters trumpeting her cause. There would be no self-declared speakers for the people, the champions of the underdog, each professing to be a leader and all demanding justice for a poor girl who was a victim of some larger subplot orchestrated and carried out on a society filled with helpless victims.

This was no thunderstorm, and the light rain Esther's death brought would do little to cleanse the stain left this night. She was nobody. Even those who watched the evening news or read the brief lines in the paper would quickly go back about their disinterested lives, perhaps momentarily disturbed before returning their rapt attention to the vapid lack of social contribution of their favorite celebrity. No one would write a book about Esther.

The Field Lieutenant showed up at the same time as the first homicide detectives.

"Go back to the car," I told Stevie. I pulled my digital recorder out of my pocket and pressed the record button. "Tuck this in your shirt. If he says more, we'll have it on tape. Don't ask him any questions. If he grills you, just defer to Homicide. Tell him they'll let him know exactly what's going on when they talk to him."

Stevie took the recorder and placed it in his shirt pocket before leaving. Sergeant Roosevelt walked over to Martinez and reviewed the briefing sheet I'd drawn up. All he wanted to do now was be prepared so he wouldn't look like an idiot when it was his turn to work. I stood nearby just in case he couldn't figure things out.

"I guess we're in the hurry up and wait mode," Martinez said. "Sure went to shit fast. We were just about to try and sneak in some dinner. I'm starving."

"You didn't eat before work?"

"I got three kids, the wife works weekdays, and I gotta commute from Temecula. Not much time for me before work."

"You get any sleep?"

"Standard four hours. I'll be glad when we're back to working weekends."

"I bet. Don't know how you do it."

Martinez shrugged. "You gotta do what you gotta do. I can't afford a decent place in the city, and the transfer list for Northeastern's way too long." He nodded toward the house. "Is she pretty dead?"

I shrugged. "I couldn't tell if she was pretty when she was alive."

Martinez laughed. "Sick motherfucker."

What could I say? If we didn't have our gallows humor, we'd all be standing around crying. The situation was traumatic. That didn't change just because you put a badge on. I'd seen plenty of bodies, more than a person should in a lifetime. Death was a stress to be dealt with. Cops did it by joking.

"Hatch."

I turned to find Detective Ronald White walking my way. The desk had made him a little heavier over the years and the stress of the job had thinned his hair some, but he still had that same goofy duck walk.

Ronny and I were from the same academy. When we had tear gas training, they put us in a little house, one at a time, and gassed us until we felt like each painful breath was restrained by barbed wire wrapped tightly around our young lungs. Then we had to walk out of that house without assistance, eyes burning, tears flowing, snot tendrils that wouldn't let go hanging from our noses to our knees. He was there to catch me when I stumbled back into the clean air of the outdoors. Snot and all, he held me up until I could stand on my own. We had become cops together, and even though many years had passed with long months without contact, we shared a bond. I trusted him to this day.

Where my career had been shift after shift on the street, his led him into investigations. That was what he always wanted, what he liked to do, and he was good. He was in a suit and tie with his little spiral notebook in hand.

"Ronny, you couldn't investigate your way out of a paper bag. Don't tell me they put you in Homicide."

He smiled at Martinez. "You have to work with this crusty old bastard?"

Jess nodded.

"Sorry, man. Cut him a break. He suffers from a special medical condition."

"Special condition is it?" I asked anxious to hear what I had this time.

"Oh, you know you do," he said to me. To Martinez, "Old Hatch has this rare genetic make-up that causes strange things to happen in nature. He is what's called a fecal attractor, shit magnet if you will. My life exists, my job exists, only to clean up the splatter of a mess that seems to gather around him."

I shook his hand when he got close enough. "Good to see you, Ronny."

"Good to see you, ya old fool."

"We're both old."

Ronny looked around. "Apparently so, don't recognize anyone."

"Times change fast out here."

"No kidding, two months in Homicide and the gray hairs doubled. What have you got?"

Ronny and I walked over to the sidewalk, away from the prying ears of others, and I told him the whole story. He would hear everything in the briefing, but he wanted his news from the source. That's what made him a good detective. His single goal was to clear cases, to find answers. In order to do that, he knew he needed help.

No matter how much talent an individual might possess, they can't do everything alone. Ronny relied on others to act as his net. The broader he could spread that net, the more he could catch. And when others helped, he was quick to share whatever accolades fell upon him with those who made it possible. I could give a shit about the accolades, but I'd help him any way I could.

When business was finished, we switched to the important stuff.

"How's your wife," I asked.

"Good. A little unhappy about all the callouts, but I think she'll get used to it."

"How long you been together now? You were married in the academy."

"Coming up on twenty years. My oldest graduated already."

I groaned.

"That's not the half of it—she's going to UCSD. Got a scholarship, but even living at home I know I'm gonna hate to see how much this is gonna cost. To be single and rich like you. Wanna adopt her?"

"She look like her mother?"

"Fuck you, you still with that one girl?" The question trailed as he searched for her name. It didn't surprise me, there'd been a few over the years.

"Michelle," I said, completing his sentence. "Yeah, nearly a year now."

"You gonna marry her or what?"

"Dunno, not sure I should mess with a good thing."

"Marriage is a good thing. Twenty years, man. Even with the bad times, I know she's there when I get home."

I smiled slightly, warmly. He might be right, but his case seemed the exception, and the thought of giving up half of everything I'd ever worked for scared the hell out of me. I'd seen a lot of guys my age starting over or spending long years having to coordinate child custody with people they didn't like. My way seemed easier.

"Perhaps one day," I conceded.

Ronny's head jerked. "Looks like my boss is here, better get back to work."

He headed toward the small crowd of suits forming next to the crime lab van. As soon as they were all present, Sergeant Roosevelt would read the briefing and they could go to work. Several hours would go into photographing, searching, and collecting any evidence from the house.

I recovered my laptop to start writing my report. They'd want that before the night was done. Since I was the first one here, I had the most to account for. I wanted to be accurate, complete.

I wrote. The block around me was a kinetic swarm of activity that reminded me of ants searching an area for crumbs—there was slow, steady movement, but no bit of ground went uncovered. Cops were knocking on doors trying to find a neighbor who might have seen something, detectives were crawling around on the floor of the Anderson's filthy house, reporters were trying to find prime shots for their evening newscast, and neighbors were wandering anywhere they could get away with. Not a bit of it seemed exciting.

Ronny spent a few minutes talking to the husband, Aaron Anderson, who was still in the back seat of my car. He let him out, and I loaned him a cigarette to give him. After a few minutes, Ronny was off. An hour later, the homicide sergeant asked us to transport Aaron down to Headquarters so they could talk to him some more.

Mr. Anderson was quiet most of the trip, the gravity of his situation, the sudden shift in life weighing firmly upon him. He finally spoke as we were pulling into the front lot at 14th and Broadway.

"I'm in a world of shit, huh?"

A glance in the rearview mirror, and I could see that he was looking at me. People do that—they gauge us just as clearly as we do them. It was easy to tell the veteran, and Mr. Anderson knew that's who'd most likely have his answer.

"Sir, I'm not quite sure what you mean," I lied. One way or another, he was in the spotlight. I knew it, he knew it.

"Bullshit, man. They think I killed that bitch."

My instincts fired. I ached to see where this would go, but now wasn't the time. Homicide was preparing to interview this man, and I didn't know what they did or didn't have on him. As much as I might want to get into his head to look for answers, it wasn't my place. Not right now.

"Mr. Anderson, I really don't know much about what the detectives are thinking. I'm just the patrol guy, they don't tell me much. They're who you need to talk to."

"You're not listening to me, man." He slumped back in his seat. "She never listened either. She'd listen to that bitch from work but not me."

"Sorry, sir. I'm just not the guy with the answers. You need to talk to the detectives."

"Fuck you then. You cops never do help people."

CHAPTER 5

WE SPENT THE NEXT three hours smashing our asses in the Homicide office. I'd have played Solitaire on my laptop, but the folks in New Technologies blocked it so officers wouldn't waste time playing games. I tried to talk to Stevie, but after a few minutes of struggling to find common interests, we both gave up. He quickly drifted into the world of text messaging. My report had taken maybe an hour to write. The remaining two were spent staring at walls, looking at cubicles, and drifting between thoughts. My curious nature remained in church-like restraint. Something about this office made you feel less than free to move around.

The only place you felt less free to roam was Internal Affairs. I think the current terminology is Professional Standards Unit. Hard to say, the name might have changed again. You never can tell, old names sometimes disappear to fit some rising star's new vision. This was Headquarters, but at some point it had become the San Diego Business Center. Perhaps I needed to get out more, but the last time I checked, we were the police and the central building was always Headquarters. Why you'd need a different name was beyond me. Some things might need changing, some don't. The old names are still good enough for me.

My thoughts shifted to Aaron and the two detectives who had taken him when we arrived. I wanted to watch the interview, see what he had to say, but they were gone before I could ask. To simply walk back and observe, even if he couldn't see me, would get me an ass-chewing if I didn't have permission. Whatever my interest, I wasn't about to blow a murder investigation because I was curious.

Three hours was a long time, and I had to wonder if he was confessing, spilling his guts about their bad marriage and the fight that put him over the edge. That's how these things usually went, but I couldn't get over the other possibilities. Maybe he was involved and he paid someone to kill her, to make it look like a burglary. The real story could be anything—rarely was it complicated or intricate.

My thoughts passed away like smoke from a Marlboro when the Homicide Sergeant came into the office and told us we could leave. He collected our reports and didn't seem inclined to talk, so I pried. "He saying anything yet?"

Sergeant James, a stocky man with a shortly trimmed mustache, was just a couple years senior, but every time I'd ever run into him he always spoke like there was a decade between us. "Just working out a timeline. Nothing yet."

"You think he killed her?"

Sergeant James shrugged. "We really don't make a decision this early."

If the shrug didn't tell me what I wanted to know, the tap dance around an answer sure did. I wasn't in the loop, and he wasn't going to put me there. We returned to the Mid-City station. I told Stevie to have a good weekend. He headed toward the lockers while I started for the report room.

I found Murphy staring at his computer. He turned; his eyes were glazed and bloodshot. This had been a longer night for him.

"Still here?" I asked. "I was just going to submit my report on your deal."

"Tryin', man. I'm so tired I can hardly see straight." His shirt was still torn.

"What'd you get into?"

"Same bullshit. That dumb bastard made my night a living hell."

"Turned into a bit of a cluster?"

He nodded. "He fought me every step of the way. Higher than a kite, we had to restrain him to get blood while he spit and thrashed and bit at everyone. I found dope in his shoes, had to impound that. Finally got to jail, they rejected him cause he said he wanted to die. Took three hours to get cleared at Mental Health, and we had to fight him again there. I just got to my report about a half hour ago. At least it's Friday."

"Anything I can do to help?"

"No, man. Thanks for offering though."

I printed a copy of my report and gave it to him. As I got to the door, Murphy spoke again.

"Hey, John."

"Yeah."

"Thanks for being there tonight." He hesitated as if the words fought to climb up his throat. "I thought he had me. The only thing I could think of was that this bastard was going to get my gun. I didn't even see the other guy until he was running. If things went on any longer, I'd have had to shoot that dumb bastard or he'd have had me. I was almost outta fight."

"You did fine."

"Just the same, a shoe full of dope ain't worth dying over."

"I have faith you'd have survived."

"Don't know if that would be the better option. I can imagine the headline, 'Cop kills unarmed man in fistfight.'"

"It didn't come to that. Don't sweat it."

He nodded. "You're right. Coffee's on me next week."

"Fair trade."

"You da man, Hatch."

"Oh no, you da man. You are a super SWAT, ninja-god, don't ever forget that. I could only hope to be you. In fact, when I'm reincarnated, I hope it's as your t-shirt just so I can be close to you."

Murphy laughed and went back to his report.

I hit the locker room and changed into my standard, non-working garb—a Hawaiian shirt and blue jeans. It never hurt to be prepared. If the day came when I lost my job, I could walk onto any used car lot in the city and be dressed for work. If things got too unbearable, I could just hop onto a plane and step off into my tropical paradise.

I was on my way out when I saw Stevie sitting on the bench in front of his locker. Seems this had been a hard night for more than just Murphy. Stevie's elbows were on his knees, his head in his hands. He didn't even see me standing at the end of the aisle.

"Don't you have a home to go to?"

Stevie looked up slowly and then started when he saw it was me. "What, ah . . ." He was dumfounded, his face ashen white.

The anger I'd felt earlier washed away in an instant. "You've never seen someone dead before? I mean other than the autopsy they do in the Academy."

He shook his head. "Not like that. What could she have done to deserve that?"

"Not a thing."

"Then why? Why would some fucker do that to a person?"

"It just happens that way."

His voice raised, "We were three blocks away."

"And we got there as quickly as we could. She was dead long before we had a chance to do anything."

"What about her neighbors? Nobody called."

"Who knows, this is East San Diego. People are used to hearing all kinds of things, and they learn to ignore them. Maybe no one heard anything. Bad things happen."

"How can you be so okay with this?"

I sat down on the bench next to him and thought for a moment. I spoke softly. "I'm not okay with this. I don't think you should be either. But you do need to find a way to accept what you can't change. Life is brutal and unfair. The only promise we get is that one day we will die."

"Well that's fucked up."

"Yeah, how did you think it would be?"

Neither of us spoke for several long seconds. I knew what he was going through, but I just couldn't find the words to help. So many years, so many bad things, I just couldn't remember what it felt like to have your image of the world stripped open in such a raw manner.

"My first was Willie Baker. Old Willie was a transient, never did much of anything to anybody, didn't do much for anybody either. Willie just spent his days by the dumpster around 70th and El Cajon, behind the hotel drinking his forty ouncers. I'd talked to him a bunch of times, took him to Detox nearly as often."

I paused. The images of that night stretched long fingers across many years to reach out and touch me. The moment was as clear in my head as the night it happened. "I rolled up on Willie one night about two in the morning. Someone had beaten the living shit out of him. He'd tried to fight back, so they stuck him in the chest with a knife."

Stevie interrupted, "Why?"

"Dunno. The only call we got was the neighbor complaining that Willie was screaming and they wanted us to deal with him. The shitbird who killed him never got caught. I crouched next to

Willie and did what I could while the life bled out his chest.

"He couldn't speak in the end, maybe he didn't have the energy—maybe he was drunk. All I know is while I was waiting for the medics, while I held his balled up jacket against the hole in his chest, he just sat there staring at me with this pleading look like I ought to be able to perform some magic to fix the bad things. Up 'til the very end when his eyes glazed over and the death rasp they make forced the last bit of air out of his lungs, he never looked away. There was nothing I could do but keep him company."

When I thought my eyes might start to water, I turned as if I heard someone come in the other end of the locker room. When they didn't, I turned back.

"To this day, I can't drive behind that hotel and not see Willie's eyes looking up at me. That's the job you signed up for, kid. The world is a harsh, sucky place. You want to work the streets, that's something you'll need to reconcile. If you can't, get out while you're young enough to do something else."

Stevie remained silent. I got up and put my hand on his shoulder. "Go home. It's been a long night. These questions don't need to be answered right now."

I started to walk down the aisle when Stevie spoke. "Can I ask you something?"

"What's on your mind?"

"Well, you know, some people talk."

"This job, everyone talks. Rarely anything good."

"Yeah, this isn't good."

"Spill it."

"I'm just trying to figure something out. You don't seem like the asshole some people make you out to be. I mean, sometimes, but not like right now."

I smiled. "The greatest trick the devil ever pulled was convincing the world he didn't exist. You heard that saying before?"

"Yeah, well maybe."

"Don't let me fool you. I'm every bit the asshole people say."

I walked out of the locker room. It wasn't the first time someone said, that but I'd long quit worrying over what people thought. That some didn't like me was no news flash. I'd rubbed a lot of folks wrong over the years, and they ranged from trainees to chiefs.

Stevie had learned a lot tonight. He was changed, and nothing would take him back to the way he'd viewed life twelve hours ago. A light in his eyes was gone. The glimmer would return—at least I hoped—but his look would never be quite the same. A night like this changes a man ever so slightly, irrevocably, and years of little changes like that take their toll. I had no doubt that if little Stevie managed to grow from baby cop to veteran, he'd have his share of people thinking he was an asshole as well.

I made it to my Ford Explorer. Once inside, I rolled my neck and started the engine. The bad things had come out tonight. There was a day when I'd have run to the bar with the others and we'd drink them away. We'd douse the bad things with a bit of booze and reinforce our fragile self-confidence by bragging about the big things we'd done.

Gone are the days of Wambaugh's Choirboys. The old guard has been replaced. Though I have little doubt some folks still make it out for a drink after work, such events are no longer the nightly occurrence they used to be. And as a whole, we were better for it.

I don't remember those days, not like the streetwise thirty-plus year guys who are retiring now, but I grew up with those vets. They were where I am now, and in two days my first partner—one of that old guard—would be off to what I hoped would be a long retirement with little in the way of bad things.

As I drove to the entrance of the parking area, the gate opened automatically. Almost free. A couple seconds more, and I'd make my mad dash through East San Diego. With any luck I'd be through without someone shooting up the streets in front of me. Every night was the same thing, those few minutes of uncontrollable puckering in the nether regions. At least I had plenty of gas. I wouldn't have to stop at the first station and have some doper approach me for a dollar before realizing who I was.

As I eased out the gate, a car pulled to the curb next to me. The passenger door popped open. I jammed the Explorer in park and jumped out. I wasn't about to get gunned down leaving the station. My hand instinctively reached into my shirt and wrapped around the handle of my pistol.

An Asian woman got out of the car. She was maybe forty and still fully dressed. Didn't people sleep any more? Day and night they flock to the station and do everything possible to flag down a cop so they don't have to call and then wait around their house. If they had so much free time in the middle of the night, you'd think waiting wouldn't be a problem. As is often the case, I was wrong.

"S'cuse me, you police?" She nodded yes as if this was a given.

I scanned her quickly and then the car. There was an old man in the driver's seat looking at me with eyes indifferent to whatever urgent thing she was dragging him here for. I couldn't see anyone in the back seat.

"Yes, Ma'am, what can I do for you?" I did a quick look down the street to see if there was a patrol car I could dump this on. No one was around.

"We give somesing to you?"

Oh shit, she wants to turn in some gun, or dope, or burglary tools or some other silly thing she doesn't want to deal with. I didn't want it either.

"What do you have? I'm actually headed somewhere," I said leaving out that I was going home. "I'm not sure I can take it."

She reached into the car and the hand on my gun tightened. There is no escape. Mid-City's a place with its own gravity and you need a blind eye or a powerful force to get free of the strong grip that tries to keep you there.

The woman retrieved a large box and I groaned quietly. A whole bunch of stuff I'd spend the next hour impounding because that would be quicker than waiting for an on-duty unit.

She set the box down in front of me. "We found in alley."

"Take a step back. Let me see."

I crouched to look. The flaps of the box were folded so the top would remain closed. I tugged one corner fully expecting my arm to be blown from my body in the resulting blast. A bit paranoid, but you get that way after a while.

The flaps popped open and the streetlight overhead lit the inside of the box. There was a moment of hesitation as the little creature's eyes adjusted. "Mew," was all it had to say. Aww. Hell no. She could call Animal Control. What was I going to do with a kitten?

I started to close the flaps and the little thing began to protest and jump at the walls of the box. Its claws scraped frantically at the cardboard. "Ma'am, I'm not sure . . ."

"Please," she interrupted. "I don't know to call."

Her eyes pleaded, and I didn't have a clue how to explain the way to call Animal Control. At this hour, I wasn't inclined to spend thirty minutes trying.

I nodded. "I'll take care of it."

"Sank you, sank you," she said before running to her car. They were gone as quickly as they'd arrived.

Before anyone else could seize on the opportunity to take hold of my night, I grabbed the box and put it in the back seat. My prisoner and I were away in a flash.

I made it to the freeway while my passenger wailed in protest. The beast was annoying, and I wanted to turn up the stereo, but the volume I'd need would hurt both our ears.

If he was living in the alley, he was probably hungry. I stopped at a 24 hour grocery and picked up some food and litter. Where to put the litter gave me pause. I didn't want to buy too much for a creature that wasn't going to stay. The top of a Moet Champagne box would work. He could crap in style. I also grabbed a half-a-dozen stupid cat toys unsure just what it was a kitten would need to stay occupied. I certainly couldn't have him crying like he was. I wouldn't get any sleep.

"What a damn day," I said aloud, and he shut up. I caught the clue, and we made small talk the rest of the way home. The last thing I said as we pulled in the driveway, "Don't get too comfortable. Tomorrow you go to Animal Control."

CHAPTER 6

I WOKE TO A THIN crack of bright sunlight beaming through a narrow gap in the thick curtains. When you get to bed at four in the morning, you don't need the first hint of sunrise killing the remainder of your night. Heavy drapes are a requirement.

I rolled over and squinted, my eyes straining to focus on the glowing red numbers on my clock. As usual, I slept late. The life of a bachelor. However, today I had plans. I was meeting Michelle for lunch, and I wanted to practice at the range. If I was going to get the cat to Animal Control, I'd have to hurry.

I flipped off the covers and slid my feet over the side of the bed. As I stood, my body protested—a daily event. Starting with the tendons in the back of my heels, the stiffness worked quickly up my calves. Shooting pain fired through my right hip and my knees cracked. I froze while my body adjusted. The stiffening moved to my lower back. The first three steps were more a crippled stagger than a walk.

There's a price you pay for wearing that heavy gun belt.

The seat of a Crown-Vic didn't help. With a cage in the back, there's little leg room. What you have is further restricted by the computer, a seatbelt mount and the handcuff case at the back of your belt. Getting in and out of the car does little but torque your knees.

Twenty minutes in a searing shower helped ease the aching stiffness. As I made my way to the kitchen, the persistent mewing of my captive echoed from the garage. I ignored him while I set up the coffee pot. The crying didn't stop.

I walked back down the hall. Mine was a moderate, three bedroom house built years ago on the southern end of Mission Hills with a two car garage and a laundry room. There was a central hallway that ran past the bedrooms, a hall bathroom, and into the kitchen and dining room. A large living room with a fireplace lay just beyond the kitchen with floor to ceiling windows that looked over downtown. At night the view was pretty spectacular, and I felt fortunate to have the place.

When I opened the garage door, something scampered away and then stopped. The black and white kitten sat and stared at me a moment. I was about to step closer when the fur ball darted between my legs. It was gone before I could even turn.

I closed the door and followed. The cat moved like fury unleashed as it dashed into the living room, ran in circles, jumped on the couch, then over the couch, and darted though the kitchen and back down the hall again. He disappeared into a bedroom.

Must be mental, I thought, and went for my coffee.

I poured my first cup, and then I heard what sounded like the pounding of a small kettle drum as the kitten came charging back down the hall. How could anything so small make such a thundering racket?

Hitting the kitchen tiles at speed, his back legs veered sideways. In a split second he lost all traction, went down on his side and started to slide. When he stopped, he jumped up and started to run like one of those cartoon characters that runs in place for a moment before taking off like a bolt. He was nuts.

The black patch over his right eye made him look like a little pirate. Liberated from East San Diego, he was running in my house like a wanted parolee afraid to go back to the joint. We called people like that Parolees at Large, or PALs.

I took my cup of coffee and headed to the back patio. Pal could run around all he wanted until it was time to go to the bad place. Surely someone would want to adopt a fuzzy mental pirate.

I crossed the kitchen and paused at the baby grand piano that sat hunkered in the open space meant for a formal dining table. The thought of sitting down to play pulled at me, but I decided coffee was the priority.

I opened the French doors to the covered patio and stepped outside. The morning was warm and the thick, sweet smell of jasmine cut through the hazy smog that hung as a leftover from the morning commute. The trickle of water over rocks and the small splash as it gurgled into the fish pond was the only sound. The neighbors were all off to their nine-to-fives, and the morning was mine.

Sometimes I thought about a normal life, a nine-to-five, a wife, a family, a dog, and a summer vacation. It would be nice to come home and have people waiting to see you, to show you their latest school project. That's the life I had growing up, the life I always thought I'd have as an adult.

But even with the family and the house in the suburbs, cops never had the normal life. I'd heard the guys talk. With shift rotations, court callbacks, days off in the middle of the week, cops could sometimes go days without seeing their families. Some found a way to make it work, others didn't. I admired the ones who did.

Despite my intentions, life had never worked out that way. Perhaps Michelle would change that, but I'd long ago given up dreaming about what could be and simply accepted what was. Mine was a good life. I didn't have to worry about a roof over my head, or braces, or college, or any of a number of things the other guys seemed to have to stretch into a salary that just didn't quite go far enough. Some moved out of the city to places they could afford and managed their incomes sparingly. I didn't envy their miserable commutes. I envied the newer guys even less. I didn't know how a kid like Stevie would ever afford a home.

At least I could find peace here in my garden of solitude filled with palms, tropical plants, some hibiscus and a couple of plumeria bushes. I was always surrounded by color and sweet smells. This was my little bit of the islands, and I spent nearly every morning here or at the piano. That was my balance. It kept me sane.

I turned on the radio. The coffee went down good, and I lost track of time. Pal crept cautiously into the yard like a little jungle cat. When he discovered the cool grass, he started to roll and twist in it. Seemed he'd found paradise as well. And then, in a moment, he was off and swatting his paw at the big fish in the pond. He scampered away when they came up to investigate. Predator or not, they were nearly twice his size.

After finishing my second cup, it was time to go. Pal started when I moved. He darted back in the house and disappeared, small enough to hide in some nook. I would find him, but that might burn up my morning. I still wanted to shoot. I moved his food, water, and litter box into the laundry room. He'd have to wait.

Just as well. If I took him, I'd have to drive, and today was a fine day for riding. I grabbed some spare clothes and headed to the garage. In addition to the Explorer, I had two bikes, a Honda VTX, and a Goldwing.

I opted for the Goldwing with locking saddlebags where I stowed my extra clothes and spare helmet. Lunch with Michelle would surely turn into dinner, and then I'd stay at her house. Maybe we'd go to a movie. Tomorrow we could ride up the coast and be back in time for Jack's retirement party. Then a notion of responsibility struck. Staying at Michelle's wouldn't be an option if I didn't lose the beast. I considered making another attempt at a capture. No time. We'd have to come back here tonight. Maybe I could give the thing to her. I backed the bike out of the garage.

The officers who worked at the Range gave me little in the way of their usual hard time over how much Department ammunition I was using. Then again, I wasn't burning their ammo, police ammo. I was burning mine. I was carrying a new gun, and apparently the budget hadn't accounted for such things. That meant if I wanted to shoot, I'd best be prepared to eat the expense out of pocket.

The Department had a new Chief, and only time would tell what kind of leadership legacy he'd leave us. That didn't concern me. I was the little guy. What he did or didn't do would rarely be something I'd be aware of, but he had done one thing. He authorized officers to carry weapons we weren't previously allowed to use.

I opted for the Springfield-Armory TRP Operator. Built on a 1911 frame, it was a .45 caliber pistol whose design had survived for nearly a century. Commissioned in 1777 by George Washington, Springfield Armory had been serving America for a great deal longer. I was as confident in the company as I was in the power of a .45.

If the moment came between me and another, I wanted him stopped—quickly. The longer a threat is present, the longer people are at risk. This was the real world, and an armed bad guy on drugs didn't always stop like a kid playing cops and robbers. Beyond that, the .45 was a big, ugly hunk of steel. Sometimes the difference between shooting someone and getting them to surrender was little more than you being just a bit more scary than them. If the sight of my Springfield could discourage a deadly conflict, then I'd rather scare them into submission than shoot them into it.

Of course, with change comes the need for practice. The Beretta I'd carried had been a part of me for many years, as much a part of my daily life as carrying a wallet. I knew the gun, was comfortable with it. Now I needed to be every bit as comfortable with the new one. No good to get into a scrape and have my hands scrambling to manage a gun that functioned entirely different from the one I used to carry.

I burned through ammunition quickly, not taking time to do much other than draw and fire and then do it again as quickly as I could until I was out of rounds. I was on target, and my shots went where I wanted. It's too bad things don't work that way on the streets when your mind is trying to process what's happening at the same time as it's trying to control hands shaking from adrenaline overload. Of course, a paper target isn't very threatening, and it doesn't move or shoot back.

I spent a few minutes cleaning my gun, then stowed it in the Galco shoulder holster I wore when I rode. I had just enough time to get to the restaurant.

Downtown can be a pain, but on a bike there are a number of places you can park for free. I chose Hooters and walked through the Gaslamp Quarter to Sammy's Woodfired Grill. Michelle was already at a table in the middle of the restaurant. Considering the afternoon, I was surprised she wasn't sitting on the patio.

My pulse quickened. Something about the way her wavy brown hair brushed her shoulders. If not the hair, her soft, brown eyes got me every time.

I ran a hand through my own hair, coal black, save for the few shots of gray at the temples. Not as dark or glossy as it used to be, but I guess a lot of things faded with time. I kept it short, which minimized the motorcycle helmet-head phenomenon.

"Thought I'd beat you here," I said as I neared the table.

"Got done quicker than I thought," she answered. I expected her to start rambling about how excited her students were at the thought of a short day. She didn't. Michelle loved teaching, loved elementary school, but that got tiring just the same as any job. Perhaps going out to a movie would be replaced with a stay at home rental.

Michelle stood as I bent to kiss her, catching me on the cheek in one of those awkward, two people doing the same thing, thinking something different moments. Rather than try and correct my miscalculation with a second, perhaps more awkward kiss, I found my chair.

For a moment I couldn't do anything but look at her. That's when I noticed the difference. She looked sad. My mind worked the options. Sometimes she got this way after a run in with a parent who berated her for dealing with their child. She hated those days, the parents who did little in the way of disciplining their own children but were quick to jump on the teacher when their spoiled kid acted out.

I hated those days too. They brought joy-drowning melancholy. "You okay?"

She forced a smile.

"Tough day, huh?"

"Yeah," she said flatly.

The waiter came. We ordered iced tea, and he left.

"You wanna talk about it?"

Her expression shifted to concern. "What happened to your arm?"

I looked at my forearms, certain I'd scraped myself at the range. "What?"

"Your shoulder," she pointed.

The dark blue discoloration started just above my bicep. A tug on the short sleeve revealed a much darker bruise with ugly flecks of yellow, black and green. I quickly pulled the sleeve down while I shrugged dismissively. "Must have banged it on the car door. That happens."

"That's no bruise from a door. Let me see it."

"It's nothing."

"John!"

Shit, Mom voice. She was serious so I rolled up my sleeve again.

"Jesus," she exclaimed. "What happened?"

"I don't know," I started. Then it came to me. "Oh, I was helping Murph with a prisoner. I must have banged into the wall," I lied. "Really, I've had worse." I could tell from her reaction that admitting to worse injuries was of no help explaining this one.

Michelle shook her head. "Why didn't you tell me you got hurt?"

"This isn't hurt," I said honestly. I'd felt the dull ache a couple times while shooting but simply wrote it off as another of the litany of chronic aches that come and go. I had suffered worse. I'd spent four weeks with my chest wrapped in bandages after banging up my ribs. In hindsight, the doctor would have been the smarter course, but he might have taken me out of the field.

Eventually, I got better. This would heal too.

Michelle glared, looking for any hint of untruthfulness. She took a sip of water before speaking. "Why is it so difficult for you to tell me things?"

"Because you'll worry and there's no need."

"I worry anyway."

I shook my head. "We've been over this. Turn off your phone. I'll leave you a message when I get home so that you know I'm okay when you get up in the morning."

"I can't turn off my phone. What if something happens, something serious?"

"I'll send someone to let you know."

She fumed. "And what if you can't? John, I don't want someone knocking on my door several hours after you're hurt or maybe sometime the next morning. And God forbid that no one comes and I just have to find out from the news."

"But if you leave the phone on and I call at three in the morning, you wake up and freak out just the same. Then you can't sleep, and you're in a bad mood the next day." I leaned forward and put my hand on her forearm. "I'm not trying to keep things from you. There's just certain stuff better left at work. You have to have faith I'll be okay."

Her head bowed, eyes welled. Crying, shit, what did I know about crying?

Over the years I'd developed an ability to read people on the street. Most times I could tell what a person was thinking before they opened their mouth. Outside of work, women confounded me. I tried. I wanted to be supportive, but it never seemed to work.

Moments passed and still the right words didn't come.

They found her. "Where are we going with this?"

Time screeched to a jarring halt. I'd have hyperventilated if I could have found a way to inhale. Why did they always do that, put you on the spot with the tough questions when you're least prepared to deal with them, and then gauge your reaction? I scrambled for an answer that would satisfy her, all the while knowing any answer was double-edged and razor fine.

I tried humor, and a question. "With lunch?"

Wrong tact. "Where are we going with us, John? Be serious."

I rubbed my forehead, frustrated, hoping to buy time. "I'm sorry. I didn't expect to have this conversation today."

"Then when? We've been together long enough for you to have a clue. At work you make your decisions in an instant," she said, snapping her fingers to make her point. "Why does it have to be so damned difficult to tell me what I can expect?"

"I don't know."

"How can you not? Why is it so hard to make a commitment?"

The reasons dumped on me like a trash truck. She wasn't the problem, I was. I was damaged goods. Everything I'd seen work in the marriage of my parents was blown apart in my years on the streets. I didn't see the Brady Bunch. I saw dysfunction, trauma, and conflict. The notion of marrying a cop is a lot grander than actually living with a man who doesn't want to talk about his day, not because he doesn't want to but because he doesn't want to dump his ugly world on someone who doesn't live there.

"Michelle. I'd love to see where things go, but I can't tell you. Not right now."

"And I don't want to spend years waiting for something that won't happen."

"I need time."

"Damn," she said, wiping a tear. "It wasn't supposed to go this way. I'm not talking about time. I can give you time if I know where we're going. I'm talking about the streets, the shift work. I'm talking about building something stable, with normal hours, something that gives you a life and us a chance at stability."

Now she made sense. This was about wanting me to be something I wasn't.

"Finding some desk doesn't work like that. If a day position opened, I'd have to apply just like all the others that want good hours. My time on is no guarantee, and quite frankly I wouldn't want it if I could. This is what I do, what I want to do."

"There comes a time when you have to grow up."

Inside, I fumed. This wasn't about growing up. This was about changing who I was, changing the very things that had attracted her to me in the first place. I softened my voice but I knew what I had to say. "If I was a surgeon and had to work long, stressful hours, you wouldn't ask me to change. You might want a better schedule, but you'd accept the nature of the job even if I was getting called out at all hours of the night. Stressful hours can be managed. What you're asking me to do is change something else entirely."

The waiter delivered our iced tea and I told him to give us a few minutes. I took a drink. "When I drive to your house through Golden Hill, I see hot spots—people loitering, watching cars, looking to cut a deal, sometimes turn a trick, or maybe pawn something stolen. When we sit on your front porch so I can smoke, you watch the sunset and I watch the people walking by. If we go into a store, you see designer labels, sales, and shiny baubles—I see where the exits are and who might be a threat. We look at the world through different eyes. That won't change with different hours.

"Soldiers get to do their patrols among people they'll never see again. When they come home, they don't have to worry that the guy who was trying to kill them will end up behind them in the grocery line the next day. There's nothing I'd love more than to walk through life holding your hand blissfully ignorant of what's going on around me, but the ability to do that died a long, long time ago. Danger and me, we're a package deal. To me, this bruise is nothing more than spilled paste or crayon markings are to you. Put me on a desk, and I'll still rush out if Murphy calls for help again."

Michelle lowered her head so there was no chance at eye contact. "This isn't going to work, John."

It took a second for her statement to catch me, but when she looked up, the hurt was gone and there was a cold, insensitive glare. The tears remained, but what had been hurt now held a glimmer of anger, indifference, and she directed her discontent at me.

"I love you, and it's going to break my heart to move on, but we don't want the same things. I don't like the way being with you makes me feel."

This time the words hit like a sledgehammer. I knew what was coming. The pain hit me square in the chest, and the room pitched and spun like a Tilt-O-Whirl at a summer carnival. I began my frantic search for some way to make it stop.

"You brought me here to break up? You couldn't do that tonight?" Now there was an edge to my voice as I instinctively started to shut down. Years of doing the job teaches you to compartmentalize, to put the pain someplace else while you do what needs to be done. My mind erupted in a frenzy of thoughts. I struggled with my next move. Like "coffee to cover now," my personal life had changed in an instant.

My defenses kicked in. I would like to say they were the right ones, but who knows? Years of survival skills honed sharp on the streets have prepared me to deal with all of life in much the same way. Over time, you end up building some pretty serious battlements, ramparts, and bunkers that allow you to remove yourself from those things you don't presently wish to deal with.

Defenses didn't change if the danger was personal. This was still about survival.

"Why here?"

"I didn't want a scene."

That hurt. I thought about giving her a scene, then I thought about pleading, and then I thought about the nature of being a man, and character. There was nothing I hated more than the simpering, crying, spineless heaps who fought with their wives and girlfriends but melted into a muttering pool of "I love yous" when it was time to go to jail. I'd be damned if I was going to be that muttering heap. Maybe if I had a little less character, I'd be a lot less lonely, but maybe my problem wasn't character at all. Perhaps it was just plain foolish pride. Either way, I wasn't about to compromise.

"What about our time together gives you any indication I would make a scene?" She shook her head. "I don't know."

I kicked into interrogation mode. "Then why now?"

She didn't respond well to that, women never did. "Something changed, John. Maybe it was all those nights you were working, the days that I wouldn't see you. Sometimes it's like I'm not even a priority. Sometimes you're around, most of the time you're not. This isn't the life I want, and you won't change."

"Fine. You're free to go," I said, like a prince dismissing a serf.

Her eyes flared. "How can you be so damn cold? Don't you feel anything?"

"Apparently not," I said softly. "Would it change your mind if I did?"

She shook her head.

"Look, if you want out, I can't change that. What would you have me do?"

"But it's like this doesn't even matter to you."

It did matter, it was killing me and I wanted to tell her but my instincts fought me. I was determined that she would not see me reduced to the muttering heap. I did the only thing I could think of . . . I shrugged.

Michelle stood. She started to dig in her purse, "I have to leave." Her voice choked. "I'll give you some money for the tea."

"Don't worry. I'll take care of it."

She stopped digging and glared at me. "You're an asshole, John Hatch."

I didn't turn to watch her walk out. I wanted to, but I just couldn't. I waited until I knew she was gone, and then I took her chair. If she came back in some righteous moment of anger, I didn't want my back to the door. I ordered the grilled salmon, determined to sit in the restaurant and finish lunch. Once again, I was alone, and all I could do was pretend that everything was okay.

When I returned to my bike, I dug in the saddlebags and found the case for my iPod. I turned it on and shuffled through the list of stored albums hoping to find something. I thought about just turning the radio to the local country station. After all, with the exception of the blues, what better to listen to when you lose love? Then again, I'd only lost love. I didn't lose a pickup and a dog. Country music was out.

I found Styx, Grand Illusion. Minutes later I was headed down Interstate 8 for the East County. The seventh largest city in the country, and it was just a short ride from the center of town to some quiet country road. I needed that road, to focus on something else, to feel the bike bank into the curves, and to feel the race of the accelerator. The music played over the speakers in my helmet. It soothed me, brought me back to years when life wasn't so complicated.

The songs switched and Tommy Shaw's voice came through with haunting clarity as he launched into "Man in the Wilderness." Great, a song about the lost and lonely. Perhaps Styx was a bad choice after all.

I wasn't looking to tap emotions. If I hid them long enough, they would go away. I hit the accelerator and forced back the momentary wet blur that distorted my vision. There was no room for that. There was nothing but the road. I focused on that thought, and for a time my troubles faded into the background.

Chapter 7

BY THE TIME I'D DRAGGED myself back home from my ride it was well after midnight. Pal was waiting when I came through the door. Apparently he wasn't as mental as I thought. Now that Animal Control was closed for the day, he was back in plain view. He looked pretty skinny, and I figured he must have been on the run for some time. I poured some food and water into the kitchen bowls I'd set aside for him and made my way to the couch. I remember turning on the TV but nothing after. Exhausted sleep came quickly.

It was the middle of the afternoon when I woke up to the sound of purring and the soft, furry warmth of a content kitten curled up in the crook of my neck. I had no idea how long he'd been there, but he clearly liked the spot and was more than a little disturbed when I moved.

The shower was longer today. Not because I needed the heat any more than the day before, but because I had little in the way of motivation. My body's chronic aches were little in comparison to the crushing weight in my chest. Michelle and I had been together for close to a year, and just when I started to feel like maybe I was ready to try and build a future again, my hopes were dashed. I never saw it coming.

And now I'd pay the price. Like some heavy monster standing on my torso, his spiky toenails digging into my skin. The weight was oppressive and his claws dug deep. I could lift him off me for brief periods, but ultimately he came back heavier than before. I hated this pain. I knew it would pass, but that didn't make today any less ugly.

Pal and I repeated our routine on the patio. I needed coffee more than yesterday. Afterwards, we returned to the couch and I flipped channels for a couple hours. When I realized it was nearly six, I dug out my best Hawaiian shirt and left. Yesterday I'd gone to the Range to practice. Tonight I would say farewell to my oldest partner, my mentor.

I rode the VTX, a street cruiser that was easier to maneuver than the Goldwing. A smart move, the Range parking lot was packed. Marked, unmarked, and personal, cars, trucks, you name it. All crowded in a space far too small. Jack had always been popular. He'd earned a great deal of respect. That was clear by the number of command staff vehicles. Many of those who were now Captains and Chiefs were cops of his era. Some of the faster climbers had probably been his trainees when they were baby cops. No matter the connection, he'd given a lot to a great many people over the years.

You'd like to think, at least sometimes, that your efforts mean something, that you made a difference. When it's all done, you hope someone will remember and be thankful for your contribution. If you're real lucky, perhaps one of your silly stories will live on in the folklore of your Department.

It doesn't always happen. Nearly two thousand badge numbers have been assigned since I came on. That's more than everyone working the entire city. Cops come and go—I can't remember the faces of most and the names of even fewer. But there are some, those few who survive long enough to become a part of our history.

If you're lucky enough to be one of those, at least there is a night like this one, the night you separate from the people who have been your family for the majority of your adult life. It's on this night that for a few brief hours the people of the Department try to give back to you what you have given them.

Some don't throw parties, they just slip out of work one day and that's the last you see of them. When a party does happen, some folks don't attend. That's a shame, for this is a rite of passage. Tonight, Officer Jack Wells becomes Retired Officer Jack Wells, or as some will happily admit, Citizen Wells. This is the night when he throws his six guns in the saddle bags and rides off into the sunset.

I parked my bike on the sidewalk outside the Range Master's office and headed toward the main building. The complex was alive, music playing, people laughing and shouting. I could smell barbeque on the grill and realized I hadn't eaten since yesterday. Then I remembered lunch and was no longer sure if the pang in my stomach was hunger.

After walking through the double doors on the west side of the old stone building, I stopped to take in the massive crowd. The giant room was packed with enough people to staff a couple commands. Most didn't notice me, a couple waved and I nodded a greeting in return. I started to make my list of the people I'd need to connect with. People I hadn't seen in far too long. An event like this brings out all levels of our profession. Some come for reasons other than to pay their respects.

"John, how are you tonight?"

I turned to see Sergeant Roosevelt standing next to me with his hand extended. I shook it. "Sir." He was wearing a sport coat and tie, standing stiffly like a wedding cake groom. I looked for the post that kept him upright.

"What brings you out?"

I kept my face deadpan. "Thought I'd come drink some of Spunky's liquor and throw up on his new car."

"Spunky?"

"Jack."

He paused to think. "Oh, Officer Wells. I'm afraid I don't know him too well." His brow furrowed. "Why would you throw up on his car? . . . Ah," he forced a laugh. "That's some of your humor."

He was quick. I had to give him that. I glanced over him. "Why the tie, sir?" I was tempted to call him Sarge but reserved that title as one of honor. He'd have to make do with sir.

His look was serious, sincere. "Well you know, John, you have to make a good impression. You never can be sure who's going to be around."

"Got ya." I tried not to barf on his polished wingtips. "That's why I wore my best Hawaiian shirt."

"Perhaps." He paused again. "Anyway, I suspect the people here are already familiar with your reputation."

The way he said it pissed me off. I needed to get rid of him and find a group he wouldn't be comfortable standing around, otherwise this was going to be a long night. I eyed my diversion.

"Do you know Chief Rickert?" He was an Assistant Chief, but that didn't matter.

Sergeant Roosevelt looked in the direction I was staring. "No, not really. I mean I met him at a couple community meetings but never worked around him."

I watched as Rickert spoke to an officer and his wife. He was laughing. I hated to piss him off, and I'd surely end up hearing about the consequences of my antics, but that couldn't be worse than the torture I was presently enduring. I was confident he would forgive any transgression I might force upon him. Might cost me coffee, maybe even lunch, but he'd forgive me. I remembered his single days. His wife didn't.

I pointed to Rickert pretending that Roosevelt didn't already have target lock. If I looked closely enough, the rookie sergeant was likely salivating over the chance to meet a chief he didn't know. "He was my first sergeant. Ask him why he always keeps the back windows of his car slightly rolled down. That'll break the ice."

Roosevelt eyed me. "Why does he do it?"

"Ask him. It's a funny story. I'd hate to steal his thunder." I hoped he bought my pretend sincerity.

He did. "Ah, okay." He shook my hand and started to walk off. He stopped. "And John, try not to drink until you throw up. That's looked down upon these days you know."

"I'll do my best, sir," I said with a half salute.

He walked off and I watched. Briefly I felt guilty about what I'd done. Briefly, mind you, but I did feel it.

Rickert did days on the beach—suspension—twenty some years ago when he and his girlfriend got it on in the back seat of his patrol car. They'd have gotten away with a little policeman fantasy if he'd only rolled the back windows down. He didn't, and they sat naked in the back of his car until one of his squad mates found them. He'd forgotten the rear doors of a police car don't open from the inside. Word spread, and he got honked. Today he'd have been without a job. In retrospect I'm sure he wondered why he didn't kick out the window. Safety glass can do a job on bare feet, but they'd be healed by now.

I watched while Roosevelt approached. He waited patiently until the chief finished his conversation and then moved in for what he thought was going to be a good little bit of sucking up. Rickert reacted with all the sensitivity I'd imagined. I couldn't hear what he said to poor Sergeant Roosevelt, but his pointing finger and angry glare told me enough. I melted into the crowd before he looked back my way.

I snaked through the masses, staying low to minimize detection, and stopped only long enough to shake a couple hands or endure a slap on the back and a hello. Bill Gideon began to approach me, and then his face distorted. "Hatch, you're stirring some shit, get away from me." I did as ordered. We'd reconnect later when I was in the clear.

I was amused by the looks some gave as I continued through the crowd hunched over like an old man. My next encounter was Ronny. He shook his head.

"Stand up, Hatch."

"Nope," I said with a smile. "Can't do that." I glanced behind me, certain Roosevelt was in pursuit.

Ronny sniffed the air. "You drunk already? I don't smell anything."

"Not drunk, just gotta keep moving. Anything else turn up on that murder?"

"It was yesterday, for crying out loud."

"Yeah, and I thought you were a detective—detect."

Ronny shook his head. "It was the husband. You know as well as I do."

I nodded. "Probably. Did he admit to it when you interviewed him?"

"Not yet."

"What's your thought on the burglary angle, maybe a CIA hit? You could find yourself digging into something that'll get you killed for National Security reasons."

"My ass! Small fishes, buddy. No government, no cartel, no mysterious intrigue. We'll break this, but I got bigger fishes first. This case is about odds and resources. Until I find a reason to shift the odds to someone else, my limited resources look at him and higher priority cases. Too much work, not enough detectives. Justice moves slow for the little guy, but it does move, in a sort of painful, constipated way."

"Good job, detective," I said giving him the thumbs up. "Gotta go. I'll let you buy me a beer later and we'll talk about what you can will me when the CIA has you whacked." I left. I'd have liked to talk longer, but there was still plenty of night ahead. Right now I needed to make it to the doors on the other side of the building.

I passed a few feet from the first person I recognized from my own squad. Suzie Orwin was here with Jake Gill. She looked great in a tight sundress with the highest hem and the most cleavage possible. She was still trouble. Jake was her male counterpart. He looked like Brad Pitt. Using that and a little charm, he nailed any woman that would spread her legs for him. The crack of dawn wasn't safe around the man and he flaunted it. Perhaps if either one of them was worth a shit as a cop, I'd cut them a break, but I felt only disdain. They, of course, wondered why no one gave them any respect.

I made it out of the building and onto the back patio . . . freedom. The cool evening air was refreshing after the stagnant, sweaty indoors. This is where I would find the cops. This is where I found the barbeque. I didn't need anything more.

"Officer Hatch?" I turned, and I'm quite sure I staggered a step or two. Though I hadn't even cracked a beer, my motor reflexes were momentarily influenced.

I didn't recognize her, at least I couldn't place her face or where we'd met, but there was a familiarity about the woman. Early thirties, she was tall, perhaps five ten with auburn hair that flowed to the middle of her back. Her tan body was slim, lithe like that of a dancer, and she wore a long sleeved, white blouse and black slacks. Her features were sharp with an angled jaw, but her high cheeks rounded off and that gave her a smooth, striking look. I was speechless.

She held a cocktail in both hands, the sides of the glass dripping with beads of condensation. I was certain my forehead would soon do the same. She let go of the tumbler with one hand, then she reached down to wipe it on her pants. Excellent, this was a woman who knew what trousers were for. She extended her mostly dry hand.

I shook it without hesitation.

"Officer Hatch, right?"

My brow furrowed. I wished I could have been cooler about the whole thing, but I just couldn't place her. "Yeah," was all I could manage. I tried to say it in as suave a manner as possible, but monosyllabic responses can be neither suave nor debonair.

"You probably don't remember me. I had my hair up and was in a suit for most of the trial."

Oh shit, here we go, the lump in my throat dropped into my stomach. This couldn't be good.

She recognized the concern on my face. "Oh no," she said with a giggle. "I'm Maralyn Denoir. I work for the DA. I was the attorney on one of your cases."

Bingo! Memory came back to me. The prosecutor on the armed meth-freak I'd arrested. She did a good job on the case. I didn't remember her looking like this. "Sorry, you looked different."

"Not bad, I hope," she said, fishing for a compliment like women do when we men aren't paying attention.

I shook my head vigorously. "No. Not bad at all. To be honest, I was struck a bit speechless when you called my name. Little of that had to do with recognition. Mostly just me being somewhat captivated." I wanted to continue the compliment but my train of thought wrecked violently when Michelle came to mind. Instant guilt, like this was too quick, like I was a letch for finding this woman stunning. Nevermind that Michelle left me, I was the creep because I let someone catch my eye the very next day. Part of me wanted to think that if I'd have been a decent man I'd wallow in misery for a while.

I realized I was just standing there like a silly fool, my compliment thrown out but my rhythm suddenly lost. I tried to recover. "What brings you here?"

"I came with friends. They know the officer who's retiring or someone who knows him. I'm not sure which. They just said it would probably be a good time."

She smiled and my guilt left, replaced by small brain thinking. So what if I'm the bad guy? "It should be fun," I agreed.

"I take it you know him."

"My first partner. One of the last really good ones left these days."

She smiled again, wider this time, and spoke in a coy tone, "We still have you."

I shook my head, suddenly embarrassed. "No, I'll never be a Jack Wells."

A red headed woman I didn't recognize ran up and grabbed Maralyn by the arm. "Can you excuse us?" She turned to Maralyn. "Come on, there's someone I want you to meet."

Maralyn looked at me, but I couldn't read the expression. It appeared like she was looking for permission. "Will you be around for a while?"

"My plan is to wake up in the target shed and not remember tonight. I'm not going anywhere soon. Go," I said. "This looks pretty urgent."

I turned to the smaller groups at the picnic tables outside the main building and quickly found several people to talk to. Old friends were everywhere. Nights like this renew our bond.

With the exception of adding points to my boss's blood pressure, most of the quibbles, the daily bickering, the back-stabbing and the stress would simply go away for a while. By Monday afternoon the gossip mongers would have spread every sordid tale of every little thing anyone did that could be bent, twisted, or used against them. We are a Peyton Place, after all. With so many marriages, divorces, remarriages, and all that falls in between, our family tree doesn't branch much. Oftentimes we were our own worst enemy. But that would be Monday.

Tonight I was content to talk with friends. The stories come out on a night like this. They start off small, but they don't end that way. Everyone has to build on the last story told. If you've been around long enough, it's a battle to find something bigger, better, or more dangerous. Then it needs to get gory. We can't make it through a conversation without talking about the nastiest things we've come across. In our strange, twisted, microcosm of a world we laugh at every bit of danger and misfortune.

While we talked, I kept an eye on Jack. The crowd around him never lessened. I thought about waiting my turn, but couldn't. He was talking to the old-timers, men and women who'd spent more years around him than I had. This was their time.

Without warning, Mike Spellman took the microphone. A huge man, Mike was six-six and well over two-fifty. He and Jack had been on the same amount of time and were old friends. The task of being emcee fell to him. There was static, and then a screech, and then his deep voice boomed over the microphone. Quiet Mike was his nickname, but there was nothing quiet about him.

As Jack stood beside him, Mike spoke of the early years. How they'd been so much fun, nothing like today. Everyone clapped. Jack's head bowed, embarrassed. At six four, he was no small man, but he looked like a child next to Quiet Mike. He was enjoying himself, even though he never was one of the glory hounds. Just as well, we had enough of those.

After a couple embarrassing stories, including the one about the toothless transient who had the hots for Jack and called him Spunky, Mike quickly turned the microphone over to the Chief. He spoke from his scripted list about the extraordinary career of Jack Wells, a nice, respect-filled tribute that paid homage to a veteran cop.

Then the parade began, continuing by rank and time in service. There was a hierarchy to observe. Jack had been an honorable cop, and whether they knew him or not, there seemed to be no end to the chiefs, captains, lieutenants, and crusty ancient detectives who wanted their moment to speak gushing praises into the microphone. Some were genuinely touched. Others simply wanted to attach themselves to his memory in a public forum, hopeful that some of the respect he'd earned would attach to them.

I waited my turn, for Mike Spellman to ask if there was anyone in the audience who had something to say, some story to tell. I had a lot of stories. We'd been in car chases and fights, we'd put murderers, robbers, and rapists in jail. I owed the man a great deal. He taught me more about being a cop than anyone. I wanted him to know that.

The procession continued—minutes turned into a half hour and then an hour. The audience, though enjoying the stories, was ready to get back to drinking and socializing. Hope dwindled. Suddenly, I was gripped by the fear that I'd be the one person who said too much, the last person not saying something new, just barfing out what has already been expressed. My feelings might be heartfelt, but there comes a point when enough is enough. I could bear the fear, but I couldn't be the one to diminish Jack's moment.

Then I noticed Sergeant Roosevelt had worked himself into a front row spot. He wanted to be seen. If I spoke I'd have to deal with him when I finished. I didn't care to talk to the man again tonight. He could have my ass on Monday.

I thought about what I could do, something different. I considered taking the stage and borrowing the band's keyboards. A song, Ray Charles, "Hit the Road Jack." That would be amusing. Then again, I might just embarrass myself. I didn't want to look the fool any more than I wanted to be the last guy repeating the same speech.

My indecision cost me my opportunity. When I'd thought about the party earlier in the week, this wasn't what I pictured. Somehow I'd hoped for more, to give an old friend credit for all he'd given me. I'd hoped to be able to let others know just how good a man was leaving our service. It wasn't meant to be. Of course, that's the way of life. Rarely does the fantasy of what we expect meet the reality of what becomes.

CHAPTER 8

I FOUND SOMETHING TO DRINK and moved away from the crowd. I needed a smoke, and I'd left those in my saddle bags. As a whole, this had been a rather crappy week. Suddenly the lack of motivation that had me flipping channels on the couch had returned.

As I walked back to my bike, I passed the Field Lieutenant's car. Bright and shiny, brand new, this one hadn't seen a thousand puking, spitting, kicking, foul and nasty prisoner transports. It was unlikely a bad guy ever sat in the back seat. Of course it wasn't set up for one. He was a supervisor. He didn't even have a cage in the car.

Steve Buckard was the Field Lieutenant tonight. I'd known Steve since he was a patrolman in the field. A nice guy, but sometimes he made himself too easy a target. I noticed he'd left the door unlocked. Maybe he was in a hurry. Maybe he felt safe in the parking lot of the police range. In either event, I was compelled to address his lack of safety-minded thinking. The ten year old in me would have screamed the remainder of the night if I denied my duty.

I looked around and there was no one in view, at least no one looking my way. I opened the door and pushed down on the lock. Then I sat in the front seat and started tampering. I turned the stereo and police radio volume all the way up and then flipped the switch to activate the emergency lights and siren. Nothing happened but when he started the car, everything would roar to life, and that should scare the living crap out of him. Since it was a warm night, I turned the control to heat and set the fan on high.

I hit the switch for the trunk hoping the garage guys had failed to disconnect it. They hadn't. Too bad, the neutral kill switch was in the trunk of the car. All I needed to do was rap on the side of it and his cruiser wouldn't start until the reset button was pressed. Such a simple device designed to help prevent an explosion or fire in the event of a rear end collision. To cops, it was a toy. Hit the neutral kill switch and then watch while the rookie tries to figure out why his car won't start. Lieutenant Buckard was no rookie, but it was one more thing to remind him to lock his car.

I closed the door and walked away. I found my bike and dug into the saddle bags for a fresh pack of cigarettes. I always brought them to an event like this. If I ended up drinking, even a beer, I'd want smokes. That's just the way it works.

I sat down on a bench near my bike and fired up. The first drag tasted like smoke from a camel turd. I took a sip of the cold Pepsi I'd brought from the party. It washed away the taste and the second drag was better. The band started and music played in the background. I could hear a couple shouts but mostly it was rather quiet where I sat.

Jack's voice broke my peace. "I saw you come in, and then you were gone. Thought maybe I missed you. What you doing out here?"

"Keeping an eye on Lincoln-4's car."

I turned to see a broad grin cross Jack's unshaven, time weathered jaw. It was my bet he wouldn't shave for a few months now that he no longer had to. The hair on his head might be flecked with gray, but that didn't mean the beard was. One could hope.

"He left it open, it wasn't my fault," I shrugged.

"You turned everything on."

This time I grinned. I tried not to, but the inner ten year old demanded as much.

"You don't know how to make friends, do you?"

"Apparently not."

Jack moved toward the bench. He had a commanding presence, his body and swagger similar to that of the Duke himself. His deep voice resonated clearly with a bit of a drawl. "Mind if I wait for the show?"

There was plenty of room but I slid over just the same. Jack sat. He had a fresh beer in his hand and he opened it. "What are you drinking?"

"Pepsi."

He coughed. "Cops don't drink Pepsi, not at my party." He stood and dug into the pockets of his Dockers. "Here, I brought extras just in case there was a delay getting back to the bar. People won't seem to let me move anywhere tonight."

"It's your night."

"And I'm glad you made it." He nodded. "Why the Pepsi?"

I cracked the beer and took a swallow. It tasted good. "Been a long week. I didn't figure booze would do anything to change that. Something about an ass-chewing you gave me on 'The three B's.'"

"Booze, broads, and bills, nothing's changed. Get you in trouble every time."

I raised the can. "Then here's to trouble. Seems to be finding me with frequency." I took out another smoke and lit it.

"Gimme one of those," Jack begged.

"Aww, hell no." I shook my head. "You've got your health to think about. You need to beat the odds, my friend. Thirty years of hard work means you need thirty years of pension. Since most guys get five, you need all the help you can get."

"One ain't gonna kill me."

"It's the ones that follow. I'll not be responsible."

"Agh," he grunted with as much drama as he could conjure. "And what good is retirement if I can't enjoy it?"

He had a point. "All right, but I ain't contributin'. I'm gonna set this pack on the bench next to me. If you happen to steal one, it's on you."

I set the pack down.

"Oh look," Jack said as he reached right down and took one out. "The things you find." He lit up and took a long drag. He held it like some teenage pot fiend, and then exhaled. "Tastes worse than I remember."

There was a sound of movement. Instantly silent our attention turned to the booby-trapped patrol car. We waited to see if the Lieutenant was returning. It was just a couple walking to their car. We took a drink of beer and another drag from our cigarettes as they crossed the lot. They didn't see us. We should have had water balloons.

I recognized the moment and made for my opportunity. "I'm glad you found your way out here. I wanted to come up when they were telling stories, but the line just didn't seem to get any shorter."

As I was about to thank him, he interrupted. "Bunch of hogwash. Most of those stories never happened, least not the way people remember." Jack crushed out his smoke and dug another from the pack. "Enough about me, what's bothering you, John?"

He always called me John. To nearly everyone I was Hatch but never to him. It was always by first name and he always spoke to me like the older brother I never had. The concern in his eyes was genuine. Jack Wells was as crusty and sly an old dog as there ever was, and yet he never talked down to me, never treated me like some naïve kid, even in the days when I'd been worse than naïve . . . I'd been clueless. It was a gift he had.

I paused, distracted from my train of thought. What I was going to say drifted away and images from my week flashed across my brain like flickering images from a music video. None of it made any sense, it was just sensory overload.

"Where's that young teacher?" Jack asked. He was not to be deterred, and by her absence he'd likely already figured out the bulk of my worries.

I took another drink and reached for the smokes. "Seems she didn't like my life."

Jack nodded. "At least she didn't have to marry you to figure that out."

"There is that," I agreed. Jack knew better. He'd paid years of child support to a woman who waited a full five years to decide she didn't like his life. She did like his house and the monthly payments he made. Maybe I had some luck after all.

"That's too bad. She was a nice gal." He drew a breath. "Bet that smarts a bit."

"Enough." I wanted to say more, to open up, but words just didn't come.

"What else?"

Isn't that enough? I thought. He knew better, could read me better than anyone.

I shook my head. "Sometimes none of it seems to make any sense, Jack. Why we do this to ourselves, why we endure the bullshit."

Jack rubbed some ash on his slacks. "Now you're talking, boy. Let's talk bullshit."

That was Jack, no beating around the bush, just get right down to it and speak. "I have this new sergeant, Roosevelt."

Jack laughed openly, deeply. "Sorry, man, heard the rumblings in the hall. He's that five year wonder off the last list, isn't he?"

"Yup."

"Yeah, met him earlier. Never before tonight, but he showed up at my party. Suck-ass! I'm sorry you got stuck with him. Things will surely get worse before they get better. You think of transferring somewhere else?"

"You're a load of joy, aren't you?"

"Not telling you anything you don't already know. You stay, it's gonna be a battle. It's always that way. Been there myself a time or two."

"Don't understand why he can't just let up. It's not like I don't work."

"You do. He just doesn't understand the work you do, why you do it. If you're waiting for him to get ten more years of field experience, things ain't gonna happen. You can't change what is. What else is on your mind?"

Damn but his intuition was right on. "It's not just him. Suddenly I can't seem to figure out half the cops around me. It's like a new breed from some other planet."

Jack nodded but said nothing.

I felt compelled to explain. "For example, yesterday, Sergeant Wonder put me with a guy named Buckman. Good kid but he's barely twenty-two, still lives at home.

"We went to this cover-now, cop on the ground fighting for his life, and Stevie charges off after some rock-monster who runs. Leaves me alone to fight this guy with an already winded cop. It's like he's on full speed all the time. When we're not doing something, he wants to be doing something. He's not sure what, just something. He's never content with what is. When we're driving around he spends most of his time with his head down looking at the computer or checking his cell phone to see if anyone left him any messages. The world could be crashing around him, and he wouldn't know it until the dispatcher sent him the radio call."

Jack busted out into a deep, belly-shaking laugh. I turned, sure someone was watching, embarrassed that I'd just said something wrong. We were still alone. It was a full minute, maybe two, before he regained his composure.

He slapped me on the back. "Thank you, my old friend."

"Thank you, for what?"

"All night long people been bending my ear about how I was this, or how I was that. Not a bit of it—none—was anything but lip service. You, my friend, gave me the first bit of validation I did something right all these years," he said, poking my chest.

"How do you figure?" I found myself a little angry, off center. For the first time it felt like Jack was mocking me.

"I gave that same speech, well nearly the same, to Sergeant, sorry, Chief Rickert, when he put you in my car."

My anger turned to hurt.

Jack slapped me on the shoulder again. "Don't go getting your feathers in a ruffle. You turned out all right, better than all right."

I knew he had a point, but I wasn't following him. I was blind, and I knew it. In all these years, nothing had changed, and I realized how much I still had to learn. Here, at the range, I was sending off the one man I could always turn to, who was always there for guidance. I trusted him, and this was his last night.

"Look, John, nothing's changed. When you and I started working together, you were what . . . twenty-three, twenty-four? Hardly older than that young man in your car. You might not remember your youthful enthusiasm, but I do. I remember a bright young college kid who wanted to change the world and had no shortage of ideas on how he would accomplish that.

"The first month we were together I didn't have a clue how you thought. Your instincts were good, your intentions right, but I just couldn't understand some of your perspective."

"I never knew that," I admitted. My anger mellowed, and I felt silly.

"Of course not, you were a good kid. A little naïve maybe, wet behind the ears for sure . . . but good. I figured I could fight with what I didn't understand or I could do something about it. If I didn't, you might have ended up like wonder boy, and we don't need any more of those. So I exposed you to everything I could. I did my very best to turn you into a cop."

"You made my head swim those first few months."

"Yeah, I don't doubt it, but you learned. You picked up on what this job is all about."

"And for that, I'll always owe you."

"Nonsense," Jack said with a dismissive wave of the hand, the same gesture I caught myself using from time to time, the same gesture he used to give me like a wave of absolution, forgiveness for dragging him into an avoidable situation because I didn't know how to outthink the people we dealt with. The same move I'd used to dismiss Michelle when we broke up. My stomach tightened, and I realized just how little I'd learned.

"You did an awful lot," I told him. The failure to apply that properly was my fault.

Jack shook his head and tossed the cigarette that had been forgotten and burned out in his hand. "Mine was only a small part. You did the work. You never shied away from the rotten tasks, never ran from the scary ones. You screwed up from time to time, but you always got up and tried again."

Jack paused to think, and a warm smile crossed his face. "This is a strange profession we do. It's a grim business and there are few rewards, but it's necessary and there is honor in that. There is also a price that has to be paid. Your young lady-friend is one of those costs. There's nothing you can do about it. Enjoy what you had and move on. Few will ever find someone who can deal with the strain that years of this kind of work puts on a relationship. Be glad you found out early."

"Some guys make it work."

He nodded in agreement. "Some do, but they're the exception. Their commitment to home is greater than their commitment to the streets. They're the ones who make family a priority, who will take jobs that allow better schedules. We are not them. Neither you nor I would ever survive a job where we couldn't be the cops we want to be. We live the adventure we want our lives to be. That doesn't leave much room for the family life."

"That scenario sucks."

"You can't have everything. Look at me, I tried. I thought I could be fully devoted to my job, be the best I could out there, and raise a family. My son turned out okay, but I don't remember much of his childhood. Things coulda been a lot worse. Still, I did do some things right."

"You did fine."

"Don't misunderstand me, I have regrets, but I'm proud of what my life has been. However, my days here are through. It's my time to move on, to try and have as much relationship with my son as I've had with the folks here. It's someone else's turn to carry the torch. After all, that's what this is about."

Jack paused for a moment and thought. "Not everyone can be a police officer, and of those who make it, few have the ability to be cops. Just as it was my obligation to do what I could with you, it's now your responsibility to do with others. Some will learn, those with the aptitude will excel, and others will be what they may. You can't be angry with them for failing to be the cop you'd want them to be. They just don't have what it takes. You do. Now do with these guys what I did with you."

Jack shrugged. "You better do 'cause I ain't gonna be here. We might not live in the old west any more, but that don't mean there ain't a whole lotta wilderness out there for me to wander about. Maybe I'll buy one of those Goldwings you're so fond of and see what the country looks like on the back of a motorbike."

The thought tugged at me. Perhaps I'd go with him. The streets would never be as fun as they used to be. Maybe it was time for a new adventure.

"Ooh, ooh, ooh," Jack said, his tone suddenly excited. The ten year old in him had found his voice. He pointed.

I looked toward our trap. Lieutenant Buckard was walking briskly back to his car. He had his cop face on and was no longer in the social mode. The bad things had come out somewhere in the city and his cell phone must have interrupted his fun at the party. It was time for him to get back to work.

Buckard pulled his keys from his duty-belt and reached for the door lock. He was totally unaware that he'd left it open. I inhaled and held my breath as if any little noise might alert him to our presence. Jack did the same. And then we waited.

A moment passed as Buckard sat down. We watched his silhouette as he turned to look at the computer console next to his seat. He was reading whatever call had come to him. Another couple moments and he sat up. Buckard turned the ignition, and like a car bomb, the night exploded under dazzling flashes of red and blue lights. We could hear the radio blasting inside the car. He moved frantically in the dark trying to get everything turned off.

Jack and I broke our silence and began the little girl giggle that always follows such a display. It had been a perfect plan with the exception of one small thing . . . the siren didn't sound. I had forgotten that it wouldn't work unless he put the car in gear. The rest of the plan played out flawlessly.

We were still laughing when we saw the window roll down. Buckard was looking for the culprits. We ducked and stifled our laughs. He glanced around for a moment, looking into the darkness, listening for any sound that would betray the location of those who'd just made a fool of him. Content that no one was around and it had just been some cop passing by, he put the car in drive and left the lot. We were in the clear.

Jack and I sat up and suffered a second bout of the giggles. There was no testosterone about it, we were simply reduced to children and we enjoyed the moment.

"Hello?" The greeting came out more like a question about whether it was okay to interrupt us. We looked up to find Maralyn standing a few feet away.

Jack tried to stifle his laugh, but he'd had too much to drink to put on a straight face. "Hi," I said as I stood up like a schoolboy caught drawing on the classroom table. "Ah, didn't see you walk up."

She had a smile on her face, and I sighed in relief. "You were busy. Good job, I never saw a cop jump like that."

We giggled again, and I coughed in an attempt to regain my composure. "Yeah, but we didn't have anything to do with it. Honest."

Jack nodded rapidly as if that would help convince her.

"I'm sorry, Jack, this is Maralyn Denoir. She works for the DA."

Jack stood and stretched out his hand. She shook it. "Always a pleasure when a weathered old fool like me gets to touch skin that soft again. We were just finished here." He looked at me and winked. "I better head back in. If I don't see you before you leave, let's get together sometime soon."

I shook his hand. "You bet."

"Nice to meet you, my dear," he said to Maralyn.

"You too," she said with a smile.

He started to walk off and then stopped.

"John?" This time he had a serious look about him, one I'd not seen before.

"Yeah?"

He looked at Maralyn. "If you'll excuse an old man for just a moment."

"Certainly."

"John, what do you hear when you're out there on the street?"

"I don't follow you."

"When you're in the zone and everything is going right. Like with shooting. On a good day, sometimes that pistol doesn't need sights, your hand just knows where to go and the bullets hit the paper. When you're in that place, what does the city tell you?"

I thought for a moment. "It sings to me. As surely as if I was playing a song. When I'm on, it's like I just know the next note, the next chord. I can feel the beat and know where to place my accent notes. It's natural, and things just come together."

"I knew I did something right." He nodded. "For me, it was like a rodeo. When I was there, I knew which way the bull was gonna buck so he couldn't throw me. Wasn't always easy, but if I rode smart I could tire him the hell out. Turn that same skill to those around you. Learn their song, and things will go much smoother. You don't have to like the music to learn to play it."

Jack paused a moment as if he was collecting thoughts. When he spoke, he did not pause. "It's a war on those streets. Don't let anyone ever tell you different. Men die, women die, families lose whatever it is made 'em families. Lives change in an instant. Fight the injustice where you find it. Don't ever give in, and don't ever let up. Bring the fight to them if you have to but fight just the same."

He breathed. "That said, don't you change. There's a lot of down times, but don't ever give up that part inside that makes you human. Yours is a calling, John Hatch. Think what you want, deny it if you will, but I've met few men in this world who have the courage, honor, and aptitude to stand tall and do what needs doing. There's bullshit, shysters, and men of weak character everywhere you go. Pity them when you must, show compassion when you can, but above all, stand up when it's time. That badge has all the power you give it. Learn to use it and then use it well. If you get real lucky, maybe one day you'll know you did something worthwhile."

Before I could speak, he turned and started to walk away. "I quote Connery, my friend, 'here endeth the lesson.' Good luck Johnny boy," he said with a thundering laugh. "Don't forget to live a little."

After I watched him disappear into the building toward the crowd that waited, I looked at Maralyn. "Sorry, we were just talking."

"Old times?"

"The end of old times."

A new sadness crept over me. Tonight had truly been a rite of passage. I'd expected it would be Jack's, not mine. He'd just passed the torch, and I suddenly found myself unprepared to deal with it.

"Want to go for a ride, find some place less noisy?" I nodded toward the bike.

"Is that yours?" she asked, a whimsical look crossed her face, her eyes widened.

"Yeah."

"Is it a Harley?"

"No, it runs . . . it's a Honda. Just looks like a Harley."

She paused for a moment as if considering something. I realized

I'd spoken without thinking and was suddenly embarrassed.

"I'm sorry," I thought about an easy out I could give her. "You probably brought your own car."

Her response was quick. "I did not. Hang on," she said. Maralyn dug in her purse and pulled out a cell phone. She dialed a number and waited for it to connect. When it did, she spoke. "Cindy, I left. Stay as late as you want, have fun. I'm okay. I got a ride with a friend." She winked when she said it. "I'll give you a call tomorrow." She hung up the phone. "Do you have a spare helmet?"

CHAPTER 9

THERE'S SOMETHING PRIMAL about a motorcycle's connection to a man's soul. Anyone who rides knows the feeling is about more than just getting from place to place. It's about freedom, and at the same time control. The power of the machine, the way it handles, the feel of leaning into a curve on no more than a few square inches of tread is pure pucker power. Riding can almost simultaneously deliver a moment of serene peace and a total connection to your environment, all the while forcing you to bear down and face a threat or open the gates and crap your pants.

On a bike, you can feel the road as if you are a part of the pavement, feel your center of gravity shift and destabilize when you push too far. That's why the young guys with their first crotch-rocket end up plowing into things. The speed with which the bike can move beyond their control is faster than they can react.

But often, that's what this is about—instinct. A motorcycle separates you from the world and leaves you a part of it at the same time. You are exposed and must face the challenge of being vulnerable, of overcoming an environment that both tests and refreshes you. There's nothing else like it, save working the streets.

When it comes to female motorcycle passengers, there are three types. The first holds on to some part of the bike. The second rests her hands on your waist, maybe grips some shirt in her hands. The third, like Maralyn, wraps her arms fully around you. Holding a driver that close can make it a bit difficult to drive, but I didn't complain a bit.

I downshifted, and the bike slowed as the freeway turned into a city street. Unprepared for the shift in speed, Maralyn's head bobbed forward. Our helmets clapped together. She tilted her head to the side so she could lean forward and speak in my ear. "Sorry, I wasn't ready for that." Briefly, her breath was hot against the exposed skin of my neck. A shiver ran down my spine. "Let's keep riding," she said.

She was reading my mind. I cut hard, turned down the adjacent street, and gunned the engine. The bike lunged forward, rumbling deeply under the torque of the lower gear. Maralyn wailed with excitement and leaned into me. I grinned with the understanding that the move just did more for her than me.

A moment later we were on the ramp for southbound I-5. This time I kept the gears low intentionally as I gunned the engine and raced up the ramp toward the freeway. I could feel her fingers wrap more tightly around my shirt as we rocketed forward.

I took the Coronado Bridge exit. Having stood at the apex, next to a guard rail that barely reached my knees, I've felt it sway and bounce under me as I looked for the latest jumper. I don't like heights, especially this one. But sometimes you must challenge fear to witness magnificence.

I kept the bike in the outside lane, as near to the edge as I could while we climbed toward the top of the bridge. The roadway was canted, and I had to lean to compensate. My gut was tight, and I found myself a little anxious as I wondered at the brilliance of my idea. Ours was a long fall should my passenger get scared, move suddenly, and cause me to lose control of the bike.

The world transformed in an instant. This was a bright, clear night. The marine layer still waited off the coast. The lights of the city shimmered and overpowered all but a few bright stars. The moon, a beautiful crescent sliver, glowed as if spotlighted. Towering downtown buildings loomed to our right and glowed with all the radiance of giant gemstones. The blue waters of the bay shone deep and dark.

Time seemed suspended. Fear, desire, and anticipation bounced around inside me as if they were charged particles banging about in some atom that wished only to split and release its overwhelming pulse of energy.

And then time started again. We eased our way down the latter half of the bridge and into the City of Coronado. We weaved our way through streets that just couldn't seem to stay straight and then passed the Hotel del Coronado. The hundred year old wooden structure, the hotel of Presidents, looked brand new. Moments later we were on the Silver Strand heading south. The thick, salty smell of the ocean blew across us as we rode into Imperial Beach. Then it was east on Palm Avenue and back to the I-5. We went north. To go south brought only Mexico.

Our trip had only lasted about thirty minutes, but once again we were heading into downtown. I slowed the bike and we eased into the Saturday night traffic headed toward the Gaslamp Quarter. I could park the bike at Hooter's again, and we'd be in the thick of weekend activity. Perhaps we could go to Croce's and listen to some good music. I'd like that, but I wasn't interested in fighting the crowd for seat.

I decided on the Moreland. A quiet, far more intimate venue not too far removed from the rest but much less occupied by the twenty and thirty-something bar crowd. Errol, the owner, would find us a nice, peaceful table in a corner somewhere.

We parked and went in. Maralyn kept my jacket on, her arms crossed in front of her for warmth. As expected, Errol Moreland greeted us at the front door. A man of medium height and a thin build, he had blonde hair, pale skin, and angular features. He was a Brit, and his greetings always came out more like an "Ello" than "Hello." He quickly seated us in a corner. I took the chair that would leave my back to the wall.

Maralyn ordered a Bailey's and coffee. I just took the coffee. Once we'd ordered, Errol was off about his business.

"How do you know him?" she asked.

"Just got to know him over the years. Think he was a sailor in the British Navy or something. He can be kind of crusty, but I can appreciate that. I like his food, and his place is generally quiet. Sometimes on a Friday night I like to come downtown, have a nice dinner, sit and watch the people. If not here, sometimes I'll head up to the Barnes and Noble in the valley."

"You don't strike me as a bookworm." Maralyn grinned.

Leaning back, I shook my head. "Not quite, just like a good story now and again. Mostly I like to feel the city move around me. Don't like crowds, just the energy of people out and about living their lives."

Errol returned. "My dear." He set our drinks down. "John. No merlot tonight?"

"I'm on the bike."

"Understand, mate." He straightened and then he was gone

again.

"Anyway, I don't know him all that well. I'm just a regular." I looked over at the wall and the old, upright piano with its deep, rich, polished wood. Most nights that was where I'd sit with my glass of merlot. Errol let me play anytime I wanted.

We spent the next two hours talking. Mostly it was her, not that I didn't want to talk, it's just that every time I tried to think of something, my mind blanked out. Conversation isn't normally that difficult, but my brain was somewhere else, lost in thoughts of what Jack had said and flashes of lunch with Michelle.

"This was a tough night for you, wasn't it?"

My mind snapped back to the conversation. I looked across the table. Her green eyes seemed luminous in the light of the small candle between us. There was warmth in those eyes, and I felt comforted.

"I'm sorry, I drag you away from your friends on a Saturday night and I turn out to be about as much fun as a boil on the ass."

Raising a hand to her mouth, she stifled a laugh. "Not quite the comparison I'd have used."

"What did I . . . oh, see, foot-in-mouth syndrome. Sorry if I offended you."

She reached across the table and ran her soft finger down the side of my face. I started, just a bit, an instinctive reaction to a new touch. After years on the street, it always takes me a while to get over it; to let someone into my space.

"I'm sorry, didn't mean to jump."

"You do not offend me, John." She brought her hand back up and this time stroked it along my temple. "When we were in court, I was quite taken with you. The way you walked, your confidence, the way you were able to explain yourself on the stand. I've seen the man you are, there's no need to apologize. You're going to miss him aren't you?"

"Jack? Yeah, I will."

She stroked my cheek again. I could feel her fingers drag across my beard and realized I hadn't shaved. The sweet scent of her perfume worked its way to my nose and my senses exploded. "You've got these lines around your eyes."

"I'm not getting any younger."

Her smile stayed warm. "You're not that old, and that's not what I was thinking. I'm just wondering at the things you've seen. These are character lines, nothing about age in that. A man has to earn these. I'm curious about what put them there.

"You wanted to apologize for taking me away from the party. I should be thanking you. My girlfriends dragged me there because they figured there'd be a bunch of cute, young, available cops. All they wanted was a wild night. I didn't meet a guy there who . . ."

Errol interrupted. "Sorry mates, last call."

Maralyn sat upright in her seat like a teenage girl caught necking under the bleachers during a school football game. "I didn't realize it was that late already." She looked at me, "I'd better use the restroom before they shut us out." She got up and walked away.

I stood to stretch and walked over to the long bar opposite the piano. "What do I owe you, Errol?"

He turned with his dishrag in hand. "'Ow 'bout you play a song, we call it even. Didn't drink but coffee and a little Bailey's."

"Not really in a performing mood tonight."

"Performing for who?" The place was empty. "Besides, I already closed the till."

"Limey bastard," I groaned.

"Yank," he countered with a smile.

"I'll see what I can do," I said as I walked over to the piano and pulled the bench seat out. I reached for the cover, but it was locked.

"Sorry," I shouted as I spun on the bench. "I tried."

Good thing I turned, or the keys Errol tossed would have hit me in the back of the head. I caught them and unlocked the cover. I placed my fingers on the piano and found my spacing along the keyboard, my right thumb to middle C. The notes came without thinking as I drifted into a rendition of the Eagle's, "The Long Run."

The song came out slower than it was supposed to be played, but that's the beauty of music—you can adapt to fit a mood. Mine was pensive, melancholy.

I finished to clapping. Maralyn stood behind me. "And here I thought you were a bookworm-cop. Now I find you are a warrior-bard. Play me something."

I started to put down the keyboard cover. "Oh no, I thought you were in the bathroom. Errol coerced me."

"Please," she said, dragging the word out like a kid begging a parent. "Just one song. Don't make *me* coerce you."

I slid back around and she sat on the bench next to me. This was easier. The moment belonged to Billy Joel. I went right into "She's Always a Woman."

Maralyn slid closer and reached an arm around me. I'm quite certain I fumbled a couple notes under the intensity of her stare. I was afraid my throat would dry up and I'd choke on the lyrics, but I didn't.

I finished the song and lowered the lid over the keys. I turned to Maralyn, and her gaze was unwavering. She simply sat there staring. I tried to read the look in her eyes, whether it was one of unexpected amusement or whether there was something more.

She spoke softly, but her words were firm. "You need to take me home, right now. Not my house, I have a silly roommate. You need to take me to your place. Don't even think about telling me no."

I swallowed the lump in my throat. Her words made my head swim. Fortunately, the little brain did the thinking in absence of the big brain's ability to function. I stood and tossed the keys to Errol. "Take care of yourself, buddy. I'll see you soon."

I grabbed Maralyn by the hand and led her out the door in what seemed a race to get to the bike. Just as we did, I stopped. She took one more step, not quick enough to stop with me. We stood for a moment, our only connection our hands and the arms that stretched between us. I tugged her arm and pulled her close. I didn't let go of her hand as I brought her arm behind her. Then I wrapped my other arm around her. I looked down into her eyes and she up into mine. The city was quiet save for a few passing cars.

When she realized one arm was behind her, she broke eye contact and looked back. "Am I a prisoner?" she asked with a giggle.

"Do you need to be?"

"All night long, I swear it."

I leaned into her and kissed her hard. She pressed against me and her lips met mine with every bit as much desire. We kissed for what were several long moments, and then I heard the blast of a police air horn and then an amplified voice over the PA system. "Hey Hatch, get a room." Maybe a hundred cops working a Saturday night in a city this size, and I can't kiss a girl on the street without someone recognizing me.

We separated and Maralyn's face glowed bright red. "Friend of yours?"

"Sorry," I said, "didn't know anyone would be driving by."

We were on the bike just as quickly as we could get our helmets fastened. There was no time to let it warm up, I flipped the choke and the engine started.

Traffic was light as we thundered up the freeway. To say I was on the verge of distraction was to put things too lightly. I focused the best I could and kept my eyes on the road. I was not to be deterred, and I certainly didn't need my night ruined by some drunk who just couldn't manage to see me through whiskey blurred vision.

As we pulled into the driveway, I eased the bike to a stop.

"The garage door opener, right front pocket of my jacket."

I could feel her moving as she dug for the opener. A moment later the door started to rise. We both ducked and rode under before it was all the way up.

I took off my helmet and helped Maralyn with hers. As soon as I removed it she ran her hand through her long hair.

"I must look wonderful after the wind and that helmet."

I reached out and thrust my fingers deep into her hair so I could support the back of her head with my hand. I pulled her close and whispered. "I can't imagine you looking any more beautiful." For a moment I thought I felt her knees buckle, and then she reached up and took my face in both hands as she pulled me close.

Her lips met mine and there was a near frantic nature about the way she kissed me. They were long kisses, wet and firm. Her tongue pushed past my lips in a hungry, needy way. I reciprocated every bit as eagerly.

Her body pressed against me, and she took a step forward. I backed up, my hand reaching for the door handle. I found it and we forced our way inside.

We moved down the hall toward the master bedroom, her hands grabbing and stroking my neck, the side of my face, and working their way through my hair. Our breathing was ragged, wanton. I could feel my heart pounding, was certain that the thumping had to be audible. I could feel her heart pounding against my chest.

She reached down and started to unbutton my shirt, I did the same with hers and both dropped carelessly to the floor. I slid out of the shoulder holster I'd been wearing, lowered the whole works, and then dropped it the remaining foot or so to the ground.

We both froze at the high pitched screech, and I realized I'd probably just dropped the whole rig on the cat. I flipped the switch to the hall light. Pal stood a few feet away, tail puffed, an angry, frightened, disjointed look on his face.

Our moment temporarily broken, we stood there in the hall, still holding on to each other but both looking at the frazzled kitten. "Sorry, Pal."

"Oh, how cute," Maralyn said. "What's his name?"

"Pal."

She got a strange look on her face.

"He was taken off the streets."

She nodded, recognition struck. "Parolee at Large. I get it. You're such a cop."

I shrugged and she leaned into me again, perhaps more forcefully than before. I reached forward and undid the clasp on the front of her pants. I slid the zipper down then reached around and slid my hands down her lower back. She groaned as my fingers slipped under the satin of her panties. I pushed down and her pants slid to the floor, panties and all in one swift action. She was reaching for the button on my Levi's before I was even done. My pants came off an instant later and we both used feet to get rid of our socks. I was slower and while I kicked the last sock free, she reached back and unclasped her bra. It fell to the floor and we toppled onto the bed.

For the first time in days, I felt like I was in control, even though she was on top of me directing the moment. It didn't matter. What mattered was that for whatever reason the two of us had found this common place.

We spent long minutes kissing, our hands working their way over unfamiliar territory, our senses afire with the newness of it all. There's something special, unrepeatable, about that first time with someone new. Her skin was soft like fine silk against the rougher texture of my fingers. Each touch, each stroke, sent waves of electricity through my body. Her perfume was even stronger than before, filling my chest with a wave of intensity with each deep breath of her I took in.

I reached for the drawer next to the bed and pulled it open. I dug inside until I could find what I was looking for. I pulled the condom package out, trying as well as I could not to break rhythm we'd established. The last thing I wanted to do was create an awkward moment. I didn't need to worry.

Maralyn leaned back and sat up, straddling my thighs. She took the wrapper from me and opened it. I must admit, you have to dig a woman who will put it on for you. Sometimes, there's nothing quite as difficult as trying to figure out which way it unrolls when you're in the heat of the moment.

Her job complete, Maralyn slid forward until I could ease into her. She let go a long sigh as the two of us joined into one. Slowly she started to move her hips. Without thinking, my back arched and I pushed up with my heels. My hips raised into her.

Our eyes locked, the light from the hallway just bright enough that we could make out each others features. Maralyn bent down so she was over me, close enough that we could feel each others breath, close enough that I could feel her hard nipples brush against my chest as she moved on top of me.

Our bodies moved slowly, with rhythm. All the frenzied anticipation that had driven us into the bed now slowed as though neither one wanted it to end. Sometime later and we collapsed into each other. Maralyn on her side, me flush up behind her. I held her close. Tight in my arms, thankful she was there, thankful for what she'd given me. No words were spoken. There was little I could say that would enhance what already was. I stroked her long hair until we both drifted off to sleep.

CHAPTER 10

I WOKE ALONE THINKING maybe I'd dreamed the previous night. Rolling over, I crushed my face into the pillow and caught a hint of perfume. My thoughts weren't some drunken memory after all. Either that or I'd gone too long without washing my sheets.

Reading the clock was a strain. Just after eight, no wonder my eyes didn't work. Morning sucked. I glanced at the bathroom. The door was open but the room was dark, not that I expected otherwise. A woman might sleep with you that first night, but when the time comes, she'll look for the bathroom in the farthest corner of the house.

My feet slipped off the bed. I found my pants folded neatly on the dresser. Pulling them on, I headed to the kitchen. I'd barely made the hall when the smell of fresh brewed coffee hit. Maybe my luck was changing.

Maralyn was sitting on the patio watching Pal hunt some small bug in the grass.

"Good morning." She smiled. "I didn't want to wake you, but I couldn't sleep any more." She was sitting crossways on the two person patio chair, her feet up, coffee mug held firmly in both hands. My Hawaiian shirt was large for her slim frame. I marveled at the way the sharp morning light reflected in her eyes, but mostly the flawless nature of her smooth, tan legs.

"A morning person, are you?" My words were gravelly, more

a growl than anything. I poured a cup, kept hold of the pot, and moved toward the patio.

"Not quite. Apparently I move my feet when I sleep."

I stopped, not following her train of thought but not awake enough to think and move simultaneously.

"Your friend," she pointed to Pal. "Movement under the covers is some game."

I nodded and continued forward again.

"He doesn't much pay attention to what others want. I think it's a cat thing. Sorry." I raised the coffee and she extended her cup. As I put the pot on the table, Maralyn brought her knees up to her chest to make room for me.

I sat and stared into my mug. I needed coffee but didn't want to scald my mouth. I blew across the cup and took a small sip. The inky black liquid was hot, but my tongue didn't blister and my gums didn't melt away. I'd just need to be careful.

Attention shifted, Maralyn was staring. I stared back, trying to read her thoughts.

"What?" She blushed.

The question jarred me. "Sorry," I said to buy time.

She tilted her head and her hair fell loosely over her shoulder. The movement caught my eyes and they inadvertently dropped. That brought me to the open front of her shirt. The curve of her breasts and the promise to be found in the shadowy cover of the cloth shattered my train of thought completely. I quickly brought my eyes back up hoping I didn't just get busted looking in her shirt.

Maralyn smiled. "Is that what you were looking at?"

My eyes went back to my coffee and I took a sip. I swallowed hard. What to say? I wanted to spend more time with her. I wanted to tell her how glad I was for last night, but I didn't want her to feel like I was giving her the "Don't feel cheap" speech. We'd reached the morning after, that uncomfortable place between intimate encounter and the routine of life. And I had been looking down her shirt.

Then I remembered yesterday's plans. If Michelle hadn't left, I'd hoped to go up the coast for lunch. A bit early, but maybe I could talk her into breakfast. "I was wondering if you might like to take a ride to La Jolla, maybe get something to eat."

She gave me an awkward look, then lowered her eyes and stared into her cup much the same as I'd done. Long moments passed and her attention drifted to the yard. Fear crept through me and I wondered if I said something I shouldn't have. I turned my attention back to my own coffee hoping the difficult moment would simply pass.

When her eyes did make their way back to me, I looked up.

"Look, John, you don't have to entertain me. I'm a big girl, don't feel obligated."

Shit! Now I was really off center. To pause and think could be misunderstood; to speak too quickly might sound insincere. My solution was probably the kind of thing a '90s man would do, but I had to try.

Reaching out, I stroked her cheek as I forced myself to maintain eye contact. I felt awkward, unaccustomed to dropping the walls protecting me from feeling anything that might be construed as an emotion. "I don't feel obligated. If you have some place you need to be, I understand. I'm just not quite ready for last night to end."

Her eyes sparkled and she brought her hand up to cover mine. "I need to get my car and get home." My heart sank. "But if I'm there by six, I should be okay."

She set her cup down and stood, then took mine and set it next to the chair. A moment later those long, firm, wonderful legs straddled me. My heart raced, the rapid beats having little to do with the coffee. Wrapping her arms around my neck, she leaned forward, and then her smooth lips brushed against mine. Morning or not, I was awake.

The sun was bright, and warm on my face. The Goldwing's windshield kept most of the wind away. A slight haze still clung to the coast, but the marine layer had mostly backed out to sea. Randy Travis sang a sad song on the radio, but today his melancholy tune was nothing but background noise. Today was a good day.

The road rolled out ahead and I concentrated on making the ride enjoyable. The freeway would have been quicker, but I stuck to surface streets. A few extra stops for a red light now and again, but the steeply curved, tree-lined serpentine that was Torrey Pines Road was worth the extra time. This route was built for motorcycles.

As we banked into a curve, my eyes found a big pine on the side of the road. My mind flashed back to days of training in Northern Division and the fatal car wreck that had ended with that tree. The scars remained where the Toyota's front end bit into the thick trunk, but to any other passing motorist the damage might have simply grown over into something revealing character. The memory faded as quickly, just one of several I might get from our trip through town.

As we rode, Maralyn's hands stayed in constant contact. First, slowly stroking up and down my sides, and then reaching up to run her finger down the back of my neck. I found it as hard to concentrate as I did to wish she would not be such a distraction.

Once in La Jolla it was a short walk past the small shops and boutiques lining the narrow street to a little restaurant overlooking the cove. Lots of people had my idea today. Fortunately the bulk of them were families still busy trying to find a spot to park the minivan and an easy way to carry their loads of picnic gear to the grassy lawn overlooking the water.

We were lucky enough to be seated on the front patio. The ocean breeze was thick and probably contained enough salt to trim a margarita glass. Tempting thought but too early. We ordered coffee. I'd still only had half a cup, the other abandoned for a naked romp in the shower—nearly a fair trade, even in my book.

Our conversation was date talk. Not the kind two lovers share in the bedroom, but the kind of get-to-know-you talk they do when they're trying to decide whether they are ever going to get there at all. The thought amused me. I'd never been much of a one-night-stand guy, but I was also never one to follow the norm. What happened last night was fitting, that I would sleep with this woman and then spend the next morning trying to find out whether I'd do it again. So far, the conclusion was a certainty. In fact, much of what wandered through my little brain as she talked about her co-workers and life in the DA's office was the thought that I'd really rather be naked with her.

Several times I caught myself looking around. On the street, you get used to scanning your surroundings while others talk. Time equals safety. The best way to be safe is to see things coming. I'd run into enough bad people off-duty that I couldn't comfortably sit anywhere without paying attention to the people sitting or moving around us. With any luck she'd dealt with enough cops to understand our quirks. If not, hopefully she'd give me some time before I'd get the "Why aren't you paying attention to me?" speech.

Women don't respond well to the wandering eyes. Most of the time the topic comes up the first time it happens. They see your eyes searching and think you're either not interested in what they're saying or not interested in them. Sometimes they try to find the woman who must be distracting you.

"So, John," she began.

I stopped scanning and focused. Any time a woman starts a sentence with "So" you'd better pay attention—especially to the tone in her voice.

Maralyn continued. "Enough about my silly office. Your turn."

I smiled as warmly as I could. "Your days seem far more exciting than mine."

Lowering eyes, she blushed. "I doubt that. Everyone's on their best behavior by the time they get to me. Either that or they've got their victim of society role going."

I hesitated to speak. I wasn't used to talking shop outside the office. I'd gotten used to leaving that behind me.

She continued. "Okay, then can I ask a personal question?"

Shit. "Yeah, go ahead."

"Most of the guys are younger than you, the ones in uniform anyway. The older cops seem to be Detectives or Sergeants. How come you're still just a patrolman?"

She had my full attention.

"What's wrong with being a patrolman?"

"Ah . . . well, nothing," she stammered.

I realized my response had been more bark than answer, but there was something about "just a patrolman" that always bent a nerve. Her impression was the same one most folks had. The street cop was just the guy that did the grunt work, the little stuff. The things that could be done by any moron until the exceptional thinkers, the detectives, came along to do the tough thinking.

"I just meant that you seem capable of more."

And that was always the follow-up response.

"I like the streets. We got plenty of folks get into this job and find out it's not for them, so they start looking for ways to get out of the dirty work. Quitting isn't an option, not without losing a steady paycheck. They want the money, they just don't want the job; don't want the crummy hours, the nasty dregs they have to deal with. Most of all they don't want to make the hard decisions. Patrol is the most challenging position. Nothing the same day to day, a successful street cop needs a far wider set of skills to be effective than someone in any other position. I like that challenge."

"But don't you want to work something like robbery or homicide?"

"I work them in a uniform. Nothing says I can't catch a bank robber or solve a murder. Yesterday, for example, we went to a homicide. If I wanted to solve that, no reason I couldn't. The rules don't say I only get to set up the crime scene tape. The badge gives me the same authority as a detective. Hell, same as the Chief. The only difference is clothes and a desk. The authority is the same."

She listened intently as I ranted. When I finished, she smiled. I felt like shit for reacting and was about to apologize when she spoke.

"I didn't mean to offend you, John." She paused as though she wanted to say more. Instead, she changed the subject. "Tell me about the homicide?"

"Not much to tell, really. Woman got killed. Odds are the husband did it." I left it at that. Police work isn't like coming home from the office and telling your other half about how tough you worked to broker the copy machine sale. Communication with a cop is different. On one hand, they want to know about your day, on the other, talking about the bad things is sometimes better left alone.

Maralyn leaned forward, undeterred. I forgot I wasn't talking to Buffy the wanna be homemaker, I was talking to a DA. "Really, John, tell me about the case."

I poured more coffee. She put her hand up when I moved to fill hers. When it comes to coffee drinkers, there are amateurs and there are cops. I took a sip and looked across the broad lawn topping the cliffs of La Jolla cove. The dark, blue water of the pacific struck a marked contrast to the soft spread of green grass. Hard to believe she wanted to talk about the bad things in a place as beautiful as this. She waited patiently.

"Man came home and found his wife on the floor in the bedroom. To look at the scene, seems Esther put up quite a fight, shoe marks on the walls, stuff knocked off the dresser. Hell, even her jeans left a transfer mark on the wall when she was slammed against it. Whoever beat the life out of her really wanted her dead."

"And you think the husband."

"Logical choice. Had him in the car afterwards. When my partner told him his wife was dead, his response was something like, 'Good, she deserved it.'" I left out the part where he called her a cunt. "Once they sort through the other stuff, odds are he murdered her."

"Sounds convincing," she said, her tone unconvinced. "What's the other stuff?"

"Back door was pried, some stuff set on the kitchen table."

"That sounds like a burglary."

"Or set up to look that way."

Maralyn leaned into her chair and thought a moment. "I'd need more before I'd issue on him. Sounds like maybe some burglar got surprised. Probably sound that way to a defense attorney too, and he'd only have to convince one juror."

"Could be." I shrugged. "Really wouldn't surprise me either way. Something about a burglar doesn't ring right. Usually the dopers do burglaries so they don't have to deal with people. If they were a confrontational sort . . . they'd do robberies. Who knows how long the husband had to stage things. Long enough I think."

"And what's his reason to kill her?"

"Don't think he liked her much."

"Lots of men don't like their wives. From not liking to murder can be a long trip."

"Not as long as you might think."

The notion seemed rather simple. Most of what we deal with isn't out of a book, or the movie of the week. Rarely are people as creative in real life as they are in the stories. After a while you see the patterns, the product of frantic actions and carelessness.

I continued. "I dunno, something just doesn't sing stranger to me. If beating her didn't do the job, there was the cord around her neck. If not that, then the bag over her head. I've seen burglars kill but usually they aren't the thieves, they're the sex freaks. If that's the case, more likely we'd find a pile of her photos or underwear stacked on the table, trophies, rather than something to sell. This person was venting rage. If the killer's a stranger, we're dealing with a whole other sort of animal, a predator for damn sure."

"Interesting." She sighed. "I'd still need more."

"I'm sure the details will all come out in the end."

"So what's next?"

I looked at my watch. "How 'bout a walk on Prospect?"

"No, I mean with the case."

"Aw, hell, I've been gone three days. Probably already sorted itself out."

"And if not, what's next for you?"

"That depends on what the dispatcher has waiting."

"You're not going to keep working this? What happened to solving anything?"

"Nothing, but there's good folks in Homicide, and we've got too few cops in the field. This ain't ten years ago when staffing wasn't gutted by a jacked up budget. These days it's enough to handle radio calls. That doesn't leave much time for playing Columbo. If I run off on tangents, who covers my workload?"

"I see," she said flatly, eyes narrowing. "What was her name again?"

I paused. "Esther."

"You remember her name, but you're not sure you need to stay involved? I don't buy that. I don't see you able to let go that easy. Surely you can find a way to balance your time. Maybe Homicide will figure it out. But if not, who speaks for Esther?"

We paid the bill and walked toward the cove. I spent the next thirty minutes thinking about what Maralyn said. Who did speak for Esther? Plenty of folks meet untimely ends, but this was my weekend, I was with a beautiful woman, and I wanted to enjoy what time remained. That didn't seem too much to ask, to not have to think about the bad things just for today at least. I could think about them tomorrow.

We spent the afternoon walking, holding hands, and searching the tiny shops for treasures. I forced our conversation to the back of my brain. I'd worked hard to get to the point where work didn't come home with me, but even now, one simple comment and suddenly my personal life blurred with my professional one.

Too quickly afternoon turned to evening. I opened the Goldwing's trunk and stowed the box with the small vase I'd bought Maralyn at the import shop. She'd argued that it cost too much, but she liked the design, a purchase well worth the smile.

Cool evening air brought a chill as we cruised down the freeway. Maralyn grew quiet, more reserved. I couldn't tell if she was caught up in that sad Sunday feeling that creeps up when you realize your free time has slipped by and you need to get back to thinking about real life, or if there was something more on her mind.

She spoke as we stopped for the first light into downtown. "You can drop me at the courthouse. I can walk from there."

I tilted my head back so I didn't have to yell, "Nonsense."

"Really, I'm a big girl. It's not that far."

I wasn't sure whether she was trying to make the split easy or trying to avoid the awkward last moment at the end of an extraordinary date. Either way, I didn't feel right dumping her on a sidewalk. One thing that had been instilled early on, a man simply didn't let a woman walk to her car unattended. That meant he opened doors and pulled out chairs, even if she was fully capable of doing such things for herself. To do otherwise would bother me the rest of the night.

"I'd feel better, the parkade, right?"

"No, pay lot behind the courthouse," she replied.

The light changed and I accelerated. The momentum drew her back and I didn't hear what came next. We were pulling into the parking lot before either of us had another chance to speak. On a Sunday evening, there were only a few scattered cars among a sea of empty spaces.

My stomach tightened as we idled across the lot. I never was much good with the end of a date but usually the difficulty lay in the do I kiss her or not crap. This was different. There was an inherent expectation, and I wasn't sure how far it extended. I certainly intended to ask her out again. There was something about her, an understanding Michelle never grasped.

I tried to guess which car was hers and settled on the Accord in the middle space. I turned that way. "Yours?"

"No. Corner," she said so softly I could barely make out her words.

The only vehicle in the corner of the lot was a truck. A big, red, shiny Ford. An F-250. I'd have written a truck like that off to the Fire Department, but this was raised with over-size tires. My first thought was, "Cool, we can take that to the desert." Then reality hit. The jitters in my stomach twisted into a knot.

As I reached to help Maralyn from the bike, there was a look I'd not seen before. Sadness, recognition that I was solving something she didn't want me to figure out. I retrieved her vase. I'd have said something, but I couldn't think of words to mend the rift that was quickly forming. Tears welled in her eyes and she lowered them. Though the idea was getting pretty clear, I wasn't entirely sure where we were headed. Regardless of the details, this was about to end badly. She struggled to speak.

Standing there wasn't going to make it easier. "That's not your truck is it?"

A single tear broke loose and streamed down her cheek. Part of me was busy tossing sandbags to reinforce the bunker I was building inside while the other part wanted to reach up and wipe the tear away. That was the Knight in Shining Armor syndrome, the part of me that wanted to rescue her from whatever dragon she needed help escaping. I didn't, I wouldn't. Never again. I'd played that game enough. I wasn't going to do it here, not now.

Silence hung on the air. Then she spoke. "John, this isn't what you think. I'm not his girlfriend any more."

A shard of hope glimmered like the sliver of light in a cracked doorway at the end of a dark hall. Her crying told me the door was closing. "But you're driving his truck. Do you live with him?"

Tears streamed down both cheeks. "Not like that, really. We're more roommates until he can find a place to get settled."

My reaction wasn't intentional. I bit the inside of my lip and looked away. My thoughts were scattered visions of all the things that didn't work out, all the dreams I wanted but could never quite realize. My brain grappled over whether this could be any different, if she could be any different.

"John, if you'd just let me explain. I didn't mean for things to turn out this way. Last night just happened so quickly."

I'd heard enough. Hers was the same sad story everyone used to justify cheating. The same story men used all the time. "I can't leave my wife until . . . , the marriage is over, except . . . , now isn't the right time but . . ." I'd heard the sob stories before, and I'd been the guy whose girl told them to someone else. All of it was shit.

The last thing I needed was to end up in Internal Affairs on some kind of conduct unbecoming allegation when the boyfriend found out and called the Department to complain that I was boning his woman. That's the world I had to live in, my personal life was never entirely personal. Worse yet, if IA didn't come looking for me, the whole mess would get sent back to my command to deal with. That meant wonder boy himself got to dig into things I was certain we would never discuss otherwise. Sergeant Roosevelt—the five year wonder—would use an allegation like this as his tool to crush me into submission or punish me for not cowing to him.

I'm a veteran cop, a trained observer, and an expert in reading people. Who would believe that I just made a mistake, that I didn't do something I shouldn't have? That's never the way this works. Whoever dealt with the complaint, I'd be marked from the onset and they would treat a mistake as something intentional. Even if the whole thing just went away, that wouldn't be before I'd had to answer a bunch of embarrassing questions. Welcome to a world where you're expected to live by a higher standard.

My voice was firm, cold. I strained to keep it that way. "What he is, is a boyfriend. If you live with him, if you drive his car, he's a boyfriend. I'm sorry Maralyn but I won't get in the middle of that, wouldn't have even considered the possibility if I'd have known last night."

There were a million things I wanted to say, some I knew I

shouldn't and some I knew I couldn't. I was on that line between hurt and anger, between doing what I wanted and doing what I should. My head spun, but I let the opportunity for discussion go. I got back on the bike and strapped on my helmet. Maralyn didn't move. A part of me wanted her to, wanted her to step toward me, but my logical side was glad she didn't. I fired up the Goldwing and cut hard into a turn. I was racing across the lot before my brain started to wonder if I'd really heard her say, "I'm sorry."

Chapter 11

PEOPLE TALK ABOUT HAPPINESS as if the very thought were some right, an entitlement. I have the right to be happy. I have the right to a nice house, a wife who is my soul mate, the job I want, a big screen, an SUV, and enough money that I can have Starbuck's whenever I want. It's my right. The whole concept is bullshit. If you find something that makes you feel special, just hold on. The feeling isn't permanent. Eating a carne asada burrito is happiness, but the satisfaction always leads to a messy run to the crapper. Life is tough and makes no promises.

I couldn't help but wonder if Esther thought about that while the life drained out of her. She'd found little in the way of rights.

I'd been wondering about that most of the night, dwelling as a matter of course, something to keep from fixating on my own little drama. The end of the day with Maralyn hurt, I couldn't deny that. I liked her. She was there to fill a need at the right time. Our encounter could have been a nice memory. Now the whole mess just left a spoiled feeling in my gut. The only thing I could do was to try and reject my feelings, to bury them deep in the bunkers that held a history of painful moments.

In order to not feel, I had to think about something else. Esther had become that distraction. Feeling sorry about Maralyn was a small thing when I set myself in the right context.

By the time I pulled into the station parking lot, I'd worked myself into a fully pissed off state. Not the way I liked to come to work, but sometimes there's just no avoiding it. Unless I got stuck with Stevie again, Marcus would be doing most of the talking. We had an agreement. If one of us was in a funk, the other did the contacts. That helped keep some poor soul from getting throttled, dragged out of his car when he asked indignantly why we weren't catching real crooks. Set us on a pedestal if you want, scrutinize us under the microscope while you talk about how we need to be better than regular folks, more in control of our temper. In the end we're still just people subject to all the flaws of anyone else. Sometimes living to a higher standard simply means knowing when to let your partner do the talking.

I tried to find a parking stall that wasn't too near the fence that enclosed our lot. My Explorer wasn't fancy, but it was mine. I didn't need some shitbird on the sidewalk tossing a chunk of asphalt or some nasty package on the hood. I grabbed a clean uniform from the back seat and started toward the locker room.

My thoughts shifted back to Esther. I still figured the husband was the odds on favorite, but thinking of him as a near absolute no longer sat in as settled a spot as it once had. What if he wasn't? What if we were dealing with a predator? With all that had been going on, I hadn't much thought about that until Maralyn dragged work into our lunchtime conversation.

If our bad guy was the husband, Homicide would figure out the connections quickly enough. Maybe I could help, maybe I couldn't. On the other hand, if we were dealing with a predator, some sicko, he'd need to be found, fast. They never hurt just one. They went on hurting folks until someone stopped them. The longer we waited to hunt someone like that, the more chances he'd have to do harm. That was my responsibility. I was the one on the street.

If I was wrong, if the husband wasn't the suspect and somebody else got hurt, it would likely turn out that there was nothing I could have done to prevent another victim. You learn not to own certain things that happen out here. One thing was certain, I didn't want to live with the thought that I didn't even consider alternative actions.

By the time I got to the locker room I'd decided my next step was a phone call to Ronny in Homicide. Perhaps they'd come up with something. If not, maybe he could give me a better read on where things were headed. No point getting too into this if the conclusion was already a done deal. I opened the door and stepped into the locker room.

The change happened. You don't notice the transformation all the time but today I was acutely aware of the metamorphosis. Every day you work, the process of mental preparation starts a good couple hours before you actually get there. Your thoughts start to shift from errands and hobbies to the far more real considerations of radio calls and survival.

The shift is subtle at first, something entirely internal. I used to feel my mindset change the most working graveyards when I'd try and meet folks for dinner before heading into work. There I'd be, enjoying a nice meal and yet I could barely think of a thing to say. My lack of focus didn't have anything to do with whether I had anything to talk about. No matter how much I tried there was simply no way to avoid the process. In the end, I'd spent many a night staring at my coffee cup while someone else carried the conversation.

The change is more dramatic when you hit the locker room. A police locker room is a kinetic place, men telling war stories or laughing about their weekend. Some rattle on about how many felony arrests they made during the week and others rant about how glad they are to be back at work and free of their honey-do list. Some bitch about how the Department is fucking all of us. Regardless of conversation, all are preparing to cruise the streets in a big black-and-white target not knowing if they'll return to their lockers at the end of the day. For the unlucky few, the honorable who don't come back, someone will have to come to their locker and box up the photos of the wives, girlfriends, and proud kids in their baseball uniforms.

Walking through the door, the shift is like stepping from one world into another. Much of what makes up your off-duty life simply goes on hold. You come in plain clothes, a civilian for the most part. You go through your little ritual of gearing up, getting dressed in your little blue street warrior outfit, and by the time you walk back out that door you are an entirely different person. For a cop, the locker room is like Clark Kent's phone booth. The only difference is that bullets don't necessarily bounce off your blue suit, and there's a lot more kryptonite than Superman ever encountered.

I walked as quietly as possible. I wasn't in the mood for the banter today. That didn't matter, never does. Your friends might be sensitive to whether you had a bad weekend, but cops will still bust your balls. There's no room for weakness in this place. That's how we stay sane. It's how we survive. The quiet I fought to maintain ended before I was half way to my locker.

Brad Beckett came around the corner. You'd have thought I'd have heard him coming, heard the slapping sound of his shower shoes as he trotted down the aisle, but my head was still somewhere else. I should have known to be more aware, Beckett was always running, always operating as if he were permanently five minutes behind the rest of us and in a rush to catch up.

He was headed for the shower. My inattention nearly cost me a head-on collision with a naked man carrying a towel and a bottle of shampoo. Beckett was a full six inches shorter than me, a bit stocky. Being former military gave him a different standard of locker room decorum. No part of the man maintained any illusion of privacy. This wasn't the first time he'd run around naked, and it wouldn't be the last. Considering his height and the fact that he had somewhat pointed ears, he always reminded me of a streaking elf.

Beckett stopped in time to avoid the collision. His glance was furtive as if he was contemplating whether he had time to say anything at all. He grinned, a sort of twisted, knowing grin. "Hatch, you got balls of steel, man."

I wasn't quite sure what he was talking about, but I was pretty certain his thoughts had to do with the retirement party. Some small part of me braced for the embarrassing aftermath that was about to follow. I attempted to cut him short. I growled, "Beckett, I'm not so sure I'm comfortable with you talking about my balls when you're standing there butt-ass naked and holding a towel."

Brad's head jerked when he looked down then jerked again when he looked back up. He shook his head and trotted off. "Balls of steel, man."

Groaning, I continued my trek. The day was going to be longer than expected; I'd forgotten the party. No doubt every dirty deed, every silly drunken antic was already moving through the rumor mill. Cops from Northern Division to Southern Division were already talking about variations of the same sordid stories.

I turned the corner. Marcus was already there, early like every day and very nearly dressed. He took his appearance to the extreme and dressed with an absolute sense of pride. Jenkins was further down the aisle, and I could hear Martinez yammering around the corner.

Marcus raised his right fist, holding it out in place of a handshake. "Brother John." I brought up a fist and rapped my knuckles against his. The greeting was the same every day.

"Mornin'," was all I got out.

Marcus laughed. "Guess I'm driving. Seems Brother John did some sinning."

"We're not gonna start like that, are we?"

"We're absolutely gonna start like that my fine friend. The Brotherman must know details."

"What?" I groaned. "There are no details to give."

"You had a girlfriend when last we talked."

"Apparently things change," I said as I slipped my vest on.

Jenkins looked up. "Say what? Michelle dumped you? I knew it, I figured that the second I didn't see her at the party." He nodded as though he was proud of something. "Sorry man, at least she didn't take half your shit."

Marcus watched my expression as Jenkins spoke. I shrugged. Indifference seemed the right reaction for the locker room. His right eye narrowed. I brushed off the probing nature of his stare.

"You hear that?" Jenkins said to Martinez. "Michelle bailed on Hatch."

"Don't worry, Hatch, you'll find someone," Martinez shouted matter-of-factly over the lockers, apparently undisturbed enough to feel the need to walk over and speak face to face. I'm sure he meant to show a degree of encouragement but it was unlikely there'd be a sensitive hug attached.

Jenkins spoke again. "Hey, hey, I got one for you. Digs cops, always flirting."

"No thanks."

"No, really. At least she'd be someone to go out with."

"I think I'll survive." At least they were harping on Michelle. Clearly someone was talking about the weekend, but so far there was no mention of me leaving with a DA.

"Yeah, but she'd be fun, got a rockin' body." When I didn't ask, Jenkins felt compelled to continue an effort he clearly thought would change my mind. "Her name's Anna, she's that new waitress at Denny's."

Marcus laughed out loud. His deep voice reverberated off the lockers. "You mean sawtooth? C'mon, bro, you can't be that frustrated."

Jenkins stopped dressing. He stood there for a moment like a little boy who'd just been shouted at. "What? Her teeth aren't that bad."

I looked at him, certain I didn't need a Denny's waitress with bad teeth. "Yeah, they're a bit messy."

"Shit." Marcus sighed. "Jaws had a straighter set than her."

"What would you know? You've been with the same woman all your life, probably took the first one that'd have ya. Now she's holding your nuts in her pocket."

"Oh, my poor red headed brother. When you have the finest e-bony love goddess, there ain't no more need for prowling around. Specially for one might turn you on. My wife will never be calling me her babies' daddy." Marcus closed his locker. "Sorry, Opie, you got a ways to go before you start explaining love to the Brotherman."

Turning to me, Marcus said, "I'll see if I can't find us a car that runs." A quick glance, and I knew our conversation wasn't done. You learn to read a lot in a partner's expression. Michelle might have left, I might be having a bad day, but he was there with me all the way. He'd never have to say as much, and there'd be no sappy, tear-covered conversations over Oprah. As much as they might rag on you, that was the way with cops. Before he walked away, he spoke quietly, "Brother John, might be best to avoid Roosevelt should you get the chance."

Aw hell. Not only had I forgotten the party, I'd forgotten about the five-year wonder. He might not be too keen on seeing me. My little introduction to Chief Rickert seemed funny at the time. No, I smiled, it still seemed funny. The look on his face was the only thing that'd brought me a smile all day.

I looked up and saw Jenkins standing there as though he were contemplating something. He remained silent.

"What," I asked.

He got a hurt expression on his face, "Why's the white guy gotta be an Opie?"

It took me a moment to figure out what was troubling him. "Jenkins, remind me how old you are."

"Twenty-eight in three months."

"Ever been to Mayberry?"

"Never even heard of Mayberry."

"Opie lived there. He was a red-headed white kid." I closed my locker door. "You're the only one in this room who could be Opie." I walked away. Behind me I heard Jenkins asking Martinez if he knew who Opie was.

I slipped into the main part of the station making sure to avoid any of the places Sergeant Roosevelt might be prowling. I checked my mailbox, quickly rifling through the mish-mash of routine paper that backs up on days off. Involuntarily, my body shuddered at the thought of what my e-mail might look like. There'd be a half dozen messages, but the Sergeant would have forwarded them to me, the Lieutenant would have forwarded them to those of us that worked for her, and the Captain would have forwarded them to everyone. By the time the forwarding was done, I'd have to sort through the same six messages sent by at least half-a-dozen different people. I missed the old days.

At the bottom of the stack was a phone message from Maralyn. The note said please call DA Denoir. I looked at the time. She called in the morning, clearly after she'd arrived at work. The prefix looked like a cell phone number. For someone who didn't actually have a boyfriend, I wondered why she would wait until she got to work, would call herself by title to make the message look work related, and would leave a cell number instead of her office line. I took the message, the rest of the useless paper, and stuffed the whole pile into the shredder.

I glanced at my watch on the way to a quiet place where I could call Ronny. No time. I'd have to wait until after line-up or run the risk of being late. That was probably the last thing I needed. I headed off to find a seat.

Line-up hasn't changed much over the years. I doubt we'll ever again see the days where someone brings a belly dancer for the sergeant's fiftieth birthday. Then again, we seem a bit beyond the days where we even have sergeants who are fifty. I have the boy wonder. If someone ever brought a belly dancer, I seriously doubt he'd have any idea what to do with her. Barney or Chuck E. Cheese would be more appropriate.

Belly dancers aside, line-up is much the same as they showed on Hill Street Blues. Those of us about to head the field still gather in a room while one of the shift sergeants reads a log of what has or is about to happen. Wanted posters hang on the wall. Sometimes a new crook's background gets passed around when a detective is hot for him. I'd bet you could walk into any department in the country and find line-ups are pretty similar. Probably been that way since the Centurions stood around discussing what the pesky Christians were up to.

Rarely did our briefing amount to much. Certainly the summary of daily events provided little that was shocking. I'd seen enough years of traumatic accidents, shootings, stabbings, and general mayhem that I was rarely captivated by the daily list of bad things that occurred in the command.

Every now and again the sergeant read a death notification of some retired cop. Most of the time at least one of us still remembered them, but even their demise wasn't often a surprise. Rarely do you hear of a retired cop living long enough to be forgotten. Mostly we die before our time. Some cities provide more lucrative benefits to entice a guy to stay longer, but often those few brief years of incentives only result in an earlier death and less overall benefits for the retiree in the long run. We all hope to beat the insurance actuary tables, but the truth is we don't. Unfair perhaps, but that's life.

I sat quietly in my corner and watched the room. Monday, today was a barrel day, meaning that several squads worked a shift that overlapped between days off. The room was packed. Some of us were coming back to work, others were heading toward days off. My attention turned to the crowd while I waited for the sergeants to arrive and get things started.

Suzie Orwin sat at the table rambling about something uninteresting. At least three guys paid attention to her every word, not caring what she said but hoping she might find their attention worth her time. Some guys would listen to anything, even nonsense, if they thought they'd get in a girl's pants. Suzie played that to her advantage, hoping they would overlook things like not showing up on a "cover now."

Murphy was back, his composure regained after his fight. He sat at the table patiently polishing his badge and name plate. Most of us could have done that in the locker room in about thirty seconds. Not so for a SWAT boy. Polishing brass was akin to some kind of ritual. He'd spread his stuff out on the table and would need twenty minutes more than anyone else, except perhaps another SWAT boy. To them, boots and brass couldn't be shiny enough, and they couldn't be allowed to touch a speck of dirt.

The back door opened and Eric Smith slipped quietly into the room. I couldn't tell you why he felt the need to be quiet. The room was a maelstrom of conversation. Perhaps he simply didn't want the attention. He wasn't comfortable engaging people, a strange trait for someone whose very job is to go out and talk to strangers, but we had plenty of guys like him.

Eric glanced at me, then looked away and took his seat. The door pounded open and Sergeant Roosevelt stepped into the room carrying the day's schedule. He was followed by a swaggering Sergeant Brian Rake.

Rake was an old-school cop. He drank coffee, chewed cigars, chewed tobacco, and some were convinced he chewed steel. He'd been a sergeant longer than anyone in the room could remember, and no one knew exactly how old he was or how long he'd really been around. The six hash marks on his sleeve were more than some squads had if they added their combined years of service. Those slashes on his shirt meant he'd been around at least thirty years.

If Sergeant Rake didn't like you, he told you. If he thought something was screwed, he said so. He'd been to enough calls, put enough bad guys away, and had seen enough cops come and go that no one questioned him. If he needed to put a Chief in his place, he'd do it and not give the action another thought. He was the kind of guy many folks in the administration wished would simply go away, but there were too many legends associated with his name for them to ever be able to make it happen. He wouldn't leave until he decided he didn't want to be here anymore.

Roosevelt started reading through the list of incidents that took place over the weekend. He ran down the normal litany of robberies, beatings, and stabbings that fill the book daily. There was nothing new. Then he got to one incident. "Jefferson, you were on this combative guy, you want to talk about it." There was no question in his voice. He expected the officer to speak.

Phil Jefferson started, "Yeah, ah, the other day we responded to a call of a man yelling in the street. When we got there we found . . ." He rambled on for several minutes. I half-listened to his story of another angry, mentally disturbed, and totally intoxicated person who simply wanted to be confrontational. Pepper spray didn't stop him, pepper balls fired from the air gun didn't stop him, and bean bags from the shotgun only slowed him long enough for a couple enterprising young cops to tackle him. In the end they managed a successful conclusion to an otherwise ordinary tale.

Phil continued, "When we got him in the car he worked his hands down his pants and started flinging crap in the back seat."

The room broke into hysterics. Next to a fart joke nothing can amuse a bunch of adolescent grownups like a story about flying crap. A poo-flicker. I was glad I didn't get him. I'd had enough, I didn't mind sharing the wealth. A poo-flicker's gotta be near the lowest form of humanity.

"Okay, quiet down," Roosevelt continued. "Just remember to use your personal protective equipment." He couldn't just say glove up and try to avoid getting smeared. Aesop had to pretend he was teaching us something we didn't already know.

When the room settled, Sergeant Roosevelt started reading the roster of unit assignments. Most of us worked the same beats so I only paid attention to whatever was out of the ordinary. When he got to Marcus, his assignment fit the bill. He was scheduled to work alone. I looked at him and he shrugged.

"John," Roosevelt said. It took a moment to realize he was talking to me. "You and Steven will be 831 Zebra. And John, please see me in my office after line-up."

If his demands didn't regain control after the poo-flicker story, his last comment did. All heads turned to me. The instant hush was followed by the low murmur of people muttering "Ooooh." You'd think I was back in high school with the teacher catching me shooting spit balls. I leaned back in my chair and gave him a nod. This was going to be rich. I was about to get my first ass-chewing by my new sergeant, and he'd just made sure everyone knew it.

Chapter 12

BAD DAYS IN THIS JOB never seem to improve. I was steaming when I walked out of the line-up room. Everyone knew what was going on and most kept their distance. A couple patted me on the back and asked if I'd sell them my gear, one asked if I wanted a jar of Vaseline. I ignored them and headed to the sergeant's office. There was no point putting off the inevitable. Better to let Roosevelt have his moment so I could get out in the field.

When I entered the little cubicle that was his empire, Theodore Roosevelt was seated at his desk making notes on the schedule. Without making eye contact he motioned for me to sit. I knew his failure to immediately address me was a power thing. He would speak when he was ready. Until then, he wanted obedience. A more normal sergeant would have pulled me aside or caught me in the field and addressed me away from my peers. He wasn't normal. He was Napoleon and he had something to prove.

When enough time passed, the boy wonder pushed his papers to the top of his desk and swiveled in his chair to address me. "John," he began. His voice low, patronizing. "Do you have something against me?"

"Sir, I hardly know you." I didn't answer his question but my response didn't force me to lie to his face either. Avoidance was the best way to make him play his hand. I'd have an easier time responding if I knew exactly what he wanted. This had to be about the party, I was just wishing he'd spit it out.

"Hmm," he murmured and nodded. "Did you have fun at the party?"

"Yes sir, and you?" I was right. He was gonna make me drag the words out of him but the fact that I'd embarrassed him was going to come out in the end.

"Actually I felt a little used. I think you must have found it quite amusing to set me up with your 'It's a funny story' antic."

I fought a smile. It was a funny story. "I'm sorry, did something happen?"

For the first time, his voice rose. He was well aware that I was fucking with him. What he didn't know was if he could prove what his instincts told him. "You know damn well what happened. Chief Rickert chewed my ass and told me to go away. Do you have any idea how I looked? You set me up."

"I'm sorry, sir," I said with as much empathy as I could muster. "After you walked away, I went out to see some friends. That's an old story. The Chief and I have laughed about it many times. He must have been in some kind of mood."

There was no use denying what I did. He had me. That didn't mean I had to tell him that the shame was inflicted intentionally. I'd ducked out before Roosevelt could have turned to see me. If he couldn't prove I watched, he couldn't prove I set him up. He might know the truth but this game isn't about knowing, it's about proof. If he was real committed he could order me to tell him and I'd be screwed. I was willing to bet he wasn't going to turn this into a stink that might leave him looking silly to someone else. He redirected his efforts.

"Let me ask you this, John. How come after all these years you're still just a patrolman?" He let the question hang and then I knew where we were heading. I was going to get lectured. If he couldn't prove I'd set him up, he'd berate me.

Why did being a patrolman always have to seem like a bad thing? Maralyn's words clamored in my head. There was always a tone people took, an underlying implication that patrol was simple civil service work for knuckle dragging lunks.

"I like patrol, sir. Is there something wrong with that?"

"Not if answering calls is the best you can do."

"I'm sorry. Don't we always hear how patrol is the backbone of the Department?"

"Sure, but then most guys don't have the ability to get beyond basics."

"So they're not good enough."

"Let me put it this way, the cream always rises to the top. You've heard that before, haven't you, John?"

Oh yeah, that and a number of other catch phrases. Silly little clichés guys like him always felt compelled to throw out in some vague attempt to make a point when they didn't know enough to really explain themselves. I'd heard the saying; I just wasn't aware I was dealing with a philosopher. "Yes, seems to me I might have heard that once or twice."

"You see, John, nobody just gave me this job, I earned my position."

I'd like to say I paid a great deal of attention but I'd heard the story before. He got his degree through one of those universities you don't really have to attend but once a month, and you can buy credits for things like "life experience." Then he was on to the part about how he was so wonderful he only needed two years before he was off the streets and in an administrative position that demanded the brilliance only he could provide. Two years on the street wasn't enough to even figure out how little he really knew. What twisted me even more was that in ten years he'd be making policy decisions that would affect the rest of us, and they'd be based on those two meager years of experience.

"As soon as I was eligible, I took the sergeant's test and scored in the top category. I earned this job, no one gave me anything. My hard work got me here."

Sure did, is what pounded in my head. More likely what got him attention was old fashioned ass-kissing. I simply nodded. "I understand, sir. I believe I might have been misinformed." That really set him off.

"Look, the reason guys like you don't have anything to look forward to is because you're a malcontent, worse yet, incompetent. I don't think you have to be that way, but you've got to start learning."

I couldn't help myself. "And you can teach me?"

"The Chief promoted me because we share a vision, told me himself. You're a dinosaur and unless you can beat the comet, you're going to be extinct. The future is changing whether you like it or not. If you're not with us, you're against us. It's as simple as that. All you need to do is pick your side."

"I understand." I nodded. Clearly this conversation was something best let go. That's what I understood. He was indeed a philosopher. That fact was apparent by his unending string of commonplace catch phrases. He was spitting out all the things people told him he needed to say to be an effective leader. He'd obviously spent far too much time listening to talk of leadership and too little time practicing the concept.

"Is there anything else?" I wanted to call him Socrates, but I figured he'd launch out of his chair. I was certain I could take him, but I wasn't sure I wanted to explain how the sergeant ended up on the floor under my boot.

"I put you with Steven as a chance to show me what I think you're capable of." Now he was trying to placate me. I was certain I wasn't following his method. "This is your opportunity to shine. You can rise to the challenge or you can throw the opportunity away. I'll be watching. Be the cream, John, and rise up."

I leaned back in my chair and brought my hand up so I had something to rest my chin on. He was making my head hurt. I was tired of him, but there would be no getting out of here until he was ready to release me. I could always get up and walk away, but we weren't to the point where I was willing to take that battle on.

"And one more thing, John."

I really wished he'd quit calling me that.

"It seems there was a little question regarding your actions the other day."

He had my attention again. I let the question show on my face. Not talking seemed the smarter course.

Someone mentioned you might have been a bit excessive in your attempt to capture that subject Officer Murphy was fighting with."

I didn't have a clue what he meant. "'Fraid you lost me?"

"Well, it seems you might have kicked the prisoner in the groin. You are aware that is against policy, aren't you?"

Smith . . . that wormy bastard. No wonder he slithered in to line-up just before the sergeants. He'd been busy throwing me down to Socrates. Now I understood why the little snake couldn't look at me. If either of them had a clue, they'd realize a good old nut crunch wasn't against policy, it was simply outside the written policy. There's a dramatic difference. Any cop who'd been around the block, or down to IA, a couple times could tell you that. Policy gives guidelines, and reality doesn't always follow those to a letter. Sometimes the right thing to do is improvise. Of course, that means you have to be out there and end up in a situation like that a time or two.

"Actually, what I did wasn't really a kick," I said with a shake of the head. "It was my knee and I planted in firmly in the guy's ball sack. I suspect he's still waiting for his nuts to drop. He wasn't a prisoner yet, and I still didn't have control of him."

"Well, remember, we can't just do business the way we want to. The rules are there to be followed."

"They were. You need the rundown, read my report. My actions were no secret."

Sergeant Roosevelt paused, clearly unsure which direction to go next. He'd been hoping I'd be afraid I'd done something wrong, that I needed him to protect me. My actions were outside the norm. They were also entirely appropriate considering the circumstances.

"Well, hopefully this doesn't become an issue, but if the suspect complains, we'll have to address this again."

"I look forward to the possibility. Is there anything else?"

"No, I think you've got enough thinking to do."

Not today I didn't. I just wanted to get away from him, get away from the station. No good ever came from loitering around a place where the Sergeant Roosevelts of the world lingered. I got up and started out of the cubicle, then a notion popped into my head. As much as I tried I found myself entirely unable to resist. If Roosevelt was going to consider himself a thinking man, a philosopher, perhaps he needed a simple humanities question to consider.

I stopped. "Sir?"

"Yes." He was irritated. He'd dismissed me and there I was tossing out the last word.

"There's a paper clip on your desk."

"What about it?"

"Is the value of that paper clip intrinsic or extrinsic?"

His brow furrowed. "Huh?"

"Never mind." So much for Socrates the thinking man. Buy-a-degree University must have given him a philosophy syllabus that allowed him to confuse Plato with Play-Doh. Theodore Roosevelt was not quite the thinking man I'd imagined. Apparently he'd given little thought to whether things had value that was inherent or whether they had value because we gave it to them.

I left his office and stormed through the station. A couple cops were still lingering. They stayed clear. There was no mistaking my mood or my disinterest in idle conversation.

Sergeant Roosevelt had given me exactly the kind of meeting I'd expected. With any luck Stevie would already have a car and we could leave just as soon as I loaded my gear. As I passed the door of the Lieutenant's office, I heard her soft voice call out to me.

I stopped dead. Lieutenant Ariana Lindstrom had been one of my training officers. With a name like Ariana, I figured she was better suited to being a princess than a police lieutenant. However, to know her left you feeling like she should be anything but.

Ariana was tough. She'd been promoted quickly although not nearly as fast as Socrates. She, on the other hand, had my undying respect. As a sergeant, I'd seen her stand her ground against crooks and angry citizens alike. She knew how to treat people, and she knew police work. As a lieutenant, she was fair and trusted her people to make grown up decisions.

Ariana was tall, thin, and strikingly beautiful with sharp features. Time had added some character but she was no less attractive now than she'd been years ago. Golden hair fell to the middle of her shoulders but you'd never know that to see her at work. When she was at the office, that long hair was pulled up, pinned down, and ready to head into the field on a moment's notice. She was a clear professional.

Ariana's chair was pushed back from the desk, her legs were crossed, and her hands were folded in her lap. "What's the matter," she asked.

I stepped into the office and closed the door. The action a bit presumptuous for an officer entering a lieutenant's office, but this wasn't just any lieutenant.

"I don't suppose you're inclined to rotate sergeants, are you?"

"Not particularly."

She looked at the two empty chairs across the desk. I realized I was looming over her and sat. I ran my fingers through my hair.

"Is there a reason I should move people?"

"I'm thinking things are going to go less than swimmingly between me and the new sergeant."

"What makes you think that?"

"Mostly that we just had it out in his office."

Ariana grinned. "Should I be sending an ambulance?"

"No Ma'am, I left him alive. Just don't want to work for him."

She leaned back in the chair and studied me for a moment. I could deal with a lot of different hostile situations, but for some reason her gaze always unnerved me. I'd thought about that a great deal over the years, and I never could figure out what it was that put me off center. I certainly wasn't thrown by the rank. I'd known her long before she ever had stripes or bars.

"So you don't like your new sergeant. Do you want me to talk to him?"

"Hell no, I'm not asking you to fight my battles."

"What battle? He's the sergeant, you're the officer. End of story." She shrugged.

"He's a pinhead."

She nodded. "That very well may be, but he's Sergeant Pinhead. John, it's not your choice who you listen to and who you ignore. If you don't like him, then find a way to deal with your situation."

"Did I mention that he's a pinhead?"

"You don't have to respect the man, but you damn well better respect the position."

I squirmed at the thought. This wasn't the response I'd been looking for. "Well he shouldn't be there."

"Be that as it may, he is."

"He shouldn't be."

"Then put in for sergeant the next time the test rolls around. You take the test, and I'll use whatever little bit of influence I have downtown to try and get you promoted."

"Hell no."

"Then I don't know what you'd have me do. You tell me there's a problem but you don't want to give me any sort of reasonable solution to help you deal with it. I'm not sure where to go from here. He's still a sergeant, and the Chief decided that's the way things should be. You might not like it. Hell, I might not like it, but that's reality. This organization can't just run from the streets. We need people with different skills. Since you choose to work in the field, that leaves others free to do as they wish. If they're not the best choice for our organization, there's nothing we can do but adapt."

"Yeah, well that's the kind of crap that makes this job tough. It's not the crooks that cause cops stress. It's the bureaucratic pinheads that can't tell the difference between doing what's right and doing what some book tells them to do. Add their little power trips into the mix, and you have a real fine mess."

She let me rant, and then sat patiently for a moment before speaking again. "You lead out there John. You do it every day, probably more naturally than the rest of us will ever hope to learn. The officers listen to you, they respect you. If you're not willing to put in for a position of leadership, then your job is to figure out a way to help those who have so they might figure out what to do when their time comes to lead. I know that's not what you want to hear, but that's the way it is. If you don't like it, fix it or suck it up."

I'd like to say my conversation with Ariana helped, but I left the office feeling no better than when I entered. How could she not understand? Did "pinhead" not paint the picture clearly enough? I'd known sergeants who needed a bit of help getting up to speed. Roosevelt wasn't one of them. Why was fixing him my responsibility?

I grabbed my gear bag and headed toward the parking lot. I ran into Marcus as I stepped out the back door. One look and he knew my day wasn't getting any better. I stopped and stared into the lot. The conversation with Roosevelt continued to hammer on my nerves.

"What's up?" Marcus asked, clearly unsure where he might want to start.

"Just pondering overpopulation."

"Yeah." His brow furrowed wondering about the implications of what I might say next. "Just thinking about that myself. What'd you come up with?"

"The problem is real enough."

"You got a solution?"

"Not yet. Fucking myopic sycophant has his head buried so deep in statistics and mission statements he's been rendered totally incapable of catching a real clue."

"Whatever you say, professor."

"He can kiss my ass."

"Is that all?"

I'd been scanning the parking lot for Stevie while I vented on Marcus. Taking my anger out on him was a shitty thing to do, but he wouldn't take it personally. As we spoke, I caught sight of Eric Smith driving across the lot. He gave a furtive glance my direction and then turned away as he drove past us. He was heading for the car wash.

"No, that's not all, not even the start of it." I dropped my gear bag.

My plan formed the moment I started to walk. Smith and I were about to have a discussion on respect. I angled my direction of travel so he would go around one side of the building while I went around the other. I didn't want him to see me coming.

I could hear Marcus behind me. "Don't do it, Hatch." He was the good angel on my shoulder, trying to keep me from doing something stupid. But my mind was set. The devil was going to win this round. Smith was pulling into the car wash as I came around the corner. He was looking forward, trying to steer his car into the guide rails. He had no idea I was coming.

The front of Smith's car locked in place. I pulled out my key and unlocked his trunk. That's the nice thing about using common cars; we each have a set of keys. His fate was set. There was little he could do to stop me now. He didn't have to like the way I did business. If he thought I was too forceful he should have said so. If I was a brutal, abusive cop, he could still go to the boss. That didn't mean he couldn't talk to me first, especially since he hadn't been there to see everything. If he couldn't stand up like a man, then I'd give him something to complain about.

I pulled out my baton and extended it as the trunk popped open. A slight rap against the right spot on the inside of the trunk and the fuel cut-off switch would activate just the same as if he'd been rear-ended by another car. I struck.

Smith's horrified face stared through the back window when I slammed the trunk shut. I stood straight, crossed my arms, and glared back.

Someone accustomed to stressful situations might have reacted more quickly. Smith was more creative at finding ways to avoid tough decisions than he was at finding resolutions. If he could waste enough time studying something, he might not actually have to act. But not this time. He wasted his reaction time staring wide-eyed at me rather than doing what he needed to.

Breaking eye contact, Smith looked forward. He jammed his foot on the accelerator, pumping furiously in an attempt to coax a little extra gas before the lines went dry. He was too late.

The car nudged forward, then sputtered and died as the engine used the last bit of fuel. The car wash sprayers were on. Water pounded against the front driver and passenger doors. The prisoner cage eliminated his ability to get into the back seat and climb out. He was stuck. The only way to start the car was to reset the cut-off switch. To do that he'd need to get in the trunk. To get into the trunk he'd need help or he'd need to open the door and get showered by the sprayers. I walked away.

As I headed back to the parking lot I noticed several cops standing around watching. Martinez and Jenkins were laughing so hard they had to hold onto each other to stay upright.

I looked at the bystanders and spoke loud and clearly enough so they would hear me over the sound of water spraying in the background. "Don't let me catch one of you fixing that switch for him."

CHAPTER 13

STEVIE WAS WAITING by the trunk of our car. I couldn't tell if it was fear on his face or if he was simply feeling like his day was gonna suck because he got stuck working with me. Either way, he didn't say a word as I tossed my gear bag in the trunk and slammed the lid shut.

I started the car as Stevie scrambled into the passenger's seat. He was probably hoping I'd let him drive. Not a chance. This job is about control. The longer you do it, the more you learn to control your environment. Or at least the more you succumb to the illusion that anyone can control anything.

I would let Marcus drive for half the week because I trusted him, trusted his ability to command our mutual environment. I could ride in a car with him and not have to worry about my safety, about whether he was going to overreact and plant us headlong into the grill of another car during a chase. I didn't trust Stevie like that. I was the senior officer. I was driving. End of story.

The goal was to head to 7-11, grab my coffee and his Snapple, then call Homicide before we needed to clear and start handling radio calls. Stevie changed that plan.

"Ah, Hatch," he stammered, "I need to go to Op-Support to get my taser fixed."

I shot him a sideways glance and was about to fire off a hot question about why he needed to fix a device he probably hadn't been around long enough to even use. Then I realized his problem was to my benefit. If he needed to go downtown, that would give me an opportunity to talk to Homicide in person. I modified my plan. I could get coffee in the Watch Commander's Office and then speak to Ronny.

We left the station and headed south on Fairmont to Home Avenue. From there it was just a couple blocks to the 94 freeway and then a straight shot into downtown. It took less than ten minutes.

As we arrived, Eric Smith's voice came over the radio. He spoke slowly, tentatively. "833-Yellow, is there a unit still at the station that can make it to the car wash?"

There was no response. At least some folks still listened to me.

After a moment the dispatcher responded. "Sorry 833-Yellow, no one's answering up."

This time his voice was deflated, defeat apparent. "Ten-four, could you have someone in the phone room call the garage and see if one of the mechanics can come over and give me a hand with something?"

The radio was silent as the dispatcher contemplated why he was so lazy he couldn't simply walk around the side of the building and ask them himself. After the silence conveyed her displeasure, she told him they would make the call.

The Headquarters front parking lot was full. The plate glass windows shimmered in the afternoon sun. With the exception of some new construction on the north side of the street, 1401 Broadway seemed entirely out of place. One modern building in the midst of older, rundown buildings, their sidewalks littered with the cardboard mats and the shopping carts of the transients who claimed a piece of concrete as their home.

At least it was daytime. The front counter officers would be able to deal with the drunk and mentally unstable people that wandered the neighborhood like spirits in search of a peaceful eternity. These folks were always in need of something, and they would hijack your whole day if they got the opportunity to attract your attention.

We drove down the aisle of parked cars and turned into the alcove that led to the underground parking. My attention quickly turned to the two people standing to the right of the entrance gate. I sighed silently with relief when I realized they were dispatchers, not transients.

I didn't recognize the younger blonde. She stood next to the two foot tall concrete ashtray with a cigarette in one hand and a diet Pepsi in the other. I did recognize the woman standing next to her.

Liz Campbell was a short, feisty brunette who had been a dispatcher since the late seventies. When she was relaxed, her radio voice resonated with a deep, smoky, richness I always found better suited to some sultry movie star from a 1940s mystery. Every time I heard her speak I half expected to see Bogart step from the shadows. But if you managed to piss her off, she could lay into you with the fury of a fourth grade schoolteacher. She could also make a grown man feel every bit the ten-year-old by the time she was done with him.

Mostly she used her sexy voice, but every now and again, when she needed to put someone in check, she would use the other. Liz had been around far too long to get worked up over anything major. She was as cool under fire as anyone I'd ever met. It was the stupid stuff cops said over the radio that earned her disapproval. She had no patience for idiots.

I stopped in front of the gate, and when Liz saw me she ambled around to my side of the car. I lowered the window. "We missed you last weekend."

Liz looked irritated. "Don't get me started. We had no staffing and I got stuck with mandatory overtime. I'd have called in sick, but you can't really go to a retirement party after that. Someone's bound to catch you. How was it? Jack do okay?"

"Did fine. Don't think he wanted to be there at all. We hid and drank beer."

"Sad to see him go. Seem to be losing a lot of good ones lately." She paused to scan the back seat of my car. "No prisoner? Not like you to show up during the day without a reason."

I nodded toward Stevie. "We need to get his taser fixed before you start badgering us to clear calls."

"Hell, you never have a problem clearing calls. It's the other stuff you get into that's the problem."

"I don't get into anything. Bad things just seek me out."

"Sure they do."

"It's true." I shrugged. "I'm a path of least resistance guy, a malcontent and an incompetent. Truly. Just ask my boss." I was sure my tone was laden with sarcasm, probably still held the edge of anger over my recent meeting.

"Who you working for these days?"

"Socrates."

Liz's clear lack of understanding showed on her face.

"Sorry, Theodore Roosevelt, I simply confuse him with a thinking man."

She laughed out loud. "That's not 834-Sam, is it?"

"Yup."

She fired right back. "Tell that twit to listen to his radio. He never answers when we call for him." Liz paused to think for a moment. "Disregard, he's no better when he's paying attention. Always has some kind of stupid thing to say and always wants to direct folks from his office when he really has no clue what the hell's going on to begin with. I'm sorry, how'd you end up with him?"

"Luck of the draw. It will pass. I'm sure he views his patrol assignment as mandatory duty he needs to fill until he can get himself dug into a really important office job. In the meantime he'll be a pain in my ass." My attention was drawn to the rearview mirror as another car pulled in behind me. "Look, I'll talk to you later. You can update me on all the good dirt and I'll update you on the joys of working for wonder boy."

As I started to pull forward, Liz said, "Hurry up, I'll have calls ready for you when you clear. If the twit gives you any grief you just let me know. I'll have him chasing his tail so fast he'll forget you even exist."

We pulled into the basement sally port designed for prisoner processing. The cavernous room was painted slate gray, the concrete floors were grey, and the steel beams in the ceiling were gray. Building support posts once painted bright yellow to warn you of their presence were scattered about to keep the building upright. They had grown dull and grimy and nearly as gray as the walls over time. Parking was tricky in stalls more appropriately designed for Yugos than full size Crown Victorias. The Watch Commander's office was the gateway to the main part of the building.

"I'll be in Homicide," I said to Stevie. "Meet me there when you're done."

The sally port was empty. Day watch officers had already booked their prisoners, and second watch hadn't had a chance to generate any yet. I was glad. A guy could get distracted when the area was full of police cars and people trying to get their booking slips written. This room was central to the city, and being there was usually the only time you ever got to see the folks you knew who worked in other divisions.

I looked through the small window in the steel door in front of me as I approached the Watch Commander's office. When I could see no one standing on the other side, I hit the kick plate at the base of the door with my boot. The door popped open and I stepped through before it closed.

Sergeant Scott Saunders was the day shift Watch Commander. Thirty-four years on the Department, he was less than a year from retirement. His hair was gray, like the walls outside his door, his face cracked and weathered from too many years of bad hours, bad food, and bad scenes. He looked a great deal older than a man in his late fifties.

Sergeant Saunders leaned back in his chair and pondered my arrival. Then the corner of his mouth twisted upward in a grin that had taken many years to perfect. The lines in his face deepened. He was an experienced sergeant better suited to street work but this being a young man's game, he was out of the run. The years had been hard on him. The chronic pain in his body was too much to do anything other than sit around and approve bookings. He'd stayed too long and given too much. I hoped I'd fare better in the years before my retirement.

I walked past and headed to the coffee machine at the end of the long counter. Fifty cents for burned coffee from a machine rinsed out in the same sink the prisoners used to wash their hands after they provided a urine sample. I'd convinced myself years ago that the pot got hot enough to kill whatever might grow in that sink. If it didn't, I figured it was just one way of building my resistance. Either way, it was coffee.

"Hatch, whatever you have, write slow so the night crew has to approve it."

I looked at the clock on the wall. "Why Sarge, you still have a couple hours. What if I brought something special for you?"

"It's your special things I don't like in particular."

I thought about telling him I didn't have anything, but if it weren't for some banter now and again, how could I keep his interest? The monotony of his job had to be a killer. Besides, a little uncertainty over his day seemed an even trade for the coffee.

"I'll see what I can do."

I continued down the hall to the elevators. It was midafternoon, far too early to come downtown. Trips to the heart of Headquarters always produced a risk that I'd run into some political office jockey who liked working here for the "face time" it gave them with the Chiefs. It would be a long ride on the elevator if I had to listen to someone ramble on about how difficult their meeting schedule was.

I got lucky. The only person on the elevator was some poor fool I didn't recognize. He stood in the corner with a glum look on his face and a stack of yellow folders in his arms. He gave me the required eye contact one makes when you get on an elevator, and then quickly descended back into his own little, inner world.

I got off the elevator and headed to Homicide.

The secretary looked at me like I'd breached some special temple where I wasn't wanted. "Ronny White around?" I asked. She contemplated whether she should call him or walk back to get him. A moment later she walked off.

A couple minutes passed before Ronny came around the corner. He was all smiles. "Hey buddy, what brings you down here?" he asked as he shook my hand. "Don't see you for months, then three times in a week."

"Thought maybe we could talk about your case."

Ronny stepped back and waved for me to follow. "Sure, come on back.

As we walked down the hall, he continued. "What's on your mind?"

"Just had some time to kill, thought I'd follow up a little. You guys get anything since last week?"

"Naw," Ronny said. "Told you at the party, I'm betting on the husband. He stuck to his story during the interview, but when we started to push, he decided he didn't want to talk any more. Angry guy, though, called her all kinds of names."

At the cubicle, Ronny cleared a stack of folders from the chair next to his desk and I sat down. He rifled through some more papers until he found the pile he wanted and handed them to me. "I ran his history. This guy's a real asshole. Cops have been out to his house several times on domestic bullshit. He's been arrested twice for battery on her. He's also been arrested for some bar fight where he and another guy got into it and made citizen's arrests on each other. The other guy got a ticket and our guy went to jail cause he was drunk. Probably the bigger of the two assholes that night."

I looked over the papers Ronny had handed me. Aaron Anderson's background looked like that of a lot of construction guys. I scanned through the different cases and their dispositions. Cops took reports about him a bunch of times, arrested him for about half of them. It didn't look like he ever did any real jail time other than a couple days here or there in County. Most of the cases against him were dropped. There was at least one instance, a methamphetamine arrest, where he pled guilty in exchange for probation and counseling. Then there was the assault with a deadly weapon.

"What was this one?"

"Something from a construction job. Looks like he got into it with another contractor over who should be doing what. Turned into a brawl and he ended up whacking the other guy in the back with an iron pipe. The DA didn't want to issue because the other guy was a prick too and started it by throwing hot soup from the chow wagon at him. Probably didn't help that it happened at a construction site, and out of all the people there no one saw anything."

I tossed the papers back on the stack on his desk.

"Dunno why you're wasting time, Hatch. I haven't been up here as long as some of these guys, but you and I've been around long enough to know the story. These two loved to fight. He liked to drink, did a little tweak on the side. God knows what they got into it over but she said something that pissed him off and he killed her for it. That's the general consensus with the whole team."

I leaned back in my chair and brought my hands up behind my head. My thoughts were heavy. Part of me understood everything he said, and that part of me agreed with him. So why did this one bother me?

Maralyn's voice dinned in the background, "I'd need more."

Was that it? Was it what she'd said at lunch yesterday? I knew I didn't want to put out a bunch of effort on some case that would solve itself in time, didn't want to go running off chasing things that weren't there. Sometimes that happens. You get a notion and spend all your free time searching for some shadow of a suspect. In the end it turns out you were just wearing rubber off on the pavement. I didn't like that feeling, that sense that you could have been doing something worthwhile but were too pigheaded to look at the facts.

"So what's next, Ronny?"

He waved his hand across his desk. "Shit, you see this stack of paper. We're as understaffed as the rest of the Department. We impounded a bunch of tools from his truck, anything that could have been used to pry that back door. The lab will take a look. I suspect they'll find one of those screwdrivers in his toolbox matches right up. That'll take a week or two, maybe longer depending on lab priorities. We'll re-interview him and go from there. Unless someone else's fingerprints show up in the house, the case will probably start to build against him. Until then, I'll work on other stuff."

I was about to get up, certain I was making more of this than I needed to. My ass felt like concrete when I tried to move. There was surely something I was missing. I wanted to be convinced. I wanted to believe Esther's husband killed her, then I could let go. What was bothering me was why I wasn't convinced, and why I couldn't explain why I wasn't. My mind fought to remember the images from that night, to dissect the scene and look for something I missed. Each time I thought I was on the verge of recalling something new, Stevie's voice, quoting Aaron's angry outburst, rang in my ears, "Good, the cunt deserved it."

"Do you have any photos I can look at?"

"C'mon, John," Ronny said. "I have a stack of cases, each important. Let's let the evidence clear the husband before we start looking for ghosts. I'll grant you could be right, that we need to look for someone else, but let's focus on what's in front of us first."

He paused. From his expression he clearly couldn't understand what was bothering me. I couldn't understand either. I was hoping this wasn't just the need to prove to some woman that I could do whatever I wanted in this job, to prove that I was as worthwhile as anyone who might be a detective or a sergeant. I'd been known to let my pride get in the way before.

"Sorry, Ronny, just want to look at the scene again."

He smiled. "We get paid by the hour." Ronny reached over to a stack of computer disks and filed through them until he found what he wanted. He tossed the CD into his computer and then spent a minute moving the mouse around on his desk. Every now and again he'd click on the button and something would happen. When he was done, he stood up.

"Take my seat. I gotta run down the hall for a minute. Just click on the arrows and it will cycle through the photos."

I moved into Ronny's chair once he left. Times had sure changed in the last decade. It used to be 5x7 glossies or Polaroids we used when we needed to refresh our memory. Now Esther's homicide was in full color on the monitor in front of me. I wasn't sure if I liked it, less sure that I wanted to go back to being without.

I scanned the photos not knowing what I was looking for. They started with a shot of the street sign and then an overview of the front of the house. The address was clearly displayed. From there, the photographer worked his way around the outside of the house taking shots that were closer than the first. None of the doors or windows had been tampered with. The dust, dirt, and lack of general housekeeping was layered and covered with cobwebs. The only exception was the back door. The back door had places where the dirt and grime had been wiped clear. I looked for an indication of fingerprints.

There were none.

I moved to the pry marks. They were about a quarter inch across, just about the width of a screwdriver. It made sense that a hotheaded construction worker would have access to all the screwdrivers and pry tools a person could want, but I'd seen enough people on the streets that carried them as well. The gangsters carried them for protection when they didn't want to get caught with a knife. The car prowlers carried them to break into vehicles. The tweakers carried them to disassemble their vehicles, and the hypes carried them to break into the coin holders of pay washing machines. They also used them to break into houses. Hell, everyone carried screwdrivers. They were almost standard issue in the hood.

I continued searching through the photos. Every click of the mouse brought a new image. They moved inside the house. I'd been there. This part was clear in my head. I could remember the stench of stale beer cans, cigarettes, and stacked plates and boxes of take out dinner. I looked at the DVD player on the kitchen table and at the photos of the wires where it was removed from the TV. Nothing struck me. This part of the scene looked like any other burglary where the guy got scared off. It was easily something that Aaron could have set up.

Realization jabbed me as sure a finger poke to the forehead. Maybe that's why I couldn't just accept Aaron. He was the easy choice. Had I grown that complacent over the years? Had I become so accustomed to the answer being easy that I ruled out alternatives? Or was I fixating on easy, questioning my own instinct and judgment because Maralyn had called me on my assumptions?

I clicked back to the photo of the pry marks on the door and then panned the DVD player on the table and the wires protruding from the TV. What was there that I wasn't seeing?

A new thought formed and I wondered how I'd missed it before. I'd seen the TV and the DVD player as soon we opened the door to go in and check on Esther. An image flashed of my gun breaking clear of the holster. I had never once been in that house and yet the instant I walked through the front door, I keyed in on something different, something dangerous. Had Esther been so clueless when she came home that she didn't see these things? Clueless would explain how she made it into the bedroom before she was attacked. Many people move through their lives with little to no situational awareness. Esther wouldn't be the first to walk through her house totally unaware of a threat.

My thoughts snapped back to the easy answer. Maybe Esther hadn't seen that she walked in on a burglary because she hadn't. Maybe the reason she made it all the way through the house and into the back bedroom is because she didn't know the threat would come from the man she shared her home with.

I went back to the photos of the family room and kitchen again, this time paying attention to the carpet, the walls, the tables and anything else that might be out of place or bear the mark of a struggle. I needed to eliminate the thought that maybe she was accosted as she entered the house and then dragged to the bedroom.

I found nothing new as I followed the photos down the hall, past the spare bedroom and the nasty bathroom, then into the master bedroom. The pictures rendered a cold, impersonal perspective. To another cop these would have simply been another series of crime scene photos. Not to me. I'd felt the humidity in the air that was caused by people sweating during their frantic life and death struggle. I had smelled Esther's perfume mixed with that same sweat, and I had breathed the same air that had been her last. The photos were no longer something impersonal. I was back in that room.

The computer screen faded from view as I found myself pulled into the screen, back into the room as though I'd never left. This time I was alone. There was no nervous Stevie standing over my shoulder—it was simply me and Esther and whatever missing fact I couldn't seem to figure out.

The mattress was still turned over. In this world, this place, nothing would ever change. The husband might have already cleaned things up, but in my world, in my mind, this was how the image would remain.

I looked at the marks on the wall. How much force did someone have to use to leave marks like that? I'd slammed some guys pretty hard, but never once did I make their clothing abrade off on a wall. That wasn't an action of fear, not that of a scared person . . . that was rage. What caused that kind of anger?

The dresser was nearly clear of everything. Only one small, wooden jewelry box remained. It was askew and the little drawers that pulled out from the front were open, fanned out like they had been knocked that way. I stared at the photo for a long moment. The crime itself played out in my head. I wondered who had knocked everything around. Had the suspect tossed things before Esther returned? Or had he been swinging Esther's flailing body across the room? Something in the back of my brain struggled to explain itself as I attempted to recreate her last moments. It was never that complicated. I just needed one little clue and the answers would become as apparent as the intent of drunken teenagers on prom night.

I clicked to the next photo, and there was Esther. I hadn't really taken a long look at her before. When I found her in the room, she was a crime scene. She had been a body, a person for sure, but not like this. The first time around, I'd looked only for specific things, signs of life, evidence I didn't want to disturb. I recognized she was human, but I was looking for something else. This time I was looking at the person. She seemed so small as she laid there with the plastic bag over her head and that rope around her neck.

"You see anything there you didn't see before, Sherlock?"

I swiveled in my chair—Ronny's chair. He was leaning against the corner of his cubicle.

"Nothing I didn't see yesterday." I lied. I wasn't going to break down and start telling him what it felt like to see the photos. I certainly wasn't about to bring up any half baked theories until I'd had some time to think them through, make a reasonable pitch. "I just can't help but feel like I'm missing something."

"Yeah, I kind of have that same feeling," Ronny said as he looked at his watch.

"I'm sorry." I stood up and moved toward the door. He stepped aside. "Look, you mind if I knock on some doors and talk to people? I figure you guys already did that, but maybe I'll get lucky, find someone that wasn't there when you checked." I knew I didn't need to ask, nothing was stopping me from talking to anyone, but this was Ronny and the case belonged to his team. Special units like this sometimes get worked up when you start poking around their empire. There was a time and place for pissing on another dog's fire hydrant, but I didn't think this was one of them. I figured I owed him the respect of asking.

Ronny thought for a moment, then rubbed his eyes. "Yeah, go ahead. Do me a favor though, make sure you write an A-9 on anything you do so we can account for where you've been. My sergeant will have my ass if you get out there and stir some shit we can't document down the road. You find anything, you call me right away."

"You know I wouldn't leave you hanging."

I was certain he meant his smirk to be a grin, it just didn't come across that way.

CHAPTER 14

STEVIE WAS AMBLING down the hall toward Homicide as I left. He stopped and then turned around when I passed him. We'd spent enough time out-of-service. I was ready to get in the field. The anger from my confrontation with Sergeant Socrates had dissipated to some degree, replaced by my thoughts about Esther's death and the questions racing through my head. I hoped the answers would come, that my efforts wouldn't simply be another instance of wasted time. More than that, I hoped I wasn't struggling to prove something to someone I might never see again.

The brief trip down the elevator was uneventful. As we walked out of the Watch Commander's office, I thanked him for the crummy coffee and told him I'd have his booking forms ready in a moment. We got in our car and left.

Stevie remained as silent on the trip back as he did on the way downtown. He didn't want to be in the car with me any more than I wanted to be there with him. Jack's voice echoed in the back of my head, something about mentoring, and something about setting the example. I was nearly certain I heard him say something about obligation, but that part wasn't clear as I forced myself to focus on Esther. Too many complications. I wanted things to be simple again.

Traffic was still light as we made our way back to East San Diego. I checked the computer to see what other units were up to, to see if anyone got jammed with a report on my beat while we were away. The least I could do was offer to take the call over if they had. All units were tied up, some on traffic stops. Others were going to calls, none of them on my beat. We made 54th and El Cajon Boulevard when time ran out and the day got real.

Liz's voice was steady, smooth. "I need a unit to clear for a non-breather on Beat 813. Elderly male, medics en route."

Bad days never get better. That wasn't our beat, but we were the closest. I grabbed the microphone. Being just a few blocks away meant we were likely to get there before the medics. I gunned the engine and didn't turn as I spoke to Stevie. Being a mentor was out, now it was time for more rules of seniority. First of all, I drive. Second . . . "You got your CPR mask handy?"

"Yeah," he replied unsteadily. The kid had probably never tried to revive a person, and if that wasn't freaking him out, the rule of CPR most certainly was.

"You know the rule, don't you?"

"I thought that was a joke."

"No joke, junior guy takes breathing, senior guy gets compressions. Better hope medics get there before we do."

The light changed to yellow. I stomped on the accelerator as I turned on the overhead lights and siren. Perhaps my day wasn't as bad as I thought. If I'd been partners with Marcus, he might have been able to force the issue, and I'd have had even odds at sucking face with a dead guy.

In less than a minute we were pulling up to the front of the residence. There was no need to look for numbers on houses. Our destination was clearly marked by two frantic arm-waving ladies standing on the sidewalk with yapping lap dogs.

I drove across to the wrong side of the street and parked just past the driveway to leave enough room for the ambulance. With any luck the guy had just passed out. The odds on that dwindled when I saw his ninety year old wife standing next to a crumpled figure in the garage.

Stevie popped the trunk to dig for his mask while I went over to check the man. He was on his knees, one finger wrapped in the handle of the screen door to the house. He slumped forward, his face pushed into the mesh and metal door grate. He'd been trying to get in when he dropped. I bet his heart was good and non-functional, stopped in an instant.

My ears strained for the sound of sirens. Old man, baby, teenager, it didn't matter. No cop ever liked doing CPR. The process was nasty when their stomachs filled with air, expanded, and then they barfed. At least we had the mask for that. In the old days you'd get a mouth full of grandpa's hamburger helper. Frantic family members never took it as an encouraging sign when you started vomiting next to their loved one.

I glanced at the wife as I dropped to a knee. I wished I hadn't looked at her but in a moment, all the years of hard things I'd seen, all that had toughened me to the plight of others, washed away. The poor fool was no longer just another anonymous old guy who'd dropped, he was someone who meant something to someone, and she was struggling with the realization that he might be gone.

"How long has he been down?"

A faint voice, worn gravelly, and withered with time told me five minutes.

It was probably closer to ten considering the time it took to call but I'd work with five. Either way, his chances were slim. I checked for signs of breathing, a heartbeat, any indication of a serious injury from the fall. There was nothing to indicate he'd done anything but drop straight to his knees and fall forward. Still there were no sirens.

I cradled his head and pulled his finger free from the door handle, then laid him gently on his back. It wasn't hard. He couldn't have weighed more than a hundred and twenty pounds. His skin was dry and parchment thin, still warm as I moved his arms to either side. That's when I heard the sirens. Help was on the way.

Stevie ran up with his mask. His fingers fumbled with the plastic carrying case while I began to reposition the man's head. It had come to that. Medics might be right down the street but they were still a minute away. A minute would be a lifetime if I had to spend it doing nothing while this poor old guy's wife stared at me.

I leaned forward. We needed to start.

"Give me that mask," I said as I grabbed the case out of fingers that quickly relinquished the device. I placed it over the old man's mouth. He was so frail, so gaunt in the face, that the pliable, v-shaped rubber didn't want to fit right. Whatever he had been in his day, he was a shell of that now. I leaned forward and blew twice. His chest rose and fell each time.

I started CPR myself then started talking Stevie through the compressions. He was nervous at first, probably wanted to stop when he felt the first frail rib pop. I'd been there, felt the turmoil inside as I wondered whether I was helping the man or hurting him. After a couple rounds of compressions, Stevie found his rhythm.

We stopped CPR when the medics were ready to take over. I stepped back and watched. I knew he was gone. The chance of our being able to revive him had been slim, and I thought about just calling the death right on the spot. I'd have probably done just that, but the widow would have never understood. Even if I did revive him, a guy this age would surely never regain consciousness. If he did, he'd likely be gone again by the end of the day. That's just the way things worked. Wanting them to be different was a waste of time. What I didn't want was the widow to think we didn't care enough to try. Whether he was dead or not, she needed to feel like we did everything we could.

I turned to her. The expression on her face cut my soul. There had been deep love between them, her and the dead guy. Tears welled, adding a depth to the pain, the sense of loss reflected in her eyes. No one would ever grieve like that for me. I reached up and rested my hand on her shoulder. I was sure she never felt my touch, because she didn't even remotely react. At least it let me feel like I was doing something.

I would have taken her inside, but the medics needed her there to answer questions about his medications and medical conditions. For the time being, there was nothing to do but ride out the next few minutes.

Medics continued to work. Having been through this a time or two, I could tell he wasn't responding to their efforts. I guessed they'd call a time of death any minute. What they did now was simply their last ditch effort. Perhaps they knew they weren't doing anything, but were simply giving their best show before they stopped.

The medics quit and leaned back so their backsides rested on their heels. One of them stood and softly whispered the time to one of the firemen holding a clip board. The Fire Chief walked over and told the woman he was sorry.

I spoke loud enough that I knew my voice would be heard. I tried to maintain a soft tone. "Ma'am, can you tell me your name?"

"Amelia," she said weakly. "And he is Jonathan."

I turned to Stevie and spoke softly. "Can you take Amelia inside?"

He responded instantly. "Yeah," he said as he took her by the arm. At first she didn't move, simply stared at her husband's lifeless form.

"Please, Amelia," I said. "We'll get you some time with Jonathan in a moment."

Slowly, Stevie led her out of the garage and through the front door to the house. When they were gone, I asked the medics to remove the wires and tubes. This was a natural death. There was little chance the coroner would respond, certainly no chance he'd spend time on an autopsy. Jonathan's death had been an imminent event. His own family doctor would sign the death certificate. In a homicide, the tubes and wires would remain. In this instance, nothing of the sort was necessary.

The medics understood. They weren't going to be transporting him. He would remain here until we could get a funeral home to send someone to pick him up. For someone this age, the arrangements had probably already been made. The least we could do was clean him up, make him look more natural, and maybe find him a decent place to rest until they arrived. That would allow his wife a little time to sit with him before he was taken forever.

While the medics cleaned him up, I went inside and spoke with Amelia. I thought a spare bedroom might be the choice, but she was convinced we should put him on the 1950s era, pea green colored couch in the living room. It was his favorite place for an afternoon nap.

The medics brought Jonathan in on their backboard and transferred him to a resting position on the couch. They tucked a small pillow under his head and crossed his hands on his lap. Amelia stood patiently, arms folded as she watched. Like so many of her generation, she was the picture of poise and grace. Her eyes were the only thing to betray the immense pain she felt. The fire truck left first, then the ambulance.

I brought a chair from the kitchen and set it next to the couch. Something made me think every old person in the world had this very same couch. I tried to remember where I'd seen it last.

Amelia sat and held her husband's hand while Stevie and I searched the house for whatever information we might need to complete our report. She didn't seem to mind and directed us to where we'd find things when we couldn't find them ourselves.

It took about thirty minutes to locate what we needed and to get the coroner's waiver. When that was complete, we called the funeral home and arranged for them to pick up Jonathan. They assured us they would arrive within the hour. With any luck, the daughter-in-law we'd located in Oceanside would arrive about the same time.

I returned to the living room and sat in a chair next to Amelia. She managed a warm smile, then turned her attention back to Jonathan. Stevie also came into the room. I figured he'd have found a reason to go back to the car so he could avoid the whole thing, but he didn't. He sat silently in the far corner while Amelia and I sat with Jonathan. The silence lasted several long minutes. I thought about trying to comfort her with conversation, something to distract her thoughts, but I wasn't sure what to say and I didn't want to deny her final moments with her husband.

Finally, she spoke. Her words were soft, and she sounded defeated. She also sounded angry. "Eleven days, you sweet man."

"Excuse me," I said, unsure whom she was talking to. I didn't figure she would be calling me sweet, but you never knew with old people. They had odd sensibilities.

Amelia turned and rested her hand on my forearm. "Oh, I'm sorry, Officer. You are a sweet man as well."

"I'm afraid I'm not following you."

She smiled warmly. "Of course not, here I am bleating on like an old goat. Of course you don't understand." She patted my arm as if she were comforting a child.

"What's the significance of eleven days?" The question was out before I could swallow my words. That happens in times like these, like the time I went to the suicide where the man had strung himself up by the rafters with a rope. The family didn't want to be alone and asked if I could stay until everything was through. I told them I would "hang around." You don't always select the right words when you're nervous.

Amelia turned her attention back to Jonathan. The anger in her voice dissipated. "Eleven more days, that's all he wanted. It would have been our seventy-fifth wedding anniversary."

I sighed audibly. It would be a miracle just to live as many years. I'd never figured a person could be married that long. Certainly it would never happen that I'd see such a landmark. Hell, I was lucky to make it through the end of the second day. My heart sank. Suddenly it seemed so petty to come to work upset over a woman I'd lost after only one night. It even seemed insignificant that Michelle and I made it the better part of a year. What did I know about loss?

"Miss Amelia, I'm not sure what to say." Now it wasn't Stevie stammering, it was me. "I can't even begin to imagine what you're going through."

She stared longingly at Jonathan. "Just eleven days. That's all he wanted. All the years we were together and he never once complained about a single chore I set him on. Forty years he worked to support me and the kids. He put every one of them through college, and together we've buried two of them." Amelia took a long breath and wiped at the corner of her eye. "In all that time he never once complained. Every year, on our anniversary, he would plant carnations in the front yard."

Amelia turned to me, "Carnations are my favorite, you know, especially the red ones. He would plant a bed of them every year, and when they would bloom, he would pick one and tell me that each of the little wrinkles represented another reason he was glad I married him." She stopped again and swallowed. "You couldn't get him to say a sweet thing the rest of the year, but every anniversary he gave me that. These past few years he just kept saying he wanted to make it to seventy-five. He said that was something worthwhile."

The knock on the door about brought me out of my chair. I had been so totally consumed as I listened to her that I didn't even hear the van for the funeral home pull into the driveway.

I stood and rested my hand on Amelia's shoulder. "We'll be outside if you need us. You take some time alone."

Stevie and I left through the garage to make sure there was room to bring the gurney in the house without having to go up the sidewalk and through the front door. The garage was clear, and the funeral home had backed the van up to it in anticipation that this would be the most discrete route to remove the body. When I told them what was going on, they didn't complain about waiting.

As we waited, I looked at the workbench on the other side of the garage. There was a new, pine flower box on the bench. A bag of potting soil rested on the floor below it. My stomach tightened and I wanted a cigarette.

Amelia came to the garage door a few minutes later and told us she was ready. We stood with her while the funeral home told her what she would need to do next. When they were done, they loaded old, dead Jonathan onto the gurney, put him in their van, and drove away as though they were headed to the next stop on their Fed-Ex route.

Stevie and I stayed with Amelia until her daughter-in-law arrived. We met her in the driveway. She thanked us for waiting and then rushed into the house. We didn't go back inside. A moment later, we started down the driveway to our car. We made it halfway when the front door opened. Amelia stepped outside and started our way. I turned and walked back to save her the effort. Stevie followed.

"Thank you," she said as she gave me hug. I put an arm around her, uncomfortable about the moment. When she released me, she turned to Stevie and hugged him as well. He was no more comfortable than I.

"You are good men. Jonathan would have liked you. You stayed even when you didn't have to."

And then it was done. What happened next was up to the family. Sometimes it's hard not to feel a sense of pain and loss when you enter into someone's home for something as personal as this, but when your job is through, the time comes to move on. We'd had a role to play, that was all. There would be no closure, just another radio call. As emotional as this might have been, no part was ours for resolution.

We drove off. At the end of the street, I got on the radio and told Liz we were clear. A moment later, our next call appeared on the computer—a residential burglary in one of the college area apartments. I turned left at the next intersection and headed that direction. It was the perfect call. We could take the information and then go write the burglary and the death report over coffee. It was just the kind of break I needed.

"Shit," Stevie exclaimed as he shivered visibly. "That was the suckiest call ever. Couldn't we have done that different? Maybe we could a got one of the neighbors to sit and wait with her?"

"There were lots of less sucky ways we could have handled that."

Stevie hit the recline lever on his seat and slammed the backrest against the prisoner cage behind him. "Well my vote would have been to do it. That just creeped me out. Why did you have to bring the dead guy in the house?"

"Just doing a little work on my karma."

"Huh?"

"Nothing," I replied. "Just something someone used to say when things like this came up. It's one of those things like, 'the badge doesn't make the man.'"

"It was still creepy. Didn't you have a hard time sitting there doing nothing?"

I turned and looked straight at him. "Killed me. Not the suckiest call ever but it gets honorable mention for sure."

"No, suckiest ever." He was adamant. "I'd like to hear your

idea of something worse."

We pulled into the apartment complex as he spoke. I barely had the car in park when some kid with blond hair and acne walked rapidly up to my door.

"It's about time. Someone robs my place and you guys can't get here any faster than three hours. What? Was there a special at the donut shop today?"

Maybe I was wrong, maybe this wasn't the kind of call I needed right after the last one. I know I didn't need the spike in my blood pressure. I took a deep breath and resisted the urge to put the kid in a Darth Vader grip and lift him off the ground.

"Sorry, we got delayed on another priority call."

"Oh, so someone robbing my apartment isn't a priority?"

My fingers twitched. The dark side of the force was screaming for release. I controlled it. "How about you tell us what happened and maybe we can help you now." My voice was firmer this time, my patience less intact.

"I had people over last night," is how his story began. I'd been around the college long enough to know that meant a party. People were not friends, people were drinking buddies. "I left the apartment around two to walk someone home." Literally translated, "I hooked up with a drunken college girl and went to get laid." He continued, "I ended up staying at her house because it was late and I was too tired,"—meaning drunk—"to walk home. When I got home this morning my stereo was gone."

He seemed to cool down as he finally got an opportunity to tell his sob story. I was about to help him feel like we really cared, but then he was compelled to add more.

"So what are you going to do next? I've been waiting three hours. I demand you do your job and find whoever did this. They belong in jail, and if you can't find them then you need to call someone who can."

That was it. I stepped forward, close enough he could feel my breath in his face. "Look, you 'wet behind the ears, momma still wipes your ass and daddy pays for everything you need, little college puke.' We just came from a call where some poor woman lost the husband she'd been married to for about four times the number of years you've been alive. If you think I give a rat's ass because you let a bunch of drunks into your apartment and left them unattended while you went out to get laid but passed out instead, *you* are about to get a real education. I could give a flying fuck whether you lost your stereo. It sounds to me like you have only yourself to blame."

I wasn't sure his eyes could get any wider as I barked at him. I was certain that if anyone else was out in this parking lot they could have heard every word. When this complaint came in, it would be founded.

Then Stevie stepped in between me and college boy. "Hatch, how about you go back to the car and work on that other report. Let me take this one."

Chapter 15

DEATH IS A FUNNY BUSINESS. In all the years I'd been doing this, I thought one day I'd become accustomed to the lost lives, but there were still times when reality snuck up and surprised you like a bite on the balls. This had been that sort of day.

I thought I had come to understand death, to accept the natural element of life's end, but that's just the start. Loss becomes impersonal. You arrive at a radio call, find a dead guy, do your job, and then go about your day. If you had any feelings at all, the most you'd share is a dark joke at the end of your shift. After a while, that's all death becomes—a dark joke most of the time.

Death can be intimate. Something far too many people in America have lost touch with. Stevie saw Jonathan's passing as the creepiest call ever. Amelia was comfortable sitting next to the couch for a few minutes with a man she knew she'd never see again. She was of a different era, a bygone time when people kept their loved ones in the parlor until it was time to bury them.

What I hadn't learned to fully understand were the nuances of death, which ones would get to you and which ones wouldn't. The children, they get to all of us. There's no way to avoid that except to hope the number of times you need to deal with a dead child are few and spread apart by many years.

Perhaps this is why we had a homicide unit. Maybe the separation between responder and investigator is a good thing.

As a patrol officer those final heartbeats often bind with

whatever emotions came with the call. In Esther's case, the fear of searching the house, then finding her, and smelling odors, sharing the last breath of a human life as it clung to stagnant air that reeked of old beer cans and cigarettes. The whole incident becomes a memory. Powerful and clear, but just a brief glimpse at a sensation you will remember the rest of your days.

Homicide gets involved afterwards, and the start of their job is typically the end of yours. The intensity is gone. They can imagine, they have patrol experiences, but mostly their role is separate. You each only deal with a little piece of the whole. Probably easier, I just hadn't thought about that when I started sticking my nose in things. Then again, I hadn't expected to get another death call my first day back to work.

The truly sad part about these two deaths was how they cheated people. Death took heirlooms more precious than any piece of jewelry, without regard to any honorable code. Perhaps no honor among thieves should extend to include the Grim Reaper.

All that Esther might have been was gone. That she likely wouldn't have become anything but a drunken wife who fought with her loser husband was irrelevant. Her life was hers to live as she pleased. Death robbed her of choice, of the possibility to become more, and the best thing her husband could think to say was that the cunt deserved it.

Jonathan had had everything. He'd lived a full life, raised children, lived well, and had nearly seventy-five years with the woman he loved. He even died quickly. The sadness of his story was Amelia. When a spouse dies after that many years together, the other usually follows in a few short months. To deny his dream was to refuse Amelia the peace of her final days. The good memories she carried would be replaced by the pain for the man who had given her everything yet didn't get his one last wish.

That was death.

I closed my laptop and leaned back against the rear bumper of the car. The trunk hadn't made a great desk but you couldn't be picky in the empty parking lot of a vacant business. My report was done. Perhaps not having to write any more about Jonathan's passing would mean I wouldn't spend more time dwelling on miserable thoughts. One could hope.

I tilted my head to look through the back window. Stevie was still pounding away on his stolen stereo caper. Like most new guys, he was slow to formulate his report. He'd earned the extra time today. If there was any chance at keeping that twit of a college kid from complaining, it only happened when Stevie stepped in and took over. I could give him a little credit.

I pulled a cigarette from my shirt pocket. The first drag filled my lungs, and the nicotine swept through my body like a soothing wave. I enjoyed the peace, disrupted only by the occasional gunshot that cracked randomly as someone in the neighborhood test fired a shot into the air. There would be no radio call. A single gunshot, even multiples, seldom drew much attention in this part of town. People accepted these things unless the gunfire was accompanied by screaming.

Stevie stepped out of the car as I was crushing out my cigarette. He stretched and ambled toward me. I lit another, hoping to draw a couple more minutes from my break. He stopped and looked down at the ground before lightly swinging one foot to kick a pebble out of his way. There was weariness I hadn't seen. Something was troubling him.

"I think I'm ready for today to be over," he said plainly.

We weren't even half way into our shift. Some days are like that, nothing physically taxing about them, but after a couple hours you're exhausted. I was ready for the day to end the moment college boy set me off. I was sure that would come back to haunt me. When it did, there was little I could do but confess my sins and ride out whatever punishment Socrates wanted to impose.

I gave Stevie a nod. "You did good today."

He looked at me like I was speaking some other language.

"With the kid at the college. Heads up thing to do, stepping in like that."

If he was a Golden Retriever, his tail would have wagged.

"Really, it was almost like I had a partner."

The tail slowed. "You do have a partner."

As my words replayed in my head, I realized how insulting I must have sounded.

"I'm sorry, let's not get ahead of ourselves. I didn't mean to offend you. That was good work, but a partner is something entirely different. Kind of like the difference between a cop and a police officer."

The tail stopped. "What's the difference?"

"Between which, partner and coworker or cop and police officer?"

"I don't care, either one," he said as he stopped swinging his foot. His body language changed. He shifted, feet apart, shoulders squared in my direction. He felt challenged. That was the way with young guys. Everything was about respect. A compliment wasn't good enough, they wanted to be equal.

The academy did that to them, told the recruits they didn't have to take crap from the old guys, that their opinion was just as important as anyone else's. Used to be you didn't even have an opinion until you had a star on your name badge. For every five years you give the city, they give you a star. You knew you were a legitimate part of the universe when you had at least one to add to the heavens. If you encountered one of those venerable guys with more stars than you could count, you considered them a galaxy unto themselves and you gave them the respect they deserved. There was a pecking order, and seniority meant something. Not so any more.

Stevie did a piece of good work today. I'd give him that. If he wanted respect, then he'd have to learn patience. He'd also have to learn a little bit about the universe. We had enough shooting stars, folks who wanted to get places faster than they were ready. The problem with shooting stars is that they burn out or they crush something when they hit the ground.

"Look, perhaps I'm just not being clear and that's my fault. A partner isn't just someone you get in the car and ride around with. It's a relationship. I've worked with a great many officers over the years, but I've only ever had a handful of partners. That's something that takes time and requires trust."

"Excuse me," Stevie interrupted. His tone was indignant. "You don't trust me? I went through the same background you did."

I took a long drag from my cigarette. "That's not what I meant." I exhaled. "Let me give you an example. Marcus is a partner. I've worked with him off and on for a long time. I know his moods, I know what gets to him, and I know his boundaries. I know that because we've worked together long enough to develop some history. You and me, we've worked together two days. Today you did good, but there's a whole lot about you that's still up in the air."

"Like what?"

"Like whether you're in this job to be a cop or a police officer."

"Partners, fine, I get it, but we're still all cops."

"Are we now?"

"Okay, you got me, what's the difference?"

All I'd wanted to do was give the damn kid a compliment. I hadn't really intended to get into a philosophical study of intent.

"A cop wants to be the first one at the scene, wants to be

involved. A cop will make hard decisions. He'll look at two shitty situations, make a choice, and then he'll act. He'll do that based on experience and what his guts tell him. Then he'll live with his actions knowing he did the best he could.

"A cop will take action, not form a committee.

"A cop isn't afraid to get in there and get his hands dirty. Some guys don't believe they should be required to touch a nasty person without two layers of gloves, protective glasses, and a mask. To do otherwise would be unsafe, and they shouldn't be required to go into unsafe situations unless every effort in the world has been made to ensure that they won't really face any danger.

"A cop knows that no day is safe, ever. Life is an imperfect experiment.

"Folks get into this job for a great many reasons, but the guys I've known who preferred to be called cops had a perspective that was just a bit different than those who wanted to be police officers. I can't say there's anything really bad about either type, they both fill a need. I'd just rather be a cop.

"You see, from my perspective, a police officer will tell you about his grand vision for the future of our department. He'll have a whole plan about how to fix everything that's broken. He'll be able to tell you that plan his first year in the field. A cop will take the time to learn the streets, to develop an understanding of what works before he tries to fix what doesn't. A police officer is quick to tell you he is an expert in something. A cop just knows what worked the last time."

I lit a third cigarette. "You're not really following me, are you?"

Stevie shrugged. "Some of it makes sense. Some of it just sounds like maybe you're a bit bitter."

I shrugged back. "That could very well be, but I still see a difference and that's hard to sum up in some pretty, concise package. A cop is grit, a part of the streets. He understands his environment and works as a part of it. The police officer goes into that environment as a separate entity and tries to mold it. Then he leaves and goes back to his comfy little home and talks about all the good he did for the poor folks in the world. Meanwhile, he never really understands there's no separation, just folks."

Stevie stood silently when I finished. "Like I said, you get it or you don't. Just remember, the day will come where you have to make a decision about whether you want to be a cop or a police officer. Either way is fine, just know that there's a difference."

Stevie shook his head like I was nuts. "Whatever."

"No matter what, that was good work today. I lost my cool and you stepped in and bailed me out. I shouldn't have lost control, but shit happens and that's my burden. If Roosevelt calls you on the carpet to discuss it, I expect you to tell him the truth."

I looked directly at Stevie. "You tell him exactly what you saw and whatever you remember me doing. Don't you dare lie to protect me. There's nothing you'll ever see me do out here that will get me fired. I might get in some grease, but I'll never intentionally put my job at risk. If you lie, they will fire you in a hot second. I didn't get you this job. I don't expect you to lose it for me." As I spoke, Jack's voice rang in my head just as surely as if this was years ago and he was giving me the same speech.

I took another drag of my cigarette and washed it down with coffee that had long since grown cold. "The same thing goes for kneeing that guy in the balls. Roosevelt hit me up on that earlier today. He might very well ask for your thoughts."

"I didn't see that," Stevie said breaking eye contact to look at the ground.

"That's right," I said, remembering that he'd been running down the alley after a two-bit rock monster. "Never mind that one then. Just tell the truth."

Stevie nodded but kept his eyes lowered. "He doesn't like you much, does he?"

I slapped him on the shoulder. "An age old struggle, buddy. I see cops and administrators, he sees has-beens and visionaries. He might be a police officer, but he'll never understand what it means to be a cop."

The rest of the day went smoothly. We responded to a couple of alarm calls that were nothing more than employee error or some mysterious activation neither we nor the alarm company could pinpoint. There were two calls of domestic violence, one where the woman wanted a report because she thought she saw one of her babies' daddies in an unknown model car parked at the end of the street in violation of her restraining order. The other call was a husband who got mad and threw his mac & cheese across the kitchen, splattering the food bowl all over his wife. There was probably more to that story but he left before we arrived. He'd hide out and in the morning she would love him all over again. We also managed a disturbance where some nutty lady was cussing out her neighbor because she didn't like the way the cat stared at her through the kitchen window.

Sergeant Roosevelt called a 10-17 at Hoover High. In my

language, that's a report signing session. Most sergeants did them sometime near the end of shift when you weren't likely to get another report. Oftentimes, this was a good opportunity to tell stories about your day. I wouldn't have discussed Amelia, but I could have spent fifteen minutes on a rant about the staring cat lady. What I couldn't manage was a desire to visit Roosevelt. I did a traffic stop instead. If he wanted to give me grief about not participating, I could always claim that I got tied up protecting motorists.

When we got back to the station, I drove to Stevie's car so he could unload his gear. Why he didn't just throw it in his locker I didn't know. Perhaps because he carried so much stuff there was no way he could fit everything inside a locker and still have room for a uniform. I'd have to remember to show him how to trim his equipment down.

I grabbed my own gear bag and slung the strap over my shoulder. "You mind parking the car when you're done? I'm going to go in and get these reports signed."

Stevie stood up from where he was bent over the trunk of his car. "Hey, Hatch." His tone was more humble than normal.

I stopped. "Yeah."

"About the other day," he started, then paused. "Well, I'm sorry I took off on you and Murphy. I should have stayed. I just didn't think about it quick enough."

I smiled a little. "I bet that hurt to say."

He shook his head. "A lot. I've been meaning to all day, but I just didn't know how. I knew you were mad, but what I did was wrong."

"Nobody got hurt." I gave him a pat on the shoulder. "Think of it as a lesson and try not to repeat the mistake. We all screw up. Recognizing that is a good start."

"You think Murphy hates me?"

"I think he'll get over it. You get a chance, tell him what you told me. I don't see he'll hold it against you."

I walked into the station. Perhaps there was a chance for the kid after all. I stowed my bag and headed to the report room. Sergeant Roosevelt was waiting.

"Nice of you to make it. Couldn't stop by the 10-17 like everyone else?"

"Sorry, sir. We got delayed on a traffic stop." As I expected, everything had to be an issue. I bit my tongue while anger and resentment burned inside me. This was not the time.

"Get your reports done and then see me after we're through here."

Aww, hell, maybe it was. Time to put Socrates in his place. You can be Sergeant, but that doesn't make you right.

Shit. The college kid had complained.

I looked at Roosevelt, then around the room. Everyone had stopped working and paid full attention to us. Jenkins was behind Roosevelt mimicking him. I wasn't in a mood to laugh. Roosevelt was calling me out but if he had a complaint against me, now was certainly not the time to incite him. Everyone else in the room ached for the confrontation, but they wanted me to carry the sword. The problem is that when you fall on your blade, the same cops who encouraged you will openly tell others how you made the stupid decision to act and then privately grumble about the system crunching you.

Pushing dignity aside, I sat down and logged on to my laptop. The steel toe of my boot dug into the floor as I tried to focus on taking care of my reports and not chewing my boss a new asshole. A moment later the computer booted up. I selected my reports and handed the whole thing over to Roosevelt so he could review them. When he was done, he handed the computer back to me.

"Did you really need to spend so much time on that death call?"

My blood pressure rose. Complaint, or not, I was losing patience. It had been a long day, I didn't need this. As I started to open my mouth, Ariana's voice bounced through my brain, something about not having to respect the man but having to respect the title. Perhaps it was time to take a different tact, try something I hadn't done much of before. Maybe this was the time to work on that thing called diplomacy. I could always find an opportunity to fuck with peanuthead. "It took a while for the body snatchers to get there. We couldn't leave the widow alone."

"Well, in the future, if you're going to be delayed, let me know so I can come evaluate, see if there's not a better way we could be spending our time. We could have replaced the two of you with a single man unit." My impulse was to address him in kind. If he was going to take me on in front of others then responding in front of them was fair game. That little voice of experience was yammering something about prudence being the best course until I had a chance to evaluate what he knew that I didn't.

"I'll surely let you know."

I submitted my reports and went outside for a smoke. Nicotine would fix this, at least ease the urge to be impulsive. Roosevelt would release everyone quickly enough. I needed to cool down before I went into his office to let him patronize me again.

Somehow this needed to end. As much fun as it had been to taunt the last sergeant like him, I realized the fun part was the memory. He hadn't been that much fun at the time. If Socrates already had a reason to write me up, he would have the upper hand. I'd need to move carefully. If it came down to punishing me for discourtesy, there was only so much he could do. I didn't need to add inches to the handle he used for leverage.

When my cigarette was done, I walked back into the station. The Report Room was clear. Everyone had been dismissed. I walked down the hall to the Sergeant's Office and went inside. Roosevelt was seated in his cubicle.

I didn't sit, simply stood at the entrance. "You wanted to see me." It was an effort but my tone remained calm.

Roosevelt motioned for me to sit.

"I'd rather stand, sir. My back hurts, been sitting enough today." That was a half truth, but it was time to start the power play. He wanted me to sit, I did not. He needed to learn that he could only control so much. I'd have to tread lightly, but we needed to start establishing some boundaries.

"Very well." He swiveled around in his chair and leaned back. He would have appeared relaxed but the arms across his chest said otherwise. "Why did you and Steven go downtown instead of clearing at the start of the shift?"

I paused. "He needed to fix his Taser." Years ago, I might have run my mouth about someone complaining the moment I walked in the room. I'd learned. Now he would need to bring it up. Until then, I'd have to navigate through his little mine field.

"The next time you need to leave the area, please advise me prior to doing so. It is policy."

Socrates was a fitting name. Policy. I'd played this game before. If he needed to approve every time I left the area, I'd check with him every time I took a prisoner downtown. In fact, I could find lots of reasons to have to check in. I could check in so often he would hear my voice rattling around in his sleep. Most of the time you could follow policy by the letter and a guy like him would get sick of your application of rules quickly enough. Now was not the time. I figured peace was the better exercise in discretion. He might be holding the complaint as his trump card should I start spouting off.

"My fault, I just ran straight down after line-up. Look . . ." I started in the most apologetic tone I could muster. This one was for Ariana. If there was a middle ground, it wasn't going to be my fault we didn't get there. ". . . I'm not sure how we got off on the wrong foot, sir, but I'm certain I don't want to be at odds with you. No one wins if we can't get along. You're the boss. All you need to do is tell me how you want things done. There doesn't have to be any games involved." Of course, that implied there could be. The choice was his. I was giving him the opportunity to carve out a peaceable middle ground, and I was humbling myself more than I normally would have allowed.

That threw him off. It threw me off as well. I was not accustomed to apologizing when I hadn't screwed up. On the other hand, it did me no good to have a supervisor gunning for me. Roosevelt thought for a moment. I was certain he was trying to figure out what to do next. Either that or he was about to hit me with the complaint. Whatever he was planning, I'd called him out.

"Times are changing, John. It's not like it used to be. I have a plan on how to get us to the next evolution of law enforcement. If you give me a chance, I can bring you along."

Hah! There was no complaint. If there was, he'd have pulled it out. "You're the boss. I'm not trying to get in your way, just doing things the only way I know how."

"Sometimes we have to unlearn what we know before we can learn something new."

That was Socrates. How I couldn't follow his wisdom was beyond me.

"Yes, sir," was all I was going to give. I'd left enough pride on the carpet today. "Is there anything else?"

"Yes."

Damn, played my hand too quick, the complaint existed.

"What you did to Eric was inappropriate. He was stuck in the car wash for fifteen minutes. You wasted water and could have damaged the car with your prank. That behavior will cease, is that clear?"

Oops. No complaint perhaps, but I'd forgotten about Smith. It took everything I had not to break into a wide grin. "Yes, sir."

"That will be all then," he said turning in his chair. I was about to back out of the office hoping he would accept my apology as penance and ease up. With any luck he'd forget about me and move on to his mission statements and stat reports.

Then I realized we weren't done.

"Sir," I started.

He swung back around in his chair.

"If you're going to counsel me in the future, please do so in private. If not, I'll consider it fair to respond in front of the group. Just a heads up so we don't find ourselves in an avoidable misunderstanding."

CHAPTER 16

I COULDN'T REMEMBER much about the ride home. Time was a blur, an indistinct passage of familiar streets and landmarks. This was one of those nights where my brain stayed in Mid-City while my body cruised home on auto-pilot. The only thing I could say for certain was that no one followed me.

I'd like to say lapses like this don't happen, that I can turn my thoughts off like a switch, but the truth of the matter is that the job doesn't really work that way.

A lot of highs and lows can happen in the few hours that make up second watch and adrenaline often flows frequently. The fluctuating nature of those demands requires focus, thought, and energy. The day comes at a price, and over the years this job has turned many a vibrant, energetic person into an isolated couch potato.

The doctors, those experts they bring in to tell us what makes us tick, talk about this in the stress classes. They call it some variation of Post Traumatic Stress or some other such phenomenon.

I first heard the deal in college and then again every few years thereafter in some mandatory training session or another. You can't operate at a heightened, energetic state for hours and not have to go through a depressed period of some degree to counterbalance that.

I always figured the after work down-time was the payback for all the fun I'd had. The payment I needed to make for being allowed to do real police work. The problem with that thought, real police work, catching robbers and such, that didn't seem to ever really stress me out. What got to me were the other things, the crummy calls, the hurt people that shouldn't be hurt, and most of all, some of the assholes that made the station their center of orbit. Tonight I'd pay for my confrontation with Roosevelt, for the woman who would be sleeping alone after seventy-five years, and for the college shithead that couldn't get beyond his own sense of entitlement and bad decision making.

And with all that had happened, it was Roosevelt and diplomacy that got me really worked up. Who the hell was I to try diplomacy? I sure didn't try it on the spoiled kid who didn't know any better, but I went out of my way for a guy who was supposed to be my superior, a guy who was supposed to be leading me. The absurdity of my attempt still didn't settle any better than it had when I made the decision to try. Treating people right was a leadership issue. It should extend from the top down, not the bottom up. That was how I expected him to lead, five year wonder or not.

The house was dark as I pulled into the driveway. I waited for the garage to open. The light inside was burned out. I'd need to fix that in the morning. Probably an easier task to do at the moment, but I just didn't feel like it. Fighting in the office took a lot more out of a man than fighting on the street ever did.

The garage closed behind me as I walked through the door leading into the house. A rush of cool air blew across my face as I stepped into the hallway. I shivered involuntarily at the cold, lifelessness of the place. Somehow all sense that a human occupied the place had left long before I ever got back. The hall light was on, the only light in the house. It let me see, regardless of when I came home, and it kept anyone on the outside from really knowing whether someone was there when I was away.

I started to step and caught myself. A glance at the floor made sure Pal wasn't already standing at my feet. He was sneaky that way, either there waiting when I came home or slipping silently along the baseboards at my feet. I'd nearly smashed him enough times to know better than to wander without checking. There was no Pal.

There was no one to greet me other than the cold, empty house. Realization brought a wave of both sadness and comfort each time I walked in the door at night. This was the loneliest part of the day. However, the emptiness of no one to greet me was compensated by the relief that I wouldn't have to talk to anyone. Things could be worse.

Then came the rumbling of little thunderfoot. I waited. As he came barreling around the corner his back arched, tail puffed, he began to sidestep as if he was ready to fight. He stopped cold, eyed me for a moment, then tore back down the hall into the dark. Strange animals, cats. I was quite certain I would never understand them.

I made my way to the kitchen, switched on a light, then paused and listened. Pal was lying on the floor licking his foot and made no attempt to even recognize I was there. The house was still, the air around me as it should be with no drafts from a broken window, no signs of anything disturbed. Without moving, I eyed the French doors leading to the patio then shifted my attention to the living room. Content that no one had slipped into my home in my absence, I walked to the bedroom.

My gun made the same clunk every night when I set it on the dresser, that thick sound of heavy steel echoing dully inside the hollows of the dresser as if I'd just used a big metal tong to tap on a large wooden drum. I ditched my wallet and keys as well.

The flashing red light caught my eye, a phone message of all things. For a moment the thought was exciting, that someone had called. That didn't happen as often as it used to in the days before all my friends were married, or were in between marriages. My guess was a solicitor and I'd won some amazing promotional deal. In any event, the flashing light would annoy me at some point.

I pressed the play button and went to the closet to ditch my clothes. The machine beeped and there was a long pause that followed something unintelligible, like an, "Ah," or an "Umm." My gut tightened and prepared for bad news. Someone was calling and they weren't sure how to breach the topic. I'd had those calls before, and I braced myself.

I wasn't prepared for Maralyn. Her words were broken, staggered. "Yeah, umm, John . . . I . . ." Then she seemed to regain a bit of control. "John, I knew what I wanted to say and the words disappeared when the phone beeped. Ah . . . I'm sorry about the other day. I didn't mean to hurt you. My life has been a bit complicated lately, and I wasn't prepared for you. I certainly never dreamed things would happen like they did."

She paused again. "Anyway," she continued. It sounded like her throat tightened. "I'm sorry. I probably shouldn't have called your house, especially since you didn't call back on the message

I left at work. But, at the risk of seeming like some freaky stalker chick, I just wanted to at least leave you a message and apologize, maybe explain things a little better. Take care, John."

Suddenly the emptiness of the night felt heavy. I sat on the bed. What was there to explain? I never dreamed a lot of things would happen, but they did. That was life. Sometimes we get surprised, I get it. What I don't get is cheating. If you're not happy with things, change them. If you can't change them, leave. It's that simple. You can't play both sides and expect things to not get complicated.

It was how she spoke that got me. That call had been tough to make, I could hear the strain in her voice, the words, the breaks, the tightening of the throat. It pained her to make that call. Instinctively, I wanted to reach out, to help ease her pain. Hearing her hurt made me hurt. Brief as it was, I liked Maralyn. Perhaps there was something more going on that made her life complicated, and I just needed to understand.

I picked up the phone and pressed Caller ID. Maralyn's number flashed in the little screen. The cell phone again. My thoughts deflated. Maybe I did understand. It wasn't that complicated, she just didn't want to make a tough decision and I was getting drawn into the middle of her mess. I'd suffered through Knight in Shining Armor complex enough times to recognize when it was winding up to bitch slap me. Being convinced that someone needed saving had led to a lot more pain than any other trait I possessed. I put the phone down and walked back to the closet. Not this time . . . never again. When it came to bailing women out of their self-induced, bad decision driven messes, this knight was retired.

I ditched my clothes and threw on swim trunks. Sleep wasn't going to happen anytime soon. My back ached, my hip ached, hell, damn near my whole body ached. Maybe a spell in the hot tub would help.

I walked back to the kitchen, opened the fridge, and grabbed a beer. Reaching up, I dug in the cupboard behind the coffee mugs for the spare pack of cigarettes I kept just in case my stopping smoking wasn't going as well as intended. No point being a quitter any more tonight.

Pal smashed his head into the side of my leg, then moved slowly in a figure eight between my feet. I reached down and scratched his forehead. He responded with a purr and then promptly bit my hand before running off. He might have been funny if those sharp teeth didn't startle the shit out of me enough to spill beer on the floor.

"Damn cat!" I went for a wash rag. "Tomorrow it's Animal Control for sure."

The backyard was dark, the night air cool and quiet when I finally made my way outside. I removed the cover from the tub and turned it on, lights and all. The lights in the tub weren't bright, but they were enough to keep me from slipping in the dark. I was dressed inappropriately for death. If I was going to slip and die in the dark, I'd need to go out in a way that would at least entertain the cop who came to do the report and wait for the coroner. Perhaps if I was out here in a halter-top bikini that would give him something he and the guys could laugh about. Better yet, I'd stick to the light and try to avoid a stupid accident.

The tub churned to life, the surge of bubbles bursting into a hot mist above the water line. I slid the small, round table with the battery powered stereo up close so I could have music. I should have driven downtown and spent the last hour playing at The Moreland. That might have helped. Then again, Errol might have wanted to spend five hours talking.

My body relaxed as I eased into the tub. The water was hot. Not scalding, but damn good regardless. A long day in east San Diego had a way of coating your skin with something nearly imperceptible that made you feel grimy just the same, or perhaps that grungy feeling wasn't the neighborhood, maybe it was the job. I don't know. What I did know was that hot water felt good on my aching muscles. The chlorine would take care of the grunge.

After relaxing a minute I pulled out a smoke. A moment later I drew a long drag and washed it down with a cold swallow of beer. I did have the right kind of yard for this. Not that I really planned it, I just lucked out when I bought the place. I'd made enough money on the first house I bought in the early nineties that I was able to sell that and afford this one with a view of downtown.

A lot of guys weren't so lucky. They had families and didn't make a killing on their investments. Most didn't even get to live in the city. They drove from outlying areas like Alpine, Temecula, and Chula Vista. Some lived even farther out, seventy miles one way, to afford a decent home.

As bad as the day had been, at least I had this. I could sit in my hot tub, or at my piano, and look out at the shining lights of what I thought was the finest city in the country. It's not what I had dreamed when I planned my future, when I was young and had my whole life before me.

I always figured I'd be like Jonathan and Amelia. Maybe I

wouldn't get seventy-five years, but I always thought that would be my life. As far back as high school, that's how I saw it. One day I'd be walking along and out of nowhere there'd be this amazing woman who had me the moment I laid eyes on her, that she'd feel the same for me. We'd spend our life connected, best friends. We'd have kids and they'd be good kids because we would love them and pay attention to them. They wouldn't be off running around with thugs, because we'd be better parents than that.

That had been before the years of seeing families that weren't like my dream at all. What I saw were the crack addicts prostituting themselves for a fix and screwing some John in a fleabag hotel while their small children were asleep, or pretending to sleep, in the very bed where mommy was humping away at some stranger who would pay her enough for a hit. I saw parents ignore their kids, beat their kids, and ultimately do much worse to them. Then there were the kids whose parents did nothing wrong and they turned out to be absolute shitheads regardless. Day in, day out, when I deal with families, I don't often see the good ones. Over the years, it reorients your thinking about the likelihood of raising decent human beings. Throw the standard American divorce rate into the mix, and suddenly all those youthful dreams, all those plans, have a way of becoming something more frightening.

All that aside, I still never thought I'd be sitting in a hot tub drinking a beer at one in the morning pondering the life that never seemed to happen, mourning someone else's loss by dwelling on my own. I understood what Maralyn meant when she said she never dreamed we would happen.

Over the years I'd learned a great many things about building expectations and losing dreams. Michelle led me to start thinking about what I could have, what I'd failed to make work in the past. She'd come at a time when I didn't have much hope that being a cop would bring any shot at something real, worthwhile. Michelle. Shit, nearly a year together, and all of a sudden I hadn't been thinking about her at all. A weekend, that's all it took to move on. A weekend and another pretty face. Had the walls really grown that high, the bunkers that thick?

Then again, Maralyn wasn't just a pretty face. Something about her made me feel a connection. Maybe it was the fact that she liked the lines around my eyes or that she dug the thought that the things I've seen put them there. A lot of women liked the idea of dating a cop. The concept made them feel safe. Some liked the excitement, the edge. Maralyn looked at me and seemed to see something more, as if she understood what the streets, the shift work, and the bad things could do to a person. Perhaps that came from her job. As a DA she worked with cops, so understanding them seemed a likely byproduct. Finding someone was hard enough, but finding someone who understood the demands of your life and could accept you for who you were rather than an image of who you were was an entirely different thing.

Michelle hadn't been like that. She liked the security. Maybe I was able to move on so quickly because a part of me had known the relationship wasn't right. She wanted something I could never be, whereas Maralyn seemed to want what I was. And both were destined to simply be one more memory of things that just didn't work out.

I grabbed another cigarette and lit up. I didn't much like self pity, but this was sometimes part of the price. There was nothing I could do but ride out the night. This was a chemical thing. You can't operate all day in a kinetic environment and then go home and expect to be normal. Like it or not, while I enjoyed the little things, a cold beer, a smoke, and the city view, I would also get to work through the painful memories of the day. After all, that's what this was really about. This wasn't about Michelle, or the dreams that had died. This wasn't about Maralyn, or whether I should call. This was about working off certain chemicals that got produced during the work day.

Jonathan and Amelia's story was as beautiful as it was tragic. Dealing with them came with an emotional cost, something that complicated and compounded the chemical transition. I can't understand what it's like to lose a partner after seventy five years. I do understand having love taken from you. Cops grieve loss like anyone, even when it's not theirs.

This wasn't the first time coming home was painful and lonely. The night would pass, and at some point I'd sleep. I just needed to make it there. I'd known too many folks who didn't. Guys ate their guns over this kind of shit. No matter how bad things got, there was always tomorrow. Until then, I would take comfort in the skyline.

I took a swallow of beer and lit another smoke. Keeping that pack was fortuitous, or maybe it was just experience. I realized how quiet the night was and reached for the stereo. Flipping the on switch, I recognized Little River Band immediately. That should have been my first warning. The song took a moment longer, "Reminiscing." Hell. I flipped from radio to CD and hit play. A moment later it was Eagles, "The Girl From Yesterday." I hit the skip button and it went to "Sad Café." I turned it off entirely.

I had a love-hate relationship with the radio much the way folks had with cops. Like we were never there when they needed us, the radio never played the song I wanted to hear when I wanted to hear it, but always played the songs I least wanted to hear when I least wanted to hear them. There was no point scanning stations. Perhaps I'd have better luck with late-night television.

I dried off, covered the tub, and made my way to the family room. Twenty minutes later I was flipping channels for the second time. There wasn't anything, nothing but infomercials and bad reality reruns. Even the History channel was without something worthwhile. Two-hundred stations of shit.

Correct that, *Where Eagles Dare* was starting. I'd probably seen the movie a dozen times, but you could never go wrong with Clint Eastwood and Richard Burton. It wasn't about a wife and kids anymore, it wasn't the dreams of youth, or the pain of loss. It was about stopping the Nazis. Maybe not much for some people, but it could get a lot worse than a night watching Clint in the days before he got sensitive.

CHAPTER 17

I WOKE ON THE COUCH the next morning. Pal was sleeping on the pillow over my head, and the TV was still on. I couldn't remember the end of the movie but was certain they'd successfully beaten those pesky Krauts. Clint was tough, I had faith in him. A walk to the corner coffee shop would get me right up to speed.

Yesterday's sadness was gone, resolved, worked out, safely compartmentalized, and packed away until the next night the job tapped the right emotions. I'd lived through it. The chemical imbalance of an adrenaline overload had stabilized. Today was a new day, and I was looking forward to the possibilities. I was looking forward to work.

As I sat at a sidewalk table outside the coffee shop, I wasn't sure whether I felt bad about the way I'd treated Stevie yesterday, but I was inclined to think, rather extensively, about how to turn the blowout into a learning point. Perhaps I had come on a little strong when I tried to clue him in on being partners, on what it means to be a cop. He'd certainly looked dejected when I was done. What I didn't know was whether I made a difference or simply sounded like the disgruntled grump he was convinced I was.

All I knew was that the kid needed some clueing in if he really wanted to work the streets. This was the real world, and patrol work is a lot colder than the touchy feely classrooms that quit giving failing grades because they didn't want people feeling like they weren't good enough. There was enough of that mentality;

I didn't need it in my police car. Too much hand holding. We fail the moment we teach folks that there are no losers and being substandard is acceptable. We are no longer measured by what we do but rather what we could do if we wanted to. It's not our actions that matter, it's the content of our hearts, and it's bullshit.

We don't teach reality. We don't teach the fact that failure in the real world has consequences. Sometimes that means more than repeating a class the next semester. In this business failure can mean your life. Worse yet, it can mean someone else's. I don't like hurting anyone's feelings, but sometimes you have to do it to teach them to get a grip. I just hoped my blunt tone had been the right choice in this instance.

Right or not, I figured Stevie had earned a reward, something to give him incentive. He wanted to stay busy, wanted to get involved with something, then we'd do just that. We'd hunt.

When I got to work, things were quiet in the locker room, much of the normal banter gone. Guys spoke in hushed tones. It was as though a heavy, wet blanket had been dropped over the room. My little clash with Socrates had driven home a point. He was not in this job to have fun, and he wasn't to be considered one of the guys. That dampened everyone. His actions killed morale. Until he left or settled down, guys would walk on eggshells. No one wanted to be the target of an asshole.

The whole situation was sad and didn't need to be that way. My stomach tightened, but the word diplomacy kept bouncing around my brain. I would give this a real shot. Perhaps he could be redeemed. In the meantime, I would do my job and lay low.

I got ready, checked my mailbox, and logged onto the computer to check my e-mail. It was a daily routine, and if I did it before the shift started, that left more time on the streets. Some guys worked the other way. If they could wait and check their e-mail before getting in the field after line-up, they might get lucky and avoid the first round of shitty calls that would inevitably be waiting when we cleared to relieve the day crew.

Clearing quickly was like being on the firing line of a civil war battle. If you were up front, you were the one that got blasted. Though it was a lead ball in those days—in our war it was the suckiest radio call. Because of that, some guys dragged their heels. They didn't mind if they jammed up their buddies with a shitty call as much as they did getting that rotten call themselves. It was a work ethic thing, and I didn't have much respect for the heel draggers.

There was nothing new in any of the mailboxes, nothing more from Maralyn. I made for the line-up room and sat silently reading a piece of newspaper someone left behind until it was time for our briefing to begin. People entered the room as quiet as they had been in the lockers. A couple guys from another squad laughed as they entered, but quickly caught the mood and settled down. Line-up was uneventful. Roosevelt didn't even show up. When we cleared, Stevie and I loaded our car in relative silence. I thought about apologizing for jumping on him yesterday, but then decided against it. I didn't want to minimize the impact of the point. I could make him feel less crummy by getting out there and working with him more than I could by apologizing for jumping on him. Perhaps down the road I would offer the apology. At the moment I thought it best to let things be.

The first radio call hit us, but we took the volley and continued on. In my book, that was the way it had to be. There were times you did something before clearing, errands like fixing a Taser, but mostly you got in the field and did what you were paid to do before you started on what you wanted to do. If you played it right, you could do both.

Our first musket ball was a domestic violence report, the kind of report those heel draggers wanted to avoid. Of course, this was just the kind of call I'd have preferred to avoid as well, but in the end, someone was still had to do it.

Things were much calmer when Stevie and I arrived. Both the husband and wife were still there, but they were no longer arguing. The wife answered the door. She appeared calm, but clearly a bit concerned to see us. She knew that something was going to happen in the next few minutes, but what exactly that was remained unanswered. From the bruise on her forearm, I was betting she expected her husband would go to jail today. If he wasn't injured, it was highly likely I would end up in agreement with her.

We separated the two and after talking to each of them, the husband was arrested and put in our car. He was going to jail. Though the story each of them told was different from that of the other in regard to who was the aggressor, the one thing that was common was that he had grabbed her arm in the middle of the argument. His story was defense; her story made it out of anger. Neither appeared willing to let the battle go, and each had strained to hear what the other half said, even though we did our best to talk to them separately. We decided to make some decisions for them. Tomorrow would be another day, but tonight she'd have to bail him out if she wanted to fight. Absent an independent witness that could give us another version, another option, it was about all we could do.

When we arrived at the Watch Commander, I told Stevie I'd do the crime and arrest report if he would do the booking slip and jail paperwork. Not an even trade, but we needed to shave time if we wanted to hunt. To split the work evenly would take too long. He still wrote slower than I did, and though practice would make him better, I was inclined to make sure we got him some field experience. It was kind of like having a trainee in the car, but I could manage the extra work.

By the time Stevie walked the suspect into jail, I was done with the reports. We were ahead of the standard amount of time generally taken to complete an arrest. That meant we had a little time to prowl if we could make it back to our area without getting flagged down or having to answer up to cover on a priority call. I checked the status of our squad mates and none of them appeared to be on anything pressing. The radio was only moderately active and no high-priority calls were holding. We were good to go.

My preference would have been to work on some follow-ups for Esther's death, but that task might be a little slow for Stevie. Besides that, I was trying to give him a perk. We could spend all night doing follow-ups on a homicide and walk away with nothing to show for our time. The disappointment would just encourage him to stay away from such activities. We needed something with an easier payoff. Being that he had gotten all excited last week over chasing a dope fiend, that seemed a good spot to start. Perhaps we could grab a street dealer.

In any event, something about those crime scene photos was still tugging at my brain, and I'd need to work that out before I started knocking on doors and asking questions about Esther. Until then we'd work on a street dealer. It was like fishing, sometimes you had to be content tugging out sunfish until you finally got a run at the big Muskie.

When it came to street dealers and arrests, the number of people we could grab on any given day nearly always outweighed the number actually booked. In a city where cops are outnumbered and understaffed, as much as you might want it, you couldn't get everyone.

We took the 94 back from downtown. It was quiet in the car at first, then Stevie spoke, "You seem like you're in a better mood today. You get some last night?"

If we'd have been on a city street, I'd have stopped the car. "Excuse me?"

He shrugged. "You just seem less grumpy."

"I'm not grumpy, and what I did last night is none of your business."

"So you got some then? I got some. Went down to P.B. after work. Hooked up with this hot little bartender, and before I knew it, I was knocking her headboard against the wall. Bam, just like that. Even your grumpiness will not get me today."

Jack replaced Ariana. No longer was I focused on diplomacy. Now I was listening to Jack tell me about "Booze, Broads, and Bills." Stevie just covered two of the three things that led young cops down some bumpy roads. My impulse was to give him the speech, to pass on that bit of old school wisdom we all needed to hear. The question became whether this was the right time. I figured it was not. I'd trusted Jack when he gave me that lecture. It meant something coming from him. I believed what he passed on because I trusted that he had my best interest at heart. I couldn't say Stevie would extend that same level of trust to me. It was enough that he was talking. I'd leave it at that for now and focus on the day ahead of us.

He continued before I could respond. "You probably miss those days, huh? Why don't you wear a ring?"

"Say what?" We took the Home Avenue exit.

"Why don't you wear your wedding ring? A lot of guys don't. You worried you'll tear it off in a fight?"

"I'm not married."

That took him back a step, shattered his assumption.

"I'm sorry, divorced? Lots of cops are divorced."

"I'm not married."

"Sorry, man, didn't mean to make you grumpy again."

"And I'm not grumpy."

"Whatever," he said as he shifted toward our computer.

"Stop," I barked as he was about to clear us from our last call. He started. "What? See, you are grumpy. Admit it."

I ignored him. "Don't clear just yet."

Confusion spread across his face as Home Avenue turned into Euclid.

"You want to do some police work or hurry off to the next report?"

Confusion turned to a smile. "I didn't think grumpy old guys liked having fun."

He was fucking with me. The kid was trying to play in the majors, trying to push and give back some of what I'd been giving him. I had to respect that, at least for now. I could always bring him down a notch if I had to, if he decided to try and fit in a bigger pair of pants than he was ready for.

"Seems we haven't been doing much of anything but chasing the radio," I said. "Thought maybe we'd see who might be up to no good. If you think you're up to it?"

Stevie leaned back and waved his hand. "Go ahead, let's see what you got."

It was a challenge. For a moment, my impulse was to sit back and let him show me what he had. I was pretty certain I wasn't in the mood. Little steps seemed smarter. I needed to test his limits before I started letting him run. He was still barely out of the Academy, and he could dig us into a hole right quick if I wasn't careful.

I turned east on Trojan Avenue, my mind set on the green power box on the southwest corner of 50th St and El Cajon Boulevard. The box was a magnet for any weary crook who might want to sit and wait for a target of opportunity or an easy drug sale. They often saw the police long before we saw them, but sometimes you could surprise them, twist the odds in your favor. No half-hearted, uncommitted effort was going to generate much of an arrest. Not in this neighborhood.

If you could get up on them quick enough, the guys on the green box were generally worth talking to. So much so that sitting on that box was damn near reasonable cause to detain a person. The regular folks didn't sit there because the bad guys chased them off, and the bad guys sat there 'cause they could watch for targets and still have an avenue to run away. It was their spot.

I turned the car and headed north a block away from our target. If I could make it to the Boulevard and turn right quickly enough, I could be on anyone sitting there before they had an opportunity to flee. That was the key. You had to be on folks quick, had to swoop on them before they could formulate a plan to counter you. This was a game of strategy, and if you took too long, your subject was as gone as a ghost. That was precisely why you heard the term "ghosted" when guys talked about the one that got away.

In the game of street enforcement, there was no slow approach and certainly no driving around the block to sneak back up once you'd passed someone. You needed to be ready to move once you spotted your contact. If you gave them time to disappear, they would take advantage and you'd be left standing there looking silly. He who engaged first had the best chance of staying on top. This was no secret to cops or crooks. It was the most basic rule of the game.

I put my foot on the accelerator. We had one shot. If we didn't get a hit on something and didn't get it quick, we were back in the rotation for the next radio call. Liz would forgive us if we grabbed an arrest. The rest of the troops would understand if we got tied up, as long as we didn't make a day of it.

What wouldn't be tolerated was Stevie and me out here hunting what we wanted while everyone else was busy dealing with all the calls. The troops were okay for short periods, but if you got a reputation for jamming others, for only being a felony cop, your future was limited. We didn't have the staffing for people to simply ignore the radio. On the other hand, everyone knew that sometimes you needed the chance to control your own day, if only a little. It was the balance between those ends that made up part of your reputation. If you abused the balance, there would be a price to pay.

I spoke as I started braking for the stop sign. "As soon as we come up on the corner, there's going to be a green power box to our right. If there's someone sitting on it, or standing next to it, I need you to watch their hands. If they toss anything keep track of where it goes. I'll do the rest. We get a rabbit, you sit tight unless I go after him. If I do, then we stay together. Got it?"

"Got it," Stevie said. His voice was a little higher, little tighter. From the corner of my eye, I could see him tense. The adrenaline was dumping into his system, and he was starting to charge up. That happened. He figured we were about to engage, and his mind was racing. I was hoping he would keep it reined in enough that he didn't turn in to a liability. I didn't need him running off by himself again.

We were close. In moments, we'd have something or we wouldn't. It was that simple. It got complicated only by the fact that our encounter could be something that ranged from an easy conversation to a gunfight. Odds were against the gunfight, but we were still actively looking for someone up to no good. We were doing it in an area with greater than average crime issues, and we were looking for something narcotics related. That meant possible gang involvement, and it meant possible gun involvement. Despite the odds, a gunfight still needed to be a consideration. Since we'd be getting up close, we'd also need to consider weapons like knives.

I did a rolling stop as I came upon the intersection. As soon as I could see that no one was coming, I blew through the stop sign and turned right on El Cajon Boulevard.

There he was, just as predicted—a black male sitting dead center on the box. He might have seen us quickly enough to disappear if it hadn't been for the fact that he was mid-swig on a forty ounce bottle of something in a brown paper bag. It seemed a cliché, but then I worked in a world of clichés. I love the days we get something original. In the interim, we get the bad stereotypes from an old CHiPs episode.

I almost missed the subtle pitching movement of his right hand while he lowered the raised bottle with his left. He was smooth, accustomed to being out on the streets, accustomed to being watched by the police. When he drank from the bottle, there was no tilt of the head. There was only a turn upward of the bottle. That kept the eyes level to continue scanning his surroundings. It didn't buy him enough time to get away, but it bought enough to pitch his dope. Unfortunately, dope or not, he was mine. If he was going to have any chance to take off, he needed to start running now.

I turned the wheel hard and pulled the passenger side tires up on the curb as I jammed the car into park. The front end of our cruiser faced our contact so both Stevie and I could see him without cranking our necks to the side. The public hated this maneuver, screamed about how it was aggressive and that we just ran up on people who weren't doing anything wrong. When it came down to it, they were right. It was aggressive. However, in this instance, he was loitering on a public utility box, and he was drinking alcohol in a restricted public place. He was up to at least two things I could address. There was a chance it wasn't alcohol in that forty ounce bottle. But the odds were against it, and to contact him, I only had to believe it was more likely he was drinking booze than not. To my knowledge, Pepsi hadn't started serving in that size.

Stevie and I got out of the car and came at him from different sides. His chances of getting away were quickly diminishing. The odds of my getting control of the moment were increasing at a proportionate rate.

I recognized him just a little more quickly than he recognized me.

Chapter 18

"EDDIE TAYLOR," I announced as I approached him. Stevie came around wide and blocked his route the other way. "That you sittin' on my green box?"

I knew Eddie, had known him since he was fourteen and running dope on his bike, bought and paid for by the bigger thugs in the neighborhood. To say he was a low level dealer was an understatement. Eddie never really broke into the world of distribution much beyond what it took to support his own petty habit. The funny thing about addiction is that it keeps you from being what you could have been. That truth extends to include success as a drug dealer.

Before he could speak, I continued. "Stand up for me, please. Leave your bottle on the ground." I wanted him to think this was about a citation.

"That's not my bottle," he lied.

"I saw you holding it." I took hold of his upper arm and his wrist.

"I seen the bag there and picked it up to see what was inside."

"You need a drink to figure that out?"

"I don't know what you thought you saw, but I didn't drink nothing, you're mistaken, Officer Hatch."

"Got it," Stevie announced proudly, holding a little plastic bag up so we could both see what he had. "What's this? Looks like a felony to me," he added. "You think we're stupid?"

I could feel Eddie's weight shift. His arm tensed as he realized he was moving from a ticket for drinking in public to a felony trip to jail. My anger surged at the kid. The dumb ass tossed our trump card while I was still working on stabilizing things. Stupid fuck. Now I had to deal with Eddie and his fight or flight reaction. If he was going to flee, he'd need to fight. He was gearing up for both.

"That ain't mine," Eddie blurted as indignantly as he could. "You ain't gonna set me up," he continued as a distraction while his eyes scanned for a way out. I needed to move quickly.

"Eddie, Eddie, Eddie," I said, calm and steady, a bark the first time I called his name, but more quietly each time thereafter. When I barked his name it got his attention, as I got calmer, he got calmer. If I was going to prevent a fight, I needed to reduce his tension. At the same time I needed to get control of him.

I brought his hand behind his back and applied a little pressure to his wrist. Not enough to injure him but enough to get his attention. "Eddie, relax, if that's not yours then you'll be on your way before long. Don't get worked up over things that haven't happened yet." I kept talking until I had him in handcuffs.

We spent the next few minutes playing the denial game. "Is that dope?"

"I don't know what dope is."

"Aren't you an addict?"

"Well I used to smoke grass a long time ago." It was always a game of minimization. "A long time ago," in doper terminology, could be earlier in the week, or an hour for that matter. He would speak vaguely and that way he could say he never lied to me. Instead, if I put him on the spot about using dope, he'd say he admitted using pot but never admitted anything else.

"So you've never seen meth," I asked.

"What?" He was stalling.

"Methamphetamine."

"Oh god, is that what that is? I hear that stuff's really bad. You gotta believe it's not mine. I'd never use something like that."

Now the debate, meth freaks will go all day long as if repeating something makes it true. They'll look you in the eyes and keep lying as you stack the evidence in front of them. When it comes to liars, they top the list.

Eddie was high. The facts were clear as soon as we started talking to him. Certain things happen when you're wasted, things that don't happen normally. Those symptoms change depending on the type of drug. In the end, you can't alter body chemistry without having some type of manifest effect. If you didn't, you wouldn't be high. A person could mask those effects but they could not eliminate them.

Eddie was out in the daylight, and yet his pupils were dilated beyond what an average person's would be in a dark room. In the bright sunlight, the pupils should have restricted. That was the stimulant fighting the body's natural reaction. His pulse pumped along at a hundred-thirty beats per minute, and he was sweating like he'd just run thirty blocks. They always said that was because they were nervous, but nerves don't get you like that. Maybe for a minute or two, but in fifteen minutes, Eddie's heart would still be chugging along like he was in a sprinting contest. It would probably do that the rest of the day. And he would shiver and fidget and squirm, all the while rambling on about subjects that had little to do with anything. That's what happens when you ingest a stimulant manufactured with the same stuff used to degrease the gunky buildup on motor engines.

"Eddie, you're high."

"No, really, Officer Hatch, I'm just nervous. You scared me when you come up on me like that." He tried to give me his most sincere look, but his bugged out eyes, the deep lines in his face, and the dry lips he kept smacking from thirst made his sincerity look more like a caricature.

"Close your eyes and stick out your tongue."

Eddie did as he was told. The moment he closed his eyes, the lids started to flutter like he was in a full-on REM sleep. He could only keep them shut about a second and a half. No doubt this seemed like thirty minutes to him. He also couldn't keep his mouth open.

"Stick out your tongue. Pay attention Eddie."

This time the tongue came out further. Not for long, but long enough to see that it was as dry as the concrete under my boot, despite the fact that he'd just taken a swig of beer. He was as high as they came.

The dope was his too. Stevie saw him pitch it. I saw him pitch it. The little baggie landed on the ground right next to the green box where he was sitting and it was resting on some dried, dead grass as surely as if it had just landed there. The bag was shiny clean like you'd expect after having been in a sweaty tweaker's pocket, not dirty like something left lying on the ground. He could deny the facts all day long, and maybe in his burned out little brain he would come to believe them. I, however, would not. I was going to take him to jail and let the system work out his culpability. Not that I believed the system was going to fix this poor soul's problems, but I wasn't going to let him slide either.

When it comes to street drugs, meth is as big a destructive force as we face today, up there with heroin, Oxy, Ecstasy and a handful of other world class players. There are people who say we should legalize it, use the revenue to pay for treatment. We even had a retired Assistant Chief spout that garbage. Then again, he was a man that never much had a reputation for understanding police work to begin with. He was never a cop.

We'd tried that experiment, and it seemed to me that putting a tax on cigarettes to pay for the health care costs of smokers didn't work out so well. Instead of using the money for the people who paid the tax, the government used the tax to pay for other things. Drugs would be no different, and in the end we still wouldn't be making headway. Add to that the fact that meth changed the dynamics of your brain, could be instantly addictive, and could make you very volatile. I had no desire whatsoever to see such a substance legalized. If that day ever came, I'd find another career.

Eddie kept rambling while I emptied his pockets on the hood of my car. There was no frisk for weapons. This was a full on pocket-dumping search. He was going to jail. Nothing was changing that, so the contents of his pockets belonged to me. If he had a gun, a knife, a glass pipe, or another baggie of drugs, it was all good to go.

"What's this?" I asked Eddie as I held out the open palm of my hand and showed him the gold necklace piled in the middle of it.

"That's not stolen."

I chuckled. "Now why would I think it was stolen?"

"You think I'm gonna sell it for dope."

"But you don't do dope."

Eddie paused while he thought for a moment. He'd wavered on his story. "It's my mother's chain, I'm holding onto it for her."

I almost burst into laughter. "This belongs to your mother, huh?"

"She told me to hang onto it so it don't get stolen."

At least he was trying. Chances were it was stolen. I wouldn't have put it beyond Eddie to have graduated to residential burglary. Not robbery, not yet. Eddie hadn't degenerated enough to use force to take something from another person. He could, however, sneak in and take a gold necklace when someone wasn't looking. Anything to feed the monkey.

Mom probably wasn't gonna push the issue on charges even if he was a thief, so we'd confirm the chain was hers and then she could have it back. No use making her pay any more than she already had. Having a doper for a kid was punishment enough. A kid like Eddie could be a real drain on a parent.

We loaded Eddie into the back seat of our car. I was still steaming at Stevie, so much so I felt compelled to chew on his ass a bit. I restrained myself. If diplomacy could work on a turd like Roosevelt, perhaps I could use a bit on a kid that still didn't quite have a clue. If I was going to have any chance at changing his behavior, I was going to have to build some trust. We'd discuss the issue when I was calmer and we weren't in front of some fiend that didn't need to know the kid's issues.

Stevie ran Eddie for warrants on our computer while we drove to his mother's house. Twenty-four and still living with mommy.

We were halfway to Eddie's house when Stevie spoke. "No warrants, but he's a 4th waiver until March of next year."

Not much of a surprise there. Dopers who couldn't get their shit straight had a tendency to end up in this way. When you're a 4th waiver, or simply a 4th, you have already been in front of a judge for something, typically a narcotics offense. As a result, the court will often require you to waive your 4th amendment rights in order to be freed from jail early or as a result of a plea agreement.

Those who use dope have a hard time getting away from it. Those who sell dope will generally sell more dope. It's a cyclical thing, and a 4th waiver gives the police the authority to search a person, their car, or their residence without a court order. They have waived those rights to search and seizure. The reason for the search should still be reasonable, but if I'd have known this when we first contacted Eddie, I wouldn't have needed to arrest him before digging in his pockets. The contents would have been mine for the asking.

Either way you cut it, Eddie was a done deal the moment we locked him down to talk. It was no wonder he made a move at tossing the dope while we approached. He had nothing to lose. If the meth remained in his pocket, we'd have recovered it the moment we found out about his conditions. At least now he could try and convince a judge or a jury that we didn't really see him pitch anything.

We arrived at Eddie's mother's house, a rundown, three bedroom rambler built in the forties and paid for by her dead husband's years of faithful service to the Nasco shipbuilding yards. His mother, always Mrs. Taylor or Ma'am to me, was a short, dark skinned, heavyset woman who had one of those looks that was soft and serious, gentle but menacing, all at the same time. She was sitting on the front porch sewing something as we pulled up.

"Stay with him," I told Stevie as I got out of the car and started toward the house.

She greeted me before I was halfway to the porch. "You got that no good boy of mine in the back seat of your car again, don't you Mr. John Hatch?"

"Yes, Mrs. Taylor," I said as I raised a foot on the first step of the porch and lowered my head. I don't know if that was a sign of respect or if bowing was the result of that ancient ingrained sense of fear that mothers instilled in boys who grew up more than just a little rambunctious.

"Is he staying or leaving? Never you mind, if he's in the back of your car you better not leave him with me. I swear to God I'll put a beating in that boy's backside so hard you'll be coming back for me."

"No, Mrs. Taylor, he won't be staying today." I wanted to laugh and cry for her at the same time.

"Good!" She sighed. "That damn scourge is going to take away our future. You know that, don't you, Mr. John Hatch?"

"Yes, Ma'am."

Her voice softened and I could feel the painful tremor she fought. "He was a good boy once upon a time. Seems like yesterday. That stuff's made him somethin' I don't even recognize." She paused for a long moment and stared out to the back seat of my car. Then she turned back to me. "What brings you here? You wanna search his room?" She knew the routine, had been run through it enough times already.

I stuck my hand in my pocket and wrapped my fingers around the chain. "Yes, Ma'am, while I'm here, make sure he didn't leave anything in his room that could put your house in jeopardy. You're still taking care of his daughter, I expect?"

"The joy of my life. They won't get that one without going through me."

I smiled. "The main reason I'm here is about some jewelry. Did you give Eddie some stuff to look after?"

"Yes, yes," she said after thinking for a moment. "I can't afford a safe deposit box. It's just a little old gold chain and a couple rings. I gave them to him when he promised he would put them in a good hiding spot in the house. This was when he was doing good. It was a while ago."

I stepped up on the porch and handed her the chain. She smiled and took it. "Yes, that's it. No rings?"

"No, Ma'am."

"That's too bad. Stuff's not worth much, but it's mine."

"Perhaps you could find a better hiding spot."

"I'll do that. Thank you, I know you didn't have to drive this over, not even to search his room."

Mrs. Taylor led me into the house and down the hall, past the living room where Eddie's six year old daughter was sleeping on the couch. We made it to his room, and I searched quickly. There were no drugs, just some burned out pieces of tin foil, a broken half of a glass pipe, and a bunch of paper clips stretched out straight to be used as pipe cleaners to scrape up every bit of unused residue left over after he smoked his meth. The room was dirty and smelled heavily of that pungent sweat-soaked, chemical tweaker stink that gets into everything they touch or wear. A repugnant smell. I was glad to get out of the room as quickly as I was done.

Mrs. Taylor was back out on the front porch tending to her project when I came out. I closed the heavy metal security screen door as quietly as I could so as not to wake up her sleeping granddaughter. I put my hand on her shoulder as I stepped next to her.

I held the bits of paraphernalia out in my other hand as I spoke. "Just this, Ma'am. I'll impound it so it's not in your house. I looked for those rings but didn't find anything. If I can get him to tell me where they are, I'll swing by later and let you know."

"Thank you for being respectful."

I wasn't quite sure what to say. I was taking her son to jail and leaving her to take care of his young daughter. Granted, the decisions that brought us here were his, but that didn't make the moment any more comfortable. I suspected that was true for the both of us. In the end, I settled for, "You take care of that little girl," and made my way back to the car. As mad as she was at Eddie, as cooperative as she was with me, her heart was breaking the whole time I was there. But the topic was something neither of us would ever talk about.

We delivered fidgety Eddie to jail and were clear in about an hour. The radio was busy, and we spent the rest of the night handling calls, sixteen in all. We managed a couple traffic stops and filled out Field Interview forms on six young, up and coming, want-to-be gangsters. We found them sweating and walking away from Colina Park after we responded to a radio call of Asian males fighting with sticks and knives. There was no doubt they were involved, but no one located any witnesses and no bloody victims showed up at the nearby hospitals while we took care of our business. If anyone had gotten seriously hurt in the fight, we'd find out later, or maybe we wouldn't.

We got our reports signed at the 10-17 before heading in to the station. So far, good fortune had placed me and Sergeant Roosevelt in separate locations for the entire shift. My luck continued on into the Report Room and all the way until we were dismissed. I was in the locker room when my luck ran out.

I could hear him coming, not by anything he said or did, but by the fact that guys got quiet as he walked past. I didn't know it was him, didn't make the connection with the wave of silence as it washed across the lockers until he was standing at the head of my aisle. He looked pissed.

"Sergeant," I said plainly, ready to be diplomatic. I could feel everyone in the room, their ears strained to hear, their eyes trying to burn X-ray vision through the lockers.

"Don't you patronize me. What did I tell you yesterday?"

I could feel my blood boil, it came that fast. Still, I had absolutely no idea what I did that would have him so pissed off. I could think of a hundred things I might have done, given the chance, but right now I couldn't think of a single guilty sin.

"Sir, I'm not following you."

"Didn't we have a discussion yesterday about you going off and doing your own thing without asking?"

I still wasn't sure where he was heading so I shrugged.

"You always have to be smug. I'm talking about running downtown with a prisoner when I specifically asked you to check with me before doing proactive work."

Try diplomacy. The thought raced through my head, but the words came out less than diplomatic. "Did I sleep with your wife and not realize it?"

The words weren't much, but they were enough. If there had been a rocket up Sergeant Roosevelt's ass, I'd surely just lit the fuse. I might have enjoyed watching him go airborne, but I was entirely too angry to give a fuck.

I'd tried. Diplomacy was not my game. I did my best, but I had also asked for one simple favor. If he had a problem with me, he needed to address it in private. He'd been warned.

"What did you say to me?" Roosevelt demanded.

"Look, I'm sorry. I'm pretty good in the sack, and I drag on the ground like a bull elephant so I can understand why it's got you so worked up. I wouldn't have done her if I'd known."

"In my office, right now," he screamed. His neck was red, his face flush. There were veins bulging in his forehead. I'd hit a nerve, and I went for another.

I looked at my watch, then down at my clothes. Ten after midnight, and I was dressed in street clothes. My day was done. Time to torque the man with his own beloved rules. "I'll be more than happy to see you in your office, but you're going to need to pay me four hours callback. My shift ended ten minutes ago. On the other hand, you can wait until tomorrow, and you can chew my ass for ten full hours when I get in. It's your call. I wasn't trying to piss you off, but I told you, if you're going to take me on in front of everyone, it's only fair that I defend myself in the same manner."

From the back of the locker room I heard what I thought was a gasp. If I'd been thinking straight, it probably should have come from me. Roosevelt never broke eye contact, but he paused for a moment before speaking. "I had Eric doing some important beat surveys today. I'm trying to get a handle on our problems out there. When you went out without letting me know, I had to pull him off his project."

I wanted to choke and spit. Beat surveys? That was a load of crap, another one of those tools of the clueless. An inexperienced person's attempt to build the beat knowledge most cops got with time. I might have forgiven him if he'd spent as much time on the streets as he did in the office. Then again, that would mean he'd be out there in the middle of things. That could be worse than not being there at all.

"You could have just asked the people in this room. What do you need to know? How about that Amelia and Jonathan have lived in the same house for over fifty years. They bought it when he came back from World War II and they raised a family there. Jonathan just died, but Amelia can remember when she lived in a wonderful neighborhood that wasn't on the edge of a shithole plagued by gangs and drugs.

"And Mrs. Taylor, she lives in the middle of that shithole on the front lines of the gangs and drugs. She lost a nephew to the gangs and her son—the one you are presently chewing my ass over—

to drugs. She should be enjoying her retirement, but she's taking care of her grandchild full time.

"If you want to know about what's going on out there, the guys in this room are the ones who can tell you. Show them a little respect, and they'll give you more information than any silly beat survey."

Roosevelt was dumbfounded. He stood there speechless, and I couldn't tell if it was because he was ready to come unglued or because he'd never been talked to like this before.

I raised my hands to symbolize surrender. "He ola ka pohaku," I said as evenly and pleasantly as I could.

Roosevelt shook his head, confused. "What did you say?"

"It's a Hawaiian apology. I didn't mean to piss you off. I didn't mean to offend you at your wife's expense. Are we done for tonight, or do you want to go back to the office?"

Roosevelt paused, unsure about how to handle the apology. If he was too hard on me, if he continued to push, things might get worse. He looked from side to side at the other officers watching him, watching us.

"Go home," he said. "We'll talk about this later." When he added the last part he spoke louder so every cop in the room could hear his admonishment. I had little doubt we were through. In fact, I was quite certain I'd just opened the flood gate. What was done could not be undone, and the concept of diplomacy was a thought of the past.

I closed my locker and walked out of the station. Martinez and Jenkins ran up as I was backing out of my parking space. I lowered my window.

"Holy shit," Jenkins said. "He's going to have your ass, you know."

"Let him, ain't worth much."

"What was that apology?" Martinez asked.

"What apology?"

"The Hawaiian thing."

I grinned. "Got it off a shirt I bought on Lana'i. Not an apology at all. Hawaiian just sounds pretty." I started backing up. "I just very nicely told him, 'In the rock there is life.'"

Chapter 19

THE NEXT DAY I FULLY expected to find Theodore Roosevelt waiting for me. He'd do line-up and then order me back to his office in front of everyone. From there he would spend the first part of his day, the first part of my day, talking down to me. I would get more sound advice on how I would be okay if he could mold me into his image. There'd been little chance of that from the onset, but now I'd had enough. He was a bully, and if he wanted to play with the street cop, he could have at it. I'd weathered worse, I'd manage this round. Shift change was just a couple months away. If it got too bad, I'd transfer off his squad. Until then, I'd make his life more miserable than mine. I would play until he called the truce.

As luck would have it, Socrates took the day off. I didn't know if he'd planned for it or if yesterday had been too much for him. In any event, he wasn't there, and I anticipated a better day. Even a bad day on the streets would be better than a good day in the cubicle of boy wonder, the thinking man.

Stevie and I loaded up and were clear of the sub as quickly as we had been the day before. He seemed more at ease about working with me.

"What's the plan? Maybe we can hit the green box again. Pretty good call on your part," he said.

"We got lucky. The green box has a way of giving favorable odds."

"So let's get a report and go back."

"You can't hit the green box every day, you'll wear it out, or it'll wear you out. It will be there when we need it. Until then, let's see what else we can dig up." We still had some distance to cover before I'd call him partner, but he was trying. I had to give the kid some credit.

He still wasn't going to drive.

Our first musket ball of the day was another domestic violence report. That was pretty standard, DVs were a dime a dozen in the neighborhood. When we arrived, the live-in boyfriend was gone, leaving us with only a simple report that stated it had started out as an argument over "little things." It was always over little things, and they always escalated. When she got scared and tried to call the police, he pulled the phone out of the wall. She grabbed her cell phone and he took off. There was nothing complicated. Stevie volunteered to write the report.

I volunteered us for a second call, an in progress vandalism. We were some distance away, and the suspects were gone before we got there. I listened patiently while the homeowner complained about us never being around, and then took his information and let him tell me all about the gangsters who spray painted graffiti along his back fence. When he'd calmed down, I gave him his report number and we left. I like to think the job is more complicated than that, but sometimes it isn't.

I backed into the 7-11 so Stevie and I could write. I got him a Snapple and started on my first cup of coffee. My report was simple, and I finished first. I took a quick glance at the computer screen, which showed that the Eric Smiths of the world still smashed their asses at the sub while the rest of us where out taking the lead balls of musket fire. No doubt Roosevelt would have high praise for whatever senseless project Smith was working on. I was into my second cigarette, contemplating our plan for the day, when Sergeant Brian Rake pulled into the stall next to me.

"Afternoon, sarge," I said as he put the car in park.

"So far," he grumbled, chewing on the end of his cigar. "I figured I better get a new tin of Copenhagen before it got dark and things went to shit. All these damn non-smokers will be hitting me up for a fix just as soon as we're locked down on some scene where nobody can leave."

He was the last of a breed, a time long gone when cops had grit. No one with brass on the collar would approve of him chewing on a cigar in his car, but not a one of them would ever say a word about it. "Anything else going on?"

"Aw hell, you know better. Same shit different day. Nothin' changes round here except the faces and the names at the top of the memos." Sergeant Rake took a moment to chew on his cigar. It wasn't lit, but he didn't seem to care. "Tell me about what happened with you and Roosevelt last night?"

That was old school, just the facts. There was little point easing into something when you could just spit it out. He said what he thought and did as he promised.

"You heard about that?"

He raised an eyebrow and I realized my mistake. Rake had been on since before dirt was old. He had sources that extended far beyond any normal person, probably beyond the Chief in many instances.

"Sorry, forgot who I was talking to."

His door popped open and he stepped out. "Make room, boy."

Shuffling aside, I continued, "Seems my new sergeant doesn't much like me. He thinks I'm a bit behind the curve, behind the times. He thinks me a dinosaur."

"You old," he chuckled and spit a piece of cigar. "That baby cop's barely been around long enough to figure out he can stand when he pees. What do you suppose a guy like that thinks of me?"

"I expect he'd be scared of you. I wouldn't worry 'til he was a Captain and he could order someone else to fuck with you."

"Let him try," he said in his gravelly voice. "What kinda new age nonsense is he giving you shit about?"

"Seems to think I'm out here fucking around, taking too long on unimportant issues."

He grumbled something I couldn't make out. "You clear calls quick as anyone. Put your share of shitbags in jail too. I'd take you in a hot second if I had the room for you." I knew he meant it, and I'd go to work for a guy like him in that same hot second. You could count on the Brian Rakes of the Department. They might be a little rough around the edges, but they knew the game. If they hadn't been able to adapt, they'd have long ago disappeared. That didn't mean they had to become something they weren't.

I continued. "We grabbed Eddie Taylor yesterday with dope, nothing serious but sometimes you have to do that. We were done and back in the field in just over an hour. Sixteen calls, two arrests, and a half dozen FI's sums up most of the day. No slacking on our end, but he laid into me just the same. Seems he wanted to taste some ass for not letting him know we'd be out on the one proactive arrest we found the time to work into our day. Worst of all, for some reason he felt compelled to do it in the locker room in front of everyone."

Sergeant Rake thought for a moment. "That must make it kinda hard to get shit done, a guy breathing down your neck."

"Certainly not the way I prefer to work."

"What's your plan for today?"

"Radio calls. If we get lucky, Stevie and I might get to work in a couple follow-ups for homicide."

Rake grinned, a rare gesture. "Stevie?"

I shrugged and spoke quietly. "Fits. Maybe I'm not old, but old enough."

Rake looked through the back window and gave a short nod. "Which case?"

"The woman who was beaten and choked to death last week. Our beat, thought I could at least talk to some more of the neighbors."

"Sounds like police work," he said as he walked toward the store. A few minutes later he returned with a cup of coffee and a tin of Copenhagen. He settled back into his car, started the engine, and put the cruiser in reverse.

Before backing out, Sergeant Rake pulled the cigar out of his mouth and held it between his two beefy knuckles. He glanced at Stevie who was sitting in the passenger seat typing away, then spoke loud enough so both of us could hear. "Don't sweat what you can't change, and don't let him get the best of you. Do what you need to do, just be smart about it. Between you and him, I'll lay odds on you any day. Guys like him come and go. This too will pass."

He backed up a foot and then stopped again. This time he spoke only loud enough for me to hear. "Incidentally, that weak fuck took the day off. As long as the calls get handled, I wouldn't be getting too worked up over you taking the time to do whatever you might feel needed attention."

Sergeant Rake put his cigar back in his mouth and backed out of the lot. It would be the last I'd see him for the remainder of the night. That is, unless we needed him. Then he'd be there. Until that happened, he'd be wherever it was sergeants like him disappeared until the need arose for them to reappear. He'd know what was going on, and he'd be out rolling around the streets, watching the city, but most of the time he'd be as much a ghost as the parolee you went around the block to get a second look at.

I leaned back on the car and lit another cigarette. He knew what was going on, probably knew more about our confrontation than I did. That wasn't the point of our talk. This was his way of checking on me, making sure I wasn't stressing out too much, his way of letting me vent and letting me know that I wasn't the only one with less than a little respect for Socrates. Sergeant Rake would never say otherwise, not in public, not unless Roosevelt took him on. In private, he wouldn't hold back his disdain for the man. That's what this conversation was about, that and another thing—permission to work the way I wanted. At least for today I knew I wouldn't have a sergeant breathing down my neck. Because of that, I'd make sure we covered our share of the calls.

I leaned in the car and checked our computer. There was a message from Liz. It simply said, "Be glad you're on that DV and not in Eastern, they're working a rather grizzly sounding murder-suicide." I thought about sending a reply, then figured I'd let Stevie concentrate. My boss was no doubt auditing everything anyway. No point giving him ammunition by sending chatty messages. He didn't need to know who I knew, or what I knew. He didn't need to know where my resources were. I might not have the contacts a Brian Rake did, and I might not have the rank that allowed me to make others do things, but that didn't mean I was without support. I'd keep those contacts to myself until I needed them.

I returned to my coffee. My thoughts turned immediately to Esther. If we had a green light to get some work done, I wanted to take advantage. What was it about this murder that wasn't working, why couldn't I make some connections? She was dead—strangled, suffocated, and beaten. Whoever killed her left her lying on the floor, and in an extra fit of rage tossed the mattress on top of her. Whoever killed her was angry. That still put the husband in the hot seat. I couldn't for the life of me figure out why that bothered me.

My mind drifted to another, similar deal . . . another rage killing. Jack and I had been working together at the time. We responded to a radio call from a man who came home and found two of his roommates dead in the house up near San Diego State.

When we got there, the roommate was waiting outside. He was frantic, and we couldn't understand much of what he was telling us. The only thing he could say clearly was that no one was breathing and something about brains.

We entered the house and found them in the bedroom, the man first. He was lying on his back, his head bunched up against the footboard of the bed. There was a small hole in his right temple. Around that were some burn marks. The wound was a bit jagged, and there was some discoloration in the skin that looked like a tattoo. The other side of his head was a bit more distorted and his eyes bulged outward.

The revolver was on the floor next to his right hand and his forefinger was still in the trigger guard, just the way they landed. He'd stood in the room and pointed the gun at his temple before pulling the trigger. The tattoo looking marks were from burned powder particles that cleared the muzzle with enough velocity to imbed themselves in his skin. His death made sense, even to a relatively new officer.

His young wife was a few feet away. He found out she'd been cheating on him and lost his shit. She was in the corner of the room crumpled into a ball. Her forearms were battered from trying to fight him off and there were red and blue marks where he'd beaten her viciously. She was still warm, and there were three holes in her head. He'd beaten her in his rage, and then he shot her until she was good and dead. As senseless as it was, the whole scene made sense.

As we'd walked back down the stairs, you could see the trail of tossed and broken items that started in the living room and went to the bedroom. You could tell where the fight started and ended. The whole scene was all tied up in a neat little package. That's the way with homicides, mostly.

That's when a thought hit me. It wasn't the pictures or the crime scene that bothered me. For much of the past week I'd been racking my brain trying to figure out something I wasn't seeing. It wasn't what *I* was missing but *what* was missing that got me.

I'd missed the clue that night when we responded to the radio call, missed it again when I looked at the pictures. What I wanted to see was right there in front of me the whole time. I should have picked up, got a sense, when we arrested Eddie. He should have been the contact that gave me what I needed to sort out the missing piece. The answer to my question had been neatly stashed in Eddie's pocket. I reached into the car, pulled my cell phone from the window visor, and called Homicide. With any luck Ronny would still be in the office.

The phone rang three times. I was anticipating a fourth ring and voicemail when the line clicked. "San Diego Police, Detective White."

"Ronny, Hatch, glad I caught you."

"What's up, you come up with something right at the end of my day?"

"Dunno yet, still chasing ghosts. You got those pictures there?"

"Yeah."

"Look through and tell me if there's any jewelry in the box on the dresser."

"Hold on," he said as he set the phone down. I started tapping my foot and lit another cigarette. A couple minutes later he came back on the line. "You there? Yeah, looks like there's a couple pieces in the drawers, three to be exact."

"Did you find anything on the floor?"

"Not that I remember." I could hear Ronny shuffling through some papers. A moment later he answered. "It doesn't look like we impounded any either."

"Not even in his stuff? Maybe in his truck?"

"I'm with ya, not even in his stuff. I checked."

"Don't you find it a bit odd that she'd only have three pieces of jewelry in a box with four drawers? They might not have had a lot of money, but you'd think the thing would be stacked with earrings and shit, even if it was junk. I just figured that all her jewelry had probably been knocked on the floor."

"Which brings us back to a stranger murder rather than the husband. That adds a new twist, but it still doesn't explain the anger, and that husband's an angry guy."

"Yeah, doesn't mean it wasn't him, just means we didn't find the stuff on him. Not yet anyway. That's what was screwing me up. The rage doesn't fit with a surprised burglary attempt. That nothing was missing left me to think husband. He had the rage potential and might very well have staged the house, but there was nothing to indicate he did. On the other hand, with things missing, burglary starts making sense again, but the reason for rage gets fuzzy. Somewhere there is a connection here that makes sense."

"Okay, let me check through some more photos and see if I'm just missing the jewelry. If not, I'll check into the husbands property a little more. If I don't find it there, I'll check pawn records and see if he's been selling anything. Maybe he's hittin' the tweak a little much lately or money is tight. If I can get through it all tonight, I'll give you a call. If not, I'll get with you tomorrow."

"Thanks, Ronny."

"Any time. That was a good thought. With all that's been going on, I hadn't even thought about the jewelry. It just looked like that box had been knocked around during the confrontation. Good observation. You ready to quit playing in the street and start doing some real police work?"

"You ever see me behind a desk, you have my permission to put a bullet in my head."

"It's not as bad as you make it."

"But it's not the streets. I'll talk to you later. Thanks for checking into that."

I hung up and went into 7-11 for a refill. We had things to do, and I might not get the opportunity for another cup.

CHAPTER 20

STEVIE WAS STILL TYPING on his laptop when I got back to the car. I hated to disrupt him because that would cost us time later, but we needed to get moving, needed to take advantage of our day. Sergeant Rake had given us a green light to hunt.

"Do you want to keep writing, or what?"

"Huh?" Stevie said with a start. He was too wrapped up in his report, a bad habit if you want to survive the streets. "I said, is your mother single?"

A confused look spread across his face, then changed when he realized what I said. "What the hell kind of question is that?"

"A simple one, is your mother single? Is she hot? I'm looking for something to keep me occupied on Saturday night, maybe make a headboard knock against the wall."

"Hell no, she ain't single. Not for you. You interrupted me for that?"

"No," I said plainly. "I interrupted you for something else, but you were too busy with that report to pay any attention to what was going on around you." I'd meant to leave the pay attention speech for later in the evening. I'd wanted to make time that wouldn't be confrontational, but he needed to learn.

"What I asked was whether you wanted to keep writing?"

"I'm not done."

"Irrelevant. We can come back to it. Unless you don't want to take advantage of things being quiet to do some more police work. Yesterday was good, even if you nearly got me into a fight."

"Excuse me," Stevie choked. "How do you figure?"

I tried to keep my voice calm, even. "You did a good job keeping your eyes on Eddie, even caught him pitching the dope. I appreciate that, but you lost your focus and waved the baggie right in front of his face before I had him cuffed. It was fast talking and quick cuffs that kept him from fighting. Just now you had your head so buried in that computer you didn't even hear my question."

"So I'm gonna get the grumpy guy lecture again?"

"Yesterday you might have. Today I'm not inclined to lay into you. It was a simple mistake. I'd prefer if it doesn't keep happening, but no lecture today. The rest of the contact was good, and no one got hurt."

Stevie glanced at his computer, then thought for a moment. He looked back at me when he spoke. "I didn't even think about him fighting," he said as he shook his head. "I thought you had a hold of him. Sorry."

"Don't sweat it. Training point only. Never reveal everything you know until you're ready to make it work to your advantage."

"Sorry."

"You already said that. Consider it forgotten. So are you inclined to do a little more cop shit today or not?"

"Didn't you get in trouble for that yesterday?"

"That's not the point."

"I don't want to get in trouble."

"So you don't want to work?"

"It's not that I don't want to . . ." His words trailed off and he looked back at his computer. He was struggling. He didn't want to piss off our sergeant.

Roosevelt was having his desired effect. He was developing an atmosphere of control by fear, the difference between being a leader and being a boss. The result was that self-initiated actions would suffer. Guys would be too afraid to get in trouble to demonstrate too much effective work effort. They would handle the radio, they would talk to enough people to show they were busy, but they wouldn't push and try to accomplish anything he might get after them about. They would be exactly what he wanted and nothing more. God forbid they did something to the contrary. That type of management philosophy stifled creativity and initiative.

Of course, it could be the other way. He could be one of those sergeants that just wanted his people doing proactive enforcement, one of those guys that would have you hunting petty dopers all night while the other squads handled the radio and filled the vacuum of work that needed to be done. That wasn't good either.

Roosevelt was more interested in appearance. He wanted his guys doing beat surveys, projects that had little to do with anything real. He wanted projects that gave an impression of work without having to get out there in the trenches and hunt. Unfortunately, neither way taught the new guys balance. Both neglected that area in between where the radio got handled and bad guys went to jail.

The other day Stevie had gone to bat for me. He intervened when I lost my cool on the college kid. Today was my turn. "Look, don't worry about whether I got yelled at. That has nothing to do with you. If you want to keep writing, we can sit tight until you're done. If not, we'll catch up on paper later. In the interim, we'll take advantage of the radio being quiet and do a couple follow-ups on that homicide from last week. If Socra . . . Roosevelt . . . gives you any grief, or puts you on the spot, you tell him it was my idea. I'm senior guy in the car, my heat to ride."

Stevie continued to think, evaluate risk. "We'll come back to this?"

"Even if we have to stay late. I won't leave you hanging."

He slammed the lid shut and stuffed the computer between the car seats. "Then let's go. If I never see another DV, it'll be too damn soon."

We were moving before he had a chance to change his mind. I headed toward Esther's street as I spoke. "I called Homicide. Something about that scene last week doesn't seem right. I wish I could explain it right now but I can't, not fully. Something is missing from the picture. I thought we'd go check with some of the neighbors, see if we can come up with anything more."

Concern returned to his face. "Shouldn't Homicide be doing that? I mean, the case is theirs."

"Who says? You think we can only work on DV's and vandalisms?"

"Well, no . . . but I've never done a follow-up for something like this."

"No different than a witness check for any other crime, we're just gonna talk to some of the neighbors, see if anyone is around who wasn't the other night. We'll keep a list of everyone we talk to and what they have to say, send that to Homicide when we're done. Saves them the grunt work and gives us practice on something different."

"You don't think it's the husband?"

"Probably is, but probably doesn't make a conviction. Something in my gut is telling me we're missing part of the story. If I could explain what that was, we wouldn't need to go. I can't. So I want to check some things out for my piece of mind. If further scrutiny turns into a big nothing, all we lose is time and effort. Either way, we get some good practice investigating, and people in the neighborhood get the feeling the police are actually doing something."

"So why is Sergeant Roosevelt giving you such a hard time then?"

"Fuck him." I hadn't meant for that to come out. I thought about trying to retract the words, to minimize what I said. After all, Stevie was new and there was no telling what kind of cop he'd grow up to be. It was entirely possible he'd learn to believe the crap Socrates belched, that he'd be influenced. If I went running my mouth, Stevie could very well be the one who went back to him with the details. Fuck him.

"Your sergeant thinks I'm an old school cop who just doesn't understand the way things work. He wants me to be a certain way, do things his way. If I could do that, I'd be him. I'm not. The way I work has been working for me for a lot longer than he's been around. It worked for other guys before that. Between you and me, his thoughts are a load of shit."

"So you're willing to get your ass chewed?"

I laughed. "My ass has been chewed so many times it has calluses. Get used to that. If it's not the sergeant, it'll be the public. Everything we do makes someone unhappy. If you're trying to find a way to do business that won't offend anyone, you're in the wrong job. Every arrest, every report, and every traffic stop you need to justify your actions. The best you can hope for is that your actions are the result of the right intentions. The ass chewings and the unhappiness that result are inevitable."

"Yeah, but you're not new. You're not still on probation."

"Maybe so, but I'm still the senior guy in the car. That means that, ultimately, I'm the one he'll come after. You get any flak about this, you dump the whole decision on me. His ass-chewing's are like a teething puppy. Drawing blood's an accident."

Stevie sat quietly for the next few blocks as he thought about what I said. He was still worried. There was nothing I could do about that. If he was going to continue to be a cop, he'd need to learn to let go of the worry or find a way to deal with the stress.

Small minded bureaucrats had been around a lot longer than the two of us. Considering the way the world was headed, I didn't see that fact changing any time soon.

I let him think on things until we got to Esther's street. When I parked the car, I turned to him before he could get out.

"Here's the deal. Chances are we're not going to come up with anything today. We'll knock on some doors and talk to whoever is around. Most of the time people in this neighborhood are reluctant to get involved. Maybe they're afraid, maybe they just don't like cops. Mostly they're good folks, but there's no telling what we'll run into."

I reached down to the side of my seat and pulled out a small spiral note pad. I folded it open to a clean page. "Do me a favor. Make note of each house we go to, each apartment, and keep them in the order we check. If we talk to anyone, we'll get their name and a phone number, that way Homicide can get a hold of them later. If we find someone with information that might be helpful, I'll make note in my notebook. I'll write a narrative explaining what we did when we're done."

"Wouldn't it be faster to just split up and take opposite sides of the street?"

"Yeah, we could knock on more doors, but if there's two of us, that leaves one person free to look around while the other one is talking. If I'm speaking to someone and you're watching, you might pick up on something I don't."

You could almost see Stevie's chest rise with a bit of pride. We were working something as team, and he clearly found a bit of satisfaction in that. I didn't doubt that he hated the thought of being the note-taking sidekick, but at least he felt a part of things. In reality, I just wasn't entirely comfortable setting him free to check on his own. He still had attention to environment issues.

If we did turn up something, I wanted to make sure we could document it in the best manner possible. Our work would be judged by the quality of what we turned, in whether that resulted in anything substantive or not. Since I'd done this before and he had not, he would have to follow my lead.

I typed Liz a message to let her know where we would be and that we'd be out of the car. She would recognize the nature of the follow-up, perhaps even made the connection when I put out the street. I didn't add anything more. If Roosevelt was auditing my transmissions he'd have to make the connection himself.

When we got out of the car, I walked up to the hood and leaned back against it. The afternoon had been warm, but the evening brought a cool breeze. Not enough to chill you, just enough to raise a goosebump or two on your arms. Today was certainly nothing similar to jacket weather. I'd long ago given that up, and a night like this was never wasted on the memory of bitter, cold, sunless days.

For the moment there was nothing to do but sit and watch the neighborhood. Now was a little earlier in the day than it had been when we first got the call. Aaron Anderson's truck was gone. I wondered if Homicide had impounded his ride. Where he was now was anyone's guess. The house was dark. Perhaps he was at work. Murder or not, the real world didn't allow for long grieving breaks for those who lived paycheck to paycheck. Then again, considering his background, he could still be on the upside of an extra long drunken bender. And maybe he just couldn't stand to be in the house. Whatever the reason, he wasn't there now, and the house sat quietly unobtrusive on the one side of the street. Around it, life went on.

"What are we doing?" Stevie asked.

"Just looking."

He glanced up and down the street, his eyes straining to find whatever it was I was looking at. He waited a half minute before shrugging. "I give. You see something?"

"Not a damn thing."

He sighed. "Good, I thought it was just me."

"Nope, just trying to see if there was anything out of place. Come on."

We would work our way up one side of the street and back down the other. If we didn't come up with anything, we'd clear for today and check the adjacent streets or another block when we got a chance.

Liz's voice disrupted my thoughts. "813-Yellow and a unit to clear and cover, I'm getting a report of a fight at Colina Park."

I listened for someone to answer up. A one man unit heading to a fight. Considering the park, it was probably a bunch of little thugs. Motherfucker. Just when I thought we were going to get a chance to do something worthwhile, the radio chirped up to bite us in the ass. No one was clearing to cover, and we were close enough that officer safety was about to take precedent over our desire to hunt for a bad guy. Homicide or not, we didn't have the staffing to not pay attention to the guys we worked with.

I reached up to the radio microphone clipped to the epaulet on my shirt. "831-Zebra, we'll drop and clear to cover 813-Yellow."

I was a half step to the car when Sergeant Rake got on the air. His voice rumbled over the little speaker. "823 Sam, leave that unit on their call, I'll cover on that fight."

"I'll be damned," I said out loud. I started back to the corner at a stepped up pace. "Come on, we'd better get to our shit. I don't want to head in at the end of the night with nothing to show for our efforts. Not if the sergeant is going to cover our calls. If you think Roosevelt can chew ass, you best not test Rake. Take advantage of any opportunity he gives you."

Chapter 21

WE WENT THROUGH THE first three houses and an eight unit apartment complex rather quickly. At least half the time, no one answered the door because they were either gone or just didn't want to get up and talk to us. One apartment had a loud TV blaring in the back bedroom, but the resident either left it on to give the appearance that someone was home or they couldn't be bothered long enough to get up from their afternoon fill of Oprah. I used my most obnoxious cop knock on the security screen, but still no one answered.

The one pristine house on the street was owned by a retired Navy man who had been out-of-town in his modified pick-up camper when the murder happened. From the onset, he clearly didn't have anything to offer, but we still spent a good ten or fifteen minutes listening to him gripe.

"The young people these days, not like it used to be. In my day we were too busy working. You were too tired to do drugs. These kids don't know how good they have it. You should make these kids go into the military, or put 'em in jail. That was the options we got." He spoke with conviction like I was the one with the power to make those decisions. In his mind, I was the police, and people had to do what I wanted. Wouldn't that be a different world?

There was no explaining any difference to him. Never mind that half the recommendations he had for fixing the world would have given the ACLU and the social workers something to gripe about well into the next century. I listened until we could make our escape.

Despite Sergeant Rake's help, our efforts were interrupted, and we had to leave four times as we checked the neighborhood. The first was to cover Murphy on a stop on University Avenue. He'd pulled over a car and wanted someone to watch the three occupants while he searched the vehicle. When he was done, Murph gave the driver a ticket for a cracked windshield. One of the passengers went to jail for an outstanding gang related warrant. The other passenger, also a documented gang member on probation, got off with a field interview documenting where he was and who he was with. A little bit of follow-up to his Probation Officer might cost him a couple months in county for associating with other gangsters. Tonight, he just got his name written down.

The next call was a man and a woman screaming at each other. I figured it was surely going to be our second DV of the night and that it would kill our ability to finish checking the neighborhood, but luck favored us—turned out to be nothing more than a thirty-something brother and sister still living in their parent's home and engaging in a contest of he who yells loudest wins.

"Maybe we should just clear and handle some more calls," Stevie sighed after our fourth interruption, defeated by the grind of doing one thing for a few minutes only to be torn from that task and tossed into something else.

"Just a little more," I said, suddenly feeling more like a father than anything else.

I knew what he was feeling. Working this way was tiring. Back when we had more cops, you could focus, take that little bit of extra time, but those days were gone. In a city with one of the leanest cops per citizen ratios in the country, you had to dig in, endure the disruptions if you wanted to get anything accomplished. I was as weary as he was, but something kept pushing me. Maybe it was the hope that this would turn into a worthwhile endeavor, or maybe I was just misguided in my efforts. That was the risk, and I started to get that sick feeling in my stomach that maybe I was just exerting a great deal of effort that was better spent on something else. The grind of the day was brewing an anticipation of disappointment.

"Let's just finish this side of the street. It's getting dark, and I don't want to be knocking on doors too late."

"Whatever," Stevie said. The sense of pride he'd exhibited earlier had given way to slumped shoulder submission. He wrote down the number of the apartment where we stood and waited for the next round.

We were about two thirds of the way through another eight unit apartment building, the kind of complex you find scattered throughout East San Diego. The kind of apartments slum lords built. They could get eight times the rent for a building that took up a single lot that had once held a nice house not unlike the one where the old Navy guy with all the answers lived. Each apartment faced the same way. There was a sidewalk on one side, four apartments on the ground level, and four on the upper, with a staircase on either end of what amounted to nothing more than a giant rectangular box.

A balcony ran the length of the upper level. The few plants out front were dead, long since crushed by people making their way from the alley to the street. Though there were security gates for the street and alley entries, those locks had long ago given way to tampering. There was no security in a place like this save for the heavy, metal screen door on the front of each apartment, a screen so thick that it was impossible to see into the residence from the outside. The windows were covered with wrought iron bars that were rusty and covered with flaking paint.

I knocked on the security door. The metal screen vibrated like a rattled bird cage. The clamor was answered by the yap of a small and annoying dog.

The next response was female, high pitched and raspy. "Who's there," she asked abruptly.

"San Diego Police."

My announcement was met with grumbling. The doorknob turned, and the inside door was quickly pulled open. The security door clattered but remained closed. "What," she said in a tone that was more demand than greeting. "You tell those people downstairs that Mr. Biggles hasn't made a peep all day. If they tell you otherwise, they're lying. You can tell when someone is lying, can't you mister police officer?"

"Yes, Ma'am, generally, but the neighbors didn't call." I wasn't sure if she heard what I said, because as soon as I started speaking, the lap dog started bouncing against the screen and barking at me. I expected that was Mr. Biggles.

"Mr. Biggles, you pipe down while Mommy is talking to the police officers."

I was right, and like most rodent dogs he didn't mind very well.

"What are you here about? Mr. Biggles, shush." The scolding

seemed to only agitate the creature. "Does this have something to do with those pothead hippies down the hall?" Her voice lowered and converted to baby talk, "Come on little boogaboo, let mommy talk now." Still there was no compliance from the dog.

"Oh, come here," the woman said. I couldn't see what she was doing, but there was a grunt, and then Mr. Biggles changed from a bark to a growl, then back to a bark and another growl. The screen door opened and the woman stood there holding the dog in her arms. She was an older lady, but I couldn't tell exactly what that meant. She looked ninety, but I guessed she was closer to sixty, and the years had simply been hard ones. Determining her weight was made entirely too difficult by the muumuu she was wearing.

"Come in, come in," she demanded waving her free hand at us. "Mr. Biggles won't quit barking unless you come inside. He's a wonderful watch dog," she said in that raspy voice. "Aren't you? Yes, you are a wonderful watch dog," she told ankle chewer in her baby voice. I wanted to leave.

Stevie and I stepped into the apartment. It was filthy. At first glance it was clear that Mr. Biggles and the woman spent the majority of their time on the reclining chair in front of the television. There was an old plastic TV tray next to the recliner. On it was a remote, maybe six packs of cigarettes in various stages of depletion, and an ashtray the size of a bucket. The tray which had once been white was now a yellowish gray. It made me want to toss my own pack of cigarettes in the toilet.

The couch next to the chair was covered with tabloid magazines and entertainment periodicals. There was a blanket covered in dog hair at the end of the couch nearest the recliner, no doubt Mr. Biggles' throne. The whole place reeked of old ashtray with a not so subtle tinge of dog urine.

"Sit," she said as she pushed some magazines to the side.

"No, thank you, Ma'am. I've been sitting most of the day, feels good to stand." There was no way my backside would touch that couch. I'd sat on worse. Hell, I'd touched worse, but that didn't mean I was going to volunteer. Ten seconds in that filth and my uniform was shot. I'd have an ass full of dog hair the rest of the day. Just being in this place was going to make the smell linger in my nose until long after we went home.

"Maybe your young partner then?"

"Yeah, go ahead, partner," I said with a wave of my hand.

He swallowed hard, his apprehension a little bit more up front than mine. "Ah, no, thank you . . . I've been sitting too much myself."

"Suit yourself," she said as she sat back in her recliner. "Do you mind," she asked as she grabbed a pack of cigarettes. She was quick and damn near had it lit when I told her we didn't. Stevie's frown demonstrated that he didn't agree with me. She lit up just the same.

"If not the neighbors, why are you here?" she rasped. Mr. Biggles squirmed and growled in her lap.

"We're just checking the neighborhood to see if anyone saw anything the other night when your neighbor got murdered."

"Oh my," she said, "that was a horrible thing." She lowered her voice as if merely speaking her next words might bring about reality. "You don't suppose it was one of those rapists they're always talking about in the news. Those guys that break into women's homes and abuse them, do you?"

She was serious. Perhaps he even had his sights set on her as his next victim.

"You don't think I'm in any danger, do you?"

I wanted to tell her no, but the reality of this twisted world was that you never knew. If Esther's killer was a prowler and he got startled, then surely the loud, raspy voiced woman was as much at risk as anyone. And her annoying little Mr. Biggles too.

"I think if you keep your doors locked and pay attention to anything out of the ordinary, you should be okay."

"Oh, good," she wheezed. "That makes me feel much better. I don't go out much except to get my mail and go to the store. Oh, and I go to my sister's twice a month. She lives in El Cajon. Not the street, mind you, but over in the city. That's where I was last week when it happened. I wasn't even home."

Shit. That did it. I'd gotten myself drawn into the wheezing, raspy-voiced old lady house from hell, and now I was stuck here talking to her and listening to her stupid dog bark and growl until I could make a break for it. She probably didn't get much company, and the two of us would be enough to keep her talking for hours. I'd need to get a grip on that, or we'd have to pretend we got an emergency radio call just so we could leave.

"So you were in El Cajon. Well, we'll just get your name so we can say that we talked to you, and then I'm afraid we'll have to be on our way. We need to check the rest of your neighborhood before it gets dark."

"Those people won't be able to tell you anything. The people in this neighborhood wouldn't know what to pay attention to if their life depended on it." She chuckled. "Ha ha, that's kind of funny isn't it. If their life depended on it. No, no one around here seems to care much about this neighborhood at all. If they did, they would find better things to do than make up stories about a poor old lady and her dog."

"I expect they would," I said. "I'm sorry, but I didn't get your name." I glanced to my left and saw that Stevie already had his pen out. He'd had to ask a couple people to repeat things for him tonight. He wasn't going to make that mistake here.

"Genevieve Gardenhieder," she said.

Stevie started to roll his eyes and then caught himself. "Ma'am, you're going to have to spell that one for me."

"Oh, common spelling. Genevieve is just like normal but the Gardenhieder comes from Iowa. There's lots of us there. You haven't heard the name? My father was the mayor of our town, lot of us came out here in the fifties. Certainly I'm not the first you've run into. Maybe you know my sister."

She was the first, and that was a certainty. There couldn't really be others.

Genevieve spelled her name for Stevie and then continued before he could even ask for her phone number. There was no getting out of this easy, and we were going to have to struggle to get every scrap of information we needed on a woman who wasn't even around when the murder happened.

"It's not surprising, you know. I mean if it wasn't one of those stalker rapists, it's no surprise with the life that young couple led. People coming and going all hours of the day and night—and fights, oh boy were there fights."

"Excuse me," I said. "What kind of fights?"

"The yelling kind," she said nodding rapidly. "Those two would go at it maybe twice week, sometimes more. Sometimes he'd leave, sometimes she would. Other times it would just get quiet after a while when one of them got drunk and passed out for the evening. You guys should know this. The police have been out before."

Yup, there it was, the standard thought. If one cop was out, then we all knew everything about what they did and what happened because we talk about everything that goes on everywhere. Sorry, if I didn't go out to the house myself, then chances were I never heard a thing about it. Two people arguing in their home is rarely the topic of conversation when the cops make it back to the station at the end of the night.

"I'm afraid the other night was the first time we were there."

"Ah," she said as if the idea was incredulous. "Well I'd hear them, or Mr. Biggles would, and so I'd go look through that window and you can see right into their front yard."

I looked out the window nearest her recliner. It wasn't a great view of the Anderson house, but you could see the driveway and the street. "Did you ever see him hit her?"

"I saw him push her on the driveway once. And another time they were arguing and the slutty blonde girl she hangs out with came over and picked her up. She and her husband yelled the whole time. Then she got in her friend's car and they drove off with her hanging out the window and yelling back at him all the way down the street. He threw a beer bottle at the car as it drove away even."

Our fifth interruption came over the radio as the dispatcher spoke more loudly than normal. My attention slipped from Genevieve to the radio. "I need a couple units to clear for multiple calls of a stabbing on beat 831." That was it. The call was on our beat, and we were going to need to go regardless of who else answered up. Sergeant Rake had run interference the best he could, but now it was time to get back to work.

"831-Zebra, we'll be en route just as soon as we can get back to our car," I acknowledged. Marcus, Jenkins, and Martinez also answered up. They'd no doubt beat us there, but that didn't mean we weren't going.

"Ma'am, we're going to need to leave in just a moment. This blonde woman."

"The slut?"

"How old was she? What kind of car did she drive?"

"There's a stabbing somewhere?" She'd heard the call. "Is it nearby?"

"Nothing to worry about. Please, what kind of car."

"A little red funny looking thing. You know, two doors, it looked kind of like a red lady bug."

Aw hell, women and cars. I didn't have time for this. "You mean a Volkswagen, like the old bugs?"

"Kind of but not so bubbly, more flat. And newer. The neighbor on the next block has one only it's gray and a convertible. I mean the neighbor's is a convertible, not the slutty girl's."

"Next block, which way?"

She pointed and that was good enough. I could look for the not so bubbly car after we finished with the stabbing call.

"How old was the girl again?" She hadn't answered, but that didn't mean I wanted to sound pushy, even though I was.

"Oh, same age as the one across the street, maybe a little younger, but kind of a skinny girl and she dresses trampy like that Paris Hilton on the TV."

That was it. This was going to continue for another thirty minutes. The dispatcher was airing updates, and we needed to go. Stevie got Genevieve's phone number, and we told her Homicide might call. Mr. Biggles jumped off her lap and chased us as we made our way out the door. The latch clicked shut just in time. The dog crashed against the security screen growling and barking as we made our way down the stairs and back to our car.

Genevieve had given me something to go on. It wasn't much but well worth smelling like ashtrays and dog piss the rest of the night. All I needed to do now was find a slutty blonde girl that dressed like Paris Hilton and drove a not so bubbly sports car. It was the story of my life.

Chapter 22

THE FOLLOWING DAY SEEMED a long time coming. When I got home from work, there was no down time, no depressed recovery from the emotions of the day. My brain was churning, and nothing would shut it off. Stevie and I had been up and down all through our shift. Call after call, we moved from the monotony of knocking on doors to the high pressure stress of dealing with screaming, blood soaked alcoholics. In the midst of all that, we had developed another avenue to investigate. Today, we would try to find the slutty blonde. If she lived anywhere near San Diego State, that might be our needle in a haystack.

The stabbing call that broke our interview with Genevieve had been nothing more than your standard dispute between two groups of males with nothing better to do on a weeknight than sit in a parking lot and drink too many forty ouncers. One man's buzz turned to liquid courage in the face of another's stupid comment. One of those on the losing end of a fist pounding pulled a knife to hedge his odds and thrust it several times into the side of the guy who was getting the better of him. Luck and a ribcage saved the man's lungs and heart but did little to stave off the resulting gashes.

It was pretty much a routine night in East San Diego. Nearly everyone involved in the stabbing was gone by the time we arrived, and those who remained had little to offer in the way of assistance. At some point there'd be payback, and they didn't want judgment in the form of a tidy prosecution. The sentence for this would be street justice.

Perhaps if we'd been driving around rather than knocking on doors we'd have seen these guys. Intervention, a trip to Detox, might have saved another senseless bit of violence. Then again, maybe we'd have just spent the night answering calls until the stabbing happened just the same. You could never tell, and worrying over what might have been was wasted energy in this job.

Stevie went to the hospital with an uncooperative victim while I stayed at the scene and gathered sketchy witness statements. There was little in the way of evidence. The knife, and suspect disappeared long before we ever got there. The chances of finding either were as slim as the odds that the man who had been stabbed had learned his lesson. For him, this would be little more than another night in the emergency room allowing the taxpayers of San Diego to pay tens of thousands of dollars in medical costs he couldn't afford.

A regular person would have probably died from his injuries. Not so for those who shuffle the streets in a permanent state of intoxication. If the government wanted indestructible soldiers, it should hire the street urchins. Bullets and knives might slow them down but it takes an awful serious injury or equally serious bad luck to take them out. Maybe the Navy guy had it right—enlist or go to jail.

We stayed late to finish our paper on the stabbing. I took the bulk of the report so Stevie could devote some more time to the DV he dropped at the start of the night. I held off writing about our search of the neighborhood.

I'd gone to sleep late, passed out from exhaustion when I reached a point where the adrenaline and the day's thoughts finally wore me out. When I woke, my brain kicked right back into full speed. There was more to this than what we'd seen the first night, and I liked the challenge of figuring it out. This was why I got into the job.

Esther was just another anonymous statistic in the greater scheme of things, but to someone, her parents perhaps, she was a person. Even the thick skin, the countless tragedies that numbed you, didn't change you completely. Somewhere down deep it was still hard to not care a little. Once in a while you wanted to win a battle in a lost war.

I'd arrived at the station three hours early and finished my report to Homicide in the upstairs community room where I didn't have to worry about being distracted by every cop who walked by and wanted to talk. With luck, I'd remain free of Roosevelt.

Report finished, I headed down to the locker room and dressed, then loaded a car. Liz was already on the air directing operations. I headed back into the station to run some computer checks. If I was going to find my blonde, that was a good place to start.

I sat at an open terminal and formulated a plan to search the state and local databases. I could run names of people, the times they were contacted, the people they were with, and the vehicles they were driving. I could cross reference those with information pulled from systems like the Department of Motor Vehicles. The computers in the station were a workhorse when you had very little to go on. I'd been at the computer for about fifteen minutes when Stevie walked up.

"You're kind of early for a grumpy guy," he started. "What are you doing?"

"Trying to find out more about your mom since you won't tell me if she's hot."

"Why's it always gotta be about my mom," he asked while raising his hands.

"Cause it irks you." I pushed a chair his way. "Sit yer ass down and learn something."

Stevie grabbed the chair and pulled it close.

"Why so early yourself?" I asked as he settled.

"You still had to do that report. I came in to see if you needed help."

I'll be damned. Twice in a week the kid actually sounded worth a shit. His consideration nearly made me forget the other times he'd had his head buried in another world. I almost felt bad for the mother comment.

"The report's done."

"Already?"

"Yeah, came in a couple hours ago and banged it out. Now I'm looking to see if there's anything that might give us an idea who the blonde is."

"Yeah, I was thinking about that," Stevie said raising a finger and tapping it against his temple. "First of all, the slutty Paris Hilton thing was a South Park episode, only I think Butters was Mister Biggles. I could be wrong," he said pointing and shaking his head. "But that lady, she was smelly and creepy. Second, didn't the husband say something about a friend when we were taking him downtown?"

South Park? He was using South Park to think through murder scenarios. Every generation connected to something. Jack felt like he was in a rodeo, and I heard music. When Stevie worked an investigation his thoughts drifted to South Park, and Butters, the cute little naïve kid that constantly gets taken advantage of? That was a first. My brain shifted mid-thought to the night we'd transported Aaron to Homicide. "Not sure I follow, don't remember a comment."

"Something about not listening. I didn't remember it until last night, and then just when I was about to fall asleep it hit me, something about her listening to a friend."

The comment whacked me like a slap in the back of the head. At the time, I wrote it off as nothing more than another angry comment in a string of statements that were far more incriminating. My mind strained to remember details, something about Esther not listening to him, not paying attention to him but . . . "She listened to that bitch from work."

The kid was an idiot savant—a damned clueless, bumbling, rookie baby cop with a flash of genius. The husband had been pissed off by the friend. That meant there was something going on at work, an affair perhaps. More than one person had been killed by a spouse because they were knocking boots with a coworker. Of course, more than one coworker knocked off the person they were cheating with when things went bad. Not as likely, but possible.

"Good thought, I'd forgotten all about that. I'll have to watch more South Park"

Once again, Stevie's chest rose with a hint of pride, perhaps even a little self-confidence. "Thanks. He said so many things that night I didn't remember, and then when I did it kept me up for like two hours thinking about it."

I grinned. "Kind of a good feeling, huh? Makes you feel like you're doing something right, doesn't it?"

Stevie's grin was broader than mine. "Yeah. Like yesterday, I was hating that knocking on doors stuff. By the end, I was so bored I just wanted to go do something else, a DV even, anything but keep talking to people that didn't know anything. Then we talked to that smelly lady and it all seemed like it was worth it, like we found out something important."

"Like a direction."

"Yeah, it was cool."

"That's police work. Better watch out, it's addictive. What do you want to bet your friend from work and the smelly lady's slutty blonde is the same person?"

Before I could continue, my thoughts were disrupted by the sound of Roosevelt talking to someone down the hall. My stomach tightened. Napoleon was back. That wouldn't bode well for my plans. There was still the confrontation between he and I that had to be discussed. Little chance I'd avoid him today.

"Good morning, Captain," I heard him say. He was close but not close enough that I could make out anything the Captain said in response. His was simply a muffled murmur. "Oh yes, we're doing some interesting things. You'd be real proud of how the survey is coming along."

The tightening in my stomach turned sour. Boy wonder was sucking the Captain's ass, and he didn't sound as though he was the least bit ashamed. A moment later, his voice trailed off as he wandered into whatever room the Captain had been in. Roosevelt no doubt had him cornered. A guy like him was more interested in "face time" than with actually accomplishing anything. I was glad for the reprieve.

Stevie noticed too. His grin was gone, and he looked at the door of the computer room like he expected our sergeant to walk in at any moment. I grabbed the phone. A moment later Ronny's desk was ringing.

"Detective White."

"Ronny, Hatch."

"Hey bro, sorry I didn't call you back. Things have been busy, got some new insight on the husband."

"No shit. What?"

"One of the guys found an insurance policy from late last year. Only 50K, but a lot of money to a guy like that. I'm going down to the lab in a while see if they can process the tools a little quicker. Maybe then this will start to break loose and sort out."

"Or maybe the case against him will fall apart."

"Shush, don't say that. He's got an attorney. If he's guilty, no point cooperating. I don't need you stinking my shit."

"Sorry, let me tell you what we got." I spent the next few minutes explaining the neighbor and the fights, I told him about the blonde friend in the not so bubbly car, and I told him about the comment Aaron made when we were taking him downtown.

Ronny was silent when I finished. "Fuck," he said plainly. "Seems that's a couple new wrinkles that'll need to be ironed out." He sounded disappointed. "Why you gotta ruin my day?"

"Excuse me? You don't think you'd have come up with this?"

"Well of course I do," he said emphatically. "I was just hoping I wouldn't."

"Wouldn't discover clues?"

"No, asshole, that there wouldn't be any. I don't care if it's the husband or the shooter from the grassy knoll. All I care about is a break. You guys in the field think you're the only ones getting slammed with staffing shortages. I got enough cases, all important to someone. Just hoped maybe I could catch a break, maybe not have to run around clearing red herrings."

For the first time in the last week, he sounded tired, and I realized how removed we sometimes were in the field. Detective work was a different pace, slower, but that didn't mean it was without challenges, especially in a unit like Homicide. When you're short staffed but full on dead bodies, that can mean a lot of time at work away from families and away from any semblance of a normal life.

"I tell you what, let us clear some more of the grunt work for you. Shit, this is a nice change for us, good opportunity for the kid. You get a break and we get some fun."

The line was silent.

Aaron Anderson was an angry man with a history of explosive violence. Maybe he'd found out about an affair, maybe this friend from work was putting thoughts about divorce in his wife's head. Either way, his life was a shit storm. Maybe he'd just snapped. Then again, there was the jewelry still unaccounted for. Maybe she'd already moved that out of the house, or maybe there was still a burglar. Maybe the burglar was hired. The case was starting to sing to me, things were falling into place. I just hadn't reached the bridge that tied the whole song together. There were still too many maybes. I didn't want to let go.

"Something's missing, Ronny."

"There's lots of things missing," he said, frustrated. "Can you submit your report so I can pull a copy off the computer?"

"I'll have it to you in twenty minutes."

"Thanks, and good work. Should have known that letting you play in my sandbox would leave more cat turds to scoop."

He still hadn't answered my question. "So do you mind if I go over to her work and try to locate this friend? It'll be nothing more than we did in the neighborhood."

There was another silent pause. "Hang on, let me talk to my boss."

I was moving closer to the line of interference. Homicide might be okay with me checking the neighborhood, but they might start getting nervous about doing more. Sometimes they cringed at the thought of a mere patrolman poking around their little fiefdom. It all depended on who was making the decisions and what they thought about your reputation. It also depended on the case priority. If this were high profile, I might have to find another angle. Something like this, I had a fifty-fifty chance. Either way, there was no rule that forbade me from investigating, only egos and territoriality.

Ronny put me on hold for what seemed like a mighty long time. We were getting close to the start of our shift, and I'd need to plan my day one way or another. A couple minutes later he came back on the line.

"All right. I told the boss what you developed. He was pretty fucking jazzed, if you can imagine that with Sergeant James, but he doesn't want something getting screwed up. Fortunately he knows you enough to trust you with some leeway. I downplayed what you want to do. Go look, but tread lightly, my friend. You get any indication that something is gonna get hosed, back off and call me."

"Fair enough. You have Esther's work address?"

Ronny was giving me the last of what I needed when Roosevelt interrupted us.

"John, I need to talk to you," he said loud enough to be a distraction.

"Geez, what the hell," Ronny replied on the other end.

I held the phone receiver out so Roosevelt could see it while I continued, "I gotta go. Seems the boss needs me."

"This second, can't wait, doesn't he see the phone?"

"Apparently."

"Nice, sounds like a prick."

"Absolutely."

"All right, good hunting." Ronny put emphasis in his next statement. "Call if you start slipping in shit. I'm serious."

"Already happening," I said and started to hang up.

"And John," I stopped.

"Yeah."

"The kid was right, Butters was Mister Biggles on South Park, and he was dressed in a bear outfit. Details, my friend, in a homicide it's always about the details."

"Damn, Ronny, not you too. It was South Park." I hung up. "Yes sir," I said to Roosevelt.

"What did I tell you about wandering off on your own little projects?" He spoke loud enough that anyone in the immediate area would hear him. Anger welled inside and I prepared for another round of sergeant-punking. I knew this was coming, but I was in no mood. The snide comment was nearly out when judgment caught the better of me. Stevie looked as though he was about to choke, color draining from his face. He wasn't used to this, and that pissed me off even more. Roosevelt was driving away any desire he might have at demonstrating initiative.

I wanted to make Socrates squirm, but if we were going to have any chance at not having our plans ruined by a tyrant, I'd need to placate him, at least a little. I tried the truth. In the face of confrontation, it always confused a guy like him.

"Sorry sir, you weren't here. We did a couple witness checks for Homicide in between calls yesterday. We dropped it every time a call came out."

"You were told to check with me before doing that."

I shrugged innocently, knowing the façade angered him in a passive aggressive way.

"You weren't here. Sergeant Rake said it would be okay." I hated to throw him in the middle, but considering his opinion of Socrates, I didn't figure he would have any issue putting down the complaints of a boot sergeant. In all likelihood, Roosevelt would never have the guts to even check with him.

"You don't work for him, you work for me."

I twisted his logic. "And you weren't here. I did the best I could." The last part was a lie, but it cornered him, checked his ability to retaliate . . . at least temporarily. That was good enough. We were locked in a battle that required strategy. That meant knowing when to yell and when to fuck with his head, to play with his words.

I continued. "We developed some information. Homicide is waiting for my copy of the report even as we speak." I thought about giving him the details, but that would be a moot point. This wasn't about whether we did anything right.

"Is that what the overtime was for?"

"Nope, that was the stabbing," I said. "The one we dropped our follow-up for and took because it was our beat," I added. I knew that would piss him off, rile him that I pointed out how we still managed to cover calls, but I would not get on my knees for the man. "I wrote the Homicide report on my time."

Roosevelt paused. "You're playing games with me, John. I'll not have that. You work for me. Your job is patrol." His face reddened. "If you want to play detective, then put in for the job. I don't see it happening, but that's another matter. Until then, you do things how I tell you to and let them do what they're supposed to do."

"And if you're not here?"

"You do what you've been told. End of story. I can't make things any clearer, can I?" Tension made his voice rise. "Either way, I'm here today."

Roosevelt turned to Stevie and for a moment I thought he'd lay into him. Stevie squirmed in his chair, and Socrates changed his mind. He turned and stomped away.

Stevie's grin was gone, his face paler than before. He simply stared blankly as he spoke. "We're going to get in trouble tonight, aren't we?"

"We're not going to get fired," I said as plainly.

"But we're gonna get yelled at?"

"Absolute certainty." I hadn't meant to let him in on my insubordinate plan. To keep him in the dark would protect him when the screaming started. What happened tonight would be on me. "Look, I already loaded the car. We have the evidence unit. If you're uncomfortable, tell Roosevelt you'd like a night alone. We can split up for the day if it makes you feel better. No hard feelings on my end, really."

Stevie thought on it. "But we won't get fired?"

I smiled. "Not for doing what we're supposed to."

He shrugged. "Getting yelled at ain't so bad."

"Good." I smiled. "Because I'm gonna need you tonight. If you thought we worked yesterday, be prepared to hump. I need your head in the game."

CHAPTER 23

I LEFT THE STATION to smoke. Roosevelt was going to be an asshole and nothing would change that. That meant it was time for a Plan B. If I had any hope, I'd need to get creative. The nicotine hit. I was nearly through the first cigarette when I finally calmed down enough to think.

This was about control, who had it, who didn't.

By my watch, twenty minutes to line-up. I walked to my car. To get a shot, I'd to need to walk a fine line. That meant playing by Roosevelt's rules. If I didn't, he had me. Fortunately, playing by the rules can get technical. After all, there's not just the law. There is the "Letter of the law" and there is the "Spirit of the law." Socrates had laid down the law to the letter. When I got called on the board for my actions, I was going to need to justify myself by those very letters.

It was similar to what I'd just done. He got mad at me for not checking in and I pointed out that he wasn't there to check with. Under the spirit of his statement, I knew what he meant. I toyed with his words by taking another sergeant as an accomplice. A technically correct interpretation of his statement that would cost him any battle he fought to try and jam me with discipline. Plan A had simply been to go out and find the blonde between calls. Plan B would be more complicated. My alternative would require orchestration.

From my car, I sent a message to Liz. It simply said, "Give me a call."

Two minutes later my cell phone rang.

"Hi, Liz."

"Hey, Hatch. Can't talk long, freq-6 is covering for a minute."

"Don't need much time, just need some help."

"Name it."

"That twit we discussed the other day, the one you wanted me to keep in his office and off the air."

Her voice deflated into a suspicious tone. "Yeah?"

"I need you to do the opposite. He just got all over my ass for doing follow-ups for Homicide yesterday. I need time to do some more today. If you see me dragging out calls, it's cause I'll be rushing around to make up extra time."

"Something good?"

"Could be, maybe not. I just need to be free of supervision for the night."

"And you want the twit occupied?"

"So much his head swims."

There was a giggle on the other end. "I can do that."

"I knew you could."

"It'll cost you a mocha and all the details."

"Fair trade."

"You're going to stir some shit on my air tonight, aren't you?"

"Not if I can help it. Dark Ops, my dear, plan is covert. There is no slash and burn tonight. With any luck it'll all work out quietly."

"There is no quiet with you. I'll eat early. Good hunting, John."

"Thanks, Liz." I hung up and headed into line-up.

Tonight we walked the razor blade. If I dug too deep, screwed something up, Homicide would come unglued and there'd be hell to pay. If we got caught disobeying orders and couldn't justify ourselves, Socrates would have my ass. All in all, this seemed a pretty typical way to do business. It wasn't just the balance between radio calls and arrests one had to maintain, but the balance between doing what needed doing and doing what the Roosevelts wanted. For some reason the latter always seemed more difficult.

Chances like this didn't come often. They were there, the opportunities, but you needed to look for them. Sometimes the radio denied you. Sometimes things just didn't pan out as expected. You could hunt all week only to watch everything crumble. But sometimes, every once in a while, you got lucky enough to do a bit of work that left you feeling like a cop.

I made line-up with little time to spare. Roosevelt rambled out a litany of senseless information, and the anxiety I felt made the whole process seem to last much longer than it really did. Every minute in the briefing room ticked by at a tortured pace, and the whole while I was sure Roosevelt was a split second from dynamiting my day. When he was done, I took advantage of my reprieve and left the room immediately. There was one more thing to do before we cleared the station.

As the rest of the officers started ambling toward the locker room, I went directly to Marcus. "Grab, Murphy, Jenkins, and Martinez. Meet me by the back door."

Marcus eyed me suspiciously, and then nodded. As he walked away I heard him mumble, "Brother John is about to stir some shit."

That he was. Brother John was about to be a bad disciple.

Two minutes later the five of us stood in the back parking lot in a circle away from anyone else. This was a pow-wow. They knew we were about to conspire, and such things were best done away from the vigilant ears of the Eric Smiths of the world.

"I need a favor."

Jenkins slowly shook his head to the contrary, Martinez grinned. Marcus kept his game face.

Murphy shrugged, "Name it, you know I'm in. I still owe you whatever it is."

"I have some things to do tonight, and Roosevelt is inclined to be obstructive. I need you to help me make time." There was no point being vague. Every cop in the station knew of the rift between me and Socrates. They were all aware that helping me might draw fire onto themselves.

Martinez shrugged, "Will it piss him off?"

"You bet."

"Count me in."

Jenkins continued shaking his head, for effect. He liked to think he was trying to be a good and loyal subordinate, but the fact remained that he didn't have any more patience for bullshit than the rest of us. He just sometimes felt compelled to pretend.

"Marcus?"

"Brother John?"

I smiled. "Excellent. Look, I don't really need you guys to do anything, just cover my back if I'm not clearing stuff right away. If you have any contact with wonder boy make sure you keep him occupied. Ask for him at calls, ask for his input and direction when he gets there, just do whatever you can to keep him tied up and off my ass. Don't just ask for a supervisor, ask for him."

Jenkins sighed and quit shaking his head. "Hell, that's easy enough."

Stevie came out the back door with his gear bag. "Hey guys, what's going on?"

"Nothing," I said as I put my hand on his shoulder and ushered him away. "Thanks, we're outta here."

Martinez grinned broadly. "Just make sure we get to be there when he stomps on your balls. That'll be funny too."

"Thanks for the support."

"Anytime."

"Brother John, I'll swing by Burger King and get you an application."

A minute later we were pulling out of the station parking lot. I typed a message to Liz: "We're clearing, send us whatever you got." I didn't really want whatever was holding, but if it came down to justifying myself later on I could always pull our messages and point out that we cleared with full intentions of doing exactly what our sergeant wanted. Not only that, but we'd be able to show we were the first unit in the field.

A moment later the computer beeped and we took our first musket ball. A simple paper call, no suspect at the scene, no real likelihood that we'd end up getting tied up on an arrest. Liz knew exactly the type of call to send an enterprising officer who might need to bleed a little free time out of an otherwise routine piece of work. I wanted to send a message thanking her, but this wasn't the right time to be gracious. This was about the appearance of doing what we were told. And we were . . . sort of.

We arrived at the call and had everything we needed in less than twenty minutes. Stevie typed while I drove to Esther's place of employment on El Cajon Boulevard in Western Division. We were heading outside our area.

Circumstances often required cops to cross between commands. Socrates might have an issue that we didn't notify him, but we weren't going so far that he could turn it into something too problematic. The larger problem was that we went without notifying anyone, even the dispatcher. If something happened along the way, there'd be hell to pay. If Roosevelt got in his car and went to check the location of our report, and we weren't there, the trouble would be worse. We were off the grid, a dangerous exploit if you had to start calling for help.

Esther had worked for a temp agency doing secretary work. The main office was a small storefront in the middle of a strip mall. From there, she was dispatched to businesses in need. That meant she might have worked all over the city. My expectations about an easy end deflated. There could be a great many people in and out of that agency, and they might not have any clue about who she associated with.

We'd save time if Stevie stayed in the car and wrote, but he'd learn more by being a part of this. He was quiet, and his concern over the sneaky nature of our mission was clear on his face. He was scared he was going to get in trouble. At least he faced that fear with some balls and chose to participate despite the underlying threat expressed by the man who wrote his probationary evaluations.

We met the office manager, a white guy in his mid-forties with thinning hair and a rather gray expression. His thin frame and small belly made it hard for him to keep his white dress shirt fully tucked. I tried to get a gauge on the man, a feel for whether he might be an office lover. A guy like this seemed a real candidate to listen to the troubles of an attractive and vulnerable female employee. When I told him we were there following up on Esther, his gray skin paled a shade.

"That was horrible. We saw the papers. What happened?"

"We're still working on all the details, sir. Right now we're just trying to track down people who knew her so the detectives know who to contact." I figured that was a vague enough statement to keep things low key and not put anyone with information, or culpability, on the spot.

"Well, but of course, I knew her," he nodded. "I mean, not well, but she did work for us for a couple years. Not out of the office though." He turned and dug into a file cabinet behind his desk. After he pulled out a manila folder, he opened it and looked inside. "Yes, we have six sites that used her services. Pretty regular, I might add. At least a couple of them. She seemed a pretty reliable young lady to us."

Six places? Shit. It could take days to get through all those. There might be dozens of people we'd have to sort through to find our blonde. If that was the case, we were done. Even if Homicide would approve, I could only push Roosevelt off for short periods. This was the moment when I sometimes thought I could leave patrol. To work a lead was challenging—to have that turn into six more can be a disappointment, especially if that means letting go of the hunt. I didn't like the idea of letting go.

I returned to my first thoughts on the manager and Esther. Raising a hand to my chin, I studied at him for a moment. He shifted uneasily, then smiled nervously and broke eye contact. Perhaps his actions were suspicious, but most people did that, even in the line at Starbucks. Nobody was comfortable when you looked right at them.

"You didn't really know her then," I asked, once again testing a reaction.

The manager returned eye contact. "Well, no, how would I? She got most of her assignments over the phone. The most we see these girls is on payday, if they don't have direct deposit." He didn't seem to grab even the remotest possibility at the implications of my question. He was either clueless that I would think such a thing, or we'd need better leverage before talking again. My gut went with clueless.

"Do you mind if I write down these businesses so we can send someone to check with the people there?"

"Certainly," he said as he put the open folder on his desk and pointed out the different office contracts.

Stevie produced his notepad and started writing down names, addresses, and phone numbers while I continued talking to the manager.

"Do you know anyone she might have worked with? We'd like to talk to a blonde woman."

He shook his head. "Sorry. I really don't have a lot of contact with the workers. Sheila does most of the calls and sends them out to their jobsites. This is very sad. Does she have a family, or, ah ... did she?"

"Just a husband."

"Well, he must be devastated."

I looked out the office door to the woman at the front desk. "Is that Sheila?"

"Yes, would you like to talk to her?"

"Please."

Sheila was a young, Hispanic woman in her mid-twenties, a little heavy with even heavier eye shadow. She had three dots tattooed on her hand between her thumb and forefinger. It meant "My crazy life." Sheila had grown up in the neighborhood, probably a high school education and a couple kids from some young thug she met when she was younger. She was nervous about being called into the office. I didn't figure that had much to do with Esther's death, probably more to do with her background.

"Sheila, these officers are here about Ms. Anderson."

Sheila continued to eye me distrustfully.

"We're looking for a blonde woman that might have been friends with Esther, maybe worked out of this office. Can you think of anyone like that?"

"We got a lot of girls like that, sorry," she huffed. The inflection in her voice still held some of the slang tone of her days in the neighborhood. "I don't know who her friends were."

I racked my brain trying to find something more that might help, something distinctive. We didn't really have much. Calling her slutty would be inappropriate by any standard, and comparing her to Paris Hilton probably meant little to a girl from the neighborhood.

"Neighbor said she hung out with a blonde girl who drove a little, red sports car."

Sheila shook her head.

Then I made the silliest statement I'd likely ever made during an investigation. I felt foolish but we were about done. "They said it was kind of bubbly but flat on top."

The lights come on. "Cindy, duh, I'm so stupid sometimes," she said bouncing with excitement. "A red Miata. Not so bubbly. Your person don't know cars. I love the Miata, it's so cute." She stopped bouncing, suspicion returned to her voice. "You don't think she's involved," was more challenge than question. "Do you?"

"Huh, no." I smiled, almost too stunned to continue. Leave it to a girly description of a not so bubbly, bubbly sports car to strike a nerve with another woman. We'd checked down the street the other night for any car that might match that description and hadn't come close. I never thought of a Miata, and I couldn't say I remembered even seeing one when we looked.

Sheila continued while the manager dug through the file cabinet.

"Yeah, I saw her car one time when me and some of the girls went out for happy hour after work. I don't know Cindy like a friend but I remember that car. I was so jealous. If I could only afford one."

The manager cut her off. "Here it is, Cindy Peterson. She's not working today."

I took the file and looked inside. There wasn't much, just her work history, an address and phone number. Enough, I wrote the information down, then got Sheila and the manager's information. Sheila rambled on about the night they went out and gave us a better description of Cindy. I thought about taking more thorough statements but decided that might better be left to Homicide. We had a break. I didn't want to screw that up. We thanked them and left.

Stevie was livelier as we walked back to our car. "Cool, we got it. I thought we were done when I started writing down all those places to check. What now?"

CHAPTER 24

I CHECKED MY WATCH. Interviewing Esther's coworkers had taken about thirty minutes. Any cursory check Roosevelt might do on our status would still show us well within the normal bounds of time needed to complete a report. I'd need to check on him before continuing. When Marcus didn't answer his cell phone, I called Martinez. "What's holding?"

"Check yourself," he said bluntly. "Forget how to use a computer? No wonder Roosevelt don't like you. You used to be competent, but I've noticed you slacking lately."

"You better go tell him then," I said, ignoring the taunt. Talking to Martinez was a circuitous event. "I run status, he can track that I checked."

"Ooh, didn't think of that, sneaky bastard." I could hear the click of his computer keys in the background, and then he ran down the list of what people were doing, what was holding. "Your dad isn't even logged on yet. He's still at the sub."

"Buried in his office or the Captain's ass, no doubt. Perfect, thanks."

"I still get to see him stomp your balls, right?"

I hung up.

"Sir, you there?" I typed the short message to Roosevelt and hit the "Send" button knowing full well the transmission would never arrive. That didn't matter. What was important was what he'd find if he was diligent enough to check. He'd see proof that I tried to reach him.

I changed our location to Cindy Peterson's. I could get away with forgetting to change our location one time, but I might be pushing my luck if we did everything off the radar.

Cindy lived in our area. If we were quick we could talk to her and be clear before Socrates got wise that we were bleeding time from a call we were no longer on. The game continued. At least we were making progress.

About half way to Cindy's, Martinez got on the air. "832-Zebra, can 834 Sam make it to our stop? We have a citizen who would like to speak to him about a traffic citation." The tone in his voice was a mix of amusement and calm, practiced professionalism.

I laughed. Leave it to Jenkins and Martinez. Perhaps they did have a citizen legitimately upset over a ticket. More likely the two jokers intentionally riled the poor motorist until he was unhappy and then suggested he could talk to their boss. Most folks jumped at the chance to try and persuade a supervisor they didn't deserve their ticket. If Roosevelt couldn't respond, the angry citizen wouldn't be anything they couldn't smooth out on their own if they had to. They might push boundaries, but they knew better than to dig a hole too deep. Either way, they were buying us time.

Liz needed two tries to get wonder boy to answer.

"I'll be en route." Roosevelt sighed, his agitation over being forced to drop what he was doing evident in the tone of his voice.

Liz let him have a couple moments to start for his car before she started stacking on extra tasks for him to think about. "834 Sam, no hurry, but when you get done with 832-Z, I have a couple calls I need you to look at." She didn't have any such calls. There was rarely a time a dispatcher as veteran as Liz needed direction, and there was never a moment she needed it from a Roosevelt.

I stepped on the gas. Socrates would be busy for a while. We needed to move.

Cindy Peterson lived in a large apartment complex on the eastern end of the division. Not a fancy place by any stretch, but even cheap rent in San Diego was expensive on a temporary secretarial paycheck.

The complex itself was so large it took several minutes to find her unit. Whoever designed these massive developments to house thousands rarely gave any thought to making the numbering logical for an emergency worker needing to find the place in a hurry. Searching for her unit ate precious time. I considered taking another call, but we were here. We'd push our chances.

With no answer to our first knock, I started to worry. I knocked again and heard the deadbolt release. The door opened a moment later, and Cindy Peterson stood on the other side peering through the narrow gap created by the door's safety chain.

"Yes," she said in a passive, quiet voice.

"Cindy Peterson?"

"Can I help you, officer?" The apartment was dark inside. I couldn't read her expression through the narrow slit between door and door jam.

"We'd like to talk to you for a minute about Esther."

Her voice cracked. "I don't know anything. I'm sorry."

"Can you please let us in?"

A moment passed, and the door closed. I heard the chain slide and then the door opened again. Cindy stepped back and shuffled to the couch. She sat while we walked inside.

"Do you mind?" I asked as I sat on a chair across from the couch. She simply shook her head. Stevie sat in the chair next to me. We didn't need to worry about dog hair and urine today.

"How did you get my address?" she asked, concern evident in a slight tremble in her words. "You didn't get it from him, did you?"

"Who?"

"That husband of hers. Well, so-called husband."

"No. We got it from her office. He doesn't know anything about us being here."

"Good." She sighed. "He's an asshole. I was afraid maybe he followed us and got the address. That he sent you."

"No." I thought for a moment about what direction to take our conversation. We weren't but a minute into this and Aaron was already the asshole. The compass needle continued pointing an all too familiar direction.

We had our blonde girl. She didn't look so slutty as Genevieve said, but then she also looked like we just woke her up from an afternoon nap. Maybe she was a night person. Then again, having a friend murdered had a way of encouraging a bit of depression. This could turn sticky in a hot second, which made screwing up a real prospect. Our goal had been accomplished. We'd located the unnamed woman. Homicide would be happy. But now that she was in front of me, I wanted more.

I lowered my voice, put on a sympathetic face, and leaned forward. There'd need to be trust before she would reveal what we needed. Perhaps she would do it just because Aaron was an asshole. I could change tone and tact if needed. Until then, starting friendly seemed the easiest course. Successful interviews relied on making a connection. That didn't change if you were talking to a rape victim or the suspect who did the crime. They had to trust you. If you were talking to a suspect, sometimes they had to fear that you already knew everything you needed. In the end, this was still about believing what you told them. To lose that was to lose the interview.

In this instance, Cindy needed faith that we were on the same side. The only circumstance to alter that was whether she changed from victim to suspect. It wouldn't be the first time someone jumped from one side of the fence to the other in the middle of a relationship. If this boiled down to domestic violence between lovers, the sex of the partner became irrelevant. I'd seen enough jilted women to know they could be every bit as vicious as a man.

Cindy was taller than Esther, but lighter. That she would have the strength necessary to slam her against a wall so hard her jeans left transfer marks seemed unlikely. She could have had help. History—and prison—was filled with guys drawn to the manipulative promises of the wrong woman. The compass might point at Aaron, but I wanted the nail that would hold it down. That meant eliminating Cindy.

I spoke softly. "I'm sure you're pretty upset right now, so I'm going to try and make this as easy as I can. If you get uncomfortable and need a break, let me know and we can stop." I looked around the apartment, a woman's apartment. I found what I was looking for and told Stevie to grab the box of tissues. I set the box on the coffee table in front of her.

Cindy grabbed a pillow from the couch and brought it up against her chest. "It wasn't right. She didn't deserve that."

"I know, that's why we're here. Tell me about Aaron."

"I told you, he's an asshole. He'd get drunk with his buddies all the time but give her shit if she went out a couple times a month with me. He hit her you know?"

I nodded.

"I told her to leave him. She'd come here and cry about what a jerk he was, and then she'd go back to him."

"Did you ever see him hit her?"

"I saw him push her, and he chased us once when I came to the house and got her. He was so angry he threw something at us when we left." She started to cry. I stood and handed her a tissue. "Why did he have to do that?"

I gave her a moment. "You think he did it?"

Her tone melted into wraith. "Of course he did. Who do you think did it?"

"That's what we're trying to find out." I gave her another moment. "Our detectives are probably going to want to come out and talk to you, is that okay?"

"Will it put that bastard away?"

"It might help."

"Let 'em come. I can't tell them anything more than I told you, but if it helps punish that fuck for what he did, then I'll do whatever you need."

"Thank you," I said.

Stevie produced his note pad to get Cindy's information. He asked her the same questions he did everyone else and then closed the notebook. He waited for me to give the signal to leave.

I looked directly at Cindy, waited until she made eye contact.

"Cindy, do you know if Esther had a boyfriend?"

Her eyes narrowed as if offended, and then shifted, breaking contact for just an instant. I had my answer. Looking back to me, she spoke the obvious. "She was married." It was a statement to answer the question without answering.

"I know," I started. "And I know he was an asshole. I was there that night," I said, trying to secure our connection. "I'm not trying to do anything that will make her look bad, but if she did, it's important we know that so we don't get any surprises later on. I need to be able to eliminate every other possibility if we're going to make this work."

My mind plunged into the possibilities. There was a boyfriend. Cindy knew as much, and she was reluctant to give that up. She was afraid this would become about him, and the trial would be about Esther's infidelity. I understood the fear, but that didn't change the fact that I needed a name.

"Cindy, you gotta help me here. I can't do this alone."

The time came to test whether I made that bond of trust. Perhaps this bridge was better crossed by Homicide, but to be so close and let go wasn't in me. "Please. If it was you, wouldn't you want her to tell me anything that might help?" The guilt trip was a shit move, but sometimes the job doesn't get done without pushing some painful buttons.

Shoulders slumped, submission set in like a child who accepted they were bad for not coming clean. My chest tightened, angst tapping at my conscience as I wondered about the rightness of my maneuver.

"I never met him. I don't even know for sure there was anything between them. You know, like sexual. She just called him a friend. How can you blame her?"

"I don't blame her."

Cindy made eye contact again. Her turn, she was searching, sizing me up. I smiled warmly, acted to reassure her that I hadn't intentionally given her the guilt trip.

"Do you know his name?"

She shook her head. "I told you, I never met him. I wouldn't know him if he knocked on my front door." The tears started to well up, and I gave her a moment.

We were drawing a blank. My mind worked the angles. The next logical step was to write up her statement and let Homicide take over. That meant the end of the hunt for us. I considered what more I could get.

"Do you know where she would meet him?"

"No. She'd call from a pay phone or from here and then go. I never went."

Esther kept her meetings secret, covered her tracks. That made sense. Calling from home, or from her cell phone, would leave records that Aaron might find. The first rule of cheating was to leave no stupid traces. People got creative.

"She called from here?"

"A couple times. Once when we were out she used my cell so there wouldn't be a number on hers."

I straightened in my seat. "Do you remember when?"

"Couple months ago."

That was our break. Home phones didn't send you a listing of your calls at the end of the month unless they were long distance. My cell phone company sent a list of every call I made, long distance or not. "Do you keep your cell phone records?"

"Somewhere."

"Cindy, I need you to see if you can find the number on your statement."

"I don't know the number."

"We'll look for the numbers you don't recognize."

Cindy went to a stack of papers on the kitchen counter. While she looked, Stevie gave me a worried glance. Time was running thin. I heard Liz on the air, "I need two units and 834 Sam, if you're clear, to head to this DV on beat 811." Jenkins and Martinez volunteered immediately. Marcus answered a second later. Everyone was doing their part. We just needed things to start moving. We were past due on what we could milk from our call.

"I got it," Cindy said holding up some papers.

I moved next to her while she looked through the list of calls. There were several pages. She talked on her phone a lot. The delay brought anxiety. I needed a cigarette.

The search seemed to take forever, like she had to pause every other number to remember who it belonged to. When she was done, we had three numbers Cindy didn't recognize.

I handed Cindy my card and brought my other hand up to rest gently on her shoulder. "You did good today. I appreciate your help. I wrote Detective White's number on the back. If you don't hear from him in a couple days, call him, or call me. He's a good man, you can trust him."

Cindy stared at the card, still unconvinced she hadn't broken a trusted bond with the memory of a dead friend. As we walked out the door, Cindy spoke. "Officer Hatch. Get that bastard. Make him pay."

"I'll do what I can."

"If he resists, you have my permission to kill him. Esther was a sweet girl. She didn't deserve what he did to her."

I smiled warmly but couldn't commit to her request. Guilty or not, Aaron Anderson's judgment was not mine to make.

As Stevie and I walked back to the car, he spoke. His words stammered. "Shouldn't we be clearing? Roosevelt is going to have our ass."

"Yeah, but isn't it fun?"

"Not really." He shook his head. "No."

"Don't worry. We're about to clear and go out on an FI."

"Huh? What FI? We don't even have anyone stopped."

"We will, my young friend. You just have to have a little faith."

CHAPTER 25

THE PREVAILING THOUGHT among the young and upwardly mobile like Theodore Roosevelt was that changing job assignments every couple of years was a good thing. Working a bunch of different places made you a more well rounded and marketable officer. Problem is, guys like Roosevelt were too busy looking for the next big assignment to ever pay any attention to learning their present one.

I always figured the opposite, that if you moved every two years, you never stayed in one place long enough for anyone to know whether you could really do the job or not. You might build an impressive resume, but you never actually dug into your assignment to the depth you would if you had stayed for a while. Experience, not location, made you well rounded. What you did with that experience demonstrated ability. The key was to stay fresh, challenged. If you could do that, it didn't matter where you worked or how long you were there.

There was also a side benefit to staying in one place for a while. You got to know what belonged where, who did what, and what cycles to expect. Some old beat cops knew two, and even three, generations of people in a neighborhood. Like a mother with her children, a cop like that didn't need to work a dozen different places to know what was going on.

Stevie squirmed in his seat, worried about whether we were going to get in trouble. His brief career flashed before eyes that couldn't imagine what might become of the future. I couldn't share those concerns. We'd be clear soon and on to our next bit of legitimate work.

Afternoon was giving way to evening, and we were on the east end of El Cajon Boulevard. With that came rush hour. In this business traffic created a target rich environment you could count on to stir up at least a couple prostitutes. On a boulevard long known for such activity, there was a quick buck to be made as some husband searched out the end of the workday blowjob he wouldn't get at home.

Maybe three minutes passed from the time we left Cindy's apartment until I spotted a woman I'd contacted many times in the past. I angled the car to cut off her avenue of escape, block her access to the fleabag hotel where she made her home.

"831-Zebra, clear our last, and we'll be on a field interview at 71st and El Cajon." I chose the radio, rather than the computer, so Liz would know where we were and Socrates got the impression we were simply handling field activity.

"Ten-four," she acknowledged cheerfully. Liz added a little extra distraction to Socrates just because she could. "834 Sam, are you folks going to have a prisoner out of that DV?"

"We're still evaluating," he responded, clearly agitated by the disruption.

Stevie and I got out of the car. The woman had turned and was pretending that she needed to go the opposite direction—the ostrich, head in the sand defense. If she didn't look at us then we couldn't see her.

Our target was a white female in heels, wearing a tube top that could be flipped down for easy access, and a dirty pink skirt that surely spent more time on the floorboards of some John's car than it did in the laundry. In a dark alley her twenty years might not be hard to believe; three years on drugs and a clear look in the evening light made forty an easier sell. At this rate I gave her another couple years, tops, before prison, rehab, or death.

She'd been something in high school—prom queen or valedictorian—I couldn't remember. That promise evaporated the moment she started playing with Ecstasy. Like most junkies, the joys of weekend experimentation turned to addiction. Smoking meth, and the possibility that was her young life took an entirely new direction. If she smoked less she might have survived a few years as a stripper, but she was who she was. Teeth already rotting, and no amount of Botox would fill the deep, hard lines the streets had cut in her face.

"Cassandra, stop," I barked firmly.

She froze in her tracks.

"Come here. Don't make me chase you up and down the street."

Cassandra shuffled slowly back in our direction.

"Give Officer Buckman your information, and don't give him any shit. You understand?"

"Yes, Officer Hatch," she said, dejectedly.

I looked at Stevie. "Told you we were about to go out on an FI. Have faith, but do it slowly so I can make some phone calls."

He smiled and pulled out his field interview book.

I looked at Cassandra and waved my finger to accent my point. "Make sure you give him your real name. If you lie, you'll have to deal with me."

"I never lied to you, Officer Hatch."

"You're not talking to me," I said over my shoulder as I walked back to the car.

I looked at my watch and hoped Ronny would still be in the office. I called his number and it rang until the voice mail picked up. I left him a message to call me and then called the main office number. The receptionist answered.

"John Hatch, Mid-City, is Ronny White there?"

"Sorry, they're on a call-out. Can I give you his voicemail?"

"No, thanks," I said and hung up.

Just my luck, we had information on the blonde and a line on a possible boyfriend. If Ronny's team had been called out, that meant someone else had joined the growing list of this year's homicides. I thought about paging him. He would want to know, might not want me to do more. I could call his cell.

Another problem struck me. Cindy said she didn't know Esther's boyfriend, didn't know if he was a boyfriend at all. That didn't mean she told me the truth. If so, she might call just to let him know that we'd been there asking questions. Wouldn't be the first time someone gave us up. She might not even think she was doing anything wrong. If he was the suspect, not Aaron Anderson, that could cost us any evidence he might not have disposed of before now.

I lit a cigarette, time to think. To contact this guy without permission crossed the line of interference. If things turned out badly, my ass was on the line. But to not act could cost us the advantage. Homicide was busy. If I called now, they'd be thankful and they would take it from there. My part would be done, though they wouldn't do anything more tonight—their hands were full. If evidence got lost because they delayed, that would be their burden to overcome. No one would get blamed for that, certainly not us.

I didn't want something to get lost, and I didn't care about blame. We'd started this to do something more, teach Stevie what the streets could be. Maralyn's words suddenly came to mind, "Who speaks for Esther?" I hadn't thought about her for a couple days, hadn't thought about that conversation or the "Why are you still just a patrolman?" I'd been too focused on doing the job, and now I found myself invested, unwilling to let go of something that felt as much mine as anyone's.

I started working my way over the should/should not hurdle. Roosevelt was occupied for the moment, so he wasn't a consideration. Roosevelt could wait; Homicide was the problem.

There was only one way around that. If I continued to hunt, I'd need to be able to convince them that things developed rapidly, and since they weren't available I acted with good judgment. Staying out of hot water meant pulling this off without screwing up. That could be done. What remained unknown were the myriad of things that couldn't be anticipated.

I watched Stevie talking to Cassandra. He wasn't going to learn if he didn't do. If he listened to the Roosevelts of this world, he would never realize the potential this job had to offer. He would always work within the guidelines of some rookie administrator who never did a day of real police work in his life. We didn't need more cops like that.

I shrugged. "The hell with it," I groaned. Better to beg forgiveness than to ask for permission. That was one of Ariana's favorite lines. I could do this. The only thing I needed was enough luck to simply not fuck up.

I got back in the car and called the dispatcher line that we used to run people on. A woman answered on the other end.

"Hey, John Hatch, 831-Z. Can you run three phone numbers for me?"

"Yeah, hang on." I could hear her typing on her computer.

A moment later she was ready. The first number came back to a clothing store in Pacific Beach. The second was to a Celia Gonzalez. The third number was a bar in the Gaslamp district. Not likely she called her boyfriend at the clothing store. If she called him at the bar, I was screwed. Celia didn't sound like the name of a boyfriend, but there could be a lot of reasons for that. I tried the middle number.

"Do you have an address for Celia?"

Celia Gonzalez lived three blocks from Esther. Not a boyfriend, but a start.

"Run that address locally, and see if you get anything."

She was quiet a moment as fingers typed. After uttering a couple soft "Hmm," and "Nope" sounds, she came back. "I have several contacts. You have an age?"

"No, how about twenty-five to forty?"

"Not for Celia. I have one for her, born in fifty-six, from a burglary case. She was the victim. There's Rueben, twenty-seven. He's got several contacts."

"That's the one. Sorry, I wasn't looking for Celia. I was looking for a male." My hand tapped on my leg. I needed something, and I got Rueben. Celia was the distraction. No wonder the number didn't come back to him. My luck was holding after all. He lived three blocks from Esther, and he was in the right age range. This had to be the boyfriend. "Run him in County please."

"He has a misdemeanor warrant for dope and a 4th Waiver, bunch of other contacts for dope, petty theft, petty theft with a prior." She sighed. "Do you want me to read all of them?"

"Nope. Give me the warrant number and his description, and I'll let you have your day back."

Rueben was listed at five-ten and about two-hundred pounds with black hair and brown eyes. I thanked her and hung-up. I called the Sheriff's Department and confirmed that the warrant was still good.

Esther and Aaron both had a history consistent with drug use. If she picked one loser, she might have had a pattern of doing that. No one had seen a car leave around the time of the murder. Rueben was a thief, a doper thief at that, which meant he would be in need of a regular fix. Suddenly Aaron didn't look as good, even sort of made sense, asshole or not.

There was rage in the man that killed Esther. Maybe that rage wasn't her husband—maybe it was her boyfriend. A lot of burglars broke into homes because they lacked the guts to be confrontational. If this turned out to be a burglary, if he was the suspect, the meth could change a typical frightened reaction into something more violent. I glanced at my phone and thought about having Ronny paged.

No point in that yet. Boyfriend or not, suspect or not, we had everything we needed to go contact him independent of the homicide. He had an outstanding warrant. Better than that, he was a 4th Waiver, which meant we could enter his house and search.

He didn't need to know anything about the murder investigation. We would simply arrest him for his warrant and search his place. If we didn't find any evidence, we got an arrest and Homicide wouldn't have to look for Rueben when they were ready to talk.

The decision was clear. This was no longer about whether we should. We had every bit of authority to seek this guy out. If we played it right, there would be very little risk that we'd jeopardize Esther's investigation.

I stepped out of the car and called to Stevie. "You get what you need?"

"Yeah, I was about to run her for warrants."

"Skip it. We'll come get her later if she has any." I looked at Cassandra. "Go home. I don't want to see you out here again tonight."

"Yes, Officer Hatch," she said as she picked up an oversized purse that was no doubt filled with condoms, tissues, and a whole assortment of other things I didn't even want to think about.

"Come on," I said to Stevie.

He scampered back to the car and got in. "What's up?"

"We have another place to go."

He swallowed hard. "Where?"

"Rueben's house."

"Who's Rueben?"

I told him what I found out while we drove to the address the dispatcher had given me. When we got there, I parked around the corner, nearly a block away.

"Heads up going in. I don't know if this is going to be his place or not, but no matter. Regardless of whether he's the boyfriend, he's got a warrant, and he probably knows jail is the result of any police contact."

I typed a message to Liz and told her where we were. I asked for another unit. She sent Marcus and Mike Murphy. When they got there, I told them Rueben's background and asked them to take the back alley. It was good to have Mike there. He was SWAT. Not as good as having the whole team, but we wouldn't get that, not for a simple warrant. If we mentioned any possibility that this guy might be involved in our murder, that would bring everything to an instant, messy halt while a half dozen supervisors tried to make a decision about how to proceed.

While I talked, Mike shifted back and forth. In the locker room he was full of bravado, the typical SWAT-jock. When it came down to dealing with a potential shit storm, he nervously sorted through the different possible scenarios we might encounter. If things went bad, he'd kick into gear. The bravado would disappear until the risk was over. After that he'd tell us how he didn't worry. Some bought the façade, I knew better. I'd seen his face when I'd pulled him from the losing end of a fight.

"If he runs, watch out," I said. "This is a low grade warrant, but it's also possible he'll be our Homicide suspect from the other night."

Mike spoke, "Are they coming out?"

"Not yet. Right now he's just wanted for the narc-warrant."

"Do they know you're serving it?"

"They don't even know he exists."

Mike rolled his neck. "Fuck, Hatch. Why do you gotta do this shit to me?"

Stevie looked at Mike, "That's what I keep asking."

"Do I need to remind you who ran and helped your ass last week?"

Mike raised his hands in submission. "Didn't say I wouldn't help. Just fuck."

I gave them Rueben's description. I'd liked to have had a photo, but I wasn't going to burn more time to get one. That would require a trip to the sub, delays, and the risk of running into the boss. He wouldn't be the first warrant suspect we looked for without a picture.

The cadence of radio transmissions continued to grow busier while we briefed. If this didn't pay off, Stevie and I would need to clear. If we were successful, well we'd deal with that road when we crossed it.

"Anyone have questions?" I asked.

Marcus and Mike shook their heads.

"Okay. We'll give you a minute to get out back, and then we'll go to the house."

A moment later they were gone.

"You okay?" I asked Stevie.

"Just not looking forward to getting yelled at."

I patted his shoulder. "Relax, this is the fun part."

"Oh," he exhaled, "The fun started? When?"

"Don't worry. If this doesn't turn out, we'll clear."

"Good."

Before we went to the house, I leaned in the car and typed a message to Roosevelt. "You there?" I knew he wasn't but that didn't matter. Even if he had been, I didn't wait long enough for a response.

CHAPTER 26

STEVIE AND I STAYED CLOSE to the houses as we made our way up the street to Rueben's place. With evening still light, we were never going to be invisible, but I didn't want to be seen any sooner than necessary. A few moments could buy a lot of edge.

A simple deal, knock on the door and check for our guy—a low key operation that happens a dozen times a day throughout the city. That didn't eliminate the dangerous nature of our mission. Rueben was a junkie which made him unpredictable. He was a wanted junkie, and he probably knew about the warrant at the very least. Add to that the fact that he was probably the boyfriend of a murder victim, and a contact like this could quickly go from low key to fully shit infested.

I'd been through some variation of this scenario countless times. Usually they went easy, but looking for bad guys is dangerous business. There's no way around that. You can't call the SWAT team every time you want to talk to someone. Most of the time you just have to suck it up and accept the inherent risk. Every time we engage someone, every time we make an arrest, there is always some element of the unknown. People like to think otherwise when they second guess our actions, but in reality we're generally just working with bits and pieces of the greater picture. Usually the risk is over before the full story comes clear. Today wasn't likely to be any different.

A glance at Stevie stirred anxiety. He was antsy as we walked from one yard to the next. Adrenaline surged in both of us. Steady breathing maintained control. I was used to this. He still wasn't, and that made him as unpredictable as Rueben. He'd demonstrated as much when we found Esther and on Murphy's cover now.

"Breathe," I said quietly. "You're doing great. No big deal." We were in this together. He needed to know that.

Rueben's house didn't appear much different than Esther's. Few of the homes in this neighborhood varied to any significant degree, most built during early runs of tract construction meant to accommodate the military. Some of them dated back to the twenties, most were two and three bedroom Craftsman-style bungalows.

I knocked on the front door, and a moment later a Hispanic woman answered. She was short, a bit heavy, with dark skin and hard lines in a face that had seen a great many years of challenges.

"Hello, Celia? Is Rueben here?" I asked looking beyond her, listening for the tell-tale clatter of someone scrambling out a back door or window.

"He's not here," she said angrily.

"Okay, we're going to need to come inside and check."

"Why?" she demanded, stepping up to fill the doorway.

"I will explain in a moment. First we're going to look," I said, stepping forward decisively. The matter wasn't open to negotiation.

Celia retreated, she knew the game. Though she didn't much like the thought of us forcing our way into her home, she knew we'd do so just the same. Gripe maybe, but she wouldn't stop us. To do as much would earn her a set of handcuffs while we worked. Not my preferred method of controlling a tired old woman who probably had no idea what her son was really up to, but I wasn't going to take a chance and I wasn't going to be deterred. The longer she remained a disruption, the longer we were at risk.

"Stay by the door, please," I told her softly. Celia muttered angrily while Stevie and I made our way past her.

The kitchen and living room were clear. My Springfield slipped quietly from the holster as we moved quickly into the hallway and down to the first bedroom. I looked through the open door keeping my gun low so as not to excite Celia but to allow the muzzle to track where my eyes searched. It was a kid's bedroom, empty but for clothes, a bunk bed, and some toys. The second door was the bathroom, also empty. I pulled the shower curtain aside to make sure no one was hiding in the tub.

Stevie's breathing grew more ragged with each step. Next was the master bedroom, Celia's bedroom. The television played some show from the local Mexican access channel. I moved through to the master bath but found nothing inside.

The last door, across the hall from the master, was closed. Stevie and I stood on either side. I turned the knob and pushed. "Rueben," I called out as the door swung open. "San Diego Police." There was no answer, and I couldn't see anyone. I stepped inside and pulled the closet open. Again, there was no one.

I got on the air and asked Liz to have Marcus and Mike switch to another frequency. She no doubt switched to listen as well.

"He's gone. You guys can clear, thanks for the help."

Before they could reply, Socrates angrily interrupted. "John, Sergeant Roosevelt. What are you doing?" I cringed.

"Just checking a warrant suspect, sir. We'll be clear shortly."

His tone was angrier the second time. "Get a meet when you're done. I told you to check with me."

I grinned. "Sorry, sir, I tried but you were on that DV. I sent you a message. Check your computer."

"Regardless, we need to meet," he said taking the time to punctuate each word.

"As soon as we're done here," I said. Screw him. Let him stew. The message would be there waiting when he got back to his car. I made sure of that. How long was I supposed to wait for him to answer me? I gave him a nanosecond.

Back down the hall, Celia stood in the doorway with her arms folded—not the first time a mother glared at me like that.

"Sorry, Ma'am. Do you know where your son is?"

"He doesn't tell me where he goes, what's this about?"

"He has a warrant."

"That's old, he took care of that," she insisted, probably wanting to believe in him more than anything.

"Sorry, still in the system this afternoon. We came to talk to him about it."

"You came to arrest him."

I shrugged. "Perhaps, but if he went to court he should have paperwork. If he has that we won't need to arrest him. That seems easy enough."

She mumbled terse Spanish rapidly. I didn't know all the words, but what I understood was not good. I couldn't tell if she was speaking about me or her son.

"Sorry for the disruption. We're going to search his room, and then we'll go."

"What business do you have in his room?" The accusatory tone of her voice made me think that maybe Rueben was one of those Momma's boys, fucked up because his mother couldn't recognize her kid was a turd no matter what he did. Then again, maybe the apple didn't fall far and she knew more than she let on. "Don't you need a search warrant?"

"No."

"Then you need to leave."

I spoke more softly. "Sorry, Ma'am. I'm afraid we don't need a warrant. Your son is on probation. As a condition, I have the authority to search his home."

"This is my home," she replied firmly.

"And he listed it as his. That means I can search his room. No one has any intention of looking through your things, but I'm going to look through his."

"Whatever," she said with a dismissive wave of the hand. "You're going to do whatever you want, never mind if it causes problems for an old woman."

Now was her turn to play the guilt trip just as I'd done with Cindy Peterson. It wasn't going to work. I didn't like the thought of causing her stress, but she'd been through this before. She knew the system. Pushing to try and make me uncomfortable was the only control she had. I could stand there all day and explain, but that wouldn't make things a single bit better no matter what her motivation.

I looked at Stevie. "Watch her."

He nodded back, and then stood in the living room to make sure she didn't do anything while I searched.

Rueben's room was pretty standard for a tweaker. The sheets on the bed probably hadn't been washed in months. They reeked with that sweaty, chemical, body odor, tweaker smell, so foul even mom probably gave up on the cause. The stench permeated everything in the bedroom. I ignored the odor. Meth got bigger by the day, and there was no indication the scourge was going away anytime soon. A drug like that ensured I had a career for as long as I wanted to work.

Piles of dirty clothes, plates covered with rotten, mold fuzzy food that could no longer be identified, video game parts, and tools littered the room. During the first minute of the search, I found at least six car stereos. Rueben was a doper and a thief for sure. Every cord on every stereo was cut or had been pulled free of the car he stole it from. The man was tweaking hard. A stolen stereo wasn't worth much but enough to steady a habit. The tools were for breaking into and dismantling anything that could be sold, or exchanged, for dope.

Taking a moment, I pulled some clean rubber gloves from a sealed belt pouch and put them on. I drew a slow breath before continuing. I didn't know what I might find, but I didn't want to screw up any prints—or DNA—on potential evidence. I was equally certain there was a long list of other things I might find that I wouldn't want to touch with bare skin.

Tweakers were sex fiends, their drive amplified by a stimulant that never left them satisfied. If they could hump something twenty four hours a day, they'd try. That meant the inevitable stash of porn, and if I were truly unlucky, a pile of sex toys that had been places not worth imagining. This wasn't the kind of stuff you wanted to reach in a drawer and grab ungloved. After all, this wasn't the nice, clean stash of Joannie the lonely housewife, cleansed and neatly stored until hubby spent too much time at work. This was the unclean, objects that had been places, never washed, and coated with a mix of curly hairs, dried gelatinous films, dark chunks, and smears a person would really rather not consider.

I'd need to keep an eye out for needles too. Hazards didn't cease when the suspects weren't around.

My search was methodical, moving clock-wise around the room—easier that way than having to wonder whether I missed a place when I was done. The hot air was stifled by a closed door and the afternoon sun beating against the house. Sweat ran down my back, soaking my vest, the stench more powerful the longer I was there. I'd smell tweaker the rest of the night.

I froze and thought about what I was doing. Rueben was a murder suspect. Perhaps not officially. Hell, Homicide didn't even know he existed, but I was in his room conducting a search that could turn up evidence connecting him to Esther. The tools alone might tie him to the scene. I considered calling Ronny again. He was busy. His whole team was busy. They would want to know what I found, but they'd also want to know whether Rueben was something more than my gut feeling. He could just be a doper who lived in the same neighborhood. I'd need more.

A song drummed a beat in my head. The case was starting to sing. If I didn't wrap quickly, I'd have Roosevelt to contend with. Such a confrontation would be more difficult in the midst of something not so fully resolved. I decided to dig further, see if I could find the one piece that gave me the answers I needed.

I worked through the pile of junk in the closet—more tools, more radios—making note of each item of potential evidence in my notebook. I left everything where I found it so I could take photos before seizing anything. With luck I could connect some of the stereos to burglarized cars from the neighborhood. Regardless of whether Rueben panned out as a murder suspect, I still had the makings of a good theft case. Perhaps he had been the one in Esther's house. Maybe he even put the DVD player on the table. Perhaps he'd intended to take what he could after things went screwy. Then again, either Aaron Anderson or some new stranger could have been the murderer. Cindy Peterson still wasn't out of the question, or at least the equation.

Closet done, I moved to an old dresser. The lower drawer on the right side was his porn stash. I rifled through the stack of magazines and movies, nothing out of the ordinary. I checked the night stand drawers, then moved the lamp on top to the floor and lifted one end to see if there was anything under the nightstand itself. There was not. I replaced the lamp and moved to the bed.

More magazines were stuffed between the mattress and box spring, magazines and a balled up dirty sock. I pushed the sock to the side to look under the magazines and felt an odd shifting of weight. Still gloved, I lifted the discolored sock carefully, concerned that I'd find his stash of old syringes. I didn't want to get stuck.

Grabbing the sock by the toe, I moved toward the light. The filthy footwear hadn't been washed in nearly as long as the nasty bed sheets. When I shook, the contents dumped out on the mattress. I stepped back, taken for a moment by what had fallen out. I'd reached the bridge in this song the moment I saw the jewelry lying on the bed in front of me, Esther's jewelry. I couldn't prove that, not yet anyway, but I knew.

CHAPTER 27

TO SAY I WANTED to run back to the car would minimize the feeling of excitement surging through my chest. A song pounded in my ears as sure as if I was center stage. We were onto something.

"I'll be back," I said to Stevie as I passed by and left him in the house with Rueben's mother. I wanted to let him know what I'd found, but no point running the risk of sending her into hysterics any sooner than necessary.

I tried but couldn't smother my elation over breaking this case. Premature was a certainty, a long way from a done deal, but what we had found was important. I could feel that as sure as anything. Answers were never as complicated as they got on TV. When a case came together, the fragments of the puzzle made sense. My initial thoughts that Aaron Anderson was not our guy, that gut feeling that he wasn't right, no matter how big an ass, was replaced by the growing certainty that Rueben Gonzalez was our man.

From this point the case belonged to Homicide. They'd step in and process what we'd uncovered. When Rueben was located they would do the interview. I had little hope they'd let us be involved. If Stevie and I got lucky, they might let us help make the arrest, but the final loose ends would be tied up by the detectives. I'd be luckier yet if I didn't get some hide chewed off my backside for digging a little more diligently than they might have wanted.

I got to the car and pulled out a cigarette. The adrenaline was making me antsy. I needed something to calm the jitters. Nothing would take them away, but maybe I could shave the edge off. I'd be awake a long, long time tonight. Sleep came hard after something like this. Looking around, I realized we'd been hunting longer than I thought. The sky was growing dark. Long evening shadows stretched to fill nooks and spaces visible only in the daylight. Soon, the night urchins would emerge and East San Diego would go to shit. I felt bad that my squad would have to cover my slack. To be fair, I'd have to make it up to them tomorrow.

I called Ronny's cell phone, not knowing how deep he was into his own call, clueless about how messy a caper he might already have. The possibility existed they'd need to send a different team. My thumb moved to the end call button as I thought about calling the Watch Commander instead. The phone continue to ring. I'd talk to Ronny first. Or not. The phone went to voice mail.

"Ronny, call me ASAP. I might have our guy." I hung up and leaned back against the hood of my car to wait.

Every contact of the past week played in my mind. We'd come so far from the night we found Esther lying dead in her bedroom. Each bit of information we'd gathered—the jewelry box knocked askew, a burglary disturbed in progress, Esther's coworkers, the slutty blonde—everything had brought us here to a sock full of jewelry in some strange doper's mom's house. One thing led to another and came together like a case should.

Unfortunately Esther's choices had probably led her to her ultimate demise, far from a new story. Maybe she broke off the relationship and he got angry, killed her in a rage. Maybe the thief in him, the need for dope, drove him to break into her house and take what he knew was there for the stealing. He wouldn't be the first addiction-driven thief who stole from someone he cared about to feed a fix that was larger than whatever ethics might have once restrained him.

My foot tapped nervously. I glanced at my phone as if that might make Ronny call quicker. I could be in for a long wait. I crushed out my cigarette and lit another, then shuddered that I might be delayed until Roosevelt cleared and came in search of me. I wasn't in the mood to have to explain this and then let him direct what I was going to do next. Fuck him. I'd had enough of Socrates. He could wait until later for his pound of flesh. I took another glance at my phone and tucked it away in my shirt pocket.

Up the street, something caught my eye. I looked but only saw shadows. For a moment I thought maybe it was one of the countless cats who foraged the neighborhood. The movement was quick, akin to a cat jumping from the fence to a warm car hood. That would have been Pal's life if the little bastard had been smarter than to get caught by some lady who cared enough to help.

Whatever drew my attention moved again. I strained for a better look as a shadow shifted behind a car three houses away. No cat looking for an alley rat. This was a person, and he was watching me. I tossed my cigarette to the ground and pretended my only interest was crushing it out.

I started to move, angling to make sure I kept the car between us. If I was going to get close enough for a better look, I needed to cover ground. The fact that someone was hiding, watching what I did, meant nothing in this neighborhood. If you knocked on a dozen doors, you'd likely find at least a couple people with warrants. There were a number of reasons a great many people would be interested in why the cops were sniffing around, and not all of them were nefarious.

There was also one reason that was of greater concern than any other. We'd been at Rueben's for a while. With his background, a guy like him would never just amble right up to a house, not even his own. Less so if there was a Crown Vic anywhere nearby. Rueben would watch. He might come close like a sunfish testing the worm on a hook, but he'd never just bite down on the bait. You learn these tricks on the street, you learn more of them in jail, and you get a university education on them in prison.

I kept moving, but there was no more shadow. The dying light of day was fading fast, and seeing without a flashlight was more difficult with every passing moment. I started when my cell phone went off. I wasn't the only one.

From behind the car, the shadow stood. A man, and he only paused a moment. Long enough. I could see him, and I knew who he was the instant our eyes locked. Rueben Gonzalez had just materialized into something more than a theory.

And then it was on. Rueben bolted to the right.

I lunged into a sprint while I grabbed the microphone on my lapel. "831-Z foot pursuit northbound on 4000 47th Street." I put out his description.

He was quick, more so from meth and adrenaline than any fitness regimen. I had a vest and twenty pounds of gear to contend with. I'd need to push. If he ghosted, I'd have to stop and start locking down the area with other cops so we could search for him. They'd be coming, as keyed in on the words "foot pursuit" as they would have been on "cover now."

The world shifted and bounced. Tunnel vision restricted peripheral sight as my eyes focused on my prey. I strained to cover the distance between us. Though gaining ground, I wasn't sure I could get to him before he darted between houses. I reached to grab the small flashlight from my belt. I'd have preferred my heavier Streamlight, but that sat on the front seat of my car. I'd have to make do.

Rueben looked back to see where I was, stumbled, and nearly lost his footing. That brought me closer. I squeezed the microphone and my radio screeched as another unit stepped on my transmission to advise they were en route to my call.

"Stay off the fucking air and get your ass here," I mumbled under my breath.

Rueben cut to the right and started heading for a fence between two houses. Fuck! If he cleared that fence, the chase was done. I was alone. I wasn't even sure how close my nearest cover unit was. If I lost sight of him, I knew the risk that came by bounding over fences into unseen territory. He was a homicide suspect, official or not. I had to keep that in mind. It wouldn't do me any good to go hurdling over a fence only to find him waiting on the other side with a gun. That would end things right quick. He was important, but he wasn't worth dying for. There'd be another day if it came down to that. Not so if I didn't use my head.

I tried the radio again, and put out our change in direction. The microphone popped out of my hand and came unclasped from my lapel. It swung out of reach and dangled off the wire connected to my radio. To stop would be to lose him. He was at the fence and having trouble clearing the top. If I could get to him, the chase ended here.

With a groan, I sprinted the remaining feet and was on him as he pulled himself atop the fence. I grabbed his legs. He pushed off the fence and fell back on top of me. His weight and the momentum of his fall broke my footing. I was going to the ground. I held on to his shirt and took him down with me. Better than standing over me so he could kick me in the head.

I grunted when I hit the ground and heard him do the same. He spun and started flailing his arms. The fight was on. He was shorter than me, but he still had some weight. The meth hadn't thinned him out as much as I'd have liked.

I drove a fist in his side, and he groaned. He responded with an elbow to the side of my face. My head rang. It was a good shot. I hit him again. "Stop resisting. You're under . . . arrest."

"Fuck you," he said as he spun on his side and kicked me in the lower leg. The grazing scrape from his shoe hurt but didn't seem serious. I tried to return the favor by showing him what a steel toe could do to a shin. I missed.

Rueben continued to flail while I scrambled to get control of his arms. If I could lock them behind him, I'd have leverage. He twisted one arm free and punched me in the shoulder. I could hear sirens, but they sounded a good way off. In the old days I'd have had ten cops by now. Not any more. This was the price for running a lean department.

I tried to bend the one arm I still held. A quick twist behind his back, I'd have another shot at that leverage. He squirmed the other way and my move had no effect. Then his free hand hit me in the side. My vest absorbed much of the strike.

I brought my forearm into his jaw and his head rattled with the blow. He responded with a knee to my side. Still no one showed up. I'd just sprinted a block, and now I was scrambling on the ground with a scared, drugged up suspect. Each time I grabbed an arm, his strength to resist surprised me.

"Stop . . . resisti . . ." I grunted.

"Lemme go."

"No."

He rolled onto his stomach, and I dropped across his back to try and weigh him down. If I could just hold him, pin him to the ground, I could wait for help. He used his arms and legs to push me up. I tried to get an arm around his neck to choke him unconscious. No luck. I toppled off, and he seemed to stand instantly.

I spun on the ground and scrambled to my feet, but not before he had a chance to bring his foot into my chest. I groaned from the blow, but once again the vest took the brunt of the strike.

I swayed as I got my footing. Rueben's fist glanced across my forehead and right eye. I couldn't tell if the warm wetness that followed was blood or sweat. I grabbed for my collapsible baton but it wasn't in the holder. I tried for the pepper spray, but that was gone too. If he found either of those items on the ground before I could control him, this was going to get downright sticky.

I shifted my weight forward, lunged two steps into a tackle, and took Rueben back to the ground. My forearm scraped along something solid.

Rueben brought a knee up between us and tried to force me

off. I could feel him pushing me back, and I drove my fist into his stomach. He still pushed. I hit him again. He pushed. I hit him again. He just wouldn't stop.

I could feel my breathing start to get ragged. A minute could be an awful long time. This needed to end. Without help I was in a bad spot. Each blow I made hit hard. For a normal person my strikes would have done something. But he wasn't feeling any pain. The drugs were fueling his fight, and it took everything I had to stay with him.

The sirens grew closer. I drove my elbow hard into his chest. He grabbed my shirt and pushed me back as he scrambled to stand. The cell phone in my shirt pocket started ringing again. Ronny. He had no idea I was in the struggle of my life with his suspect.

Time was running out. Fear that he might get the better of me started to creep up the back of my neck. If I wore down too much, lost my wind, if my muscles fatigued, my options would run short. You can move from able to fight to exhaustion very quickly. I had no light, no pepper spray, no baton. If Rueben gained ground, this could instantly turn into a shoot scenario. I didn't see any indication he would quit until I wasn't a threat. He might run if I just let him go, but then again, he might turn around and bring the fight back to me. I wasn't about to give him an opportunity to gain high ground.

I pushed, and he rolled onto his side. Rueben was nearly half up when I brought my arm over his shoulder and across his chest. If I could just get an arm around him, I'd have my gun clear, and I could hold out a little bit longer. With any luck I could squeeze the shit out of his nuts with my other hand. Doper or not, a good old nut grab always helped in a pinch. One thing was clear. I was going to need help to get him handcuffed. Drugged up suspect or not, I was walking out of this.

Movement blurred across my peripheral vision. Rueben groaned, and air rushed out of his lungs as Stevie delivered a full on sweeping kick to his chest.

The cavalry had arrived, and it was the last person in the world I'd have ever thought it would be. Rueben toppled to the ground. I scrambled clear but grabbed his arm in the process. I twisted it behind his back and dropped down on top of him. He groaned again as my knee landed on his lower back. That had to crush a kidney.

Stevie came down on the other side, resting his knee on Rueben's neck. Neither of us worried whether we were hurting him. Too fucking bad if it hurt. Fighting hurt. I held his arm, and Stevie brought the other one back. He pulled out his handcuffs and quickly got one on Rueben's wrist. A moment later he worked his hands around so he could get the other cuff on the wrist I was holding.

My breathing stayed ragged as I drew big gulps of air. The vision in my right eye went cloudy, and I wiped at it, writing if off for sweat. This one had taken me for a ride. I was content to simply kneel on Rueben until another officer got here to give us a hand.

"Nice kick," I said, squinting at Stevie.

"I was going to try something else, but sometimes you have to improvise to end a thing quickly. Some grumpy guy told me that. Same guy who flipped when I ran off after someone by myself."

Grinning, I reached up to my forehead. So much for sweat, blood stained my fingers. That was gonna hurt later. "He doesn't sound so grumpy, and the rules aren't so simple, are they? The only thing on the streets that's black and white is our car."

I could hear the racing engine of a Ford heading our way. I pulled on the cord and recovered my radio microphone. Took a deep breath, then let it out slowly. I was spent, worked up, and wore out but there was another rule that had to be followed. No matter what happened, how banged up you were, how frightened, you could never let anyone hear it on the radio. It was kind of a contest, who could be the coolest on the air.

I inhaled and spoke steady in the transmitter. "831-Zebra, suspect in custody."

CHAPTER 28

THE NEXT FEW DAYS passed more quickly than I'd have liked. My fight with Rueben had been harder than I knew at the time. Adrenaline did that. My face was cut, swollen, and bruised, and my right leg scraped raw—knuckles and forearms were cut up and tender. Recovery used to seem easier. Things change when you hit thirty. Start closing on forty and suddenly the aches don't leave as fast.

I found out later that when I went after Rueben, the world stopped in East San Diego. Cops dropped reports, let traffic tickets go, rushed from whatever they were doing to come to my aid. I wasn't one to call for help, and they knew that if I was asking there was real need. Sirens might have come from a distance, but the sound of them was a cavalry bugle that had given me the strength to fight. I might have been alone on the ground, but I wasn't alone in the world. I had family, brothers and sisters who would risk everything to bring me home safely at the end of the shift. They came, even Roosevelt.

Socrates had been a bundle of nerves and stress, but even he knew better than to turn that moment into an ass chewing. The paramedics arrived and checked out the damage, first to me, and then Rueben. They'd pushed for me to go for X-rays, and I declined. This wasn't my first fight, and certainly not my worst. Scrapes would heal. A hot shower and a couple bandages would suffice. I hadn't intended on anything more. I could return to work tomorrow. My command thought otherwise.

Sergeant Rake pulled me aside. "You're off the rest of the week. Don't make me kick your ass to make that happen." His statement was a violation of the letter of every workplace violence regulation. The spirit of his statement was, "Go home and rest." I was pretty certain he wouldn't make good on his promise, but a part of me decided it was best to give him the benefit of the doubt.

Homicide sent a detective to evaluate what we'd found. Someone else collected the evidence, and I was sent home without the opportunity to finish what I started. Despite orders, I came in the next day and finished my report as a matter of pride. Battered or not, I wasn't going to lie down. Paperwork done, I spent the weekend watching the new release movies I never got to see in the theaters. Pal was glad for the beating I'd taken, and took full advantage of several days on the couch watching movies together.

When I returned to work the following week, the bruises had turned green and yellow, and the scrapes had crusted into scabs. I still looked like hell, but I was good enough to function.

The evidence in Rueben's bedroom had sealed the deal. Aaron Anderson identified his wife's jewelry, and one of the screwdrivers in Rueben's pile of tools matched the pry marks on the back door of the house. Most people got rid of items like that. You don't have to be a genius to realize they could put you in prison. Fortunately, tweakers had a hard time getting rid of things. The lab quickly confirmed the pry tool. Getting results was much easier when you had a probable tool and a deadline for court.

Rueben hadn't been the boyfriend anymore. By his account, Esther broke up with him the week before he killed her. Perhaps she got tired of his shit, or she found someone else. Maybe she wanted to give her marriage another chance. We would never know. His need for drugs brought him to Esther's. He knew the house and he knew he could get some things there to pawn for a fix. The only thing he didn't know was that Esther would come home early that afternoon. He was cornered, and she was angry. That made him angry, and the fight was on as quickly as it had been with the two of us. Considering the strength he demonstrated when he turned on me, I had no doubt he was fully capable of tossing her around and choking the life out of her.

Esther's was a simple story in the end. They always were. This wasn't CSI. I didn't feel special, didn't feel like Sherlock Holmes. There were a lot of cops that could have done the same thing. Homicide would have figured everything out, ultimately. The tape recorder I'd given Stevie the night of the murder had captured everything Aaron told us in the car. A detective would have found that tape when they sorted through what had been collected. The statements would have sent them down the same path, but where they had many murders, we had only one. Time was on our side.

The satisfaction came in knowing we were a part of the process. In exchange, we would spend time covering calls so other cops had an opportunity to do the same. That was the balance, and it was important to maintain. The job of a street cop can't be all tickets and reports, and it can't be all about catching the Ruebens in the world. There would be a lot more of the mundane before there was another Rueben.

I returned to work early, eager to be back. Stevie and I had a court appointment in the afternoon. Capturing Rueben forced Homicide to quickly clean up the case for preliminary court appointments. In this job time is only on your side until you put someone in jail. Once that happens then you need to be prepared to start presenting your case. The alternative is to release your suspect until you have you shit together.

Today was a hearing that would determine if Rueben would move toward trial. No one wanted him on the street, so we'd need to bring life to Esther's death. Even if we convicted him down the road, in a few years he'd be back out, harder than before, better trained by the university of California penal system. Until then he would be a convict with a number. The justice wouldn't match the offense, but he would answer for his actions. As a result, maybe someone would find peace.

I walked toward my mailbox and was almost past Ariana's office when I glanced inside and saw her talking to Socrates.

"John, can you come in here please," she said in a tone that meant we were about to have one of her discussions.

I stopped, tilted my head to crack my neck, and then walked in the office. I looked at the empty chair next to Roosevelt and spoke to her. "Will I be staying long?"

"Have a seat."

I pulled the chair to put extra distance between wonder boy and myself. My first day back hadn't even officially started and I was in the grease. Some things never changed.

Ariana waited until I settled. "How are you feeling, John?"

That was how it should be. She might lay into my ass with some sharp teeth, but her first thought was about my welfare. I could suffer the rest. Roosevelt wouldn't even make eye contact. If he'd been any kind of man, we would have worked this out in private. Not so, he'd need someone else to do the hard work.

"I'm fine, lieutenant. Thanks for asking."

She smiled, but that quickly faded. "John, Sergeant Roosevelt has been discussing some issues with me. He feels you are a disruptive influence on the squad, and that you are actively trying to undermine his authority."

Guilty, I thought. I chose my words more carefully. No use pleading out. "Lieutenant, Sergeant Roosevelt has been on my ass since the moment he took over the squad. To be honest, I think it's about personality and control. He has no personality, and power comes from ability, not position."

That brought him straight out of his chair. "John, you have done everything you could to do exactly the opposite of everything I've directed you to do. When I tell you to check in with me, you ignore me. When I tell you to handle calls, you initiate your own little projects. It is not your job to determine priorities."

I shrugged. I would have argued, but yelling would never anger him as much as being dismissive. "I disagree, sir. That's precisely my job. I'm the one who needs to balance my day, the one who knows these streets, who knows what I can handle and what I cannot. If the job isn't getting done, then we have an issue. I'll compare my workload to anyone you want to put me up against. If I'm deficient, then I'll correct my behavior."

I let that soak, then continued before he could start another tirade. "As to the disruption, I'm sorry. I'll have to disagree there as well. You asked me to check in. I complied. When you weren't here, I talked to Sergeant Rake, who was. I sent you a couple messages my last night here, but you never answered. You were still at the sub and not even logged on when I sent the first. The second time you didn't get back to me, so I exercised initiative. I'm sorry if you feel that's disruptive, but sometimes things develop out here and the pace gets quick. In the absence of immediate supervision, the city pays me to make independent decisions."

I lowered my voice, softened the edge. Time to patronize. "I know you're a newer sergeant without a great deal of street experience. Maybe you should consider some place slower until you find what works. Mid-City can be a lot to manage."

His face ignited red, and the vein in his forehead pulsed. I'd just turned the table. This wasn't about my being disruptive, but his competence. I hoped that worked.

This time he pointed his finger—well, waved to be more precise.

"That's exactly the kind of smug attitude I'm talking about. You do everything in your power to undermine me."

"Sir, I'm trying to figure out what you want. We are, after all, in the lieutenant's office, and I'm here on my time. But, if you want to speak about undermining someone, perhaps we can start with the fact that since day one you have not only jumped my shit, but you did it front of my peers with the full intention of embarrassing me. You did it even after I asked you not to, after I asked you to address your issues privately. Who is undermining who?"

"I was addressing issues promptly, and it was always professional. I never embarrassed you, I . . ."

Ariana spoke firmly and cut him off. "Theodore."

He shut up and sat. I cringed. She spoke in the same tone my mother used when she demanded my full attention.

"I want him disciplined," he added with a wave of his hand.

Ariana leaned back and crossed her legs before folding her hands in her lap. "I'm sorry, Theodore, but that isn't going to happen today. My counterpart in Homicide called this morning to make sure I knew about the work John did for them. He said John was working with their approval, and that if we didn't write a citation he would do it himself. How am I supposed to discipline John when he's doing what someone else wanted? I'm afraid a Homicide lieutenant trumps a patrol sergeant in this case."

She took a breath and let her words sink in. "The two of you have issues, clear enough. If need be, we can alter the schedule at shift change. Until then, I expect you to work things out like properly civilized human beings."

"But . . ."

"No but, sergeant. Your points are noted. Now, if you'll give me some time, I have additional issues to discuss with your officer."

Roosevelt lowered his head. "Yes, Ma'am." He got up and sulked to the door.

"Please close that, will you? The rest of the station doesn't need to hear."

My stomach dropped and tightened into a ball.

She watched through the window until Roosevelt walked off. After that she sat quietly for what seemed like a very long time. "This is a fine mess you've stirred up."

"Me?"

She nodded. "Do you forget who you're talking to? He pissed you off, and you wound that baby sergeant up like one of those cymbal clapping monkeys."

"He's a fucking slapnut."

"Absolutely, and you're John Hatch, streetcop extraordinaire. You played him, you manipulated him, and you turned this whole damn thing against him. Now I have a brand new sergeant that's ramped so tight he might never loosen. He's looking for me to back his play, and I have to turn around and tell him I will not. That's a fine spot, indeed."

"I tried to be nice. He took me on, and I was about to punk him out in front of everyone, but your speech about diplomacy stopped me. He wouldn't let up. All I wanted to do was my job. It's that simple, always has been."

"Well, regardless who drew first blood, quit picking at the wound. Stay away from him for a while and let things calm down. Can you do that?"

Again, I shrugged.

"Can you try?"

"Yeah." I nodded. "Because you asked, not because he deserves it. Respect is earned."

"Go on then, and good luck in court. Fine piece of work. I'm glad you're okay."

I walked to the door. Ariana spoke as I grabbed the handle. "John."

I turned.

"Nice job covering your trail, but don't count on that 'slapnut' being as dumb as you think. He won't likely make the same mistakes. Make sure you thank whoever helped you pull it off." She smiled.

"I don't have the remotest idea what you mean," I said, walking out the door.

When I got to the locker room, Stevie was getting ready. "Nice face."

"Come on, hurry up."

He looked at his watch. "We have plenty of time before court."

"Yeah, but we have something to do first."

He looked confused. "What?"

"Time to work on our karma."

I started toward the back door. He grabbed his gear and scrambled after me. We picked an available patrol car and drove to my Explorer. I pulled out the bundle of red carnations and quickly put them in the trunk of our cruiser, and then looked around to make sure no one saw them. There would be no end to the questions—and grief—I'd get if anyone saw me with a bouquet of pretty red flowers.

"Where we going with those?" he asked as we left the station.

"Amelia's."

His forehead wrinkled, and he shook his head.

"The woman whose husband died. Today would be their seventy-fifth wedding anniversary. Jonathan always brought flowers. Might be a sad day if someone didn't." I wasn't sure whether it would be sadder if someone did, but figured the risk was worth the effort.

"You're a softy," he mused. "Seems the grump ain't so grumpy after all."

"Shut the fuck up." He did, but sat in his seat beaming like a kid with a secret.

When we got to the house, the garage door was closed. I retrieved the flowers. "Come on, I'm not doing this alone."

Stevie shook his head. "Nooo, you go."

"Move."

He followed a step behind me all the way to the front door. I knocked and waited for an answer. I knocked again. Amelia was old. I had to allow some extra time. When no one came, I got a sinking feeling. Perhaps she was still with her family.

A neighbor next door swept her driveway. I handed the flowers to Stevie. "Wait here."

I walked over to the woman and she stopped working.

Nodding toward the house, I asked, "Do you know when she'll be home?"

"Amelia?"

"Yes, Ma'am."

She shook her head. "I'm sorry, officer. She died a couple days ago, both of them in a week." The words hit like a punch in the stomach.

She sighed. "I guess Jonathan's loss just took her will."

"Thank you," I said and walked back to the house where I took the flowers from Stevie.

"What's up? She not home?"

"Yeah."

I walked to the side yard and opened the trash can, about to toss the bouquet when I saw a plastic bottle half buried in the rubbish. Retrieving it, I tossed the lid, and then walked over to the water spigot. I put the flowers on the front door step.

Walking to the car, Stevie said, "I'm sure she'll like them when she gets home."

We drove to court in silence, me in somber reflection and Stevie still riding the thought that we did something sweet.

Ronny and his team were already at the Hall of Justice. After a short discussion with the DA—who thankfully was not Maralyn—all but Ronny, who was lead investigator, were ordered to wait in the hallway until called. One at a time the bailiff ushered us into the courtroom to testify. I was last. Considering the morning, an afternoon smashing my ass on the hard, wood benches in the courthouse should have been considered a given. It's not like you could relax, not in uniform. You couldn't go more than a couple minutes without getting eye-fucked by some crook walking down the hallway.

When it was my turn on the stand, I walked the prosecutor through what happened, from finding Esther to fighting Rueben. The public defender asked little. I thought he was going to go at me when he started with, "Is this type of investigation something you do often?" But he let that go. Beating a cop up on the stand was a good strategy in front of a jury, but in front of a judge who was just trying to make an early evaluation about whether the evidence was worthy of trial, it was an effort wasted.

Aaron Anderson sat in the audience and watched. When my testimony was done, I returned to the hallway so the public defender and the prosecutor could argue whether we had a case. I waited to hear the judge's decision.

The door burst open and Ronny blew into the hallway followed by a line of people all trying to clear court and get on the road before afternoon traffic got too busy.

"Bound over," he grinned with a nod and wave for me to follow.

"Good job," he said away from the crowd. "Sorry you couldn't sit through the rest. You know he copped out, don't you? He admitted it in the interview the night you arrested him. When the adrenaline and meth wore off, he got all weepy and shit."

"That answers why the defense was testing how often I've done this."

"Gotta have someone to go after. He'll plead, but if he doesn't, I expect I'll be the evil detective who grilled him until he cried and admitted to a crime he didn't commit while you fucked up the crime scene. Damn, if we ain't bad people."

I was satisfied as I watched the crowd continue to funnel out of the courtroom. Aaron Anderson came out, glanced at us, and then continued down the hall.

"What's up with that?" Stevie asked ask he joined us.

"What?"

"He was the primary suspect. We found the guy who killed his wife, and he can't even say thanks?"

"You were looking for a thank you?"

"You'd think," he said shaking his head.

"We're just two cops, and he didn't like us much that night. Don't expect your efforts will ever mean anything more. If he's thankful, it's with the system. You want a snuggly hug and a shiny star, find an elementary school teacher."

I shook Ronny's hand. "Thanks for letting us play."

"No, thank you guys. I appreciate the good work . . ." he looked at Stevie, "whether Aaron Anderson does or not. I figured it was him, and that's a lesson for you. Don't ever get too locked in one thought, or you'll start missing the truth."

We left Ronny and started for our car. Time to work. There would be radio calls waiting. Today was our turn at the musket balls. We owed the guys a couple rounds from the front line.

The door opened as we approached a courtroom. I stopped to let people exit. Maralyn stepped out carrying a stack of folders, as surprised as I was to be standing there face to face.

"Hi, John." She smiled warmly. When she saw the scrape on my face, she gasped. Pulling one hand free of the stack of papers she reached up as though she were going to touch my injuries. Why women did that, I'll never know. They always want to touch the wound. She stopped and brought her hand back down, sensing that her move had been presumptuous. "Are you okay?"

"Yeah, it's nothing, really. A simple shaving accident."

Stevie looked at her, then quickly at me, and then back at her.

I wasn't prepared for this. "How are you?" I asked, unsure what else to say.

"Good. You got a minute?"

Stevie looked at me. "Go on, softy man." Then he turned to her. "Be careful," he said with a nod. "He's sensitive." He got a broad grin and walked down the hall.

"He's a little mental," I said. "Pay no attention to him."

"Did you get my messages?"

"Yeah, look, I don't know what you have going on, but I'm not comfortable being in the middle of something."

"There is no something. I just didn't cut the strings like I should have. I'm sorry. He's gone now though. When he got home, we talked and I told him he needed to move out. It wasn't what it seemed, John. I'm sorry about the way things started, but I'd really like to see you again. Do you suppose we could start over?"

I wanted to but starting over never seemed to turn out as good as the thought sounded. Maralyn had taken me by surprise, but I didn't want to be her transition relationship. I wasn't much of a rebound guy, and if she was one that didn't leave until the next guy came along, I wasn't much for that either.

She broke eye contact in the moment that lingered.

I gave in. "Maybe we could get coffee some morning."

She looked up and fought back a smile like she didn't want to seem too eager.

"I'd like that."

We lingered another uncomfortable moment. "I should get back to work," I said.

"Yeah, yeah, me too." She smiled. "Call me when you're ready. And try to be more careful when you shave."

I returned to Stevie.

"Ooo, the grumpy man got a girlfriend." He laughed, amused at himself.

"Are you through?"

He stifled his joy. "Yeah. What's the plan?"

"How 'bout we just take what comes?" He fell in step beside me.

"Okay, but I was thinking, maybe we could get a cup of coffee before we clear."

"You drink Snapple."

"Yeah, but you don't, and it makes you less grumpy."

"Coffee is good. 52nd and El Cajon?"

"Yeah," he said agreeably.

"How 'bout you drive today?"

He stopped, grinning broadly. I rolled my eyes. "Don't go thinking this makes us partners. You're hardly more than a silly trainee for crying out loud."

"Whatever."

The day was barely starting, and it had already been too long. I'd been chewed out by Roosevelt and put in my place by Ariana. I slipped out of real trouble by the short hairs on my fuzzy nuts. I brought flowers to a dead woman for a seventy-fifth wedding anniversary that would never happen, and I sent a murderer to trial for the death of a woman that hardly anyone really seemed to give a rat's ass about.

All in all, it seemed a pretty typical reflection of my life. Nothing ever came easy, a whole lot of effort for a few simple things that shouldn't be as difficult as people made them. I would enjoy that cup of coffee, and I would reflect. Not all of it was bad. At least today I took a solid shit.

ACKNOWLEDGEMENTS

No book is an effort of just one person. Thank you to my wife, my parents, and my family for all of your support. Thank you to Jean Jenkins who encouraged me to write something that drew on my experiences and has been my editor and advocate every day since I first put down words. To Michael Steven Gregory for his friendship and for the years of helping me, help others realize their publishing dreams. To Bill Frew, my partner and friend, thank you for your insight and willingness to always help me tell a better story. To the long list of readers whose feedback helped polish this book, Dan Scheuermann, Mary Harrison, Kevin Ammon, Debbie Farrar and Chris Kilby, to name a few. To the countless staff, friends, and conferees of the Southern California Writers' Conference for their inspiration and desire to keep publishing and storytelling alive. To Bill Lewinski for showing me what law enforcement could be. To ZOVA Books, Matt, Dan, Molly, and the others, for their ambitious desire to promote writers. And finally, to the men and women of the San Diego Police Department; it has been an honor to work with you. Your efforts are appreciated, even in times when it seems that they are not.

To those I've forgotten, I'm sorry, and you'll just have to wait for the next book.

ZOVA BOOKS
LOS ANGELES

zovabooks.com
zovabooks.blogspot.com
facebook.com/ZOVAbooks
twitter.com/ZOVAbooks

Made in the USA
Lexington, KY
21 March 2012